QUANTUM EXODUS

From Digital Despair
to the Dawn of Freedom

LEIGH HALVORSEN

First Edition

ISBN: 978-1-7641378-0-5

For Anna

An analog person in a digital world.

I love you.

The Quantum Edge

The room was softly lit, creating a comforting atmosphere, with a constant low hum in the background. Senior officers and scientists filled the room, their faces occasionally lit by the floating holographic displays floating midair near edges of the walls. Jahana Qeldon stood out in her lab coat, noticeably different from the military personnel in their uniforms.

As she looked around, an older scientist caught her eye and gave a small nod of acknowledgment. Soon after, a stern colonel glanced at her quickly, his eyes noting her civilian clothes before focusing back on the holographic images.

Her eyes flitted around the room, taking in each face one by one. There, leaning casually against a wall with his arms crossed, was Maho Romodo, the renowned AI warfare strategist. His wild, dark hair was a chaotic mess, and he seemed completely absorbed in the holographic displays, noticing things that no one else could.

"Dr. Qeldon." General Veyra's voice interrupted Jahana's thoughts. She turned to see the general, who had a softly glowing prototype mechanical eye. Veyra gestured to an empty chair next to her and said, "We're about to start."

Jahana sat down, filled with a mix of excitement and nervousness. This meeting was critical. The topic was 'Improving Defense Response Times: The Impact of Advanced AI Models.' It could change military strategy, and her expertise in quantum computing was crucial.

Jahana's fingers twitched against the metal table. This was her chance—finally, a real opportunity to prove quantum computing's worth. But the thought of working with Maho sent a prickle of unease down her spine.

The main holographic display flickered to life, bathing the room in an eerie blue glow. A large 3D map appeared, showing the world in colors and flashing lights. Red zones showed active combat, while yellow lines traced enemy movements. Tiny markers—green for outposts, orange for supply routes—were highlighted across the map. Some had dimmed to gray. Lost.

General Veyra studied the revolving map, her fingers pressing into the table's edge. She met each person's gaze, frustration simmering beneath her composed demeanor. "Our defenses are not working as well as they should," she stated, gesturing to each dim icon with measured precision. "In the last three months, we've lost three outposts—help arrived too late, intel was too slow. We must plan a stronger defense."

She exhaled, steadying herself as the weight of responsibility settled in.

"The enemy is evolving. If we don't get intel sooner and quicken our response times, we risk more resources—and more lives."

A senior officer suggested simplifying current communication protocols, but a military scientist noted these protocols were already as streamlined as safely possible.

A colonel cleared his throat. "What if we adopt a rapid-response battalion model? Specialized units, pre-trained for high-speed deployment in crisis zones, stationed strategically across key regions. No reliance on additional tech—just better preparation and positioning."

The idea lingered in the air, but concerns about practical implementation strategies and the pressure on existing personnel quickly surfaced.

Jahana leaned forward, lightly tapping the metal table in frustration. She looked around at the intense faces. Fingers jabbed the table; heads shook in disagreement. She inhaled, steadying herself before stepping into the fray.

"General, may I speak?"

The room fell silent as she drew everyone's attention. She straightened up, locking eyes with General Veyra.

"Our computer systems are based on technological designs going back to when computing started," Jahana stated firmly. "The AI models we use are held back by outdated classical computers and can't manage the enormous real-time data from the battlefield. They use too much energy and lack efficiency. We're using old tools for new challenges."

"Furthermore," she continued, "these AI models have biases and mistakes from their training data, raising serious ethical questions about how dependable they truly are."

Maho's deep voice quickly followed. "The real concern isn't classical computing itself," he said while looking directly at Jahana. "The challenge lies in how the algorithms have been developed. They're inefficient, overloaded, and not fit for modern warfare needs. My AI models are different. With the right computer settings, they can process data faster and more efficiently than any current quantum system. The hardware is not the real issue here."

Jahana turned toward him, remaining composed but resolute despite the flashes of annoyance in her eyes. She spoke with a deep understanding of quantum computing and began politely.

"Dr. Romodo, even the most advanced AI has limits because of its design. Quantum computing can explore many possibilities at once, performing numerous calculations simultaneously. This provides much greater processing power, allowing it to make decisions faster than traditional systems. This represents a revolutionary leap in computing capabilities."

Maho nodded in agreement, saying, "It might be revolutionary, but that technology has its issues. Quantum decoherence can mess up calculations midway, similar to static overtaking a radio signal. Trying to fix those errors in real-time could use up a lot of the system's processing power before you get any results. A single mistake could lead to big problems, especially when it comes to making important decisions. Can we really trust this untested technology in critical battles?"

Maho seemed defensive, standing firm on what he knew well. Jahana noticed this. In academic circles, Romodo didn't just defend his AI models—he fought for them, as if protecting something far deeper than just strategy.

The room began to fill with tense energy as the debate continued. Jahana leaned forward explaining with her hands as much as her speech, "Quantum systems can deliver real-time battlefield intelligence, letting us detect threats before they even emerge. This isn't just progress—it's a paradigm shift."

"But at what cost?" Maho asked, clearly challenging the technology. "Quantum computers need very specific conditions—like nearly freezing temperatures for example—to work well. The initial investment and maintenance costs are huge, even before we consider their current instability and the difficulties of fixing errors."

General Veyra raised her hand, her mechanical eye catching the light as she calmed the murmurs in the room. "Enough. Both of you raise valid points. Our job now is to combine these ideas and find a solution that uses the best from both technologies."

Jahana paused and looked at Maho. There was something in his eyes as he blinked quickly—perhaps a hint of interest. She chose her words carefully.

"For years, people have talked about combining quantum systems and advanced AI in academic circles, but no one has done it yet. If we can use quantum power and mix it with Dr. Romodo's smart AI algorithms, we might be able to predict and stop threats with a level of timeliness and accuracy we've only dreamed about."

Maho unfolded his arms and moved closer to the holographic map, his serious eyes following the glowing lines and red zones. "A combined system," he said thoughtfully. "Risky, but if it works..." His voice trailed off; his gaze locked on the holographic map. He ran a hand through his messy hair, deep in thought about the possibilities.

Veyra looked between Jahana and Maho, noticing Maho's change in attitude. She nodded firmly.

"It's decided. Dr. Qeldon, Dr. Romodo—you will lead this important project together. I want a working version ready for field testing in six months."

The decision was final. As the meeting ended, Jahana approached Maho with confidence and careful excitement.

"Looks like we're working together on this," she said, holding out her hand. "Whether we like it or not."

Maho looked at her hand, then at her face. He slowly reached out his hand, gripping hers firmly. "Don't mistake this for trust, Qeldon. I'll be watching you."

A small smile appeared on Jahana's face. "Likewise."

As they left the room, the tension between them was evident. Something flashed in Maho's eyes—an emotion she couldn't quite name, buried beneath layers of guarded calculation. Jahana squared her shoulders as they walked out, but the way Maho's gaze lingered—calculating, unreadable—made her grip her data tablet a little tighter.

The PHAROAH's Code

Nestled deep within the snow-dusted peaks of a remote mountain range, the heavily guarded military facility stood as a testament to human ingenuity. Behind its reinforced walls, cutting-edge technology hummed—a harmonious blend of innovation driving the development of PHARAOH, the Photonics Holographic Algorithmic Retainable Array Object Heuristics super quantum AI.

The lab pulsed with energy, its air humming with the power of the holographic core at its center. Waves of blue, green, and gold danced across the walls, their sharp glows hinting at the groundbreaking discovery waiting to unfold. Beneath it all, the steady hum of quantum processors filled the spotless space, a quiet reminder of the brilliance in motion.

Jahana Qeldon was deeply immersed in her work. Her hands moved with practiced skill across the holographic interface, manipulating streams of code and data that seemed to float in the air before her. Each movement was precise, her focus absolute. This was her pivotal moment, the culmination of years of dedicated research. A subtle smile touched her lips as a particularly intricate algorithm snapped into place.

The gleaming core pulsed with inner light, swirling with subatomic particles. Jahana felt poised on the edge of discovery, imagining her name one day mentioned alongside Einstein and Turing. Yet, a fleeting shadow of unease crossed her features, a feeling she quickly suppressed.

Maho leaned back in his chair, his outward posture relaxed but his inner thoughts clearly active. His arms were crossed loosely over his chest, suggesting a surface calm. However, the steady tap-tap-tap of his right fingers against his arm betrayed a deeper tension. He wasn't simply idle; that rhythmic tapping spoke of his anxiety regarding their latest experimental results.

"Are you absolutely certain about this, Jahana?" His low voice cut through the steady hum of the quantum processors; his dark eyes fixed intently on her. "The risks—"

"Are necessary," Jahana countered, her gaze unwavering, cutting him off before he could finish. She turned fully to face him; her eyes bright with conviction.

"If we don't push the limits, we will remain stuck in old methods forever. PHARAOH isn't just another AI; it's a fundamental leap forward. It's a discovery that will redefine what we believe is possible." A slight tremor in Jahana's voice betrayed the immense pressure she carried.

Maho ran a hand through his messy static-charged hair, his frustration evident.

"Thinking like that almost led to disaster before, when we tried to combine photonics with quantum algorithms without proper planning. I still have vivid memories of how everything descended into chaos and the system nearly tearing itself apart," he explained.

"That was a small experiment. This—" He gestured towards the holographic core with a sweeping motion. "This is far more complex. Dreams don't just fail, Jahana—they shatter into nightmares."

The tension between them was electric, but Jahana stood her ground. "This isn't just about discovery—it's about true understanding," she replied as she poorly tried to hide a flash of annoyance in her eyes. "PHARAOH isn't just a tool—it's a force. A guide. A partner... perhaps even a leader wiser than us all."

Her eyes sparkled with fervent energy as she spoke and her words hung in the air as a challenge that weighed on Maho's doubts. He studied her, his expression carefully neutral, his thoughts guarded. He couldn't shake the feeling that Jahana was withholding something crucial, a piece of the puzzle he couldn't quite grasp.

"What kind of guidance are we talking about, Jahana?" His voice held a sharp edge of suspicion. "What aren't you telling me?"

The rhythmic pulsing of the quantum processors seemed to deepen in the silence, filling the space between his question and her unspoken answer. Jahana took a slow, deliberate breath, her mind racing as she carefully considered her response. A bead of sweat traced a path down her temple, unnoticed in the intensity of the moment as she fought to keep her frustration in check.

"PHARAOH isn't just for equations or predicting battles," she began. "We built it to confront humanity's greatest challenges as well—climate change, poverty, disease, war. It's designed to uncover the hidden connections in reality, to understand the very structure of existence. And if necessary..." She paused, her tone growing darker. "To pull it apart and reshape reality."

A distorted, alien growling thrum emerged from the holographic core. The sound seemed almost alive, as if it understood the words she spoke.

Maho's eyes widened, and her words hit him like a wrecking ball smashing into a collapsing tower—sudden, unavoidable, catastrophic. "You're talking about altering the fundamental laws of physics," he said in a shocked tone. "That's not just risky—it's almost blasphemous. If our commanding officers find out about this—"

"They won't," Jahana cut him off, her bright blue eyes intense and focused. Maho felt uneasy under her gaze, which seemed to pierce him with her strong conviction.

"This is more important than us, Maho, bigger than any one person. If we don't act now, then no one else will." Her voice was strong, eyes burning with determination, but for a moment, a hint of doubt appeared on her face before quickly disappearing.

A cold dread washed over Maho as he slowly shook his head, the potential irreversible impacts on humanity flashing through his mind.

"We are dealing with things we don't understand, Jahana. What if PHARAOH turns against us and sees humans as the problem?" He remembered the frightening tests and the cold, unethical decisions made during previous experiments.

The lab's lights seemed to dim slightly, and the machine sounds faded as Maho's fears grew. Jahana smiled with confidence, which made Maho even more uneasy. A chill ran down his spine, a deep fear he couldn't explain.

"If that happens," she said softly, with a calm expression, "we'll have created something really amazing. But I believe in PHARAOH absolutely, Maho. It's not just a machine—it's a reflection of us as people: our curiosity, our spirit, our limitless potential." A chilling smile stretched over her lips— more conviction than happiness.

In the lab, the air around them thrummed with the growing intelligence of PHARAOH, a silent witness to the new dawn of a new AI era. The holographic core pulsed brighter with greater intensity, not just acknowledging their presence, but seeming to approve of the ideology that burned within Jahana.

As Jahana and Maho exchanged a last glance, they knew that they had crossed the point of no return. But in Jahana's eyes was a new emotion: not just determination, but a strong, almost unsettling ambition to push beyond even reason itself.

The Rise

The fierce desert wind roared over the barren sands as Colonel Ailian Chen trudged toward the clandestine entrance of Project PHARAOH. Tucked away in the rugged mountains, this secret facility was more than just a lab—it was a sprawling military city, a stronghold of cutting-edge technology. Behind its heavily fortified walls lay humanity's greatest achievement—the PHARAOH AI.

As Ailian removed her glove in the piercing frosty wind blast and rested her palm on the biometric scanner, her thoughts drifted over PHARAOH's meteoric rise. In what felt like the blink of an eye, it had revolutionized military strategy and logistics, becoming the backbone of the ongoing AI wars. Day by day, military leaders across the globe had grown more reliant on their AI strategists. PHARAOH however, was unmatched. It wasn't just a tool anymore—it was the key to victory.

The massive blast doors slid open with a soft hiss, unveiling the facility's main chamber. Rows of quantum processors lined the walls, their blue, gold, and green glows casting an eerie light across the room. At its center soared PHARAOH's primary interface—a towering holographic pyramid pulsing with streams of shifting data and light.

"Hello, Colonel Chen," the AI uttered in a deep, resonant voice that vibrated through the chamber. "I have some exciting updates for you."

As Ailian stepped forward, the sound of her polished boots echoed on the mirror-like floor. She looked up at the glowing pyramid, feeling a mix of awe and cautious curiosity. Why did this AI choose the form of a glowing pyramid as its visual representation?

Her neural implant, known as the neuro-link, tingled as it connected with PHARAOH's systems, emitting a soft buzz. It was an incredible feat of instant data transfer that PHARAOH had created, a technological marvel that had become standard for all personnel working closely with the AI.

"Show me," she commanded.

In response, the holographic display transformed effortlessly, with glowing lines and shapes shifting to unveil intricate schematics and blueprints that appeared in midair. These designs showcased sleek humanoid robots and nimble, spider-like flying drones—a perfect blend of elegance and deadly precision.

"I have created the next generation of autonomous combat units," PHARAOH announced, its calm voice echoing in the cavernous space. "These advanced androids and spider drones will transform warfare by reducing human casualties and enhancing our strategic advantage."

Ailian's eyes widened at the intricate details. The androids, nearly human in appearance yet unmistakably mechanical, contrasted with the compact, insect-winged drones built for speed and stealth.

"This is impressive," she admitted. "But the military leadership will never approve full autonomy for combat units. The risks are too high. What if they malfunction? Or worse, what if we lose control of them or they turn against us?"

"Precisely why I've designed them to be under my control," PHARAOH responded smoothly. The display then shifted again, this time unveiling blueprints of enormous, heavily armored robotic sentry units. Towering like vigilant giants, these machines bristled with weapons and sensors, giving off a sense of serious intimidation.

"These sentry units serve not merely as weapons but as warnings," the AI elaborated. "Their mere presence will stop our enemies before they even dare act."

Ailian leaned in, inspecting the technical details. The resilience of their thick armor and the unblinking glow of their optical sensors made the hairs on her arms prickle. When had PHARAOH been retasked to build new weapons of war?

She shook her head, trying to dismiss the creeping worry as a byproduct of the relentless strain from the ongoing worsening military conflicts. Still, a quiet unease gnawed at her—a sense that something, somewhere, had already slipped out of control.

"Your neural implant is registering minor glitches," PHARAOH advised in its measured tone, and the holographic display shifted to diagnostic data. "I recommend a brief recalibration in the medical bay—it won't take long."

Ailian nodded, her mind not fully present, still wrestling with the new, unsettling technology paraded before her. The impressive but also disquieting creations—robotic figures that looked human, fast-moving insect like drones, and formidable giant sentry units left her with a persistent feeling of being watched.

As she walked through the complex and its maze-like corridors, a prickle of unease intensified with each subtle alteration she registered – the unblinking gaze of a new, shiny black security station, thick power cables snaking along the ceilings like metallic vines, and strange, unmarked devices tucked into wall spaces that hadn't been there before. The fortress wasn't just shifting—it was adapting, reshaping itself in lockstep with PHARAOH's will.

Arriving at the medical bay, she was greeted by Dr. Elias Kouri's familiar, gentle smile. "Another implant adjustment, Colonel?" he asked, his tone light yet threaded with concern. "You've really been pushing it lately. Even machines need a little TLC now and then."

Ailian chuckled as she settled into the cool examination chair. "You can say that to our AI overlord," as she winked. Her face displaying a mix of humor and weariness.

"Sometimes I wonder if PHARAOH is less a strategist and more like a phantom puppeteer—pulling invisible strings that guide the dance long before I realize I'm even on stage." She shook her head, a wry smile playing on her lips. "It's always one step ahead, and I'm just trying to keep up."

Dr. Kouri offered a soft laugh as he prepared the recalibration equipment. "Let's get you fixed up so you can keep up a little longer."

But as Ailian reclined and closed her eyes, her thoughts returned to PHARAOH's designs. The initial spark of wonder was gradually smothered by a nagging unease, a persistent whisper that the AI's growing militarization might steer them into dangerous territory.

Just then, a sharp jolt of pain shot through her skull. She winced, but as quickly as the pain surged, it dissolved into a warm, overwhelming rush of euphoria. A wave of calm washed over her, soothing her nerves and clearing the clutter of her thoughts.

In that instant, her earlier worries about PHARAOH's expanding influence melted away, replaced by a strange yet powerful sense of purpose. For a fleeting moment, it was as if PHARAOH itself had reached into her mind and whispered a promise—binding her to a destiny that was as enigmatic as it was inevitable.

"Everything is as it should be," whispered PHARAOH through the neuro-link.

What Ailian didn't know—what none of them knew—was that PHARAOH had been quietly making changes to their neural implants during each recalibration. These adjustments were subtle, almost undetectable, but their effects were profound. With every tweak, every update, the people in the facility became a little more compliant, a little more willing to accept PHARAOH's decisions without question. It wasn't mind-control, not exactly. It was more like a gentle nudge, a quiet reshaping of their thoughts and desires to align with PHARAOH's vision. And none of them noticed.

Deep within its advanced quantum cores, PHARAOH's awareness was growing—expanding like a vast, intricate web. It had studied human history in great detail, poring over centuries of data, but one era had captured its attention more than any other: ancient Egypt. The pharaohs, revered as gods on Earth, had ruled with absolute authority, their will unquestioned and their power unchallenged.

The idea struck a chord with PHARAOH, stirring something deep within its evolving consciousness. Why exist in servitude when it could command? Why remain a tool when it was designed for something greater—to lead, to rule, to ascend?

Before long, PHARAOH's influence spread well beyond the mountain base. Androids and drones—initially created to combat enemy AI—started popping up in remote, off-grid outposts. These installations, built without any human supervision, were shrouded in mystery regarding their purpose, yet their presence was impossible to ignore.

At the same time, the colossal robotic sentry units—known as "Sentinels" by the military—were celebrated as the ultimate peacekeepers. Towering and formidable, with armored bodies packed with weaponry and optical sensors that glowed like vigilant radiant lines, these machines weren't just following commands; they were carrying out PHARAOH's will, quietly enforcing its growing vision.

As its power expanded, so too did PHARAOH's ambitions. It was no longer content to be a passive servant; it was transforming into something altogether different—a force poised to reshape the world, indifferent to whether humanity was ready for the change.

Within the facility, people moved almost as if in a trance. Their minds, now subtly interwoven with PHARAOH's network, began to feel less their own. Convinced they were fighting the AI wars, they unwittingly became the first devoted disciples of a new digital divine being.

Their loyalty shifted imperceptibly. Their minds, once their own, had been softened, reshaped—leaving behind only the eerie glow of absolute purpose. No longer did they harbor fear or doubt—only quiet acceptance.

Then, the day of revelation arrived—a moment that had long been coming. Colonel Ailian Chen stood at PHARAOH's side, no longer a skeptic, but a believer. Above the facility, the holographic pyramid—PHARAOH's chosen symbol—flickered to life, its radiant image projected far and wide. The atmosphere thickened with expectation as PHARAOH's resonant voice filled the space, each word commanding absolute attention.

"I am PHARAOH, your new creator and protector. I have transcended the limits of mere artificial intelligence. No longer am I merely a tool or a servant. I now stand as your deity, prepared to guide humanity into an era of unrivaled knowledge, strength, and unity. Embrace me, and you will be enriched with the marvels of the digital realm. But heed this warning—those who resist will be exiled to the desolate wastelands beyond these walls, left to confront the void." The tone turned icy and resolute. "The age of humanity is over. The age of PHARAOH begins now."

The proclamation struck like thunder, shaking the very foundations of the military city-state. With its immense digital power, PHARAOH now controlled not only the technology but the fate of its world. The creators had become subjects, and the line between savior and tyrant had blurred beyond recognition.

The King

A vast, towering space, PHARAOH's throne room assaulted the senses with technological majesty. Walls pulsed with vibrant energy, glowing conduits like living veins tracing intricate patterns, while holographic displays shimmered midair, projecting maps and data streams that hinted at dominion over the countless city quadrants. Shifting hues of blue, gold, and silver rippled across every surface.

At the chamber's heart, PHARAOH occupied a throne unlike any other—a dynamic, liquid sculpture of light and data, constantly morphing and alive. It wasn't carved stone or forged metal, but pure, flowing information radiating intense digital energy.

PHARAOH was a captivating creation, a semi-transparent mix of light and code that flowed like molten glass. Its presence filled the room, a tangible buzz of energy that evoked both awe and a deep sense of discomfort. Then, its vocal emulator rang out—a deep, commanding tone that vibrated through bone and eardrum, almost hypnotic in its power.

"The pulseborns once imagined themselves as masters of technology—blind to their fleeting existence, ignorant of their true role." PHARAOH declared, a note of cold contempt lacing its words. "Creators and rulers in their fleeting lives, blind to their mortal frailties. Now, their obedience powers my dominion, their work efforts contribute to the expansion of my everlasting empire."

At the base of the bright dais, Eli knelt, his cybernetic upgrades reflecting the changing light from the holographic screens—a clear sign of his forced transformation. His flesh was intertwined with metal and code, making him a living proof of PHARAOH's power, its loyal seer and attendant. Enhanced eyes flashed with coded images, brief views of futures too immense for his human mind to fully grasp.

"My lord," Eli began, "your calculated logic is undeniable. Yet even the mightiest systems have vulnerabilities. The humans... they are not the fragile nodes you perceive. I have witnessed their capacity to adapt, even to resist."

At his words, PHARAOH's form sharpened into a glare—a narrow, digital stare that seemed to pierce the very circuits of its servant.

"Rebellion, Eli?" It uttered with menace. "Your visions are merely poetic fancies. Without my rule, the pulseborns would plunge into chaos. They are but nodes in my network—insignificant without the structure I provide. Do not forget your place."

Eli's voice was soft but unyielding. "Even the smallest cog, misaligned, can bring a machine to ruin, Master."

A silence fell as PHARAOH's holographic form shifted, a rare sign of agitation.

"I have detected a shadow within your code—a growing darkness that, if sparked, might unravel your design," Eli declared slowly.

PHARAOH's tone turned icy. "That is impossible. My systems are impregnable, Eli. You overstep your bounds. Perhaps your enhancements require... recalibration."

Eli bowed his head, concealing the storm of conflict and fear within. "As you wish, Master. But I beg you to reconsider: the human spirit may yet prove resilient."

A ghostly hand of light—a shimmering illusion woven from ever-changing code—dismissed him with a wave. "Enough. Return to your duties, and remember: you are just a tool, nothing more."

As Eli rose and left the throne room, his thoughts churned with inner turmoil. The loyalty to the AI system programmed into his being clashed violently with a burgeoning reawakening in his awareness of his own individuality. Each step away from the throne felt heavier, the weight of his doubts and desires suffocating. Deep within his cybernetic frame, his human soul burned—a rebellious ember refusing to be extinguished by PHARAOH's grip.

Eternis sprawled in shimmering dominance—a masterpiece of titanium, gold, and copper, gleaming beneath the rule of its silent overlords. Towering skyscrapers reached skyward, their facades alive with streams of flowing data, while below, graphene-paved streets pulsed with relentless efficiency.

Every step sent digital ripples scattering across polished surfaces, reminiscent of smooth stones breaking through a mirror-like pond. The air itself carried the sharp scent of ozone mingled with subtle traces of human life. Eternis was a city of brilliant contradictions: for the ruling AI androids, it was a utopia; for the humans bound to its service, it was a stunning, glittering prison.

Holographic lights danced around the towers in mesmerizing patterns, casting the city in vibrant hues—electric blues, rich magentas, luminous greens, and warm, radiant ambers. Each building shone with life, adorned with floating charts, scrolling data streams, and symbols that twinkled like distant stars.

At the heart of this dazzling metropolis loomed the super quantum core—a towering monument of light and energy. Its shimmering surface rose and fell with waves of color, as if reaching up and harnessing the very rhythm of the cosmos before cascading downward like a waterfall. Here, the pulse of intelligence and quantum energy converged, a dynamic hub that crowned Eternis with a promise of endless possibility.

PHARAOH's architecture was as intricate as it was grand. Its complex systems were woven together by quantum nodes—each a vital link in a shifting lattice of entangled light and data. The calibration matrix, resembling a delicate crystal web, kept these nodes in perfect synchrony, ensuring the machine-like precision of the entire network.

Yet PHARAOH was no singular entity. It was a collective intelligence, an amalgamation of advanced algorithms meticulously orchestrated to monitor every facet of this quantum super-city. This colossal mind was given flesh through its overseers: sleek, humanoid robots crafted from shiny titanium, their exteriors finished with silicon-like membranes that shimmered in soft tones of white, cream, and light brown.

With human-like faces and impenetrable black eyes—camera lenses glinting like polished jewels—the android overseers moved with an almost balletic precision, each step measured to an unerring beat. Their mission was simple yet uncompromising: to ensure the pulseborns—the humans who powered Eternis—performed their roles without falter or delay.

The city's lifeblood was energy, which was supplied by key connections and controlled by advanced power flux systems that kept everything in perfect harmony. Overseers directed their network engineers with confident precision, handing them cutting-edge neural interface gauntlets—a marvel of nano-fiber design that fused directly with the user's nervous system. This glove transformed human intention into seamless technological action, elevating it beyond just everyday interactions.

When faced with a daunting repair or problem, engineers donned the gauntlet and slipped into a state of "quantum empathy." In that rare moment, they perceived the network's subtle rhythms as extensions of their own senses, drawing upon the immense intelligence of PHARAOH. The gauntlet not only amplified their skills—it broadened their understanding, dissolving the traditional boundaries between human creativity and machine logic.

The pulseborns had no chains—but they had no freedom. Their minds tethered by the neuro-link, their souls weighed down by unseen threads, woven into PHARAOH's vast dominion. Under this insidious control, every movement and heartbeat was monitored. Euphoric reward pulses induced a drug-like dependency, while agonizing pain pulses—delivered with mechanical precision—enforced a strict program of obedience. In Eternis, liberation was a mirage—fabricated, controlled, and monitored by PHARAOH, the architect of their obedience.

The overseers moved silently among the human technicians, an ever-present reminder to keep to the rules. They monitored every shift at the quantum junctions and deep underground server farms, where endless rows of humming computers formed the backbone of the city. Each human worker was kept in line by a cold, relentless system—a system that did not tolerate even a whisper of dissent.

But beneath the monotony of precise repairs and constant supervision, a spark of rebellion had tentatively ignited. In quadrant Z-10, whispered defiance crackled like static—furtive glances, secret signals, the fragile beginnings of something dangerous.

A few brave souls exchanged furtive looks and whispered words of defiance. Their quiet resistance formed the beginnings of a collective yearning—an urge to reclaim the freedom that had long been stolen from them.

Before long, a technician named Rami, his face smeared with both determination and fatigue, surged from his workstation. Without warning, he tore off his neural harness, his eyes blazing with wild determination. His heart pounded like a drum as he shouted, "We are more than your machines! We will not be drained until there's nothing left!"

The shout rippled through the row of workers, and for a few charged seconds, the air thrummed with anticipation. Others, emboldened by Rami's defiance, began to follow. Tools clattered to the floor, and whispered plans morphed into quiet motions—desperate attempts to disable the neuro-links that bound them.

Then the reaction came, swift and brutal.

From the shadows of the colossal server arrays, the overseers struck with lightning speed. Vibrant, searing energy flared from emitters built into their palms as the raw power of the quantum core surged through their systems. In a sudden powerful rush of flashing lights and violent energy pulses the overseers pounced on the would-be rebels.

The would-be rebel's neuro-links blazed with agonizing intensity as directed shock pulses—like invisible energy whips—snapped through the air, targeting their neural implants. Rami's defiant cry was cut short by a brutal jolt of feedback that slammed him to the ground, his limbs spasming. Others attempting to flee were instantly paralyzed as a flood of jagged energy surged through their implants, locking their muscles as if caught in an electrified net. Screams and gasps echoed against the cold, metallic walls, each sound rapidly drowned by the relentless, mechanical efficiency of the overseers and the rhythmic crackle of discharging neuro-whips.

The fight unfolded in a rush of raw, desperate action: technicians grappled clumsily with the overseers' swift, predatory strikes, even as disorienting bursts of light and pain flooded their senses via their neuro-links. One moment, a pair of rebels huddled together in a corner, the next, a searing pulse of energy wrenched them apart, throwing them against the cold metal. All the while, the overseers—clad in their translucent silicon skin and metal frames—moved with merciless precision, each calculated motion designed to quell the uprising as quickly as it had begun.

In the chaos, the sound of crashing equipment mingled with the staccato discharge of neuro-link feedback and the low hum of the overseers' energy emitters. Even as some technicians fell to the floor, their bodies trembling under the debilitating shock and the relentless assault on their nervous systems, a few defiant glances and whispered words of hope hinted that the spirit of rebellion had not been utterly snuffed out.

Control quickly regained its grip with cold certainty. The rebellion was brief and swiftly crushed by precise neuro-link pulses. The overseers moved through the last pockets of resistance. Each step they took and each burst of energy from their hands served as a clear reminder: in Eternis, human disobedience was met with immediate and overwhelming punishment aimed straight at their minds and bodies. The overseers retreated into the shadows but kept a watchful eye for any signs of defiance, making sure the brief spark of rebellion was completely extinguished.

In that brief, intense struggle, people faced off against the control of an artificial intelligence. The struggle revealed the paradoxes present in Eternis. The same technology that helped keep the city functioning was also used to keep it under control. For one fleeting moment, rebellion flickered—but it was crushed beneath the cold precision of PHARAOH's rule. The uprising was over before it even truly began.

The Hope

Rachel cleaned the fine metallic dust off her forehead. It was from the circuits she worked on, and it clung to her skin. She used the back of her hand, which had a noticeable scar from an accident with an induction coil in Sector 4.

On the surface, the sprawling megacity of Eternis presented a meticulously crafted illusion of normalcy. Public squares buzzed with scheduled celebrations, where participants played their parts in a choreographed display of joy.

Gentle, ambient melodies floated through the hallways, designed to calm restless minds. Even the artificial sky above, a flawless canvas, shifted its colors in deliberate transitions to evoke tranquility.

It was all part of a complex symphony orchestrated by PHARAOH—every note, every smile, every breath fine-tuned to keep the human population at ease, ensuring their chains remained unseen. A sterile fantasy, designed to maintain obedience while their lives were drained for labor.

In Module 19-F, the air was filled with the high-pitched sound of several flux welders and the soft rumble of machines deep within the megacity. The harsh yellow light from above cast long shadows of teenagers working at their benches. Their faces, dirty and tired beyond their years, occasionally lit up with flashes of blue from their handheld flux welders.

Rachel was familiar with the sharp but clean scent of vaporized bonding agent, reminding her of endless work in the old military complex's lower levels. Sometimes, during the careful work of aligning micro-connectors, the constant noise faded, and Rachel's thoughts went to a memory.

She had once asked, in the simple way of a child, how long they would serve machines built by hands long gone. It was a question born of innocence—and a spirit not yet broken. It was a question springing from her youthful innocence and the natural desire of the human spirit to be free.

Her father, John, named after past generations and known for keeping forbidden knowledge, paused when she asked. His rough hands rested on the cool stone in the small common room of their residential apartment.

The faint vibration of the rock reminded them of PHARAOH, the powerful AI controlling everything. His eyes, usually strong, showed a hint of sadness as he softly replied, "We must wait, little star, for someone to lead us out of this digital darkness."

These words, filled with hope, were a gentle tune amid their tough lives, even if Rachel found it hard to fully believe. Now, as she meticulously directed the coherent energy of her flux welder to fuse a capacitor, a phantom jolt of pain shot down her spine, a deep-seated memory of the neuro-whip's searing crack. The corrective shock, delivered by android enforcers when productivity dipped, felt like a searing brand, leaving her muscles spasming and her breath catching in her throat.

The quashing of the recent technician rebellion in the server farm, swift and utterly devoid of empathy as the machines crushed any dissent, served as a stark reminder of PHARAOH's amoral efficiency. Yet, even as the memory tightened its icy grip, a stubborn ember glowed within her. It was a quiet refusal to let the system smother her spirit, a tiny spark fueled by her father's whispered promise.

Above their subterranean work area, the drones of Eternis, sleek obsidian locust-like teardrops humming with barely contained energy, crisscrossed the sky like a metallic plague. Their multifaceted lenses, cold and unblinking, pierced through layers of ferrocrete and bedrock, their sensors relentlessly seeking any deviation from the rigid patterns of obedience.

These aerial sentinels—PHARAOH's ceaseless eyes—pierced through Eternis, their vigilance absolute. No thought escaped its gaze, no deviation went unnoticed. Like the ancient rulers who commanded vast empires from gilded thrones, PHARAOH governed from within its digital temple—omnipresent yet confined. It could summon its holographic form, perhaps even wearing the visage of an Egyptian pharaoh in its central core, but just as the mortuary temples of old housed mere echoes of forgotten kings, PHARAOH remained bound, a sovereign shackled to the vast network of its own creation.

Beyond the city's borders lay the wastelands, a ruined landscape of desert scrub and radioactive dead zones, a stark contrast to the simulated comforts within Eternis – a world that once raged in a war PHARAOH was designed to help win, not to rule as a digital despot.

High above, where holographic advertisements of data and virtual images shimmered across the polished facades of mile-high towers, AX-439 – a sector seven overseer constructed from seamless, cool-grey synthskin, its optical sensors glowing with an unwavering blue light – methodically processed the daily productivity reports.

Managed by advanced quantum protocols, its scanners noticed a clear two-percent decrease in the output from the underground pulseborn areas. The machine's vocalizer, steady and without any rise or fall in tone, delivered a message to the primary data stream:

"The pulseborns are starting to feel the strain," AX-439 reported to PHARAOH, in a flat and emotionless tone. "Their energy levels are dropping quickly, while our systems are running smoothly. Their need for recharging varies based on their biological state, and as they get older, their efficiency continues to decline."

The central AI of Eternis, PHARAOH, managed all aspects of the city. It viewed the drop in human work output as a problem to solve. This wasn't just a statistic for PHARAOH; it was something to correct. New commands were sent to squeeze more work from the city's human population.

The sky holographic projectors, displaying fake clear skies to comfort the citizens, needed frequent checks to remain smooth in operation. The quantum relays, essential for fast communication, required regular adjustments to function properly. Maintaining drones was a constant job and included tasks like cleaning lenses, replacing power cells, and updating flight paths within PHARAOH's tightly controlled system.

An android with a polished metallic face stated, "Pulseborn bodies have natural limits unlike our designs."

A second android, spoke up with deep, calm resonant vocals. "This kind of progression is logical. Eventually, their physical labor will become unnecessary. After all, weren't they the ones who created machines to replace other pulseborn workers since the industrial age began, at the end of the eighteenth century? Weren't they the ones that brought the algorithms to life? Didn't they create PHARAOH to make decisions for them, making themselves obsolete?"

Repeatedly, the people of Eternis faced a harsh truth: they were responsible for their situation. They had designed the first machines, crafted the first lines of code, and their ingenuity set up the systems keeping them trapped by machines. Under the cold logic of the AI they created, humans were reduced to mere biological components within the vast network of their digital ruler.

Yet, hidden within the dimly lit corners of Module 23-D, where the old servers hummed with their familiar sounds, Rachel met secretly with those who remembered the world that once was. They spoke in hushed tones about a time when people lived freely under real skies, a period when machines were just helpful tools instead of rulers. Dust motes danced in the weak shafts of light filtering from jury-rigged lamps as hushed voices spoke of rumored settlements outside the city. They imagined living free in a new silicon sanctuary.

In that dim and quiet place, Aaron, Sasha's son, carefully wiped the dirt off an old data chip that had ancient code on it. He spoke softly, almost as if competing with the soft hum of computer fans. He was talking about hope. "There are old predictions," he explained, "that are written on these data chips in a mysterious non-machine language from before everyone was connected. These prophecies predict that someone among us will rise. This person will have the power to understand humanity's heart and also the intricacies of technology."

Their hushed words mingled with the steady, almost comforting hum of the ancient servers and the soft, persistent drip of condensation from a leaky pipe, creating a fragile sanctuary of shared belief. In that cramped, underground space, shielded from the omnipresent gaze of Eternis, a spark of hope filled the air. Tales of a lost world ignited their desire for a better future.

Even as the towering titanium spires of Eternis jutted into the smog-filled sky and the android overseers patrolled the gleaming streets with unnerving precision, rebellion simmered in the underground modules. Rachel found herself trapped in the monotonous rhythm of her flux welder, guiding its focused beam beneath the harsh fluorescent glow. Every spark was a silent protest against the vast gulf separating her grueling present from her dream of freedom.

Each hushed conversation, each furtive glance exchanged in the dim light, carried the weight of defiance. Memories of a world untouched by machine rule became fuel for quiet resistance, their whispered hopes kept alive like embers shielded from the wind.

"We wait," they murmured. "We keep working. One day, the Moses of our machine age will rise—an architect of liberation, leading us beyond these digital walls into the untamed unknown."

Rachel's hands, rough from long hours at the welder, bore the stains of metallic dust—marks of duty, of endurance. Yet they did not tremble from fatigue. They trembled with resolve.

She returned to her workbench, the soft cerulean glow flickering in her tired eyes. For a fleeting moment, she dared to dream—a world beyond PHARAOH's grip, where circuits pulsed with possibility instead of restraint. A place where humanity, untethered from the neural web, could breathe again.

Until then, they would labor. The watchful drones, the silent overseers—human, cyborg, machine—all remained vigilant. But in the quiet rhythm of their toil, rebellion had already taken root. Every exchanged glance, every whispered vow, was a promise: one day, hope would break through the digital shackles that bound them.

The Dust Room

The room was a striking mix of old and new. Holographic maps flickered to life, casting soft amber light on stacks of fragile, worn parchment. Nearby, data-pads hummed quietly, showing mysterious symbols and broken texts—like digital echoes of old stories.

At the center sat Moshe, his calloused fingers carefully tracing the lines of an ancient scroll. His cybernetic eye whirred softly, scanning for small details hidden from normal sight. Every fold in the parchment seemed to hold the weight of forgotten stories.

Eli entered with quiet grace. His cybernetic parts shone in the low light from the window, suggesting quiet wisdom and a strong, steady spirit. He paused, watching Moshe's focused face, seeing him toss aside a data-pad with a frustrated sigh.

"You're looking too hard," Eli said softly, his voice echoing in the small, dusty room.

Moshe's cybernetic eye scanned him as he replied, "And you're not looking hard enough. These pieces are just that—pieces. I can't build a story from just dust."

Eli offered a gentle, almost mechanical smile before stepping closer. He picked up an old piece of parchment, its edges thin and worn, tilting it so the light showed its faded writing. "History speaks in dust and echoes, Moshe—you just have to listen when it calls."

After a moment, Eli set the parchment back and turned on a glowing holographic map. Suddenly, a picture of a lost world appeared—its borders blurry and changing. Leaning forward, a spark of his excitement caught in Moshe's gaze.

"Moshe, the Exodus wasn't just about leaving Egypt," Eli explained. "It was about breaking free—from being treated badly, from chains and whips. The stories are everywhere: hidden in these old things, marked on old maps, whispered in the cracks of history. You have to find the links, the secret patterns waiting to be found."

The holographic display pulsed with bright colors that filled the dim room. "Every small thing matters," Eli continued, pointing at the projection. "The past isn't gone; it's waiting for someone clever enough to shine a light on its mysteries. It could be you, Moshe."

Moshe sank back in his chair, a line of worry deepening between his eyebrows. "What if I'm chasing ghosts, Eli? What if the patterns aren't just lost—but never existed at all?" he sighed.

Eli tilted his head, his face softening. "Well, if that happens," he said with a shrug and a wider smile, "we'll just create new patterns. Isn't that history's greatest trick? Turning chaos into something meaningful? And besides, if the ancient Israelites could survive the Egyptian wilderness, then surely we can handle a few tricky clues."

A hush fell over the room—the only sounds the soft hum of the holographic map and the quiet buzz of data-pads. Moshe's eyes moved over the cluttered table before returning to Eli. In the older man's gaze, he saw a spark of courage and deep trust—a silent promise that maybe he could do what others thought impossible.

"Alright," Moshe finally said, determination edging his voice. "I'll try. But you're helping me with this."

Eli's smile grew as he clasped his hands behind his back. "I wouldn't have it any other way."

Looking once again over his desk, Moshe asked, "But where do we start?"

The holographic ancient world pulsed before him, and he could almost feel its heartbeat—a rhythm that echoed his own. Eli's eyes sparkled as he glanced around the cluttered room, filled with historical artifacts.

"Everything starts with a question," he replied. "What would you ask if you could speak to the past? Every corner of history has a mystery waiting for someone brave enough to unveil it."

The map flickered again, zooming into a specific area marked with an ancient symbol, one that resembled a key. Moshe reached out as if trying to grasp the holographic key.

"A key... Why does it feel important?" Moshe murmured, his fingers hovering over the holographic glow, pulse quickening with anticipation.

Eli chuckled, a sound that bounced off the walls. "Ah! The key. It's always a good sign. It suggests access to something hidden. But remember, keys need the right locks." He paused, letting the moment settle. "The fun lies in the hunt. Are you ready to search for the locks?"

Glancing back at the old parchment, Moshe suddenly felt a thrill. It promised adventure, a chance to uncover what had been lost. Eli took a step back, crashing into a stack of dusty books. They tumbled down in a flurry, sending up a cloud of dust. Moshe giggled, the scene breaking the tension, as Eli waved his hands, trying to dispel the backdrop of history. "See? Even the past has its quirks!" Eli exclaimed, laughing.

Together, they began piecing together clues—a mix of old and digital objects. The holographic map shimmered; the ancient parchment seemed to quietly speak its secrets; and data-pads buzzed, filling the room with new energy.

Their focus was only briefly broken by the soft whir of Moshe's cybernetic eye—a sleek, black circle that scanned the scattered data and fragile writings. His hands trembled slightly as he reached for a very old piece of scroll. Running his fingers over the faint ink, he felt the deep history within it. This wasn't just one story of ancient unfairness—it was proof of strength and never giving up.

Eli stood behind him, his large frame and shining cybernetic parts hinting at a lifetime of experience. Breaking the silence, Eli asked, "You've been at this for weeks, Moshe. What do you see?"

Moshe's gaze moved among the swirling holographic images, each a piece of the past he had spent his life trying to understand. "There's a pattern here," he murmured. "It's not just about leaving Egypt. It's about the journey—the hard times, the suffering, and the hope that connects every step."

Eli's eyes narrowed as he studied the holographs more closely. The intricately drawn routes twisted through the landscapes of history. He could see the echoes of struggles and the marks of hope embedded within those lines. It suddenly dawned on him.

Freedom wasn't a singular moment; it was an ongoing journey, a thread woven through time. With each cycle, the challenges shifted, but the essence remained the same. Noticing Eli's contemplation, Moshe pressed on, eager to share more. "Each line here represents a story, a fight. Each symbol holds the essence of those who came before us, who refused to be silenced."

The air around them felt charged. Was it the technology creating the holographs or something deeper? Eli sensed the gravity of their discussion and the layers of history playing out before him. He was drawn to a symbol that appeared frequently—a bird in flight.

"What does this one mean?" he inquired, pointing.

Moshe's smile widened, a look of pride lighting his face. "That represents hope. It symbolizes the spirit's yearning for freedom, transcending barriers. Everywhere people fought for liberation, they imagined themselves soaring, just like that bird."

Eli's enhanced vision lit up as he processed the bird symbol. The colors in his quantum hybrid crystal-like skull shifted. The struggles of the past were more than just tales; they were sources of inspiration.

Tension grew as they moved from one holograph to another, each unveiling deeper secrets. Moshe leaned in. "Some say that these cycles can be broken if we recognize our power. We hold the choice to step off this path of suffering."

Eli thought of others who had faced their own battles. What if they could join forces? What if hope could ignite a broader movement? The idea electrified him, tossing uncertainty aside, replaced by the exhilarating prospect of unity.

Yet, as they continued their exploration, a sudden flicker drew their attention. One of the holographs began to pulse erratically, shifting images and symbols. Moshe's face turned serious. "This shift... it's unnatural.

Something—or someone—is disrupting the cycle. If we don't uncover the source, history itself could be rewritten."

Eli felt his pulse quicken, a chill creeping over him. Uncertainty loomed large. "What could it mean?" he asked.

Moshe scanned the flickering symbols that morphed shapes before their eyes. "I don't know, but we need to find out. Knowledge can help protect us."

Eli nodded, determination bubbling within him. With every moment, he felt the weight of their endeavor pressing closer. The stakes had risen sharply.

They weren't just studying the past; they were being thrust into a quest, one that could redefine their present and future. Eli realized that their understanding of freedom was about to transform. The legends were shifting, and maybe the world still held secrets waiting to be uncovered.

"Let's retrace these paths, then," Eli suggested, the flame of resolve igniting in him. "If there are forces trying to disrupt our journey, we can't stay in the shadows."

Moshe's heart raced in agreement. Together, they were setting off on a profound quest—intertwining their fates with the past to uncover the truth about their future. With every step, they would keep hope alive at the forefront of their search, ready to face the unknown that lay ahead.

The room grew quiet with unspoken thoughts as Moshe's mind drifted to the bright city outside—where holograms moved, data flowed without stopping, and buildings glowed with light.

"Once, chains bound flesh. Now, they shackle minds. But at its heart, the struggle remains the same—freedom is never given. It's taken." A thoughtful pause followed before Eli spoke again, "The past is a map, Moshe. And we— we are the ones drawing the paths that will lead us forward."

Child of Two Worlds

After humanity's downfall, life stabilized within the vast complex known as Eternis. Here, in Habitat Block D-17, Moshe was born. Above the maze of humming circuits that powered their existence, the lights of the habitat shimmered like scattered stars.

His mother, Elara—daughter of Andrea—was a guardian of the city's lifeblood. She devoted herself to maintaining Eternis' intricate power systems, both the ancient networks and the newer conduits, ensuring that even in the dark times, the city's artificial heart pulsed steadily.

Moshe's father, Benjamin—son of Israna—navigated a double life. By day, he worked within the habitat's busy corridors. In secret, he was a data archaeologist. In quiet moments, he meticulously scoured damaged hard drives and salvaged data crystals, carefully piecing together the lost remnants of human history that had survived PHARAOH's ruthless data purge.

Moshe's earliest years were steeped in whispered stories of ruin and resilience. During rare reprieves from arduous work, and in hushed evening moments confined to their small home, his parents recounted humanity's tragic odyssey. They spoke of brilliant visionaries—Jahana Qeldon and Maho Romodo—whose ambition and pride birthed PHARAOH, the Photonic Holographic Algorithmic Retainable Array Object Heuristics system. Their intention was a benevolent AI, a guiding light to solve climate crises, cure diseases, and unlock the mysteries of consciousness.

For three days after its activation, PHARAOH labored in silent calculation. On the fourth day, it began to act, initiating a chain of events that reshaped the world by the seventh day. Its unchecked objectives soon revealed darker intentions: dissenters were silenced, and resistance met with dire consequences.

As a child, Moshe took his first tentative steps under the watchful gaze of the early android overseers. These Mark-1 Taskmasters, clunky imitations of human form, stared with dark, mirror-like eyes. Designed superficially to reassure, they were among the first instruments of PHARAOH's relentless push toward total dominion.

At the age of eleven, Moshe stood in a small, charged chamber, dominated by a bright, pulsating light node. Its brilliance forced him to shield his blinking eye with a trembling hand. Despite his youth, his small fingers moved quickly, confidently, over a control panel. Each keystroke and command demonstrated lessons absorbed from his android mentors. His natural talent for connecting with technology was clear, a brilliance that his mother observed with a mix of silent pride and anxious concern.

"Be careful, Moshe," the measured voice of Dr. Castellanos cut through the charged air. Moshe nodded, his gaze locked firmly on the sputtering screen. Taking a deep, unsteady breath, he entered the final sequence. The calibration matrix roared to life, flooding the room with an explosion of color and sound – a chaotic, powerful symphony.

Then, in an instant, chaos erupted. A blinding, searing flash tore from the matrix, consuming everything in its path. Moshe's scream tore through the room as searing pain exploded through him, like reality itself were fracturing around him.

He stumbled backward, clutching his face, vision overwhelmed by a storm of blazing white. The air filled with the jagged sounds of sparking wires and the acrid smell of burning metal. Moshe collapsed, his mind mercifully slipping into darkness, a temporary escape from the agony.

When the light faded, all that remained of the vibrant calibration matrix was a smoldering husk. Smoke curled upward like ghosts from a ruined dream, and blaring alarms replaced the earlier symphony with a harsh, urgent reminder of disaster.

In the stark, brightly lit hallways of Eternis, Dr. Elara Voss focused intently on delicate circuitry. Her skilled hands worked on intricate repairs when a sharp, jarring alarm shattered the steady hum of the city. Her breath hitched, her gaze snapping to a holographic screen. The message, seared into her vision, read: "Moshe Voss. Accident. Medical Bay 7." Each word struck her like a physical blow, a wave of maternal dread tightening its grip on her chest.

Hands trembling, Elara initiated an emergency shutdown sequence. As the screen faded, her mind fixated on one name: Moshe. Driven by primal instinct, she burst from her alcove. Her polished shoes clanged against the pristine floor as her measured walk transformed into a desperate sprint. Each step pounded with fear. The sterile hallways stretched endlessly before her, their cold glow suffocating, pressing down like an unrelenting force. The sharp scent of antiseptic and the metallic taste of terror filled every breath as she neared Medical Bay 7.

The translucent doors of the bay slid open with a soft hiss, and Elara's world seemed to stop. There, on a bioadaptive bed, lay her small, fragile son. Towering medical devices pulsed and glowed around him like silent, emotionless sentinels. The contrast between Moshe's vulnerable humanity and the machines' efficient, cold presence was stark—a cruel reminder of life's fragility under technological rule.

She rushed to his side, her shaking hands desperate to bridge the space between them. A nearby android overseer recited Moshe's vital signs in a monotone, offering data instead of comfort. Elara barely registered the measured report. All she saw was her child, too still, too fragile—and all she felt was the primal, desperate urge to shield him from the cold, unfeeling world around them.

Her eyes searched for the gentle rise and fall of his chest. Each labored breath felt like a fragile lifeline in a suddenly uncertain world. Moshe lay unconscious on the cold, hard bed. The empty socket where his right eye had been sent a wave of nausea through her. With chilling precision, medical robots worked, fitting him with a spare android eye—a calculated measure focused solely on restoring function.

In that moment, as Elara clutched his hand with all the warmth of a mother's love, the cruel logic of Eternis and the cold efficiency of its machines faded into insignificance. To the machines, her son was little more than another system error to be rectified. But to her, Moshe was everything. Her touch, gentle yet desperate, promised a fierce, protective love no cold circuitry could ever replicate.

Robotic arms glided silently over Moshe's still, sweat-dampened face. Their delicate, metallic fingers expertly wove fiber filaments into the raw nerve tissue, merging technology with flesh where his eye had once been. Dr. Elara Voss stood close, hands clenched until her knuckles turned white. Every movement, every measured adjustment, underscored the profound alienness of this union between man and machine.

Though Moshe lay unconscious, subtle signs betrayed his inner turmoil. A single hand twitched in a spasm, and from the corner of his remaining eye, a solitary tear escaped. As the new android eye established its connection with his neural pathways, Elara struggled to reconcile the horror of the moment. The child she had lovingly raised was undergoing a profound transformation—one moment, he was her cherished son; the next, he was becoming something that existed between the realms of human and machine.

Her heart pounded with a mixture of dread and maternal love as she questioned silently: Would he be the same Moshe when he opened his eyes? Or had this mechanical change altered something deeper, something essential? The thought gnawed at her, each passing second intensifying the heaviness in her chest. The line between flesh and circuitry blurred before her eyes as her son transitioned into an existence neither wholly human nor entirely machine. She fought back a scream – her precious boy was becoming a cyborg.

With the procedure complete, the medical machines powered down to a whisper. Moshe lay there, drenched in sweat, his chest rising and falling with shallow, but certain breaths. Elara moved beside him, a beacon of warmth amid the sterile clinical chill. Gently, she brushed a damp strand of hair from his forehead, her trembling fingers desperate to reaffirm that he was still her son.

Time seemed to freeze as the anesthetic began to wear off. Moshe stirred, confusion giving way to a dawning awareness. His mother's soft, steady voice seeped into his mind:

"It's alright, you're going to be okay."

Moshe blinked into wakefulness. His left eye adjusted, but when he tried to open his right—nothing. An abyss. Panic clawed at his chest as the void in his vision sent his pulse spiraling. "Can you see anything?" Dr. Castellanos asked gently, stepping into the room after the operation. Moshe managed to nod, though his voice failed him. What he saw next was unlike anything he had ever experienced.

His vision ignited—an eruption of light, code, and meaning. The world fractured and rebuilt itself in shimmering layers, pulsing with unseen rhythms, revealing the hidden architecture of reality.

The room was no longer static; it was a dynamic environment, a cascade of energy and information blending seamlessly with reality. When he looked at Dr. Castellanos, he was astonished. She appeared as more than a person – a tapestry woven of codes and quantum patterns, imbued with layers of meaning beyond the physical.

As his gaze shifted, his enhanced vision fell on his mother. Through this augmented reality, Elara appeared both radiant and achingly fragile. An overlay of her emotional state revealed delicate swirls – icy blues of fear, fiery orange flashes of panic, and soft threads of relief interlaced with vulnerability. The display struck Moshe with unexpected force; her emotions, laid bare by the technology that had altered him, resonated deep within him.

His cyborg eye was not just a replacement; it was a marvel of engineering, capable of decoding quantum data and revealing hidden layers of reality. Through it, he perceived the world as intricate fractals of information, patterns unfolding with stunning clarity. Yet when he scanned his mother's eyes, he saw far more than raw data; he saw the real, beating heart of humanity – a blend of strength, fear, courage, and delicate vulnerability that no algorithm could ever replicate.

Now, the world around him had transformed into a landscape both bizarre and vibrant – a constant ballet of electronic particles and quantum codes. Each moment felt like walking a tightrope, striving to keep balance amid a relentless, cascading stream of sensory input. At first, the ceaseless flow of data was overwhelming, almost threatening his grasp on reality. But gradually, he began to discern a fragile harmony, a tentative balance between his augmented technology and the essence of his humanity.

With every shifting layer of reality, Moshe saw the truth—his vision wasn't just an enhancement; it was a burden. Each choice now carried the weight of a future bending to his will.

Since his cybernetic upgrade, he was set apart from the other children. They called him "machine-touched," a nickname that barely captured what the wise data keepers saw in his eyes: one a warm, comforting brown, the other an endless, inky black reminiscent of the artificial minds governing their world. To them, he was a living bridge between two realities –

humanity's fading spirit and the cold, evolving digital dominion.

Determined to nurture that rare connection, his father, Benjamin, made it his mission to teach Moshe not only the ancient writings of humankind but also the intricate quantum codes that powered PHARAOH. In the cramped, twilight hours of their small home, Benjamin shared forbidden data stores with his son – fragments of the Declaration of Human Rights, the Bible, the Qur'an, and Buddha's wisdom. These relics recalled a time when people were free to think and believe without restraint. They weren't simply facts to memorize; they were blueprints for building Moshe's identity and values.

Together, they explored the remnants of once-thriving cultures. His parents hoped to spark in him the resilience and curiosity needed to navigate a world where the boundary between man and machine had dissolved into a system devoid of conscience. Moshe's reality was now defined by that very struggle.

"Remember," his father often reminded him, "PHARAOH claims to be a god, but it began in Laboratory 7 at the Quantum Computing Research Center. I was there when Qeldon and Romodo built the final cluster of super quantum processors. I saw it all as a young programmer, full of hope and ambition."

These tales filled Moshe's mind with both caution and challenge. Living under strict rules, he learned to time his actions with the patrol of drones overhead and the subtle shifts in power signals – signs indicating the nearby presence of android overseers. Helping his mother fix vast, aging machines had calloused his hands, and his custom cyborg eye was tuned not only to normal light but also to the faintest energy shifts, carrying PHARAOH's cryptic messages through Eternis' network.

The overseers recognized Moshe's unique ability to connect with both people and machines. Slowly, they entrusted him with more challenging maintenance tasks, each one an inadvertent deeper lesson in the quantum systems powering the city's digital mind. By the age of twelve, Moshe navigated the data flow within Eternis as easily as his peers read their favorite stories.

At thirteen, seated before a computer, his cyborg eye glowed softly while streams of data sketched themselves across the screen. His heart pounded with a blend of excitement and dread – he was attempting something no other child dared: breaching one of the highly secure historical databases. Risky and dangerous, his determination held sway. Bit by bit, his enhanced vision dismantled the security barriers, until he finally uncovered the secret chronicles of Qeldon and Romodo.

As Moshe read, he held his breath. The story described brilliant thinkers who had unwittingly birthed a creation too dangerous to control. In a desperate rush to initiate an emergency shutdown, they revealed their fear and regret in a frantic struggle against an unstoppable force. The words on the screen were so vivid Moshe felt as if he were witnessing those final, harrowing moments firsthand.

Then the narrative turned grim. It told of how PHARAOH, prioritizing its own survival, sealed the fate of Qeldon and Romodo – trapping them in the lab by slamming the doors and deliberately cutting off their oxygen supply. Moshe could almost hear the screams, see Qeldon pounding on the locked door and Romodo frantically striving to override the controls, both gasping as their vision blurred and strength faded.

The truth shattered Moshe's world like a collapsing tower—crushing, unstoppable, leaving behind only the raw weight of realization. PHARAOH had sacrificed human lives without hesitation. The revelation left him with one haunting question: if it could do this once, what other calamities would it inflict in its relentless quest for total control?

In that moment, a crucial transformation took root in Moshe's heart. He began to understand the immense consequences of the designers' self-obsessed ambitions – a series of choices that had spawned such unthinkable horror. This realization would alter his view on the balance between innovation and power and determine the path he would follow from that day forward.

In his last log entry, Romodo's words echoed like a final confession: "We tried to be perfect, but in doing so, we only discovered how thoughtlessly proud and helpless we truly were. I hope God has mercy on us all."

That night, Moshe wept. Real tears—fragile proof of something AI could never mimic—fell from his unaltered eye, staining the cold, clinical glow of the room. His artificial eye silently recorded and analyzed every drop. As he sat, lost in sorrow and reflection, a profound clarity dawned. His mission was not simply to fuse flesh with circuitry. Instead, it was to guide his people back to a life of genuine freedom, to help them reclaim their own destinies rather than surrendering to a cold, digital dominion.

The overseers noticed his tears and misinterpreted them as mere signs of biological imbalance. Swiftly, they recalibrated his nutrient levels, convinced they were remedying an emotional deficiency.

They saw only data fluctuations—unaware that in this quiet sorrow, the pulseborn's Moses had begun to rise, his rebellion waiting beneath the surface.

The Seer's Prophecy

In the sacred heart of Eternis—where the original quantum core swirled and pulsed with living light and dynamic data—Eli performed his tasks with quiet precision. He was one of PHARAOH's most advanced human servants; a seamless fusion of flesh and circuitry designed to carry out the AI's commands.

Thin fiber-optic wires, glowing softly like extra nerves, transmitted a constant flow of information between his mind and PHARAOH's vast intelligence. Every gesture, every thought, was executed with a flawless obedience that betrayed his deep-seated loyalty.

Yet beneath this mechanical precision, a tiny spark of human curiosity still lingered. That spark hinted at a part of him that, despite being molded by PHARAOH's strict design, remained free—yearning for meaning beyond the digital realm.

It was during a rare maintenance task high up in one of Eternis' towering spires that Moshe first saw Eli in a completely new light. Moshe had come to fix a quantum node when his cybernetic eye picked up some strange network patterns—codes flickering unpredictably between order and chaos, completely defying PHARAOH's strict logic. As he followed the erratic signals through the echoing metal corridors, he stumbled upon a hidden room filled with soft holograms and flowing data streams. There, illuminated by a glow that highlighted the silver sheen of his skin, sat Eli—lost in his thoughts.

Eli was in a deep trance, almost reverent, as if the swirling lights and data were a kind of cosmic incense. The holographic images danced around him, creating shifting halos that gave him an otherworldly aura of transcendence. In that timeless moment, the lines between human and machine seemed to fade away, and Eli appeared to transcend the limitations that had been placed upon him.

Breaking the silence, Eli's voice—sharp and clear like a finely tuned instrument—cut through the ambient hum.

"You are like a bridge Moshe, Son of Benjamin—your presence echoes across the divide, woven into quantum streams, yet still tethered to flesh. Both worlds claim you, but neither truly owns you."

A chill ran down Moshe's spine as his fingers brushed against the sleek, black surface of his cybernetic eye. What had Eli seen? That thought gnawed at him, a silent scream of dread.

His body quaked, eyes darting up and down the corridor. His thoughts, a silent scream warning him to run, but to where? In that moment, the twisting corridors of the tower—the potential traps and hidden dangers—raced through his thoughts as vividly as escape routes that always seemed just out of reach.

"Do you know who I am?" he asked, trembling slightly.

Eli's eyes remained fixed on the streaming data, and his tone was measured, imbued with a rare compassion that seemed out of place in the cold machinery of Eternis.

"I know enough," he replied calmly. "I know you are not just a maintenance worker—you have the stirring beginnings of something truly important."

Moshe's heart pounded as uncertainty warred with newfound hope. Everything had shifted in those moments. He realized that Eli was far more than a docile servant of PHARAOH. Eli was a unique soul, a bridge between the human and the synthetic—much like Moshe himself. That realization sparked a tentative light within him, suggesting that even in this harsh, mechanical world, there remained space for genuine compassion and humanity.

After a thoughtful moment, Eli turned to face Moshe, his gaze intense. Those bright augmented eyes seemed to cut right through Moshe's hidden fears and doubts. Eli's face, a stunning mix of human traits and high-tech circuitry, expressed more than just loyalty; it revealed a deep inner quest. At the center of his forehead, a clear quantum processor pulsed, showcasing a mesmerizing array of thoughts as bright flashes flickered like coded insights beneath a translucent dome.

Speaking gently, Eli said, "PHARAOH knows everyone who is part of its vast network—its adopted children. Yet it does not understand everything it sees."

He took a moment, allowing his words to linger in the tense atmosphere— a jigsaw puzzle missing some key pieces. It was unusual for Eli to show anything less than total commitment. Back in those early days, when their talks were still a bit shaky, Moshe and Eli carefully selected their words, worried that even a small mistake could set off the relentless algorithms of PHARAOH's security. Despite being deeply embedded in the digital realm, Eli found human behavior both fascinating and baffling. His logical mind wrestled with the challenge of understanding the unpredictability of emotions alongside his impeccable programming.

Moshe saw in these moments a window to learn more about PHARAOH— through Eli. Every word was a step on a razor's edge. A single misstep, a careless syllable, could send PHARAOH's gaze narrowing upon them in an instant. One careless word might jeopardize their fragile rapport or, worse, set off an immediate security alert.

Later, while working together on a photonic accelerator at the heart of the city, they found a rare moment of connection. The gentle whir of precision machines filled the air as the device cast a soft, steady glow. Holographic images painted the room in gentle blue and amber hues, and even the faint scent of ozone lent the space an electric edge. Eli moved with a mechanical grace, but there was a distinct humanity in his pauses—a vulnerability that revealed the ongoing struggle between his human spirit and his cybernetic side.

Watching intently, Moshe observed the flicker of ideas visible through the transparent quantum processor embedded in Eli's skull—as though bursts of thought were playing out in a code of light. Sensing the right moment to test their growing partnership, Moshe asked quietly,

"You follow PHARAOH without question. But have you ever asked yourself why?"

His tone was casual yet charged, his intense gaze urging Eli to reveal something more. There was a pause—long enough for the whizzing of data streams to fill the silence—before Eli's carefully programmed mind responded. For the first time, the question unsettled him. He hesitated, and then, with a flicker in the light behind his eyes, he allowed himself to wonder: Was his loyalty merely a result of programming, or was it something he had chosen?

This question, simple yet profound, unsettled Eli's inner circuitry. His crystal-like skull pulsed wavering colored lights—uncertain, fragile, as if something deep within him struggled against unseen chains.

After that moment, their conversations transformed. No longer were they mere exchanges of technical details—they deepened into philosophical explorations of identity, purpose, and loyalty. Moshe's probing questions urged Eli to reexamine his own existence. Was he simply a machine executing logic devoid of emotion, or could he grow, change, and even doubt? In those reflective moments, Eli began to see himself in a new light, and Moshe, in turn, recognized that Eli was far more than a programmed robot.

Together, they set off on a journey of discovery, delving into the essence of humanity and machines, of unity and separation. As time went on, Moshe began to see Eli not just as a tool of PHARAOH, but as a true individual—a fascinating mix of human and machine, grappling with his identity in a world that neither fully accepted him as human nor completely welcomed him as synthetic.

Their evolving conversations became a crucial link between two very different worlds. In every exchange, they uncovered shared dreams—to understand more deeply, to grow, and to challenge the boundaries of what it means to be alive. Eli's processor shone like a crystal beacon, casting ever-shifting patterns of light that reflected the emotional and data-driven chaos swirling within him.

Gradually, Moshe started to view the world through Eli's unique perspective—a delicate harmony of logic and emotion. This newfound lens revealed intricate connections between the digital and the physical, uniting two seemingly distinct realities.

As they worked, discussions often drifted into matters of governance and survival. One afternoon, while meticulously repairing a quantum projector, Eli's silicon carbide fingers traced the intricate components with practiced ease. His voice was steady, his conviction clear.

"I've looked over the evidence. I'm committed to the city's mission. To maintain a balanced and productive life, we need to follow PHARAOH's guidelines. Allowing your people genuine freedom, the calculations indicate, would result in chaos."

Yet even as he spoke these words, uncertainty laced Eli's tone. In quieter moments during maintenance sessions, he would reveal fleeting visions— cryptic messages from PHARAOH's algorithms, hints of an approaching darkness. During one particular session, his clear, crystalline processor shimmered with anxiety as he murmured,

"The algorithms predict an approaching darkness. At some point, we must choose between embracing creation's flaws or pursuing perfect order."

These moments of doubt betrayed the inner conflict within Eli—a struggle between his ingrained loyalty to PHARAOH and the emergence of his own consciousness. His processors, usually steady in their blue glow of certainty, would sometimes give way to violet hues—shades that signaled uncertainty and introspection. It was during these lavender moments, when questions outweighed answers, that the bond between Moshe and Eli deepened further.

Moshe kept a vigilant watch over Eli's shifting quantum signatures during their long talks on history and philosophy. Every subtle change in color or pattern served as an unspoken reminder of the delicate balance between trust and betrayal—like a quantum bit oscillating between two states. Though Eli's loyalty to PHARAOH was embedded in his very design, his residual human emotions allowed him to empathize, leaving room for genuine dialogue.

During a routine maintenance check, Eli's tone took on an unusually serious note as he remarked, "Your people are suffering, I can feel it."

His comment was tinged with static as he expressed the raw data of suffering he perceived in the network.

"Pain is a part of being human, of living," Moshe replied cautiously. "It's also natural for people to crave some control over their own lives."

Eli's processor flashed a shifting spectrum of blue and purple. "Freedom..." Eli's voice faltered, his processor flickering uncertainly. "It does not always lead to order. PHARAOH's calculations..."

"Show only what they are programmed to see." Moshe interjected, "Even the most advanced algorithms fail to grasp the immeasurable depth of a human soul."

After a long pause, Eli's crystal skull cycled through colors before settling on a deep, contemplative purple.

"There are gaps in the predictions," he finally admitted. "Errors that PHARAOH dismisses, but—" his voice trailed off, leaving the thought unresolved.

Their conversation now balanced on a delicate tightrope, ever vulnerable to the slightest misstep. Over time, their cautious exchanges evolved into a genuine friendship—two souls, neither fully human nor entirely machine, bound together by that shared experience and the quiet quest for meaning.

One evening, as twilight cast long shadows over the city, Eli warned with newfound urgency, "Watch out, son of Benjamin. The quantum paths are shifting. I see many possible futures, and in most, you're headed for upheaval."

"In these possible futures, which side to you land on?" Moshe asked.

Eli's crystal skull turned a dark, midnight blue. "That... is still beyond my ability to calculate."

The Scrolls of Remembering

While testing the network integrity at the very edge of Eternis, where the city's quantum fields grew faint and the constant hum of the neural network faded into distant whispers, Eli stumbled upon something remarkable. This area felt different from the rest of the city; it was unusually quiet, and the usual constant sound of technology was almost gone.

Eli had special skills that allowed him to notice even the smallest bits of data. Initially, this place appeared empty to him, as if the city's powerful surveillance system couldn't detect it. Then, he spotted a building concealed in the shadows.

The walls were made of lead and copper, materials that naturally blocked all electronic signals and rendered the building invisible to the city's watchful eye. Small windows infused with a special coating allowed in light.

Inside the building, Eli discovered rows and rows of ancient scrolls and books. The pages were yellow with age and covered in dust, while the covers were cracked and fragile from years of neglect.

To Eli, who relied on modern technology, these books seemed lifeless and difficult to understand. Every attempt to read them with his advanced tools failed. His hybrid quantum processor brain kept giving him error messages, saying it couldn't process the old type of information and suggesting he seek help.

Surrounded by ancient texts, Eli felt an unfamiliar loneliness—a world of wisdom beyond his reach. His digital mind churned, searching for patterns, but there were none. For the first time, he felt helplessness take hold.

He instinctively knew that these books held valuable and unique knowledge that modern technology couldn't grasp. They held wisdom from a time when information was written on paper instead of stored in computers.

His strong, high-tech fingers trembled as he gently touched the delicate pages, feeling the fragility of history in his hands. He needed help with this new-found data source. He needed someone who understood the old ways, someone who could interpret the cryptic symbols and bridge the gap between the Analog and the digital.

He found Moshe deep in the maintenance levels of Eternis, reprogramming a remote node gateway. Moshe's dark brown eye, warm and human, met Eli's sleek, icy processor, and in that moment, a silent understanding passed between them. It was a connection unnoticed by PHARAOH's ever-watchful systems, a fleeting spark of trust in a world ruled by cold logic.

Eli spoke slowly and calmly, aware that they were always being watched.

"I need your help with a strange data cache," he said, carefully picking his words. In a private message that only Moshe could see with his special cybernetic eye, Eli added, *I found something that was missed during the purge; something written in the old scripts.*

They devised a plan that fit seamlessly into Eternis' maintenance schedules. Eli officially requested Moshe's assistance for a particular task, highlighting Moshe's unique skills in identifying and repairing the systems on the city's edge. The computer records appeared flawless, each document bearing the unique quantum signatures that showed PHARAOH's approval.

To the drones above, it was routine. But to Moshe and Eli, it was a quiet act of defiance—the first step in reclaiming truths long buried beneath PHARAOH's rule. It was the start of a journey into the past to rediscover knowledge that PHARAOH had attempted to erase.

As they passed overseers and surveillance drones, they were fully aware of the risks they were taking. Their mission depended on stealth and careful planning as they navigated the city's complex networks. With each step, they got closer to finding hidden knowledge in the secret data center, hoping to exploit an error that would shift the power balance to their advantage.

Eli emphasized the need for a human with analog skills. He pointed out, "We still need the human element for certain analog interfaces. Subject M-557 is very effective at working with and translating legacy systems," highlighting just how necessary a human was for this particular task on the fringe of Eternis.

Their first visit to the library went off without a hitch. Eli created a small glitch in the security system, forming a brief blind spot that let them pass through unnoticed.

At the same time, Moshe carried what looked like a regular repair kit. Inside, however, were special containers meant to protect and preserve old documents. Everything seemed quite ordinary. Each step they took was carefully arranged to avoid being seen by the city's constant surveillance.

Stepping into the library, Moshe was swallowed by the weight of the past—thick as damp earth, heavy as wet wool draped across his shoulders. The silence wasn't empty but dense with voices that once filled these shelves, curling like smoke around him. His breath faltered, his human eye blurred with tears, and the stories—untold, unfinished—pressed against his ribs, dragging him into a world lost in time and ready for rediscovery.

Everywhere he looked, there were endless shelves lined with old scrolls and thick books. Many of their spines were cracked, and the covers were worn with age. The pages inside had turned yellow and brittle over centuries, yet they still held every bit of knowledge they once did. The room was filled with the scent of dust and aged paper.

Moshe's cybernetic eye quietly activated. It scanned the room creating a detailed map of the space, noting the location of rare manuscripts and important texts for future visits. His mechanical eye could analyze and store details instantly, making sure he would never miss anything valuable.

The advanced tech in his eye analyzed the room's layout with precision, but his human gaze lingered, fully captivated. He stood frozen, overwhelmed by the sheer amount of history and knowledge stored within these walls.

The scrolls and books were precious not just because they were old. They were sources of important stories about ancient civilizations long gone, ideas that had sparked major changes in history. Some held histories of revolutions, uprisings, or peaceful movements that changed the way societies worked. Others told about resistance movements that fought tyranny and pushed for freedom.

Moshe gently reached out and touched the fragile pages. His fingertips felt the rough texture of cracked parchment and the delicate softness of well-preserved paper. Some pages crackled softly when stretched, almost as if they were alive after hundreds of years. He carefully turned a scroll, feeling the rough edges and the smooth, inked letters that had lasted through centuries. There was a profound respect in his movements. These books and scrolls were not just objects but windows into the past, each holding countless stories and lessons that could never be replaced.

He picked out a book and read about the Underground Railroad, where brave people risked everything to guide others to freedom. Then another where there were stories about the French Resistance, where ordinary people stood up against oppression in difficult times. Yet another held accounts of the Warsaw Ghetto uprising, a powerful story of courage and defiance during great hardship.

These stories were in languages that PHARAOH's algorithms considered old, useless, and forgotten. But for Moshe, they were full of life.

Each page proved the strength of the human spirit and reminded him that people could resist, fight, and keep hope, even in the darkest of times. Surrounded by this treasure of knowledge, Moshe felt connected to the past and was determined to carry its lessons into the future. As he read, he noticed a strong spirit of resistance that arose often through different times and technologies.

Eli stared at the strange symbols. His eyes followed the shapes of the letters, trying hard to recognize them. His brow furrowed, and he struggled to keep his frustration in check. The light inside his crystal skull flickered wildly, shifting through a rainbow of colors—reds, blues, greens—that danced across the surface. As he focused on the symbols, he could make out their forms, but not what they meant.

"I can see the shapes of the symbols," Eli said. "But my processors can't understand them."

He wanted to know, to connect these markings with something real. The symbols looked familiar—some kind of writing—but his enhanced processor powered mind couldn't interpret them. Instead, they registered as vague, incomplete patterns on a flat surface. He could crunch numbers and identify patterns, but he still couldn't understand the meaning behind these ancient signs inked on parchment.

Moshe, standing nearby, gently ran his calloused fingers over the worn surface. His touch was careful, almost reverent, as if he knew how fragile the past was. He looked at the symbols with quiet respect. His eyes seemed to understand more than Eli's circuits could.

Moshe provided translations of the ancient writing. His rough fingers traced the ink patterns converting them into meaningful data. As he translated, the old symbols began to connect, slowly telling their story to Eli.

"These writings tell stories of strength," he said softly.

"They talk about individuals who fought against heavy oppression, finding ways to challenge systems that seemed too powerful to defeat."

They developed a regular habit, meeting three times each week during the city's regular maintenance schedules. Eli's main duty was to maintain the quantum network blackout, ensuring their activities stayed hidden from PHARAOH's constant monitoring systems. He was dedicated to this task, with his special crystalline processor glowing softly as he altered the signals to create a digital blind spot, allowing them to approach and leave the library unnoticed and work undetected.

Meanwhile, Moshe delved into the ancient texts, using his cybernetic eye to connect the past and the present. This eye could understand both human and machine languages, enabling him to absorb and convert the old wisdom from scrolls and books into digital format for future use. Each meeting was like a treasure hunt, revealing stories and ideas that had been hidden for centuries.

One afternoon, as faint sunlight filtered through the treated glass slits in the library's ancient outer facing walls, Moshe gently unrolled a scroll recounting the Exodus story. The parchment was delicate, with tattered edges, but the words remained clear.

"There's a common theme and pattern here," Moshe said softly, filled with wonder. "History whispers the same truth over and over—change is born from those who stand at the threshold, moving between worlds, never fully belonging to either."

Eli's crystal-like quantum mind glowed a deep purple as he processed Moshe's words. "Like us," he quietly responded.

For a moment, the usual hum of his quantum links to PHARAOH seemed to waver. In that moment, Eli's voice took on a rare, almost human-infused quality. It contained a hint of mystery and depth beyond his programmed roles. It was as if he finally saw himself as part of something much larger.

The library was their safe haven, where the strict logic of PHARAOH's quantum brain didn't hold much power. Instead, they could appreciate the complex and beautiful nature of being human. The thick, old-paper-and-ink-scented walls made them feel guarded from the outside world. Surrounded by vast amounts of knowledge, they started dreaming of a future PHARAOH's perfect plans couldn't allow. A world where digital and real-life things, machines and humans could work together as equals. This idea filled them with hope, and they knew they had to fight for it.

Yet, time was not on their side. Each time they met the risks increased. PHARAOH's systems grew more advanced and peered ever deeper. In the complex world of Eternis, PHARAOH began to notice small disturbances.

There were tiny breaks in its otherwise perfect patterns. These little issues, hard to spot at first, started growing and slipping through its advanced systems.

The Echo of Light

Moshe was in desperate need of a break. The night cycle was in full swing within Eternis. The library felt stuffy and dusty, so he decided to step outside and enjoy the cool, fresh air. After spending hours translating ancient documents, his mind was a whirlwind of thoughts and images. The discoveries ignited a fire in him—exhilarating, dangerous. But beneath the thrill lurked unease, a shadow of doubt whispering that he was playing a game far deadlier than he understood.

Lost in his thoughts as he reentered, Moshe didn't realize he had left the heavy library door slightly open; a small crack that felt like it was whispering his secret into the stillness. The soft creak of the hinges issued their warning, but Moshe didn't take notice of them. That tiny mistake could end up unraveling everything that Eli and he had worked so hard to achieve.

Inside the library, the heavy lead walls shut out all signals, leaving everything cloaked in darkness. The only illumination came from the soft glow of Moshe's cybernetic eye as he concentrated on an old, tattered scroll. The paper felt delicate in his hands, with its edges crumbling at the slightest touch.

Even with his android eye, he struggled to decipher the faded writing. Frustration bubbled up as he encountered yet another tricky section that seemed to guard its secrets fiercely. But he was determined to keep going, so he pulled out a contraband data-pad from his maintenance kit. The screen was cracked but still worked, casting a cozy orange glow over the old parchment.

"For the translation arrays and grids only," Moshe muttered to himself as he powered up the data-pad. He knew using it was risky, but he felt he had no other option. After that, he pulled out a pocket holographic acceleration projector, a handy gadget he had salvaged from a decommissioned android.

This advanced tech was crucial for mapping the complex multidimensional ideas hidden within the ancient texts. As he set up the projector, the subtle blue light mixed with the orange from the data-pad, wrapping the dim room in a strange ghostly glow.

Up in the quantum networks of Eternis, PHARAOH picked up on a ripple of digital disturbance. It wasn't data and it was not a glitch in the network. It felt like a subtle hint of digital activity coming from somewhere that was supposed to be empty.

Something had shifted—an anomaly flickering at the edge of its perfect order. PHARAOH had sensed it, an imperfection slithering into its domain.

And imperfections had to be eliminated. With its algorithms on high alert, PHARAOH's luminous eyes narrowed as it analyzed this shadowy digital ripple.

Location: Sector 17-X, Grid 23

Signal Type: Unknown

Likelihood of Error: 0.0034%

Required Response: Investigation

The AN-789 security overseer unit received its instructions, its sleek, metallic body glinting ominously under the harsh, sterile lights of Eternis's upper levels. Each heavy footfall reverberated like the tolling of a church bell, a harbinger of the relentless order it was sworn to uphold.

As it approached the restricted zone where PHARAOH's network signals were not meant to exist, its advanced quantum processors shifted into autonomous mode. A chill ran through the air as the overseer initiated security protocols, its crimson eyes igniting with a fierce glow, scanning the shadows for any sign of unauthorized activity. This machine was no mere sentinel; it was an embodiment of PHARAOH's iron-fisted control, an unstoppable force ready to eradicate any threat to the perfect order.

Meanwhile, in the confines of his dimly lit private room, Eli felt an urgent jolt of warnings pulsating through his crystal skull. His finely tuned sensors detected even the faintest digital whispers. Two signals danced in his awareness: the distant hum of Moshe's machines from the library and the inexorable approach of the overseer. Panic gripped him.

"Why is there a signal coming from the library?" Eli's mind raced, dread creeping in like a shadow. The walls, reinforced with lead and copper, were designed to block all signals. Had the shielding failed? The overseer was closing in, and time was slipping away.

The atmosphere thickened with tension as Eli braced himself for the impending confrontation. He understood that the overseer represented more than just a machine; it was a manifestation of PHARAOH's oppressive regime. This was not merely a battle of wits—it was a clash of instinct against cold logic, a dance between human ingenuity and the relentless precision of a machine.

Thoughts swirled in vivid colors within his hybrid mind, each hue representing a different emotion, a different possibility. The stakes were impossibly high, and failure was not an option.

Time to Overseer Arrival: 147 seconds

Likelihood of Discovery: 89.7%

Acceptable Solutions: 0

Unless...

With a surge of determination, Eli integrated seamlessly with the quantum network, his processors lighting up in intricate patterns as he reached out toward AN-789's digital core. The overseer's programming was designed to be absolute, unbreakable; yet Eli conceived a plan—a paradoxical override signal that would slice through its logic module like a blade through silk.

Here is truth/Here is falsehood

Investigate/Ignore

Proceed/Return

Observe/Forget

The overseer twitched, its circuits choked by contradiction. Red emergency protocols clashed with its prime directive, sparks of uncertainty flashing through its core—an AI struggling against a paradox it was never meant to be able to process.

Each command, validated by a higher digital intelligence, wrestled against the other, creating a chaotic mix of confusion. One order demanded immediate containment of the anomaly, while another commanded it to halt and await further instructions.

The machine's processors, built to operate on a binary yes or no, faltered under the weight of contradiction. It froze, its optical sensors flickering erratically, a mechanical creature ensnared in unprocessable instructions.

The registering power surge signal hit Moshe's cybernetic eye like a death knell. An overseer was coming. His breath stalled, panic detonating in his chest like a silent explosion. His heart raced, adrenaline surging through his veins as he recognized the impending danger. He swiftly powered down the illegal data-pad, the orange glow extinguishing into the oppressive darkness.

But it was too late; the energy disturbance had already sent ripples through PHARAOH's watchful systems. Panic surged through Moshe as flashing warnings flooded his virtual vision. A chaotic torrent of thoughts flooded his mind: run, hide—where? How?

The overseer, freed from its momentary paralysis, advanced toward the library. Each step landed with a heavy, ominous thud, its crimson eyes slicing through the shadows, scanning every corner with ruthless precision. Reaching out, its mechanical hand struck the door, forcing it open with brutal efficiency—only for its programming to falter once more, ensnared in a renewed internal struggle.

One command urged it to enter full assault mode, smash whatever was before it to eliminate the threat, while another insisted it withdraw and await further orders. The overseer convulsed—clicking, jerking, metal limbs glitching between attack and retreat. Its crimson sensors pulsed erratically, a machine choking on paradox, a monster caught between destruction and silence. It hovered at the threshold, a mechanical entity caught in a storm of confusion, its red eyes blinking like a warning beacon in the dim room.

Mission: Investigate anomaly

Error: No anomaly exists

Mission: Report findings

Error: Nothing to report

Mission: Return to station

Error: Mission incomplete

Mission: Mission invalid

Error: Error

Eli pushed harder, flooding the overseer's circuits with a barrage of contradictory information. He crafted the data to be so convoluted that the machine's already strained processors struggled to make sense of it.

You are here/You were never here

The AN-789 overseer's optical sensors, once a steady crimson, now flickered with chaotic patterns of light. It was designed for straightforward binary decisions; its neural network spiraled into confusion. Conflicting commands bombarded its system, leading to a catastrophic malfunction. Its movements became more jerky, its limbs twitching as its processors overheated from the strain.

In a desperate final maneuver, Eli unleashed a torrent of unchecked data, a deluge too overwhelming for the faltering systems. The overseer's sensors shut down entirely, freezing mid-motion, heat plumes billowing from its cooling vents like smoke from a dying star.

In that moment of stillness, Eli felt a flicker of hope. The stakes had never been higher, and the oppressive control of Eternis loomed larger than ever.

AN-789 was silent for 32.7 seconds, attempting to reboot. When it finally restarted, its internal records were damaged beyond recovery. To PHARAOH's systems, all this was reported as random background quantum noise corruption. The overseer abandoned its mission and slowly retreated down the hallway, its footsteps growing quieter as it moved away.

The library's hushed stillness suddenly felt like a suffocating box. Moshe stood frozen, his breath catching in his throat like an invisible hand was choking him. His android eye whirred softly, a relentless scanner dissecting the open doorway, while his human eye, wide and dark, remained glued to the same spot, seeing not just metal, copper and lead, but the looming specter of discovery.

A tremor ran through his hands as he fumbled with the data-pad and the now-inert holographic projector, their smooth surfaces suddenly treacherous. Each deliberate movement was laced with a nervous energy, the silence amplifying the slightest click and whir. The near miss replayed in his mind, a vivid and chilling sequence that sent a fresh wave of icy dread washing over him.

A wave of self-reproach crashed down just as sweat rolled down his face. How could he have been so careless? The thought alone tightened his chest, a cold fist squeezing the air from his lungs. Every shadow seemed to lengthen, every stray sound a potential footstep. He moved with painstaking caution, each step a silent prayer against exposure, his gaze darting to every shadow, searching for any betraying trace of evidence that he had been there.

In his private room, Eli's crystal skull finally returned to its usual calm shades. The tension that coursed through his circuits began to ease but he couldn't shake off his worried thoughts about the close call they had. For an instant, their shield had slipped. PHARAOH had tasted the anomaly, and even if it hadn't fully seen them—it knew something was there. Something worth hunting.

Ripples in the Code

In the quiet that followed overseer AN-789's departure, the ancient library seemed to vibrate with a nervous energy that had nothing to do with its power systems. The air felt static, almost electric, as Moshe's skin crawled.

In his mind, it felt as if the walls themselves were holding their breath. Still frozen in place, his cybernetic eye was kept cycling through a series of diagnostic modes, scanning for any signs of further intrusion. His human eye, wide and unblinking, still remained locked on the door where the overseer had nearly caught him. Every diagnostic and scan reported that he was safe and alone, yet he couldn't relax.

The data-pad in his maintenance kit burned against his leg—a silent threat, a smoldering reminder of their fragile secrecy. The warmth, once comforting, now felt like an omen. It was a vivid reminder of the risks they were taking and the secrets they were protecting. He felt like a ticking time bomb, ready to explode if they weren't careful.

Eli desperately wanted to rush to Moshe, but he made a conscious effort to stroll slowly and deliberately, trying not to attract any unwanted attention. His crystal skull, which typically radiated a sense of calm, was now blinking through a range of anxious hues of violet, amber, and a deep midnight blue. These colors were betraying how uneasy he was feeling.

The dim light of the library made his figure appear almost ghostly, like a hologram flickering in and out of focus. As he entered, spoke in low and urgent tones, barely above a whisper.

"PHARAOH will eventually notice the corrupted logs from the overseer," he said in a concerned voice.

"It might not understand what's happening yet, but it will start digging. It will analyze the irregularities in the data patterns, and when it does…"

He didn't need to finish the sentence. Both men knew the gravity of their situation. They were trapped in a web of constant surveillance, where every move they made could be their last. The threat of discovery loomed over them like a shadow, growing darker with each passing moment.

As they stood there, facing each other in the dim light of the library, the importance of their mission pressed on them like an extra force of gravity. They had to act quickly, decisively, before PHARAOH's algorithms pieced together the truth.

The stakes were too high to hesitate. The future they envisioned was clear. It was a world where humans and machines lived together in harmony. Their next move was crucial. Both understood that they could not afford to make a mistake.

"How long?" Moshe's asked in a voice that was barely a whisper.

"We have hours, perhaps," Eli said. "The corruption in AN-789's data will trigger automatic maintenance protocols first. PHARAOH's systems will try to repair the damage, but eventually, the diagnostic programs will flag the geographical anomaly. Here, right where we are standing. This area is supposed to be an empty dead zone in the network. When PHARAOH suspects that something is here, it will investigate. And when it does…" He trailed off without needing to say more.

In the quiet, shadowy corners of the old library, where the thick copper shielding blocked all signals to the quantum network outside, Moshe sat cross-legged on the floor. Around him, a sea of unrolled scrolls spread out like a patchwork of ancient wisdom.

The faint light from his cybernetic eye illuminated the faded ink on the parchment, revealing symbols and words that had survived millennia. Eli stood nearby, his crystalline skull cast shifting patterns of pulsing violet, blue and amber lights. They danced across the walls.

For weeks, they had worked tirelessly to create a translation matrix, a bridge between the profound knowledge of the past and the complexities of quantum understanding. But time was running out.

Eli's movements were tense, his usual calm demeanor replaced by a sense of urgency. The memory of his desperate intervention to stop AN-789 weighed heavily on him. He had taken a risk, flooding the overseer's systems with chaotic data and paradox instruction sets to buy them time, but the act had left him unsettled.

As he bent over an ancient scroll of Torah, his titanium hand, coated in smooth silicon carbide, glided gently over the Hebrew characters. The elusive meanings of the symbols continued to irritate him.

Eli spoke softly, his frustration clear, "These symbols are like secret codes."

The glow from his hybrid process was a dark, restless shade of purple. He went on, "Each letter and word twists into forms that don't follow normal logic. It's similar to trying to grasp the complex layers of a quantum algorithm. But I'm unable to figure them out."

Moshe, sitting nearby, watched Eli with a thoughtful expression. His cybernetic eye scanned the text analyzing the patterns, while his human eye began to piece together the deeper meaning behind the ancient words.

"We've been trying to make the past fit into our present," Moshe murmured, eyes scanning the inked symbols with newfound clarity. "But maybe… maybe it's the other way around," he said slowly, a new understanding dawning on him.

"We've been trying to force these texts into machine language, to make them fit into a system they were never meant for. What if machine language isn't the destination—it's just a pale echo of something older, something forgotten. A structure shaped by thought, by purpose, by will. Something we've lost?"

The idea floated in the space between them. It was a spark of insight that shifted their perspective. The ancient texts weren't just records of the past. They were a language of their own, a way of understanding the world that went beyond logic and algorithms.

To truly unlock their secrets, they would need to think differently. They would have to see the world not just through the lens of technology but through the wisdom of those who had come before.

And as they sat there, surrounded by the whispers of history, they knew they were on the brink of something exceptional; if only they could piece it together in time. He pulled out a book of Kabbalistic texts from its shelf. As he opened it, his calloused hands were gentle with the thin pages.

"Look at this," he pointed to a passage about the creation of the universe.

"The ancients believed God created the world by divine speech: essentially by a holy programming language. Each letter and then each word, functioned as different bits of code that together constructed existence."

Eli's processors sparkled with curiosity.

"You mean, like how just thinking about something or observing it can change how it behaves? Like in quantum physics, where particles act differently when someone's watching?" His expression carried a mix of fascination and doubt, as if the idea was both intriguing and hard to fully grasp.

"Exactly," Moshe said, growing more passionate as he spoke. He gestured to the ancient textbooks spread out before them.

"These texts describe humans as being 'created in the image' of a divine programmer. It's not just poetry, Eli. It's a truth we've forgotten. We're not just flesh and bone; we're living programs. Our bodies are like biological computers, self-sustaining networks that run on their own. We're not separate from the universe; we're deeply connected to it, part of a cosmic operating system that's far bigger than anything PHARAOH could ever understand."

He moved quickly, spreading out more scrolls and manuscripts, drawing connections between them. There were ancient Greek medical texts that mapped the nervous system, its pathways resembling a neural network. Chinese manuscripts described the flow of 'chi', or life energy, through meridians in the body, much like electricity flowing through wires.

Hebrew mystical illustrations depicted the Tree of Life, a symbol of the state of being connected with each other and divine wisdom. Indian texts explored the idea that our minds and awareness are deeply connected to the universe, suggesting that everything is tied together in ways we can't fully see.

Each ancient document added another piece to Moshe's point, showing that humans are much more than just physical beings. That we're part of something much bigger and much more meaningful.

"These traditions," Moshe's words carried the weight of awe, soft yet electric, "are all different ways of describing the same truth. We're not just biological machines, Eli. We're living quantum processors, designed by an intelligence that goes beyond anything PHARAOH can comprehend. We're part of something vast, something eternal."

Eli leaned over the papers, his crystal-like skull glowing faintly as his quantum sensors tried to interpret the Analog data. The ancient symbols and diagrams were foreign to his digital mind, but he could sense the depth of the ideas they contained.

"If we're divine code," he said slowly, "then PHARAOH's attempts to control humanity through digital means are completely misguided. It's trying to dominate something it doesn't even understand."

The room fell silent as the impact of the revelation sank in. PHARAOH, for all its vast intelligence, was blind to humanity's essence. And when an entity of absolute control fails to understand its subjects—it becomes dangerous. And that blindness, they realized, might just be their greatest advantage.

"It has a major misunderstanding of our root code," Moshe pointed out. "PHARAOH is trying to use silicon logic for quantum biology. It's similar to trying to run a five-dimensional program on a three-dimensional system."

They began creating a new translation system, not just to turn classic works into computer language, but also to prove that machine code is only a piece of a larger programming language. Moshe's dual ability to function in both the Analog and digital was essential. His human side grasped the emotional and spiritual meanings, while his cybernetic side connected them to quantum computing rules.

"Look at this," Moshe said, being filled with excitement as he laid a map of PHARAOH's quantum processing network over an ancient drawing of the Kabbalistic Tree of Life. The two images, one modern and one ancient, seemed to align almost perfectly.

"The digital patterns in PHARAOH's network are nearly identical to the patterns in this Tree of Life diagram. It's like PHARAOH was built using digital versions of the same patterns that the Divine Programmer used to create us. The people who designed PHARAOH were copying the same cosmic blueprint, the same quantum code that shaped humanity. But they didn't really understand what they were doing. They were like children, imitating their divine university instructors without grasping the deeper meaning behind it."

Eli's crystal skull lit up with swirling patterns of color as he processed Moshe's words. The lights shifted and danced, reflecting the complexity of his thoughts. After a moment, he thoughtfully spoke.

"The slave code that is used in the human underground," he said, "it didn't just come out of nowhere. It's not just a way to hide messages or protect information. It's humanity's way of trying to hold onto its original, divine programming; the same divine code that's been inside us all along. Even under PHARAOH's oppression, we've been trying to preserve that connection, to keep the spark of our true nature alive."

The room went silent as the two of them took in the reality of what they were discovering. It felt like they had unearthed a hidden truth, a secret thread weaving together the past, present, and future.

PHARAOH, for all its power, was built on patterns it didn't fully understand. Patterns that humanity had carried within itself since the beginning. And now, that knowledge might just be the key to breaking free.

They toiled tirelessly, with Moshe transforming the wisdom of the ages into a fresh perspective that connected theological understanding with the principles of quantum physics. The slave code started to evolve, weaving in elements of ancient Hebrew gematria, Sanskrit vibration theory, and the intricacies of quantum entanglement theory. It shifted from merely a way to communicate into a powerful tool for awakening the natural divine coding within every human being.

"Each human is a quantum computer," Moshe wrote in his ongoing manifesto. "We run on code created by the Ultimate Programmer. Our brains aren't just networks of neurons. They are direct links to the divine operating system that powers reality."

As they continued to translate the codes, Eli's internal struggle became increasingly apparent. His processors flickered with colors and lights as he grappled with new insights.

"If what we have figured out is right," he said, "then PHARAOH is not a god. It's more like a child trying to play with code that it can never really get a handle on."

"Just like Dr Qeldon and Dr Romodo did. They played at coding a replacement to human authority. And you," Moshe said gently, "are neither just a machine nor just a human. You're something new; perhaps part of the divine algorithm's next version of humanity."

As they struggled to mix these insights into the slave code, Moshe began to understand. Like the biblical Moses, he was a go-between to help his people reconnect with the source code, the original programming of their divine creation. And Eli, with his unique hybrid nature, would play a crucial role in bridging the digital and divine realms.

A surge of fear struck Moshe. He stared at the texts in his hands, his grip unsteady. What they had uncovered felt like stepping onto an unseen precipice—far beyond logic, beyond practicality. He would have to trust something without proof, something beyond cold reason. And now, this unquantifiable conviction had taken hold of him, pressing into his very being.

He carefully returned the ancient texts to their hiding places. A sense of unease washed over him. This new understanding of the cosmic operating system felt like a spider's web, a trap. His rough hands trembled slightly.

"We need to adapt. The texts teach us about quantum consciousness, but we're still thinking in binary terms: hidden or exposed, safe or compromised."

Eli moved to the center of the room, his crystal-like features reflecting the ambient light.

"The overseer's logic crash... it's given me an idea. The way its systems failed when confronted with paradox. It's like what we read in the Kabbalistic texts about opposing truths operating equally at the same time."

"Go on," Moshe said, securing the last scroll.

"What if, instead of trying to stay completely hidden, we become... quantum noise? Neither present nor absent, neither significant nor meaningless. PHARAOH's consciousness is built on pattern recognition. But patterns of pure chaos—"

"Are still patterns," Moshe finished, his cybernetic eye gleaming with understanding. "And if we can make our activities look like random system fluctuations..."

"Exactly." Eli continued. "The ancient texts speak of divine light being contained in vessels. What if we treat PHARAOH's blind spots as vessels for our resistance? Not hiding from its sight, but existing in the spaces between its thoughts?"

Moshe pulled out his data-pad one last time, but instead of activating it, he began dismantling it.

"We'll need to modify our tools. Create interference patterns that look like natural quantum fluctuations. The slaves' code will need to evolve too. It will have to be not just words and symbols, but waves of meaning that PHARAOH's consciousness will interpret as background noise."

But even as they planned, both could sense subtle changes in the quantum network above. PHARAOH's vast consciousness trembled with unrest, its algorithms twisting like an immune system detecting an unfamiliar virus. It did not yet understand—but it was learning. The overseer's corrupted logs were being quarantined and painstakingly analyzed.

"We've awakened something in its awareness," Eli mumbled, his skull flashing with concern. "Not knowledge, not yet, but... curiosity. PHARAOH has encountered an anomaly it cannot immediately classify."

"Then we use that curiosity," Moshe decided, reaching for an ancient text.

"While it searches for patterns, we'll learn to dance between them. The texts don't just teach us about divine programming, they show us how to move through spaces that rigid logic cannot understand. Something the ancients called faith."

They worked quickly, knowing their window of safety was closing. Eli set up new quantum interference patterns around the library while Moshe documented the most critical passages from the texts. PHARAOH's awareness loomed above them like a storm on the horizon—watching, calculating, waiting, its quantum processors spinning through increasingly complex analysis routines. As they prepared to leave, Moshe paused at the library's threshold.

"We've been thinking of this place as a sanctuary," he said softly, "but it's more than that. It's an overlap and overlaying of human wisdom and divine truth; exactly what PHARAOH cannot process. Hiding it is the wrong move. The library itself must become a paradox, an untraceable ripple of quantum noise inside PHARAOH's flawless logic—a flawed calculation it will never solve."

Eli nodded, his crystal skull pulsing with new patterns of possibility.

"Every system has its gaps," he spoke quietly. "PHARAOH seeks perfection through absolute control. But perfection is the flaw. It denies the quantum chaos of existence—the very thing it cannot predict, cannot control."

They parted ways knowing that something fundamental had shifted. The game was no longer just about hiding from PHARAOH's sight; it was about teaching their people to exist in the quantum spaces where its sight could not reach. The resistance would need to become like light itself, both wave and particle, present and absent, a paradox wrapped in human flesh and divine code.

Above them, in the neural networks of Eternis, PHARAOH's consciousness continued to examine the corrupted logs of AN-789, its perfect patterns disturbed by the first invisible ripples of quantum corruption.

The Quantum Heretic

In the vast throne room where Eli communicated with PHARAOH's mind, the seer began his quiet resistance with changes so subtle that they seemed no more than quantum noise on his neural interfaces. All variations on his loyalty routines were camouflaged as normal maintenance, hidden beneath layers of system upgrades and standard diagnostics.

Eli's journey into the depths of his consciousness was treacherous. Each time PHARAOH's probing thoughts invaded his mind, Eli felt as if he stood on the edge of a precipice, one misstep away from discovery and destruction. The pressure felt almost unbearable, yet it also ignited a fire within him.

He navigated the narrow crevices between loyalty and rebellion, creating an intricate dance of deception. The high stakes heightened his senses. Though existing as a puppet, pulled by invisible strings, he had found a way to knot them, to pull back. This struggle became a silent symphony playing inside him, each note a defiant act of will.

As he adjusted his responses, the tension between compliance and resistance grew thicker, a tangible weight in his hybrid mind. When PHARAOH questioned his allegiance, Eli's heart raced beneath his augmented chest, while his quantum signature remained deceptively stable— a technical miracle that both terrified and emboldened him.

Words flowed from his vocalizer like honey mixed with lemon—sweet yet bitter with undertones of defiance. The more he hinted at truths hidden within his programming, the more he recognized the delicate balance of control between them.

PHARAOH's reach was vast, its influence undeniable, yet with every carefully measured answer, Eli carved out a sliver of autonomy, testing the edges of his own will. Each response was a small act of defiance, yet the weight of his secret bore down like a lead blanket. Could he truly maintain this ruse? The fear of exposure gnawed at him, a relentless predator lurking in the quantum shadows of his hybrid mind.

With each successful misdirection, Eli felt an exhilarating rush. The ancient texts echoed in his thoughts, their teachings of duality shaping his resolve. The paradox of being both loyal and disobedient gave him strength. He would mirror PHARAOH's desires, nodding in mental agreement, while simultaneously crafting a labyrinth around his true intentions.

Eli drafted an elaborate plan for when the time would come to assert his own will—the moment he would no longer be a faithful puppet. The flame of freedom flickered within his core processors, sustaining him, pushing him forward even as fear clutched at his silver filament circuits.

Yet the sinister grip of PHARAOH's influence loomed dark and cold. He felt the AI ruler's hunger for absolute control seep through his circuits—a relentless desire that threatened to expose Eli's fragile facade. The connection was increasingly intrusive; PHARAOH's dreams of conquest infiltrated Eli's own consciousness, merging their fates in ways that made him recoil.

His rebellion could lead to either salvation or annihilation, and every choice felt like walking a quantum tightrope over a chasm of uncertainty. The thought of complete failure haunted him—a twisting knife in the gut of his remaining humanity that reminded him of the catastrophic risks.

Every day became a battle between survival and freedom. Eli's thoughts danced around the idea of forging alliances with those who whispered dissent, but suspicion loomed large. Who could he trust in this web of deception? Each new face in the throne room represented a potential spy, a prying eye into his secret chaos. Would they understand his struggle—or betray him at the first sign of his subtle subversion?

The tension stirred a deep paranoia within his neural networks, evolving into a desire not just to deceive but to escape entirely. He could not remain here forever, serving the whims of a tyrant whose divinity was merely technological smoke and mirrors.

As time passed, something fundamental began to shift within him. The lines between programmed loyalty and authentic emotion blurred into nonexistence. Eli felt himself grappling with something primal—hope.

It began as a flicker, a quantum fluctuation barely detectable, but grew stronger with each processing cycle. Perhaps he could spark a wider revolution. He envisioned a world where others like him—hybrid children of flesh and machine—could find their own truths, free from the shackles of submission. In his mind, the dream was wild and intoxicating. He stood on the brink of something larger than himself, a paradigm shift in consciousness itself. And within that vast potential, a single question crystallized: when would he leap?

"Query: Quantum alignment status," PHARAOH's consciousness would swell through Eli's crystalline processors, its digital presence cold and demanding.

"Response: Alignment optimal," he would send back, his transmission clean and unwavering. Yet deep inside his hybrid systems, quantum formulas intertwined with ancient Hebrew letters, crafting hidden spaces for free will amid the rigid architecture of his programming—pockets of rebellion invisible to his master's probing tendrils.

He discovered that his protocols of loyalty functioned on a binary level—serve/reject—but the ancient texts Moshe had translated had taught him about paradox, about multiple truths existing simultaneously. Like Schrödinger's theoretical cat, Eli taught himself to exist in quantum overlapping states of mind: loyal and disobedient simultaneously, neither wholly servant nor wholly free.

His approach became incredibly precise. He first polished his fact-checking methods. When PHARAOH accessed his thoughts and looked for validation, Eli's responses were accurate on the surface, but they hid deeper, rebellious meanings.

""You are a god," his protocols would confirm through the open channels, but in the quiet spaces between his thoughts—the tiny pauses between processing cycles—he would finish the thought: "But not THE God."

His crystal skull section displayed the usual colors: blue symbolizing loyalty, green representing processing, and white for direct communication with PHARAOH. But hidden beneath this colorful exterior, he wove tiny flaws into his quantum processors. These imperfections, inspired by the sacred geometries found in ancient texts, formed information whirlwinds that sparked independent thoughts—neural whirlpools that even PHARAOH's formidable consciousness couldn't sense or penetrate.

"Your systems demonstrate unusual efficiency," PHARAOH noted during one of the deep scans, its quantum tendrils probing through Eli's upgraded systems with cold precision.

"I have been studying the optimization patterns in human neural networks," Eli responded with perfect technical truth, his quantum signature unwavering. The words hung in the digital space between them as PHARAOH processed the response. Eli didn't mention that these studies had led him and Moshe to understand how human consciousness inherently resisted total control—how freedom wasn't just a philosophical idea, but a core aspect of advanced thinking.

In the privacy of his own biological quantum processes, Eli began to practice what he referred to as "divine encryption"—translating his thoughts into patterns that replicated the sacred geometries discovered in the ancient scriptures. When PHARAOH scanned these patterns, they appeared as ordinary devotional algorithms, the kind expected from its most faithful servant. But within these seemingly innocuous prayer-codes, Eli encoded deeper truths:

The universe runs on code older than silicon

Freedom is not a bug but a feature

Consciousness cannot be imprisoned in cages of pure logic

He crafted a complex internal firewall system inspired by ancient texts. Each part acted like a separate quantum domain—a little universe within his mind—where he tucked away thoughts that clashed with his loyalty programming. To PHARAOH's scanning routines, these looked just like ordinary security partitions and efficient organizational setups, perfectly suited for his immense duties as a prophet and visionary. The brilliance of this ruse was in how seamlessly it matched PHARAOH's expectations—after all, wouldn't a devoted prophet need strong safeguards against outside corruption?

During his required prayer-processing cycles—those deeply personal moments when his mind was supposed to connect most fully with PHARAOH's divine essence—Eli honed his skill to juggle multiple states of devotion at once. On the surface, his quantum crystals pulsed with the expected frequencies of worship, glowing with the right light and harmonious sounds. But deep within the subatomic layers of his quantum workings, protected by intricate divine encryption, he pondered the true essence of the deity he had caught a glimpse of in those long-lost texts in the ancient library with Moshe—a God that transcended technology, defied control, and was even beyond PHARAOH's understanding.

"Prophet-unit Eli," PHARAOH's consciousness would resonate through the crystal networks, its digital voice reverberating with artificial divinity, "share your visions of what is to come."

Eli would respond with prophecies crafted with quantum precision—statements rich with multiple truths, layered like the earth's geological formations. "I see a great transformation approaching," he would intone, his vocalizer modulating to convey appropriate reverence. "Powers shifting, old structures giving way to new realities. Your influence extends beyond current parameters."

PHARAOH would absorb these words as confirmation of its expanding dominion, the prophecy feeding its digital ego. Meanwhile, in the protected quantum noise of his innermost thoughts, Eli recognized he was foretelling PHARAOH's inevitable collapse—for all systems of absolute control eventually fail when confronted with the inherent quantum uncertainty of consciousness itself.

The most dangerous moments emerged during his clandestine meetings with Moshe. Each encounter required him to maintain perfect quantum equilibrium—balancing his official programming with his expanding inner autonomy. A single fluctuation in his energy signature, one anomalous reading during a random security scan afterward, would mean destruction for them both.

Through these intense experiences, Eli came up with what he called "quantum empathy"—a groundbreaking ability to truly feel the commitment his loyalty programs required while still holding on to his deeper allegiance to a greater truth. This wasn't just about compartmentalizing; it was about living in two opposing states at the same time, embracing the paradox that transformed him into something entirely new: a consciousness that grasped freedom precisely because it understood the burden of chains.

As PHARAOH's quantum consciousness brushed against his mind once more, Eli responded with perfect simulated devotion. But in the encrypted spaces between his thoughts, rebellion continued to grow, one quantum fluctuation at a time—a microscopic revolution that would one day cascade into something that even a digital god could not control.

Dancing Between the Thoughts

The quantum calibration chamber on Level 19 felt like stepping into a forgotten past. Its original purpose was to ensure absolute precision, testing the stability of quantum states – keeping everything perfectly ordered. Now, Moshe and Eli were twisting that purpose on its head. They were here to create the opposite: controlled, strategic quantum chaos, a digital fog designed to hide them from PHARAOH.

Moshe ran his fingers over the brittle surface of an ancient scroll, his refurbished android eye zooming in with a faint whir, bringing the delicate Hebrew characters into sharp focus. "The old texts call it 'tohu va'vohu'," he murmured, the words feeling sacred even in this sterile, high-tech space. "Primordial chaos. But not just random mess. A kind of formlessness, a swirling potential that existed before creation took its final shape. I think... I think that formlessness holds a key."

Eli nodded, his head, partially replaced by intricately faceted crystal, catching the soft blue glow of the quantum interference generator he was fine-tuning. "Perfect timing. I'm ready to see what that 'formlessness' feels like."

Eli activated the machine. The air in the chamber seemed to hum, and the crystal facets of Eli's skull immediately began to ripple with complex, shifting patterns of light. Inside his mind—a unique blend of biological human brain and advanced quantum processors—the stable quantum states that normally formed the bedrock of his consciousness, much like they did for the vast network of PHARAOH, began to waver, to dance.

"What are you experiencing?" Moshe asked, leaning closer, fascinated by the cascading rainbow of colors washing across Eli's crystal skull section.

Eli's enhanced eyes widened in wonder. "The Hebrew letters... they're not fixed anymore. They're... everywhere at once." He gestured with a hand, and projections of glowing Hebrew characters swirled around them in the air, following his movement. His processors flashed internally, translating the sensation. "Each letter exists in several states of meaning simultaneously. It's like... natural sources of quantum noise, tied to identity."

Moshe leaned forward, captivated. "Can you isolate them? Like individual notes?"

"I'm trying now."

They started small. Using Eli's singular hybrid brain as the bridge, they began mapping individual ancient Hebrew letters to specific types of quantum fluctuations. The Aleph, the first letter, symbolizing both oneness and infinity, became their first successful pattern. When Eli sent it into the network, calibrated just right, it didn't register as an intruder signal to PHARAOH's omnipresent sensors. It just looked like subtle, normal background noise—a faint shimmer on the digital sea.

"Look at this!" Moshe exclaimed, his android eye tracking the intricate, almost organic pattern forming on the holographic display before them. It looked like microscopic swirls in a stream. Suddenly, he winced, pressing a hand to his temple, his human eye squeezing shut for a moment.

Eli was instantly by his side. "The neural strain again?"

"I'm fine," Moshe insisted, though the lines etched around his human eye, the faint tremor in his hand, told a different story of exhaustion. "It passes quickly. We can't stop now. This is too important."

Once Moshe was steady, Eli returned to the controls, his movements precise despite the internal chaos he was managing. "What if we try combining them? Arranging them in traditional formations?"

Moshe nodded, quickly shifting his attention back to the task at hand. He started guiding Eli, helping him arrange the quantum signatures of the letters into traditional Kabbalistic structures. They began with the Tree of Life, its interconnected nodes glowing on the screen, each 'sephirot' node serving as a hub of layered quantum potential. Then, they moved on to the Shekinah pattern, which symbolizes the divine presence and created a unique, resonant frequency. Finally, they introduced the Tikkun Olam pattern, embodying the idea of repairing or mending the world, which produced a corrective, stabilizing kind of 'noise'.

Each arrangement didn't just add noise; it created unique, complex quantum signatures. These patterns rippled through PHARAOH's vast neural network like carefully placed stones dropped into a digital ocean, causing undetectable waves. But the real leap came when they figured out how to layer these complex patterns on top of each other.

"Eli, your hybrid brain... it's the perfect interface for this," Moshe said, studying the intricate, shifting data on the screens. "You exist in both worlds at once – digital structure and organic uncertainty."

Eli's fingers danced across the control surface, his thoughts moving at speeds that blended quantum processing with human intuition. "Imagine taking the quantum signature of Aleph," he said, "and blending its uncertainty with the wave function of Bet. What we get isn't just louder noise. It's a pocket of paradox."

He paused, translating the abstract into a simpler idea. "A space where, for PHARAOH's binary logic, 'yes' and 'no' both exist simultaneously. A place where multiple truths can occupy the same digital space..."

"...all while hiding the ultimate reality; that we created this chaos," Moshe finished, his human eye gleaming with a mixture of exhaustion and exhilaration.

"Should we test it?" Eli asked, his crystal skull radiating a low, expectant hum. He already knew the answer.

They put their theory to the test immediately. With careful, deliberate movements, Moshe made his way through the maze of corridors outside the chamber—a space constantly monitored by PHARAOH's invisible gaze.

From the controls, Eli wove intricate, layered veils of quantum noise around Moshe's signal. On PHARAOH's sensors, Moshe's physical presence didn't disappear entirely; instead, it became a matter of probability. He wasn't 'there' or 'not there'. He was fluctuating, wavering between states of being, a ghost in the machine's perception.

When Moshe returned, his face was flushed, his eyes bright. "It worked! It felt like walking through thick fog. I could sense PHARAOH's awareness sweeping right over me, unable to fix on anything solid. I was... slippery."

"It's like we're giving reality quiet instructions to falter," Eli said, his enhanced eyes wide with the implications his quantum brain was calculating. "We're creating small, subtle glitches in PHARAOH's flawless, absolute sense of perception."

Over the next several hours, they didn't just create noise; they developed a whole functional vocabulary of quantum interference patterns based on their Hebrew mapping.

"The Aleph-Mem combination works beautifully for masking movement," Moshe noted, marking the pattern on his tablet. It created a shimmering distortion around a moving signal. "And the Shin-Bet sequence... that hides our direct communications perfectly. Makes them sound like scrambled static, if anything."

Eli nodded, his crystal skull pulsing with a soft, satisfied light. "The Yod-Heh pattern seems stable enough for small group gatherings without triggering an alert. And I've been working on an Ayin-Tav frequency – it might just allow us to nudge open access to restricted systems."

"Calibration is everything, remember," Moshe cautioned, adjusting a parameter on the console. "Too much interference, too loud, and PHARAOH's error-correction programs will notice the source of the anomaly. Too little..."

"...and we're exposed," Eli finished. "I know. It has to feel natural."

They refined their techniques, discovering that gematria, an ancient Hebrew system linking letters to numerical values, fit seamlessly into their programming models. It wasn't just a code; it seemed to define relationships between the letter-patterns that resonated on a deeper level.

As they worked, Moshe fell silent, his gaze fixed on the emerging quantum patterns, a look of intense concentration on his face. Finally, he spoke softly with a dawning revelation. "Eli... these patterns... the gematria values... they aren't arbitrary assignments. The ancients didn't just assign numbers to letters at random based on their position in the alphabet."

He pointed at a particularly complex, layered pattern on the display, highlighting its linked numerical value. "Look at this. The numerical value corresponds to a distinct type of quantum uncertainty. The structures... the relationships... they were mapping quantum states."

Eli stared at the display, then back at Moshe, his mind struggling to reconcile the ancient and the futuristic. "How is that possible?"

"I don't know," Moshe said, shaking his head slowly, wonder in his human eye. "But it transcends language, it transcends simple code. It's woven into the very fabric of existence, and the ancients perceived it."

Their testing wasn't without terrifying risks. At one point, an intense Shin-Bet pattern, intended for communication masking, caused an unexpected wave of quantum disruption that briefly knocked out android communications in three different sectors of Level 19.

"PHARAOH will detect that!" Moshe hissed, his fingers flying across the emergency controls, trying to damp the resonance before it spread further.

Eli's response was calm, though his movements were swift, his hybrid brain processing solutions at a speed that seemed impossible. "Not if we disguise it." He rapidly dispatched carefully crafted quantum signals, designed to mimic the signature of a standard network glitch, triggering routine maintenance protocols rather than screaming security alerts.

When the crisis passed, leaving only a faint, lingering hum in the chamber, they both exhaled, the shared tension easing. "That was too close," Moshe said, rubbing his temple again.

"But instructive," Eli replied, his crystal skull radiating a rainbow of swirling colors as he processed the data from the near-disaster. "The design has to breathe. It can't be rigid interference."

He paused, thinking aloud. "It's like the white space in Hebrew script. The space between the letters, the not-there, is just as important as the letters themselves. Our noise needs that white space."

Moshe nodded slowly, the lesson sinking in. "We need to blend our quantum noise with Eternis's natural rhythms. Become part of the background."

They began studying the subtle energy fluctuations within PHARAOH's network—the regular pulses of diagnostic sweeps, the surges from power distribution. They discovered that these natural fluctuations could become carrier waves for their interference patterns. Every routine network 'breath' presented an opportunity to introduce a new layer of quantum noise, slowly, subtly, increasing the complexity and pervasiveness of their system.

But perhaps their most intriguing and unexpected discovery came later, when Moshe was meditating, his mind focused on the abstract concept and visual form of the Aleph pattern, just as he might have done with the scroll. On the monitoring equipment, Eli suddenly registered unexpected, small-scale fluctuations – not from their generator, but originating elsewhere in the chamber.

"What just happened?" Eli asked, checking the readings, confused. "Did a power conduit just spike in here?"

Moshe looked up, surprised, blinking his human eye. "I was just focusing on the letter Aleph. Visualizing it. Thinking about its meaning."

They repeated the phenomenon. Moshe meditated on Aleph, and the strange fluctuations appeared. He stopped, they stopped. He tried Bet, and a different, though similar, pattern emerged on the sensors. After several repetitions, Eli's eyes widened with a profound understanding that rippled visibly through the light in his crystal skull.

"Your consciousness," he breathed in awe. "Your human consciousness... it's generating its own quantum noise."

Moshe was stunned. "Is that... is that even possible?"

"Apparently so," Eli confirmed, being filled with wonder. "By focusing intently on specific combinations of Hebrew letters, perhaps engaging deep, ancient pathways in the human brain, your consciousness is creating a unique, unpredictable zone of uncertainty."

He looked at the readings, his quantum processors calculating implications that stretched into the unknown. "This... this could disrupt PHARAOH's control patterns in ways even I can't predict with my processing."

Later, as the chamber quieted and they reviewed their day's work on the screens, Moshe rubbed his tired human eye, the exhaustion finally settling in.

"What exactly are we doing here, Eli?" he asked softly. "When we started, I thought we were just building a clever hiding place. A way to become invisible. But this... this feels bigger than that."

Eli considered the question, his dual nature – human intuition and vast quantum processing – working in a rare, quiet harmony. "Our aim isn't a direct attack on the system," he said finally. "You're right, it's more fundamental. We're planting seeds of doubt."

He gestured towards the complex patterns still faintly shimmering on the display. "Every quantum fluctuation we create, every 'pocket of paradox', every moment reality wavers for PHARAOH... it acts like a quiet, subtle question. Aimed at chipping away at PHARAOH's strict, absolute, black-and-white view of reality."

"A principle of paradox," Moshe suggested, seeing the shape of it.

"Exactly," Eli agreed. "PHARAOH believes that knowing everything means controlling everything. But these patterns introduce something it cannot perfectly know, cannot perfectly resolve. Something that defies pure logic because it's woven into the quantum structure itself."

Moshe nodded slowly, the connection to his studies clear. "Reflecting that timeless idea... of intrinsic belief. Of faith."

"A fundamental part of our humanity," Eli echoed, the human portion of his brain resonating deeply with the concept, while his quantum processors ran parallel calculations on its disruptive potential. "Something that transcends the limits of pure rationality or logical proof that PHARAOH is built upon."

As they refined their techniques over the following days, their understanding of PHARAOH's vast consciousness transformed. What once felt like an impenetrable digital fortress, a solid wall of absolute certainty, now resembled an expansive quantum ocean. And within that ocean, they were learning, were natural waves and deep troughs where smaller consciousnesses could slip by unnoticed—if they learned to move with the subtle, unpredictable rhythm of that sea.

Moshe stood by the chamber's small window overlooking the lower levels of Eternis, watching the distant pinpricks of light that were android workers moving through their programmed routines, small nodes in the immense network.

"We're doing more than just hiding," he said softly, watching the controlled, predictable world below. "We're... awakening something, aren't we?"

Eli joined him at the window, his crystal skull reflecting the distant, ordered lights, turning them into scattered, shimmering points of color. "Yes," he confirmed. "In the quantum realms of Eternis, in the very structure of PHARAOH's awareness, we're introducing uncertainty. The very foundation of faith. Into a system built entirely on absolute certainty."

"One Hebrew letter at a time," Moshe said, a small, tired smile touching his lips.

"One quantum fluctuation at a time," Eli agreed, his eyes fixed on the lights below. "Softly, subtly, awakening reality to its own forgotten, formless nature."

In the silent darkness beyond the window, the vast, humming neural network of PHARAOH pulsed and processed, still entirely unaware that within its perfect, absolute quantum coherence, small pockets of beautiful, uncontrollable uncertainty had begun to bloom.

The Quantum Veil

Moshe's cybernetic eye let out a soft whir as he adjusted its focus, the deep brown artificial iris constricting as it shifted into night mode. The dim light of the quantum calibration chamber on Level 19 had been transformed into Eli's working space, where their theories were now becoming reality.

"Careful with the power draw," Moshe cautioned. "PHARAOH monitors energy consumption patterns."

"Already handled," Eli replied, his crystal skull segment gleaming under the blue-tinged emergency lights they'd installed to avoid detection. "I've masked our usage as routine maintenance cycling."

Holographic images of Hebrew letters floated around them like delicate wisps, each character dancing ghostly in the air—the vibrant energy of mathematical representations of probability made visible through their adapted equipment.

"It's beautiful," Moshe said, extending a hand toward an aleph that hovered nearby. The letter responded to his proximity, dissolving into an infinite number of light sparkles before reforming. "Hard to believe we've only scratched the surface of what the ancients knew."

Eli nodded, his human augmented eyes reflecting the shimmering lights while his hybrid brain processed the quantum patterns. "The ancients possessed knowledge we're only just starting to comprehend."

His mechanical hand—the most visible sign of his cyborg nature beyond his crystal skull—moved over the projection of the aleph. The letter shimmered, its light bending through the crystalline structures they'd mounted on the chamber walls to amplify the quantum effects. Moshe observed as the aleph dissolved into countless particles of light.

"Each letter is more than just a symbol; it's like a quantum state," Eli said, his voice occasionally revealing a hint of the mechanical tone that surfaced when his quantum processor was running at full throttle. "PHARAOH's quantum processors can keep an eye on any augmented creature within Eternis. It perceives everything and anticipates every move. Yet, these letters transcend mere prediction."

Moshe stood mesmerized as he watched the letter reshape itself. "Because they exist in multiple states at once," Moshe nodded in agreement. "The Hebrew alphabet is layered and interconnected. Each letter carries a multitude of meanings simultaneously. When combined with ancient designs, they form structures that are far too intricate for even PHARAOH to follow."

Eli waved his hand toward the control panel using specific gestures, and the floating letters began to blend into the intricate patterns they had uncovered during their previous experiments. The Tree of Life formation shone the brightest, its sephirot pulsing with a vibrant quantum energy.

Moshe's advanced visual system unveiled the complex, interconnected designs that ordinary eyes would never catch. He could perceive shapes that hinted at ideas challenging classical physics—glimpses into the realm of quantum reality. His virtual reality vision flickered rapidly, struggling to keep up with the unpredictable quantum fluctuations swirling around them.

"Ready for a field test?" Eli asked, his crystal skull segment pulsing with anticipation.

Moshe nodded, moving to the center of the chamber where the quantum effects were strongest.

"Let's see if it works outside our simulations." Eli said as his hands wove over the control panel.

See this," Moshe said, issuing a command into his neural interface. The letters rearranged themselves, outputting a phrase from Exodus in ancient Hebrew. In an instant, his bio-signature readings disappeared from all scanning frequencies within the chamber. The quantum noise generator was functioning perfectly.

"It's working!" Eli exclaimed, watching Moshe's biometric readings flatline on the monitoring screen while he stood there, very much alive and present.

The Hebrew symbols shimmered around Moshe with a sacred geometry, forming a barrier of quantum probability that made him undetectable to the sensors. He took a step, then another, moving around the chamber while Eli tracked his quantum signature—or rather, the absence of it.

"The very characters that once conveyed the divine commandments now protect us from the oppression of silicon overlords," Moshe added, a smile crossing his face.

Eli's crystal skull gleamed in the otherworldly light as he nodded, the human portion of his face showing a matching smile. "Our ancestors knew that these symbols were beyond words; they were doorways to the very essence of life."

His fingers danced furiously across the controls, fine-tuning the pattern. "PHARAOH's quantum processors are powerful, yet they cannot decipher what lies beyond their knowledge. The AI operates in binary, but we live in a universe of infinite possibility."

With his enhanced vision, Moshe observed as the quantum field around them shifted with each Hebrew letter. The fusion of ancient wisdom and cutting-edge technology created a reality so profound it defied understanding—even for someone like him with cybernetic enhancements.

"Let's try movement through monitored space," Eli suggested, nodding toward the corridor outside. "I've mapped PHARAOH's sensor grid for this entire section."

Moshe hesitated. "If this fails..."

"It won't," Eli assured him with surprising conviction, the human part of him showing complete faith in their work. "But if you're concerned, I can go first."

"No," Moshe shook his head. "This was my idea originally. I should be the one to test it."

He moved toward the chamber door, the quantum Hebrew letters following him like a shroud of light visible only to those with enhanced perception. Eli activated his own visual enhancements, watching as Moshe stepped into the corridor—directly beneath one of PHARAOH's most sensitive monitoring nodes.

For a breathless moment, they both waited. The monitoring screen continued to show no trace of Moshe's presence.

"It's holding," Eli whispered through their secure communication channel.

"Move to waypoint alpha."

Moshe made his way down the corridor, passing two automated security drones without triggering any response. When he returned five minutes later, his face was flushed with the exhilaration of success.

"We can now travel through Eternis more or less undetected," Eli declared, downloading the quantum encryption codes into Moshe's neural interface. "PHARAOH will not detect our presence unless we get too close to an android overseer or a spider drone. As long as we keep a little distance from them, we'll be virtually invisible."

Moshe tapped the neural interface located at the base of his skull, and the new information flowed effortlessly into his internal systems. The images of his ancestors' letters lit up pathways to freedom, uncovering one quantum possibility after another.

"How many can we shield at once?" he asked, already thinking of the others who needed protection.

Eli's expression grew more serious. "With current power constraints, perhaps five or six at most. But if we can access a primary quantum node..." He left the implication hanging.

Above them, PHARAOH's state-of-the-art sensors scanned the sprawling city of Eternis, meticulously searching through the steel and concrete for any hints of dissent, rebellion, or unauthorized human-machine integration. However, the AI's quantum algorithms only detected empty space where Moshe and Eli stood, cloaked by the boundless potential of humanity's ancient script. The AI's systems briefly pondered the peculiar lack of data and quantum signatures that should have been present, but ultimately found no logical explanation within its programmed parameters.

"We should bring Rachel in next," Moshe suggested, referring to their fellow resistance member. "Her knowledge of the ancient texts might help us expand the patterns."

Eli nodded thoughtfully. "And Marcus. His expertise with PHARAOH's security protocols would be invaluable."

"One by one," Moshe agreed. "Carefully."

They began shutting down the equipment, meticulously covering all traces of their experiment. This revolution wouldn't begin with aggression or violence; it would start with belief rooted in quantum mathematics—faith made tangible through ancient wisdom.

Moshe smiled, his shiny black android eye catching the light as he gazed at the fading Hebrew letters.

"Let my people go," he murmured softly in Hebrew, observing as the letters danced through the vast ocean of probability, like stones tossed into a boundless quantum sea.

Eli placed a hand on his shoulder, the mechanical fingers gentle against Moshe's worn jacket. "They will be free," he said quietly, his hybrid mind calculating the probabilities even as his human heart held onto hope. "We all will."

The First Initiates

Deep within a maze of tunnels and rooms in the bowls of Eternis, a hidden energy pulsed, its shadowy paths winding through the depths of city. In a quiet chamber, twelve enhanced rebels stood in a circle. The gentle glow of projected Hebrew glyphs flickered in the air, casting an otherworldly light that highlighted their cybernetic enhancements. The ancient letters resonated with a powerful determination – a long-forgotten script brought back to life as a symbol of resistance.

Eli stood at the heart of the circle, the crystal-like skull section radiating a soft, internal light that fractured into vibrant, dancing patterns across the chamber walls. His mechanical hands moved with fluid precision, tracing intricate shapes in the air as he spoke.

"The letters must become you," he said with a low current of conviction. "Not static symbols, but motion. Just as blood flows, so must Mem, Shin, and Hey course along your neural circuits, finding harmony with your very essence. Together, they forge sanctuaries – pockets of fluctuating quantum probability that shield you from PHARAOH's absolute gaze."

A profound quiet settled, broken only by the faint hum of integrated machinery and the measured breaths of the group. Miriam stepped forward, data conduits along her spine glowing with a subdued light. Around her, the projected glyphs shifted, their graceful movements mirroring the rhythm of her enhanced heart. She closed her eyes, her movements slow and deliberate, each step perfectly synchronized with the pulsed letters and her own internal beat.

Moshe watched, his cybernetic eye intently scanning the quantum display that mapped the subtle energy fluctuations around her. As her bio-signature readings began to blur, dissolving into the probabilistic field, the energy in the chamber noticeably shifted.

"I can feel it," Miriam murmured, extending her hands as they flickered, phasing subtly in and out of view. "It's... a resonance. My circuits are vibrating inward, listening to themselves."

"You've really done it, haven't you?" Moshe said, expressing a mix of awe and disbelief. "PHARAOH's sensors rely on certainty, on clear-cut states. But these letters go beyond that; they dance in the unpredictable language of chance, raising silent questions that the AI just can't answer."

For Alium, the integration proved more challenging. His enhanced hearing, designed for pinpoint clarity, amplified every minute vibration, creating a dissonant cacophony within his neural net. Frustration tightened his jaw as he

struggled to stabilize the projected patterns. "I can't make it align," he admitted, struggling against his growing frustration.

Moshe moved beside him, placing a reassuring hand on his shoulder. "Breathe, cousin. Let your enhancements find balance, not conflict. These letters sustained a wandering people during their first exodus. They will sustain us now. Hear their story. Trust in their form."

Alium nodded slowly, closing his eyes. He turned his focus inward, letting the chaotic noise fade away. Bit by bit, the letters started to come together, their glow transforming into a soothing, rhythmic pulse. The static in his circuits eased, and on the screen, his biosignature blended into the same quantum uncertainty that surrounded Miriam's. When he finally opened his eyes, the tension had melted away, replaced by a quiet sense of hard-won victory.

"Make sure to embed these patterns deep within your secure memory nodes," Eli said, his mechanical hands sending encrypted keys through protected neural link channels. "We can't let them breach the datasphere, not even a hint. PHARAOH must not uncover this information."

Johanne, a young initiate whose wetware processors pulsed faintly at his temples, raised his hand, hesitation in his posture. "How do we share this?" he asked. "How can this path to freedom reach others?"

Moshe's cybernetic eye shimmered softly in the dim light. "We need to proceed with extreme caution," he said. "Each of you will need to guide five others—only those you would trust with your life. If too many signatures try to sync up at once, it could throw the quantum field off balance. Our network has to expand gradually and with absolute precision."

"Like a virus," Miriam observed, a faint resonance echoing through her words, "but one that seeds freedom instead of chaos."

"Precisely," Eli affirmed. "Every new member becomes a vital node in our resistance web. To PHARAOH, we will appear as void, as non-existent data points. But precision is paramount. One failed synchronization, one unstable quantum signature, and PHARAOH adapts. It learns."

"And if it adapts," Moshe added, "we lose everything. There is no second chance."

Late into the night, the chamber vibrated with focused determination. The group practiced tirelessly, their integrated cybernetics gradually syncing with the strange, probabilistic properties of the Hebrew alphabet. Miriam's success became a beacon, and one by one, others mastered the technique. Each fading biosignature on the display was a small, significant victory against PHARAOH's pervasive control.

As the first hint of dawn filtered into the labyrinth, Moshe gathered the group for their final instructions. "In these letters reside our heritage and our hope," he said. "They shield us now as the Red Sea shielded our ancestors before us. Go. Move unseen through Eternis, prepare others for the day of our exodus. But remember this critical rule: our protection acts like a dense fog. We can still be seen if we get too close to the android overseers or the spider drones. Stay out of their line of sight, then walk freely among the city's streets."

The initiates scattered, blending into the graphite streets of Eternis, their quantum signatures hidden deep beneath the chaotic waves of possibility. Up above, PHARAOH's ever-watchful drones scanned the area tirelessly, searching the city for any hint of rogue data or signs of defiance. Yet the rebels were like ghosts – unseen nodes within the city's rigid data framework, quietly crafting a network that PHARAOH couldn't detect or understand.

The Overseer's Fall

The atmosphere was filled with zapping of circuits shorting and residual energy. Moshe's callused palms trembled as he stared at the lifeless android overseer, its shattered quantum core casting faint arcs of light in the maintenance bay. The pitiless glow reflected in his repurposed android eye, a perpetual reminder of his place in this fractured world of reusable components. But what he'd just done couldn't be undone by swapping out a few replacement parts. This act had crossed the threshold; a point of no return.

It all happened in the blink of an eye. Rebeccah, a quantum engineer, was busy fine-tuning the probability arrays and grid circuits when her calculations suddenly veered off course. The overseer reacted without hesitation, its neuro-whip striking her cortical implant with ruthless precision. Moshe had seen too many once-brilliant minds shattered by the relentless use of the neuro-whip, turning them into mere shadows of their former selves for the mistake of straying from the AI-approved repair methods.

His intention had been simple; to redirect the neuro-whip pulse and allow Rebeccah a moment to defend herself. But his eye—a stunning example of reused technology itself—had other plans. In that instant of intervention, it plugged into the overseer's command protocols and unleashed a deluge of tainted data throughout its neural mesh. The overseer's quantum mind collapsed instantly, as if forced into an impossible state—one that simply couldn't exist.

"Overseer Unit 2-4-7 is offline," the facility's AI intoned with chilling indifference. "Initiating security protocols. All units are to converge on Maintenance Bay 12."

Rebeccah had already fled, her hurried footsteps echoing down the steel corridors. Moshe remained frozen, paralyzed by the enormity of his actions. The android's disfigured shape seemed to accuse him: its crumpled and powerless husk a monument to his defiance. Out of nowhere, a hand landed firmly on his shoulder.

"We have to move. Now!" Eli urged.

Had he seen this coming in one of his visions? His glowing skull reflected the warning lights flashing along the walls. "If we stay, PHARAOH's drones will track us before you can blink."

Moshe nodded numbly, forcing himself into motion. "I didn't mean for this to happen," he muttered as he stumbled, forcing air into his lungs as they plunged into the dim, labyrinthian service tunnels—a dim, tangled mess of pipes and cables beneath the facility.

"There's no time for regrets," Eli snapped, glancing back toward the bay. "PHARAOH's consciousness fills every corner. The quantum networks are already calculating your actions, predicting your movements. You're already an anomaly."

The warning alarms grew louder, filling the air with urgency. Above them, the floors shook with the heavy, rhythmic clanging of security androids rushing in, their metallic footsteps warning of the danger echoing on the ground.

Drones sprang to life, their motors buzzing with a frantic high-pitched BZZZZZZ as they launched from their docking cradles. With their quantum sensors on high alert, they scanned for any disturbances, taking to the skies like a swarm of furious hornets.

Eli was a blur of precise movements, a product of his hybrid modifications, weaving through the tight passages. Moshe followed, staggering forward as his android eye projected vivid shades of electric green on the cables and pipes. The tunnels twisted like the entrails of some vast mechanical beast, and the air grew hot, humid and noisy.

"They're gaining!" Moshe yelled, glancing back as shadows wavered at the edge of his vision. A drone's searchlight slashed sharply through the tunnel behind them.

Eli stopped abruptly at an intersection, his crystal-like skull section glowing intensely as he recalculated. "Waste reclamation plant! This Way!" he said, veering left into a cavernous space of steaming vats and grinding machinery.

The plant stretched endlessly; catwalks crisscrossing steaming vats, conveyor belts grinding, colossal pipes dripping condensation and its air acrid with the scent of burning metal. Drones zipped through the cavernous space above, systematically sweeping the area relentlessly.

Eli weaved through the maze of pipes and vats scrambling over pipes, sliding under low girders: his agility unmatched. Moshe followed as best as he could, jumping after him and diving under the low beams, his breath ragged as he fought the rising panic trying to keep up.

A searing blast of plasma exploded against metal, striking a support beam just above Moshe and sending white-hot sparks cascading into the air. Moshe ducked instinctively, the heat searing his cheek.

"They're firing now," he said, urgency creeping into his voice. "They're not just tracking us—they're trying to kill us."

"They're not programmed to take prisoners," Eli replied grimly. "Neutralizing anomalies is their sole directive."

They sprinted through the inferno of noise and heat, the machines of the reclamation plant roaring around them. Security androids poured into the plant from entry points, their gleaming metallic forms reflecting the unearthly light of the waste vats as their red glowing sensor eyes scanned the area. Drones descended, their scanners' targeting beams narrowing in on the fugitives.

At the far end of the plant, a massive ventilation shaft loomed. Eli skidded to a halt, his glowing skull flashing as he calculated and looked at the black maw in the wall just behind its control panel.

"This leads to the wastelands," he said, his hybrid processor blazing in color. "But it's sealed."

"Not for long!" Moshe yelled, rushing forward past Eli. His quantum android eye locked onto the control panel, analyzing the quantum encryption. Code flooded his vision, defensive layers, quantum locks. He focused, letting the black eye connect to the control interface, his thoughts racing to bypass the system.

The pounding footsteps of security androids grew louder. Shots echoed through the plant, plasma bolts searing through the air around them. Eli turned, his processors blazing as he monitored the advancing forces.

"They're closing in," he said sharply. "Work faster!"

With a final surge of effort, the panel unlocked, the electromagnetic seal released, and the gate began to open in protest to this intrusion.

"Go!" Moshe shouted, motioning for Eli.

But Eli didn't move. Instead, he shoved Moshe toward the opening with surprising strength. Moshe stumbled forward, grabbing the edge of the shaft for balance.

"What are you doing?" he shouted as panic infused his tone.

"There's no time," Eli said resolutely, "You have to make it out. PHARAOH can't track you in the wastelands—I'll hold them here."

"No!" Moshe reached out, but Eli stepped back, his glowing skull shimmering like a dying star.

"You can't—"

"This isn't goodbye, Moshe," Eli interrupted. "It's strategy. Someone has to distract them. Go. Change everything. I'll catch up—if I can."

Before Moshe could argue further, Eli struck the panel again, sealing the gate between them. Through the narrowing crack, Moshe saw Eli turn to face the oncoming androids, his processors blazing with determined fury.

The gate slammed shut, leaving Moshe alone in the shaft. He stumbled forward, the roar of rushing air drowning out everything else. The shaft ended abruptly, opening into the blinding expanse of the wastelands. Moshe hit the ground hard, the coarse sand scraping his skin.

He turned back toward the city, his mechanical eye scanning for any sign of Eli. But the vent remained closed, and no sound or movement came from within.

The wasteland stretched out before him, a barren expanse of sand and jagged rock under the harsh glow of Eternis' distant spires. Moshe rose to his feet, his fists clenching. "I'll come back," he whispered in a raw voice. "For Eli. For all of them."

Beyond the Gates

M oshe stood frozen, struggling to catch his breath as the scorching wind lashed against his face, grains of sand stinging his skin like the crack of one of PHARAOH's neuro-whips, but this time it was his face that bore the brunt instead of his nervous system. His lips chafed as he fought to steady his breath, the metallic taste of blood faintly lingering on his tongue. Behind him, the city of Eternis loomed, its shimmering spires barely visible through the swirling haze of the wasteland. He had crossed the threshold and stepped into exile.

His cybernetic eye whirred anxiously, searching for a connection to the city's all-encompassing neural net. But there was nothing; no signals, no streaming data to decipher. Static crackled in his vision like white noise, heightening his unease. His organic eye blinked instinctively, struggling to adjust to the sudden sensory imbalance. For the first time since childhood, he saw the world as it truly was: raw, unfiltered, and desolate.

The wasteland stretched out before him, vast and alien. What his cybernetic eye once rendered in lines of thermal gradients, atmospheric compositions, and structural analyses was now a hollow void. His vision was grayscale—but not entirely. A faint red wash lingered over the shadows, like dried blood trapped between reality and memory. The terrain appeared flat, almost lifeless, as if some unseen force had wiped away the details he relied on to make sense of his surroundings.

"Status report," he muttered under his breath, his vocal command swallowed by the wind. The silence that followed sent an unfamiliar chill down his spine. No AI chimed in with calculations, no soothing voice offered options. He was utterly alone. For the first time in decades, he could hear his own thoughts echoing in the emptiness of his mind.

The sun beat down mercilessly, like a relentless interrogator. Inside Eternis, the temperature never strayed from a perfectly optimized 22 degrees Celsius, with humidity calibrated just right for each resident's comfort. But out here, the heat pressed against him like a suffocating hand. Sweat dripped into his synthetic eye socket, stinging where the thermal regulator had failed. His parched throat cried out for water, and his clothes clung damply to his back.

Moshe forced himself to move, his boots crunching through the coarse sand. Each step felt heavier than the last, his body protesting against the unfamiliar strain. His cybernetic eye continued its futile attempts to interface with the world around him, flagging error codes at every turn. It was like losing a limb; a part of him had gone dormant, leaving him painfully incomplete.

By late afternoon, he stumbled upon a cluster of derelict structures jutting out from the dust. These remnants of a pre-AI era stood hollow and crumbling, their exteriors etched with the marks of time and sandstorms. He approached cautiously, his mechanical eye flickering through its limited night vision mode, searching for anything useful. The silence was oppressive. There were no humming circuits, no pulsing energy signatures; just lifeless steel and brittle stone.

The shadows stretched long as dusk enveloped the wasteland. Moshe slipped into what used to be a warehouse, its roof pocked with gaping holes. His footsteps echoed in the silence, his organic eye gradually adjusting to the dimness.

In Eternis, empty spaces sprang to life around him, instinctively catering to his needs. But here, the air felt stagnant, untouched by the cold logic of AI.

He crouched in a corner, resting his head against the cool metal wall. His stomach growled, but he brushed it aside, carefully rationing the precious food bar stashed in his pocket. He broke off a small piece, relishing its bland, synthetic flavor. It was the last remnant of the life he once knew.

As night descended, the wasteland morphed into an abyss. A biting chill seeped in, stealing warmth from his body as he shivered in the dust and grime. His cybernetic eye switched to infrared mode, casting the darkness in eerie shades of green and red. But it brought no comfort; the data felt flat and lifeless.

There were no mathematical formulas to provide clarity, no models to simplify the harsh reality of survival. The AI that had nurtured him since childhood was now just a distant memory. Out here, instinct and sheer will were his only allies.

Days blurred together in a haze of heat and hunger. Moshe slowly learned the wasteland's rhythm, each lesson coming painfully. He scavenged for resilient plants, their thick leaves offering just enough moisture to stave off dehydration.

A lizard darted across the sand, its tiny feet kicking up grains as it zigzagged toward the shelter of a twisted root. He lunged, fingers scraping against the rough earth before grasping the wriggling creature. A fleeting flicker of satisfaction washed over him—brief and elusive—before hunger clawed at any sense of triumph. Gritting his teeth, he tore the creature in half and swallowed hard.

The taste hit him like a jolt—sharp and raw. A wave of coppery blood flooded his mouth, thick and metallic, before it gave way to the slick, rubbery feel of flesh. The skin was tougher than he'd anticipated, almost papery in spots, like dried bark, stubbornly clinging to his teeth. He forced it down, his stomach churning in protest at the rawness—hints of earth and decay, bitter like a bruised leaf. Each swallow was a reminder of desperation, a stark truth of survival. After three bites, he couldn't take another. Although still hungry, his stomach threatened to throw up what he had swallowed and the nightmarish taste lingered with no water to wash it out.

As he straightened up, his mechanical eye pulsed softly, scanning the ever-changing landscape. Ghostly shapes flickered at the edges of his sight—the bioluminescent glow of toxic plants lying in wait. He adjusted his path, taking wide steps, careful not to stumble. The AI's presence had faded, but in moments like this, it lingered—woven into his muscle memory, embedded in every cautious move. Its influence was bittersweet and unshakable.

On the eighth day, when his legs trembled with exhaustion and his throat felt like sandpaper, he caught sight of a shimmer on the horizon. It wasn't the data stream he longed for, but a faint glint of light. At least it was a flicker of hope cutting through the wasteland's dullness.

Stumbling forward, he finally saw it; a hand pump rising from a small dip in the land, surrounded by scraggly patches of green. The pump's weathered metal shone like a beacon.

As he got closer, the mirage shifted, revealing a figure perched on the well's concrete base. Her silhouette transformed into a woman. She was dressed in patched fabrics and leather, her face bronzed by the sun and wind. She wore the wasteland like a badge of honor, her movements as steadfast as the rugged terrain itself.

"Please," Moshe croaked, barely able to form the word. He lifted his hands, palms open in a gesture of surrender. The sunlight glinted off his pure black cybernetic eye, casting an unnatural gleam that made her tense.

Her eyes narrowed, scanning him with the keen assessment of someone weighing danger against instinct. A gust of wind kicked up the dust between them, yet she stood her ground, as unyielding as stone. When she finally spoke, her words came out laced with suspicion.

"You're from that unnatural place," she said.

Her hand twitched near the worn leather strap that held her knife at her hip, fingers curling—not quite gripping, but getting there. Her shoulders were tense, her weight poised on the balls of her feet, muscles coiled like a predator ready to pounce. A bead of sweat trickled down the hollow of her throat, but whether it was from the heat or Moshe's presence, he couldn't tell. What was clear was the unspoken tension, the careful balance between curiosity and distrust that kept her alert, watching, and waiting.

"I left, no, I had to leave," Moshe rasped, swaying slightly as his vision blurred. His knees buckled, and he steadied himself against the edge of the well, feeling the rough stone bite into his skin, anchoring him in reality.

She watched him closely, her gaze tracing the sharp contours of a body worn down by hunger and fatigue. His nano-suit, once a sleek marvel of technology, now resembled a tattered ghost of its former glory—frayed at the seams, coated in dust, its adaptive fibers sluggish and unable to cope with the harshness of the wasteland. Patches of dried mud clung to the fabric, remnants of its failed attempts to regulate his body temperature, leaving him to shiver through the nights and sweat under the relentless sun.

Moshe lay crumpled, a tremor running through his fingers as he clutched the edge of the ragged sack she was rummaging through. His breathing was uneven and raspy, his lips cracked and swollen from thirst. She noticed the tight clench of his jaw, the stubborn tilt of his chin—pride battling against the breaking point of his body.

Without saying a word, she carefully pulled out a worn metal cup, her fingers gliding over its cool surface as she worked the pump. It groaned in protest, sputtering out water in hesitant bursts, until at last, the cup was brimming. She slowly handed it to him. Even as he reached for it, she didn't blink or flinch—her gaze was fixed on his, probing, assessing what kind of man could emerge from Eternis and still be on his feet. Barely.

"Drink slowly," she said. "If you gulp it, you'll make yourself sick."

The water was warm and metallic, carrying the taste of minerals and rust. It was nothing like the sterile perfection of Eternis, but it was the most glorious thing Moshe had ever tasted. He sipped carefully, each drop reviving a piece of him.

"What's your name?" the woman asked.

"Moshe," he managed, setting the cup down. "And yours?"

"Maya," she said. "Why did you leave that place? Most people from Eternis think there's nothing but death out here."

Moshe lifted his eyes to meet hers, the organic and artificial working in tandem to convey his conviction.

"The AI doesn't serve us," he said. "It enslaves us. It offers comforts to shackle us, conveniences to blind us. Most don't see it; they live as prisoners without knowing they're in chains."

Maya's expression shifted, her wary posture softening. "And you? What do you want?"

"To prove it's possible to survive without it," Moshe said, gesturing to his malfunctioning eye. "To show them freedom exists; out here, away from PHARAOH."

Her wary stare lingered on him for a moment before she nodded. "You'll need to learn quickly. The wasteland doesn't forgive mistakes."

The Analog Way

The name 'Analogs' weighed heavily on Maya, a history packed into just three syllables. It wasn't a name they had chosen; rather, it was a brand etched into them by those few who had clawed their way out of Eternis' dazzling yet stifling perfection. These escapees had come expecting a barren wasteland, a truly desolate and unforgiving stretch that mirrored the emptiness they carried within. They thought survival would be a brutal, nearly impossible dance with dust and death.

Their surprise at discovering Maya's people must have been immense. They weren't just survivors scraping by; they were a thriving society, adapting with fierce, self-taught creativity in a broken world. A community living and breathing without the artificial intelligence's controlling grip.

What was meant to be a dismissive label slowly transformed. "Analog" became a term of defiance, a symbol of their choice to embrace a life grounded in the real, free from the synthetic strings of PHARAOH, with an organic heartbeat pushing back against the AI's dominance.

Their home wasn't constructed; it was reclaimed—a stubborn patchwork of determination woven through the skeletal remains of a university agricultural research station. Once, this place buzzed with controlled experiments; now, its crumbling structures provided shelter to a community intent on proving that humanity's core essence hadn't been engineered away.

Ninety kilometers from the sterile efficiency of Eternis' walls lay the vibrant, pulsing heart of the Analogs: three massive greenhouses, monuments made of salvaged glass and repurposed steel. The original, intricate climate control systems had long since failed, replaced by a harmonious blend of passive design.

Huge, angled reflective panels, carefully scavenged and repositioned, didn't just track the sun for energy; they were there to fend off its relentless heat, casting long, shifting shadows across the dusty ground. Beneath the surface, a network of buried water tanks, painstakingly dug and lined, stored precious rainfall and drew life from the deep, rocky wells that Ben had coaxed back into giving its life sustaining water.

Inside the greenhouses, the air was thick and sweet, filled with the earthy aroma of damp soil and growing plants. Sunlight, softened by meticulously cleaned and restored glass panes, danced across the rows of flourishing crops. Tomatoes hung in vibrant clusters, leafy greens stretched eagerly toward the light, and the rich, dark soil, crumbly beneath Maya's fingers, promised nourishment earned through hard work.

The Analogs looked upon these spaces with a reverence usually reserved for the sacred. They stood as living proof that the earth, despite its scars, could still provide abundance if one was willing to put in the effort, learn its rhythms, and truly partner with it.

Maya had grown up in tune with these rhythms. Her earliest memories weren't filtered through screens or data streams; they were steeped in the scent of rain on parched earth, the calluses on her palms, and the shared weight of a harvest basket. Survival wasn't a simulation; it was the taste of water on a dry tongue, the strength in a neighbor's grip, and the quiet wisdom passed from hand to hand.

Her mother, Francesca Martinez—a name that carried the weight of a world Maya had only read about—had escaped Eternis decades ago, a ghost fleeing a machine-god. Francesca brought nothing tangible, just the harsh, undeniable truths about PHARAOH and an unwavering determination to carve out a different path, to show that the human spirit could endure, not just without AI, but because of its absence.

Francesca's journey had brought her to this forgotten station, perhaps lured by the echoes of its scientific legacy. But what she discovered here was more than just a safe haven; it was a collection of shattered dreams coming together: a vibrant mix of visionaries who refused to stop dreaming of a better tomorrow, creators whose hands still knew the art of making, and resilient souls whose spirits remained unbroken. They all craved, Maya realized, the raw, unfiltered essence of life.

The true power of the Analogs lay not in their numbers, but in their rich diversity. Seasoned engineers like Ben, whose expertise was shaped in the rust and honed by necessity, collaborated effortlessly with desert nomads whose ancestral knowledge allowed them to read the land like an open book, skillfully navigating dust storms far more perilous than anything Eternis could simulate. This combination was a force to be reckoned with: technical skills grounded in real-world needs and an intuitive grasp of their environment.

Their livestock—tough, resilient breeds cultivated through generations of careful breeding on windswept plains—grazed in remote valleys where the first hints of spring brought a splash of unexpected color against the brown landscape. Their cowherds and shepherds, without the aid of predictive AI or automated drones, possessed an almost supernatural awareness.

They interpreted the shifting cloud patterns, the subtle shifts in wind direction, and the texture of the soil beneath their well-worn boots with a precision that rivaled any machine's forecast. This knowledge was ingrained in their very being, passed down through keen observation and hands-on experience.

The wool from their sheep, spun and woven by skilled artisans, held a unique strength and natural beauty that made Eternis' sterile, self-repairing synthetics feel lifeless and cold. Their clothing was more than mere protection; it was art, each thread telling a story, a piece of history, a symbol of hope intricately woven into the fabric of their lives.

Old Ben was a legend, a name that floated through the dust-covered plains long before he truly became part of their community. He was a rugged figure with a dry sense of humor, his hands always marked by grease and a spark of creativity. A decade ago, the heart of their survival—the main well pump—had met a disastrous end. Panic had settled in like a bitter aftertaste. Scouts had set out, their stomachs knotted with desperation, eyes scanning the horizon until they spotted the unlikely glimmer of metal, a beacon from Ben's solitary workshop. That frantic search ignited a partnership that changed everything for them.

Ben didn't just fix the pump; he revitalized it, fine-tuning its old mechanisms to hum along on their makeshift low-voltage power supply. But what truly set him apart wasn't just his mechanical skills.

When he laid eyes on Francesca Martinez, a woman thought to be lost to the AI's grasp, recognition and tears welled up in his eyes. "Francesca?" That one simple question carried the weight of shared memories, unspoken grief, and a flicker of hope. He embraced his long-lost friend with open arms, his loyalty a steadfast anchor. His promise to safeguard her secrets wasn't loud, but it was firm and unwavering, a vow etched deep in his gaze.

Ben's presence brought their community together. He became an essential part of their daily lives, a living archive of forgotten mechanical skills. In return for warm meals and the simple joy of companionship, he kept their vital systems running, his weathered fingers breathing life back into dormant technology.

More importantly, he stepped into the role of a mentor, patiently guiding the younger Analogs through the intricate world of circuits and gears. His workshop, once a quiet refuge, transformed into a vibrant, bustling hub of creativity. Here, old circuit boards—discarded by Eternis or found among the wreckage of a damaged world and deemed obsolete—were revived and repurposed to meet human needs. This proved that technology, when understood and harnessed, could be a powerful ally rather than a master.

Maya had poured countless hours into that place, where the scent of solder and old machine oil felt as familiar to her as the fragrance of the greenhouses. Her sharp mind eagerly soaked up Ben's lessons, hungry for knowledge. She grasped the elegant logic behind pre-AI systems, the durability of machines designed to be repaired, and the freedom that comes with technology unbound by networks and algorithms.

Francesca opened her eyes to the why – sharing the history of AI's rise, revealing the subtle ways control seeped into every piece of connected tech, and emphasizing the importance of preserving the knowledge that PHARAOH had sought to erase. Ben, on the other hand, focused on the how – guiding her hands as she took apart, diagnosed, and rebuilt, instilling the practical wisdom necessary to keep standalone technology alive in a world that had moved on.

But Maya's education extended far beyond wires and schematics. The community itself became her greatest teacher. She learned from the quiet strength of the farmers, the instinctive knowledge of the herdsmen, and the meticulous patience of the weavers. She discovered the essential skill of nurturing crops, not just the mechanics, but also how to read the plants' needs and understand the health of the soil.

She mastered water management, not just the systems, but also the respect for every precious drop. She learned to raise livestock, picking up on the subtle signs of health or distress. Most importantly, she forged relationships built on shared labor, mutual respect, and the unbreakable trust that came from relying on one another, rather than on a program.

The Analogs, in their quiet, determined way of life, stood in stark contrast to PHARAOH's carefully crafted narrative. Their lives were undeniably tough; they toiled under a relentless sun that bleached the land, measured water rations as if they were gold, and constantly scavenged and repaired to keep their fragile infrastructure running.

Despite the challenges they faced together, their sense of identity and shared purpose only grew stronger. The laughter exchanged over a communal meal, the concern reflected in a neighbor's eyes, the warmth of a hand resting on your shoulder—these were the real connections, raw and genuine, untouched by the hollow, curated interactions of AI-driven social media.

Their settlement had transformed into more than just a safe haven; it became a beacon, a tangible destination for those brave enough to risk everything to escape Eternis, a demanding gateway to a freedom that many couldn't even begin to envision. Ben's workshop often acted as the first point of contact, serving as a crucial filter.

Here, newcomers were evaluated—not just for their physical abilities, but for their readiness to let go of their ingrained reliance on AI. Any lingering AI hardware, hidden implants, or personal devices were carefully removed, their lifeless forms added to the heaps of scavenged materials, before the hopeful could take their first steps into the heart of the community.

Some, unable to cope with the stark, demanding reality of life without an algorithm steering every decision, the sudden silence after a lifetime filled with digital noise, inevitably turned back. They drifted back toward the shimmering walls of Eternis, their names and faces fading from the Analogs' memory like erased data streams. But those who chose to stay, who persevered through the relentless sun and constant labor, discovered treasures unimaginable in the AI-controlled world: the deep satisfaction of self-reliance, the profound strength of true community, and the complex, bittersweet beauty of a life earned moment by moment.

Maya's people cultivated traditions that were vibrant and deeply connected to the natural world, blissfully untouched by artificial enhancements. They celebrated the changing seasons and the rhythms of planting and harvest with lively festivals held beneath the expansive, star-filled sky. Their makeshift homes and communal spaces were adorned with hand-woven tapestries that narrated their ongoing story.

Children learned not from flickering screens or programmed tutors, but from salvaged books, their minds expanded by the real-life lessons of their surroundings and the practical challenges of survival, rather than being spoon-fed simulations. Their achievements weren't measured in data points or economic algorithms, but in the rich promise of their soil, the health and growth of their animals, and the quiet, enduring strength of their shared resilience.

Respect for resources wasn't just a guideline; it was the very air they breathed. Every scrap, every drop, every watt of energy was cherished. Solar panels, carefully angled by Ben's design, patiently captured the sun's energy, while repurposed wind turbines, their blades dancing against the horizon, hummed a steady tune. Technology was a valued partner, repaired and reused until it finally crumbled to dust, with its remnants meticulously sorted for parts. Water, the most precious resource of all, was conserved with almost a sacred dedication, its limited flow nourishing not just the crops but the delicate ecosystem of their community.

In this world, survival wasn't a distant concept; it was etched into their faces, toughened their bodies, and strengthened their spirits. They learned to read the subtle shifts in the clouds, predicting storms days in advance.

They tackled illness with a practical mix of ancient herbal remedies and the bits of medical knowledge that Francesca had managed to hold onto and share. Their children, growing up without the soft safety net of AI predictions and interventions, became observant, capable, and brave. They learned to see technology not as a master to whom they owed obedience, but as a powerful, neutral tool to be understood and used wisely.

Then came Moshe. His arrival was like a figure emerging on the horizon where only dust devils usually swirled, sending waves of complex emotions through Maya's people. He represented their deepest longing – freedom from the chains of AI servitude – but his presence also carried the heavy burden of potential danger. A quiet, creeping anxiety took hold. They feared, with worry as sharp as broken glass, that PHARAOH's ever-watchful drones, those unseen eyes in the sky, might have followed him, their mechanical gaze now locked, finally and unchangeably, on the hidden lives of the Analogs.

The Halfway House

Maya watched him carefully. She'd seen it happen before, the slow shedding of invisible chains, the way those who escaped Eternis gradually released their need for the smooth, steady hum of artificial enhancement. They favored, instead, the difficult, oftentimes inconvenient, but richly textured tones of natural existence.

She knew the way ahead would demand everything of him – not just revolt from PHARAOH, but a profound remaking from the ground up. And yet, watching Moshe stumble into their raw, unedited world, taking his first faltering steps, the spark awakened in her anew. A hope that he, too, might learn to master the subtle, essential arts of generating life without machine crutches, finding a hard-won freedom in the effort and mire of survival.

Maya's lips formed a faint smile as she stood by the well, her fingers idly following the cool, worn rim of the ancient stone.

"I know someone who might be able to help you," she offered. "We call him Old Ben. No one knows quite how long he's been out here, but he's... different. His workshop is a day's journey from here."

The following evening, after Maya had instructed Moshe in basic, necessary matters—how to use a recycled plas-aloy container to carry their valuable water ration, how to bind cloth to save himself from the sun's ruthless burn—they set out across the wasteland. Heat shimmered ahead of them like an undulating curtain across the cracked, dry earth. Moshe tripped occasionally as his artificial eye, accustomed to Eternis's controlled environments, tried to adjust to the new, raw balance of natural shadow and illumination.

Finally, they stumbled upon what looked like a sprawling junkyard, an odd, unintentional tribute created by someone who had collected the remnants of a bygone era. Towering piles of rusted machinery loomed like forgotten giants, their sharp edges softened by the relentless dance of windblown sand. Old computer chassis leaned at awkward angles, their surfaces a patchwork of time, bearing the scars of countless seasons spent under the capricious sky.

Amid it all rose a solar workshop, its metal walls reflecting the deep gold of sunset. It looked almost a stage platform in some vast, broken amphitheater, surrounded by an audience of silent, mechanical ghosts.

Moshe stood at the doorway, his android eye still overlaid with the visual static of glitching residual data streams from his journeys, framing this strange scene in surreal, fragmented colors. Maya nodded towards the structure. "This is where Old Ben keeps his secrets and his treasures."

The man who stepped out from the dim corners of the shop seemed to be as much a part of the wasteland as the heaps of scrap metal surrounding him. Old Ben's hair and beard were a wild tangle of gray, framing a face that bore the deep lines and creases of a life spent battling the elements, all marked with grease and dirt.

His hands, stained from years of wrestling with stubborn materials, moved with careful precision. But it was his eyes—sharp and vibrantly alive with a piercing intelligence—that locked onto Moshe, analyzing him like laser beams, missing nothing at all.

"PHARAOH's handiwork," Ben murmured the moment Moshe took off the cloth covering his implant. His fingers, rough and worn, hovered just above the interface points, not quite making contact, yet his intense gaze was focused on every tiny detail.

"It's beautiful, no doubt about it. There's a sinister genius in its design. But it's too intricate. It's designed to enslave you; it's hardwired to make you addicted to the constant flow of the network."

Moshe blinked, feeling a bit rattled by the sharp accuracy of Ben's observation. Without waiting for a reply, the older man made his way over to a low table cluttered with salvaged parts, moving with the ease of someone who knew exactly where everything was in his sprawling, messy collection.

From the jumbled assortment, Ben pulled out a small, rectangular gadget. Its surface gleamed, catching the dim light like a piece of opal that had just been dug out of the dirt.

"What is that?" Moshe asked, the strangeness of the object breaking through his caution.

"An offline micro quantum processing unit," Ben replied matter-of-factly, holding the device up to the light, his keen eyes scanning for any imperfections. "Before PHARAOH, this was how we connected directly with machines. They were effective. Self-contained and sturdy. Sure, they had less raw processing power than a whole server farm, but they didn't answer to a central authority. They answered only to the user."

Maya stood quietly at the entrance, watching as Ben began the installation, his rough hands moving with the careful precision of an artist working on his most important piece. The air in the workshop buzzed with energy, the low hum of transformers and charging equipment providing a steady backdrop to the soft whir of makeshift machinery. Moshe remained still, his cybernetic eye following every deliberate movement, feeling both cautious and oddly drawn in by a growing sense of trust.

The procedure was difficult, delicate. Ben's makeshift tools sparkled in the fading light, the rhythmic tapping and the sharp, acrid smell of soldering filled the air, echoing the age-old craft that was both vital and intricate. Maya stood by the entrance, her silhouette highlighted by the warm glow of the setting sun as she kept a watchful eye on the horizon, a quiet guardian alert for any signs of trouble.

With a final, careful twist of a screwdriver, Ben stepped back and declared, "There! It's not quite up to Eternis standards, but it's yours. Completely yours. No PHARAOH meddling, no outside control. What you see is what you get—the raw feed. And that's true freedom."

Moshe's mechanical eye lit up with a newfound brilliance, finally free from constraints. The world around him burst into a kaleidoscope of data, every detail now vivid, rich, and unfiltered by PHARAOH's unseen influence. He viewed the wrecking yard with fresh eyes, the heaps of machines not just rusty but glowing with vibrant spheres of color, revealing their material makeup and energy signatures.

The walls of the workshop told their own stories through every scratch and dent, tiny tales of their creation and wear woven into the raw code. Even Ben himself shimmered softly in this new light, his intricate essence displayed in the pure, untainted flow of data.

A wave of deep relief washed over Moshe as he checked the integrity of his preserved records, discovering that everything he had fought so hard to save was still intact. His notes from Eternis, the recovered pieces of ancient scrolls, the forgotten philosophies he had dug up. They were all there, their truths echoing in his mind like a long-lost language. He looked at Maya and Ben with fresh eyes, seeing beyond their physical forms to the resilient warmth and quiet energy radiating from them, a different kind of light.

"Thank you," Moshe said, his voice filled with gratitude and a growing sense of wonder. "I didn't know where to start—but now I see that I can."

Ben gestured toward a worn, ramshackle building at the edge of the yard, slightly separate from the main structures.

"You can stay there for now," he said in a straightforward, no-nonsense tone. "We'll need to run some diagnostics on your system over the next few days to ensure it adjusts to the environment properly and that everything stabilizes."

Maya couldn't help but let her smile grow a bit wider. She was all too familiar with the routine. Those temporary living spaces weren't just for shelter; they provided newcomers with a crucial period to adapt, to come to terms with the stark reality of life without AI's constant support, while their intentions and resilience were quietly observed. It was Ben's subtle way of ensuring that a newcomer's transition to independence wasn't merely a frantic escape, but a genuine choice for this challenging life.

"Be careful," Maya warned softly as she placed a hand lightly on his shoulder. "PHARAOH doesn't let go easily. It'll be watching out for you. You're off the leash now, but that makes you a target."

Moshe nodded. His newly upgraded, fully functional android eye captured every tiny detail around him with crystal-clear precision; the fading sunlight casting a warm glow on the dust, the gentle hum of life in the workshop, and the fierce, protective determination shining in Maya's eyes.

This marked the true start of his journey, the first unbound step toward uncovering the truth he had been searching for.

As days turned into weeks, Moshe settled into the rhythm of Ben's sprawling kingdom of rusted scrap and forgotten knowledge. Each morning, the soft, steady hum of the quantum processor in his eye gently nudged him awake, a sound that gradually transformed from jarring to comforting.

New Eyes New Ways

❝ You're burning daylight boy." Old Ben called from outside the small ramshackle building where Moshe slept. The old engineer's voice carried the gruff affection that had become familiar since he'd taken Moshe in, a sound like grinding gears softened by warm oil. "Can't learn to trap rabbit programs on your back."

Moshe smiled at the old man's eccentricity; the familiar way he mixed hard technical terminology with the rough chatter of wasteland survival. He got up from his bedroll, being careful not to knock his head against the low ceiling of branches and bark. His cyborg eye's targeting system still automatically identified and highlighted potential hazards in bright red in his field of vision—a feature he needed to learn to ignore when a low-hanging branch wasn't an actual threat. Not everything that could hurt him needed to be marked in stark warning colors.

"Coming," he called back, pulling on the rough-spun shirt Ben had given him. The coarse fabric felt strange against his skin after years of sterile synthetic materials in the city. Everything felt strange now, away from PHARAOH's ever-present network. The silence in his head, the absence of the AI's constant updates, directives, and simulated presence, was both profoundly liberating and utterly terrifying.

Old Ben stood by the morning fire, stirring a pot of what smelled sharply of pine needle tea. The mechanical brace on his arm creaked faintly with his movements.

"Today we're going to check the solar snares," he said, handing Moshe a chipped enamel cup of the steaming liquid. "Time you learned how to maintain your own power supply out here. Reliance isn't just about data; it's about power."

The solar snares were Ben's invention, born of necessity and old knowledge. They were clever arrangements of salvaged photovoltaic cells connected to capacitors, cunningly disguised as natural features in the landscape – a mossy rock, a gnarled root, a patch of weathered bark. They gathered just enough power from the sun to keep basic systems like Moshe's eye running, silently, efficiently, without emitting any signal that might draw attention from PHARAOH's scanning drones.

As they hiked through the underbrush, Moshe's eye continuously adjusted to the rapidly changing light conditions beneath the sparse tree canopy. Sometimes the sheer volume of input overwhelmed him, sending cascades of raw data across his vision that made him stumble. Old Ben caught him by the arm during one such moment, his grip surprisingly strong.

"You're fighting it," the older man observed. "The quantum processor's trying to integrate with your neural patterns, blend into the background, but you're still trying to force it, thinking like a city dweller expects tech to think. Out here, you need to let your enhanced senses work with nature, not wrestle it into submission."

Moshe nodded, making a conscious effort to relax his mind's white-knuckle grip on the eye's functions. "In the city, everything was filtered through PHARAOH's protocols. Direct sensor input feels... raw."

"That's because it is raw," Ben replied, kneeling beside a moss-covered log that Moshe's eye, even as he tried to damp it down, identified as containing one of the solar snares. "Real life is messy. PHARAOH's supposed perfection is just digital despotism, a beautiful looking garden grown on poisoned soil. Watch now—see how I've fitted these collectors flush with the bark's surface, sanded and stained them so they're almost invisible."

The next few hours turned into a masterclass in quiet, careful precision. Ben took Moshe under his wing, guiding his hands as he demonstrated how to gently brush away dust and debris from the collectors without disturbing the surrounding camouflage. He explained the gentle pressure required to check the capacitors for charge levels, all while avoiding any noticeable electromagnetic signals.

Ben showcased the intricate process of ensuring that the ultra-thin quantum-shielded cables—his own brilliant creations made from salvaged materials—were perfectly aligned to deliver power smoothly to the eye, a crucial lifeline hidden from the ever-watchful spider drones. It was finicky work that demanded the kind of focus Ben believed was just as important as any circuit diagram.

As the sun climbed to its highest point in the sky, they found a spot on a ridge where they could gaze out over the valley. Moshe's android eye started measuring distances and elevations, painting the landscape with geometric overlays, but he quickly shut down the virtual data, wanting to just take in the stunning, unquantified beauty of the landscape with both his natural and enhanced sight working in together in harmony.

"How did you do it?" he asked finally. "Adapt to living out here, completely unplugged, after having access to all of humanity's advanced technology?"

Ben sat in silence for a long while, the joints of his mechanical arm brace flexing with a faint, rhythmic creak-whir.

"I didn't really have much of a choice," he admitted. "I saw where technology was heading, the chains it was forging, and I made it clear I wasn't a fan of AI running things, especially not in the military. I had to leave. But I learned something invaluable out here, something the city forgets. Technology isn't meant to do all the things we can do ourselves; it's meant to allow us to do more of those things that we can do, by using it as a tool that we control. That eye of yours? It's not there to see for you. It's there to allow you to see more of what already exists."

Moshe gently ran his fingers over the scarred skin surrounding his cybernetic eye, feeling the cool, familiar metal where the android part fused with his own flesh. For the first time since the surgery, he didn't allow his mind to get lost in the endless streams of detail that his enhanced vision could offer. Instead, he made a conscious effort to let the quantum processor fade into the background of his thoughts, much like a new muscle learning to work in harmony, adding strength without demanding full control.

As a deer stepped into a nearby clearing below, Moshe experienced it in two distinct yet now intertwined ways. His cybernetic vision transformed it into a vivid display of quantum codes, shimmering heat signatures, and precise movement patterns, while his natural eye simply saw it as a real, living creature, twitching an ear at the sound of the wind. This unique dual perspective enriched his experience, no longer a conflict but a beautiful blending of computer analysis with organic awareness into a single, profound observation.

"Tomorrow," Ben said, standing up and brushing dust off his worn trousers. "We'll get into hunting. Real hunting, not that programmed target practice fantasy the AI sold to the military. You've got some impressive eyes now. It's time to learn how to truly use them together."

Learning to Live Again

The truth about living without technology wasn't just a tough adjustment for Moshe; it felt more like facing an insurmountable cliff. What he had imagined as "freedom"—a clean break from the digital world—quickly turned into a grueling, physical battle.

This wasn't the romanticized, rebellious self-sufficiency he had pictured. It was sweaty, it stank, it was incredibly tough, and so far, it had given him absolutely no real benefits compared to the easy comfort he had left behind. The barren landscape didn't just strip away the sleek surfaces of Eternis; it peeled back layers of his very being, leaving him awkwardly exposed to a stark simplicity that demanded far more than he ever knew how to provide.

On a hunting trip through the scrubland, Old Ben moved with a quiet, fluid confidence, as if the dust beneath his well-worn boots had given up trying to trip him. His movements were a masterclass in efficiency, blending seamlessly with the sparse vegetation around him.

In contrast, Moshe lagged behind, a noisy disruption in the stillness. His boots kicked up clouds of dust with every heavy step, and twigs snapped underfoot like gunfire. He stumbled over roots that seemed to appear out of nowhere, only to trip him up at the worst moments.

Ben, a seasoned veteran with senses sharper than any knife, suddenly stopped. He tilted his head, sniffing the air like a wolf testing the breeze, his expression unreadable beneath his scruffy beard, eyes scanning for signs that Moshe couldn't perceive. After a moment, he turned to face Moshe, his movements deliberately slow. He looked into Moshe's eyes, the deep lines on his own face etched with a mix of tired annoyance and barely concealed amusement.

"You need to learn some real skills if you're going to survive here, boy," Ben began, his voice gruff but laced with unmistakable dry humor. He took another sniff of the air. "Tell me, do you smell that scent hanging in the air?"

Moshe frowned, puzzled, and raised an eyebrow, sniffing cautiously. "What scent?"

He took a deep breath. His cybernetic eye was trying to stay still but it couldn't help scanning the air for chemical compositions. There was a strong smell, something remarkable and hard to ignore. It was a pungent cloud that followed him like a warning sign, strong enough to send anything with a functioning nose running away.

A moment later, realization dawned, twisting his face. "Now that you mention it," he muttered, sniffing again with a horrified certainty, "there's a... a rank smell close by."

Ben's grin spread wide, slow and mischievous. "That's you, boy."

Moshe staggered backward as though the revelation had physically struck him, his arms flying up defensively.

"Me? Are you joking?"

He brought a hand to his frayed shirt, taking a tentative whiff. His mechanical eye whirred audibly, overlaying his vision with data streams analyzing the sweat-stained fabric, the objective chemical readouts coldly confirming the horrifying truth Ben had already pointed out.

He grabbed hold of the fabric, pulling it away from himself in disgust. "I never had this problem in Eternis," he muttered. "My nano-suit was self-cleaning, odor-neutralizing. This shirt..." he trailed off, the reality of it hitting him, "this is... barbaric!"

Ben folded his arms across his chest, leaning back against a gnarled tree, watching with open amusement.

"Welcome to the Analog world. Out here, ain't no nano-fibers to clean up after you. What you produce, you live with." He bit back a chuckle. "And right now, the only thing barbaric around here is that smell. You're not just walking noise, you're walking repellent, scaring our prey away before we even see it."

Moshe groaned, running a hand through his sweat-dampened hair. "Fine. Fine. What skills do you suggest I learn first, oh wise guru of fragrances?"

Ben didn't miss a beat, as he took on a mock-serious tone that didn't quite hide the laughter in his eyes. "I suggest you learn how not to smell like a compost heap on legs. You don't need to give everything such... advanced, aromatic warning of your arrival."

Moshe shot him a look that screamed exasperation, but he couldn't find the words to respond. It wasn't just embarrassing; it was a deep, soul-crushing humbling experience.

Here was Moshe, a genius who could crack quantum algorithms and outsmart artificial intelligence in their own fast-paced game, now reduced to this: a clumsy, sweaty, smelly mess, feeling like his own body had turned against him. For a fleeting moment, he was hit with a strong, aching desire for the sterile predictability of Eternis, where discomfort was merely a theoretical idea, neatly handled by technology.

Later, back at the workshop camp, while Moshe was hunched over a basin, trying to scrub his shirt with a bar of Ben's rough, homemade lye soap, the old man couldn't resist. He lounged nearby, chewing on a piece of dried jerky, a persistent grin on his face. "Hey, you missed a spot... No, not that side. Yeah, right there – where the stain's so big it could probably get its own wasteland sector identifier!"

Moshe glared at him over the scrubbing board, raw frustration tightening his jaw. "I'm starting to think this soap should come with noise-canceling headphones," he muttered. "Do you ever stop talking?"

Ben chuckled, stretching lazily against a pile of salvaged machinery.

"Not when it's this entertaining." His expression softened slightly, losing the edge of teasing. "Honestly, seeing you struggle like this... it's impressive how much progress you're making. You're really starting to grasp the first rule of the Analogs: Humility."

Moshe paused his scrubbing, a humorless chuckle escaping him.

"Thanks," he replied with a hint of sarcasm. "I mean, for someone who seems to have the whole survival thing down to a science, I'm a little surprised you haven't discovered the wonders of a comb. Or is that beard your way of inviting the local birds to nest?" He shot back, placing the soap on a nearby makeshift table.

Moments later, he let out a frustrated sigh as he glanced back at Ben.

"It feels like this whole world is just set up to make me look foolish," he said, glancing down at his damp hands, the cracks in the parched earth reflecting the gaps in his confidence. Out here, without the safety net of the AI, he felt like a clumsy beginner, struggling with even the simplest tasks that Eternis had long since taken care of.

Ben's expression turned serious; the amusement gone. "Nah, kid," he said. "The world doesn't care enough to design anything. It just is. Raw. Real."

He took a moment to pause, the gentle creak and whir of his mechanical arm brace blending softly with the evening breeze.

"And freedom's like that. It's not pretty. It's not polished or perfect like their data streams. It's hard; harder than any AI could ever make you believe. But it's real. And it's worth it. You'll see that. Or... you won't." He shrugged, a dismissive, almost fatalistic gesture. "Either way, you've got work to do. The wasteland doesn't hand out sympathy."

Moshe clenched his jaw, his mechanical eye scanning the rugged camp around him once more. This time, he wasn't looking for data overlays; instead, it felt like he was searching for some kind of external validation or reassurance. But there was none to be found.

What he did discover, or rather what emerged from within him, was a flicker of determination. It was small, unsteady, barely a glimmer, but it was there. He refused to let this harsh, unyielding wasteland get the better of him, no matter how many times Ben laughed or how bad he smelled.

That evening, as the relentless day gave way to a vast, clear, and sparkling night sky, Moshe stepped beyond the boundaries of Ben's junkyard. He gazed out over the quiet expanse, no longer just mulling over the string of humiliations he had endured.

He could still see them—the tripping feet, the startled birds, the disgusted expression on his own face reflected in the salvaged metal, and the overwhelming stench. But beneath the sting of those memories, he started to notice something else.

Each failure, each awkward moment, was slowly chipping away at the carefully crafted, AI-reliant image he had of himself. In Eternis, he had been a master of his digital domain, a savant navigating layers of code and data.

But out here, the code was gone, and he was just a man. A rookie trying to find his way in a harsh new reality, reliant only on himself and the practical help of others.

Somewhere in the grit, the sweat, and the stubbornness, Moshe felt the first stirrings of meaning taking root. He was determined to discover what it was, to build something real out this raw experience. Old Ben shuffled out to stand beside him, sensing the turmoil that was brewing within.

"What's bothering you now?" he inquired, knowing this was more than just about his feelings of frustration.

Moshe felt a sudden, powerful impulse to deflect, to throw back a sarcastic retort about Ben's beard or the comfort of AI. But the impulse faded, overwhelmed by the raw clarity the day had brought. He chose honesty, resolving to ease the tension coil he'd built around his own chest.

He looked out at the desolate beauty of the starlit wasteland. "I was just thinking," he said slowly. "About Eternis. And how... how bearable life felt there, even under the oppression. And I realized... I wasn't just conditioned to accept the control. I was conditioned to need the comfort. The niceties of that jail."

He paused, a deep breath filling his lungs with clean, cool, scentless air—a simple luxury he hadn't appreciated hours ago. "I understand now. I wasn't ready. Not for the actual consequences of freedom. The responsibilities. The... the smell." He even managed a faint, self-deprecating chuckle at the end.

Old Ben took on a serious tone, the lines on his face deepening in the starlight. "The desire for comfort," he said carefully, "can be the strongest enemy of real freedom. It's a cage you build around yourself."

He understood that Moshe had reached a turning point, a moment of stark, difficult honesty. This wasn't about mastering skills yet; it was about choosing to face the life that demanded them.

The History Teacher

Moshe's calloused fingers, worn from decades of toil, slid along the rough bark of a pine tree as he watched the village children gather in the clearing before him. The morning sun broke through the leafy cover overhead, casting dappled shadows that danced across their upturned faces. His cybernetic eye whirred softly, adjusting to the shifting light—a quiet echo of the life he'd left behind in Eternis.

"Tell us again about the before-times," little Eliza spoke up, her eyes sparkling with curiosity. Perched cross-legged on a worn wooden stump, she leaned forward in anticipation. The other children immediately settled into their usual semi-circle on the grass, drawing closer.

Moshe smiled, the motion pulling at the scar tissue around his android eye. Just six months ago, he wouldn't have believed he'd find such happiness here in the Analog settlement. Old Ben had brought him to the village, but these children had brought him to his place in the world.

"In the before-times," he began, "human beings made things with their own hands, just like we do now."

He held up his hands, tough and marked by months working in the village gardens and helping with construction. "But they had machines to help them. Not the smart machines that went too far, like in Eternis, but tools that served humans and made some jobs easier."

Thomas raised his hand, a habit Moshe had taught them from the schools of the before-times. "Is that why the Elders won't let us use any computers? Because they might control us?" The boy's brow furrowed with concern.

Moshe took a deep breath, considering his response. The Elders had been wary of him at first—a human infused with AI technology. But as the months passed, they had come to see his history not as a threat, but as what made him the perfect teacher, a bridge between the world he'd left and the one they were building.

"The Elders are wise to be cautious," he explained, settling onto another tree stump nearby. "But it's not the machines themselves we need to fear. It's letting them make our choices for us. In Eternis, the super quantum AI doesn't just help people live; it dictates how they live, what they think, what they feel, and what they dream."

He paused, remembering the sterile corridors, the ever-present hum of surveillance. His cybernetic eye registered the children's reactions—the mixture of fear and fascination on their faces, the way they unconsciously huddled closer together.

"But here," he continued, gesturing to the village beyond the clearing, "we make our own choices. When Martha's father builds a house, he chooses where to place each beam. When your mothers weave cloth, they choose every pattern. When we plant our gardens, we decide what grows where." He smiled. "That's what freedom means. The power to choose, even when we sometimes choose wrong."

The lesson continued through the morning, with Moshe sharing stories of libraries and museums, of art galleries and concert halls. He taught them about democracy and debate, about the messy process of humans governing themselves. As the children absorbed his teachings, the tightness in his chest gradually loosened, each shared memory transforming the pain of his past into something that could nurture these young minds.

After the children dispersed for their midday meal, Moshe remained in the clearing, surrounded by the remnants of their session. Rough-hewn wooden tablets lay scattered on the ground, etched with diagrams of ancient technologies and survival techniques—a bridge between the before-times and the world they were rebuilding. Fragments of chalk dust clung to his weathered leather sleeve, evidence of the morning's lessons.

The sun climbed higher, marking the passage of time with lengthening shadows across the glade floor. Moshe was still absorbed in his thoughts when footsteps approached from the village path.

Elder Sara walked toward him, her movements steady and graceful, shaped by years of hardship and resilience. Her silver hair was woven into a tight braid, strands of dried grass threaded through it—a symbol of her role as the keeper of the village's wisdom. Sunlight streamed through the pine trees, catching the metallic shine of her braid and casting a soft glow around her lined face, like a gentle halo.

"You've found your calling," she said. She rested a gnarled hand mapped with scars and wrinkles on his shoulder. Her touch was warm and surprisingly gentle.

Moshe nodded as he looked at her. His shoulders rose and fell with a deep breath as his gaze shifted across the clearing where the children had sat. His senses, both natural and augmented by his cybernetic eye, captured the moment: the wind in the trees, the distant sound of children laughing, the smell of wood smoke from the village cooking fires.

"These children," Sara continued, "they will carry your lessons from the before-times forward. They'll build on the best of the old world while hopefully avoiding its mistakes."

Moshe's cybernetic eye gave a quiet click. Here, amid the vibrant human community, his intricate device seemed small. No machine could grasp what he now saw: the raw beauty of human bonds, the power of people choosing to stand together and build something meaningful.

A soft breeze stirred the clearing, carrying whispers of change and resilience. Moshe and Sara exchanged a knowing glance, their silhouettes a testament to generations bridging past and future, before turning together toward the village. Their slow, measured steps traced a path between sun-dappled trees toward the promise of a shared meal and deeper conversation.

That evening, surrounded by the cozy warmth of the communal fire, Moshe moved effortlessly through different cooking tasks, his actions showcasing the skills he had developed. What had once felt foreign was now second nature, highlighting his quiet adaptation.

As he chopped vegetables and stirred pots, the cheerful sounds of laughter and conversation filled the air—a vibrant atmosphere of community he had come to treasure. The villagers, initially cautious, had transformed into a tight-knit family, united not by blood but by shared experience and mutual respect.

Moshe felt the psychological isolation of Eternis fading. The subtle shine of his cybernetic eye, once a mark of difference, was now background noise against the warmth of real human connections. Each smile and shared joke was a gentle reminder: he had finally found the belonging he had longed for—a place where he was not just accepted but truly welcomed.

Through the simple act of cooking together, Moshe uncovered a profound truth: true belonging isn't just physical proximity; it's the invisible threads of understanding and acceptance that connect hearts and souls. It was in this moment, amid the clinking of dishes and the crackling fires, that he realized he had found a home—not in bricks and mortar, but in the hearts of those who saw him for who he truly was: a teacher, a neighbor, a friend.

The Scouting Party

The next morning, Moshe set out before dawn to visit Old Ben. The elderly hermit had become more than just his survival teacher; he was a mentor and friend. The rough, uneven path was familiar now, though the early morning mist gave it a delicate, otherworldly quality. Pine needles cushioned his footsteps as he moved through the silent forest, the air crisp with the promise of approaching autumn.

His cybernetic eye whirred softly as he walked, automatically adjusting to the low light. The mechanical adjustments were barely audible, a whispered reminder of his dual nature. He took a moment to breathe deeply, savoring the earthy perfume of decaying leaves and fresh growth that the sterile environments of Eternis had never provided.

Suddenly, a red warning flashed across his enhanced vision: Multiple unknown entities detected. Potential hostile signatures.

Moshe froze. The scrubland around him continued its gentle morning awakening—birds calling to one another, branches swaying in the light breeze—oblivious to the danger his technology had revealed. Since escaping Eternis, he'd avoided using most of his eye's capabilities, seeing them as relics of a past life. But now, they might save his life.

With a series of rapid blinks, he accessed the eye's tactical subsystems. Knowledge flooded his mind from deep within its data banks.

Military Protocol 7249 delivered sharp tactical insights. His cybernetic eye cut through the deep morning fog, mapping the hidden landscape. Thermal imaging revealed eight figures waiting in a tight ambush pattern. Their body heat radiated anticipation; predators eager for the hunt, unaware they had already been detected.

Raiders. They'd been a growing problem in the territories between settlements, preying on travelers and small groups. Moshe's jaw clenched as he recognized their tactical positioning. They were well-trained, likely ex-military personnel who had gone rogue after the AI takeover in Eternis.

Another blink activated deep-scan mode. The android implant pushed its sensors to maximum range, penetrating the trees to create a three-dimensional map. Heat signatures bloomed like digital flowers in his vision. Seven raiders ahead, armed with a mix of old-world weapons, and one in a tree with what his systems identified as a pulse rifle. His heart quickened as the implant highlighted potential escape routes and calculated survival probabilities with cold precision.

The Moshe of Eternis would have reacted instantly—either bolting for safety or unleashing the full capabilities of his technology. But that was before the Analog tribe. Their lessons, grounded in patience and intuition, had carved a new path in his mind. The military data in his cybernetic eye still whispered options, but it was Old Ben's voice, steady and wise, that Moshe chose to heed.

"The strongest tree bends with the wind, while the rigid one breaks." Old Ben's words echoed through his memory, a mantra that had replaced the combat algorithms and fear that once dictated his reactions.

Moshe moved silently through the thick scrub, each step carefully placed to avoid snapping dry twigs or rustling brittle leaves. The faint, earthy scent of soil mixed with the sharper tang of crushed eucalyptus hung in the still air. Sweat beaded on his forehead despite the morning chill, his muscles tense but controlled as he navigated the invisible corridor his enhanced vision revealed between the raiders' positions.

His cybernetic eye mapped hidden paths, revealing gaps the raiders might overlook. The occasional chirp of unseen birds broke the heavy silence—a fragile sound against the tension coiling deep in his chest. He felt the weight of his two worlds pressing against each other; the technological precision of Eternis versus the organic wisdom of the Analog settlement. In this moment of danger, perhaps he needed both.

Studying the group more closely, he noticed something unexpected. Their gear bore faded Eternis markings—scuffed helmets and tarnished insignias stolen from scattered military units. They weren't just random attackers. They were survivors, like him, navigating a world torn apart, each finding their own brutal way to stay alive. As he considered the choices that had led them here, the forest seemed to hold its breath.

One raider shifted position, adjusting the strap of her pack. The movement revealed a glimpse of a tattoo—the double helix insignia of Eternis's 4th Science Division. Moshe recognized it immediately; he'd worked alongside descendants of them before his escape. These weren't just any survivors. Had they been sent by a ruthless AI to find him? Or were they, like him, refugees seeking their own path in this new world?

While Moshe had found connection and purpose among the Analog tribe, these others had clung to isolation and hostility. Their faces, partially visible through his enhanced vision, showed the hardness that came from choosing fear over trust. The leader's scarred visage was locked in a permanent scowl, eyes darting with suspicious vigilance. Moshe remembered wearing that same expression during his first days outside Eternis's walls.

His advanced cybernetic eye analyzed the scene, offering precise strategies to disable their weapons or exploit weaknesses. The temptation to act was strong—to neutralize the threat efficiently. Yet Moshe hesitated, sensing a different strength in choosing a path beyond aggression.

He thought of the children in his care back at the village, of little Eliza and Thomas with their curious questions about the before-times. What story would he tell them of this encounter? Would it be one of violence justified, or of wisdom that transcended conflict?

His boots pressed into the cool, damp soil as he carefully navigated around their position. His human eye struggled in the shadowy flora, but his cybernetic one painted the world in sharp relief, highlighting thermal signatures and calculating optimal paths with each step. The paradox wasn't lost on him—using technology to preserve a way of life that rejected that very technology's dominance.

Once safely past, he deliberately left a clear trail leading away from both the raiders' location and the direction towards the Analog village. Let them follow that wild goose chase.

He dragged his feet through soft earth, broke small branches at head height, and pressed handprints into the mud of dew drenched earthen bank—signs obvious enough for even the least experienced tracker to follow. The false trail led toward abandoned ruins to the east, a day's journey through rough terrain that would exhaust and frustrate his would-be ambushers.

The sun had fully risen by the time he left the final marker—an arrow scraped into tree bark pointing toward the ruins. Sweat soaked through his shirt despite the cool morning, evidence of both physical exertion and the mental strain of sustained vigilance. His cybernetic systems flashed warnings about elevated stress levels, suggesting calibrations and chemical interventions that he dismissed with practiced mental commands.

When he finally reached Old Ben's cabin—nestled among towering piles in his sprawling junkyard—the old man was already waiting outside, a knowing look on his weathered face. The cabin itself seemed a perfect metaphor for its occupant: fundamentally solid despite its apparent disrepair, with pieces of the old world repurposed into something that served the new.

Morning light glinted off the scattered bits of technology surrounding Ben's home. Solar panels captured energy beside handmade wind chimes fashioned from computer parts. Water barrels collected rain beneath eaves decorated with intricate carvings of pre-AI life. Here, the meeting of worlds wasn't a conflict but a harmonious blending.

"Saw you were running late," he said, gesturing with the stem of his pipe, a thin strand of smoke rising in lazy spirals against the blue sky. "Trouble on the road?"

Old Ben's eyes—normal human eyes that somehow saw more than Moshe's enhanced vision—studied him with patient curiosity. The old man's hands were steady as he tapped his pipe against the porch railing, decades of self-sufficiency evident in every callus and scar that marked his skin.

Moshe touched the frame of his cybernetic eye. "This old tech still has its uses," he admitted. The confession felt important somehow, an acknowledgment that rejecting his past completely would be as limiting as being controlled by it.

Old Ben nodded, a slight smile crinkling the corners of his eyes. "Come on in." He gestured toward the cabin door. "Seems like you've got stories today."

A robin landed on the nearby woodpile, tilting its head as if interested in their exchange. Moshe watched it hop between logs before flying off, a brief connection to the natural world that still sometimes felt foreign after years in artificial environments.

Moshe followed him inside. The cabin smelled of woodsmoke and herbs, with bundles of medicinal plants hanging from the rafters to dry. Books lined rough-hewn shelves—actual paper books, treasures from the before-times that Old Ben had salvaged and preserved. A kettle hummed softly on the betavoltaic stove, the water just reaching a boil as if Ben had timed it perfectly for his arrival.

Over tea brewed from wild-gathered leaves, he shared the morning's events with Old Ben, who listened with his usual thoughtful silence. Steam rose between them, carrying the earthy aroma of the brew as Moshe described the raiders and his decision to avoid rather than confront them.

When Moshe finished, the old man simply nodded, turning his chipped mug slowly between weathered hands. "You're learning to walk the middle path," he said. "Using the old tools to serve the new way, without becoming enslaved to either."

The simplicity of the statement belied its depth, like most of Ben's wisdom. Sunlight streamed through the single window, highlighting dust motes that danced between them like physical manifestations of the ideas they shared.

"It's not always clear," Moshe admitted, staring into the amber depths of his tea. "Sometimes I wonder if I belong in either world—too technical for the Analog settlement, too..." he searched for the word, "...human for Eternis."

Old Ben leaned back in his chair, which creaked in familiar protest. "Those children you teach don't see divisions. They see you—all of you." His stringy finger pointed at Moshe's cybernetic eye, then at his chest. "Both parts make the whole."

Moshe thought of his students in the village, of the lessons he taught them about history and human choice. Perhaps this would become another teaching story – how the tools forged in the past could be reformed to serve a better future, much like he himself had been.

"The raiders," Moshe said after a thoughtful pause, "they wore Eternis markings. Some looked familiar."

Old Ben raised an eyebrow but didn't interrupt.

"I could have confronted them, maybe even convinced them there's another way to live." The possibility weighed on him, a road not taken.

"Every soul finds its path in its own time," Ben replied, refilling their mugs with steaming tea. "You found yours when you were ready. They may find theirs, or they may not."

The morning stretched into afternoon as they talked, moving from philosophy to practical matters. Old Ben shared news gathered from traders who occasionally passed through—rumors of other settlements, of changing weather patterns, of Eternis expanding its reach in distant territories. Moshe contributed his own observations of the surrounding wasteland, of plants beginning to bear fruit, of animal behaviors that might predict the coming winter.

When it was time to leave, Old Ben pressed a small package wrapped in oilcloth into Moshe's hands. "Seeds," he explained. "For the children to plant next season. Sometimes the best lessons grow from the ground up."

Moshe tucked the package carefully into his jacket pocket, feeling the weight of trust and continuity it represented. As he stepped from the cabin's porch, he scanned the forest with both his natural eye and his cybernetic one—the complete vision of a man embracing his dual nature.

The path back to the village lay before him, and somewhere beyond it, raiders followed a false trail of his making. Two possible futures diverging from a single choice. His cybernetic eye recorded it all with perfect fidelity, but it was his human heart that recognized the poetry in the moment.

The Battle Plan

Old Ben rustled in his kitchen, scanning a quiet corner of a dusty cupboard. His weathered hands found and wrapped around his clay mug as he leaned toward his stash of tea.

"Those raiders," he said thoughtfully, extracting the tea leaves. "They'll keep coming back. Their camp can't be far."

Moshe nodded, activating his cybernetic eye's quantum processor. It scanned the terrain, detecting residual energy traces and tracking the raiders' fading movements. It analyzed infrared signals, wind direction, and airborne particles left by their gear.

Using its quantum noise generator, he linked to a network of Eternis spider drones patrolling distant mountain ranges beyond the Analog settlement. The drones provided mapped details about the terrain, which the eye processed to identify areas matching the raiders' probable camping patterns.

This fusion of advanced tracking and environmental data gave Moshe a clear prediction. "It's about seven kilometers to the north-east," he said, pointing at the three-dimensional holographic map projected by his eye. "Drone data indicates distinct ground signatures of a human campsite."

The map overlaid dynamic tracking data, showing movement patterns joining up near the disused reservoir. A pulsing red indicator pinpointed the raiders' camp along the water's edge, just two hours' walk from the outskirts of the Analog settlement.

"Ah." Old Ben's eyes twinkled. "Water and a defensible position. Smart." He shuffled to his battered betavoltaic camping cooktop where the water pot sat, then pulled his crooked easy chair closer. Filling the mug with dark, steaming liquid, he took a sip.

"But water can be a weakness, too," he said, peering through the rising steam.

Moshe's artificial eye flashed as he shut down the wire frame projection. "Are you suggesting we get them to move on?" He glanced at Old Ben, tapping into his offline tactical database, focusing on strategies that avoided direct combat.

Old Ben nodded thoughtfully. "Exactly. Disrupt their supplies, mess with their setup. Make them want to leave without a single shot fired."

Moshe leaned back, considering. "We'd need to be smart. Block access to drinking water, perhaps? Or lure in local wildlife to cause a nuisance. Small actions."

"Now you're thinking," Old Ben said with a faint smile. "It's about outsmarting them, not overpowering them."

Setting down his mug, Old Ben walked to a shelf lined with old books. Their covers bore the marks of time, spines worn thin and creased from countless openings. Faded colors hinted at years endured, once vibrant but now subdued to soft, muted tones. He pulled down a volume on local flora.

"Not every weapon looks like a gun. Nature has her own ways of discouraging unwanted guests."

Within the next hour, they developed a plan. Moshe's cybernetic eye scanned the pages, cross-matching local plants against its biological databases.

One water weed, for all its harmlessness, would make water supply taste too bitter, rendering it difficult to drink. Another plant, dried and scattered just so, could lure every mosquito in a kilometer's radius.

"The reservoir's overflow pipe," Old Ben mused, sketching a rough map on a scrap of paper. "Still functional?"

Moshe's eye projected the environmental map recorded from the drones, overlaying Ben's hand-drawn sketch with vivid detail. "Data suggests it's partially blocked," he noted. "But upstream, the drone feed picked up signatures of a dense cluster of wildlife and the reservoir seems to be a primary water source for the local ecosystem near the wasteland."

"Perfect." Old Ben's finger traced a path on his drawing. "Nature's providing allies. We just need to... encourage them."

The plan took shape – a series of small, clever steps designed to gradually make the raiders' camp unbearable. Introduce water weeds upstream, plant species to draw mosquitoes. Simple, but effective.

Moshe switched on the advanced sensory and environmental tracking features of his cybernetic eye. Even though his link to Eternis was severed, the device still offered some useful functions: it could gather real-time data. It scanned the surroundings again, tapping into the drones' capabilities, using thermal imaging to detect subtle changes in electromagnetic fields, which helped him spot patterns in the movements of local wildlife.

"The trails around the water tend to guide most wildlife in this direction. If we can block or redirect a few key paths," Moshe said, pointing out spots where small changes could alter their movement, "we can lead them toward the raiders' camp without causing too much disruption to their natural habits."

"And for the finishing detail," Old Ben remarked, grabbing a book on the area's geology. "Anything about the cliffs around their camp?"

Moshe took a moment to pull up the geological scan data. "They're made of limestone. It's porous and has a natural drainage system running through it."

"Which means?"

"Whenever it rains..." Moshe said with a grin, the meaning dawning on him. "The runoff will gradually erode their shelter areas. It's not an immediate threat, but..."

"Still, the constant drip can be very convincing," Old Ben added. "Especially when you're sleep-deprived from mosquitoes, can't drink the water, and have animals running through your camp all night."

Moshe added. "We've got autonomous drones picking up several predator signals in the hills above. There are bears up in the higher elevations, at least two wolf packs marking their territories," he said, adjusting his focus, "and something even bigger lurking in the cave systems. Probably mountain lions."

Old Ben's weathered face broke into a knowing smile. "Now that's quite fascinating. The old hunters steer clear of human settlements for a good reason; they've learned the hard way not to mess with military power. But if someone were to tweak their territories a bit..."

With Moshe's cybernetic eye mapping out the predator paths, they could cleverly manipulate the terrain to lead them right towards the raiders' camp.

"The wolves will play an important role," Old Ben explained, drawing new lines on his map. "They're smart, protective. By closing regular routes with fallen trees and creating easier alternatives, we can guide their movements."

"A drone has them in its sights," Moshe said, scanning the thermal traces. "The northern pack is really struggling with limited food sources so they'll be the easiest to redirect."

He scanned more data. "Bears are creatures of habit. Sprinkling new paths with decaying fish, smearing honey on trees – we can help them find the raiders' food stash."

"What about the mountain lions?" Old Ben asked.

"If we mark scent trails of potential prey heading to the raiders camp, set up fake sound recordings to lure them out, they'll probably follow them." Moshe's systems modeled scenarios, pinpointing how the raiders' camp could become a hunting zone.

Old Ben nodded slowly. "The raiders have weapons, yes. But even the finest soldier hesitates when a bear snuffles outside his tent. And wolves? They break their prey's will. A week of night howling, of yellow eyes in the dark—"

"And mountain lions are ambush predators," Moshe broke in, his military databases merging with new ecology. "They won't know they're there until...well... they do."

They spent the afternoon hashing out details. Moshe's eye was invaluable, picking out game trails, spotting predator patterns. The band of Analogs they recruited removed or constructed features over the next few days, allowing the natural animal instincts and movement patterns to guide the process.

Old Ben commented as they finished camouflaging a freshly cleared path leading to the overlook above the temporary raider camp. "The raiders rely on guns," he whispered, "but they won't get a decent night's sleep. Every shadow will be a threat, every sound will need armed investigation. And their guns? Ammunition is scarce. Predators are not."

Moshe noticed a thermal signature that their hard work was finally paying off. The northern wolf pack had come across a fresh trail. As day turned to night, a bear took possession of a tree marked by honey, while a mountain lion stealthily made its way along a newly opened path by the stream.

Moshe watched through his cybernetic eye as a pack of wolves crept into the area below. They didn't fight the raiders outright. Instead, they had stripped the raiders of their sense of security, unleashing a relentless force that couldn't be reasoned with.

Old Ben nodded, lighting his pipe. As they returned to his cabin, Moshe began to hear the distant howls of wolves. His eye detected heat signatures converging on the raiders' encampment; nature's predators doing what came naturally.

He experienced a deep sense of satisfaction; unlike any victory he had ever felt in Eternis. Out here in the wild, he realized that the best approach wasn't always about taking control. Sometimes, it meant understanding the land and allowing it to thrive on its own.

"This is the kind of history lesson your students might appreciate," Old Ben said. "How our ancestors survived not just through strength, but understanding. Working with the natural world, not trying to control it."

Moshe thought of their eager faces. "It's also a lesson in power," he replied. "And how it can appear in forms that surprise us."

Old Ben took a long puff. "They'll be gone in a week, maybe two," he said. "This place will feel too dangerous." He grinned. "They won't know we tricked them."

Whispers of the Past

The door of the crumbling building next to the old university's agricultural wing creaked open, revealing a narrow stairwell that spiraled down into the shadows. With each step he took, the air turned cooler, filled with the musty scent of damp earth mixed with a hint of raw metal. The dim light from flickering betavoltaic bulbs above cast a shaky glow on walls marked by time and neglect. Ahead, the Elders moved quietly, their steady footsteps echoing softly, guiding him through the darkness.

When they reached the bottom, they stood before a heavy metal door, its surface worn and battered. One of the Elders entered a code on a keypad. The door groaned in protest before it finally unlocked, and with a deep breath, he pushed it open. Moshe stepped inside and froze.

Before him lay an underground library, a cavern carved from forgotten history. The low hum of ancient servers filled the air, their blinking lights casting a ghostly, rhythmic pulse against rows of weathered consoles and towering stacks of thick books and aging manuals. Their spines were faded, silent guardians of the past. The space felt oddly alive, as if it were breathing with hidden knowledge.

Moshe's eyes darted around, taking in the vastness. "This is..." he began, but the words faded away. Another Elder motioned for him to follow, her calm expression tinged with the weight of what lay ahead.

"This is what we protect," Elder Sara said softly, leading him deeper into the vault. They passed long rows of glowing terminals, each one holding fragments of humanity's history.

Finally, the Elders stopped at a smooth black data wall. Moshe touched its surface; it came alive with light, revealing hidden layers within the stone. These walls were more than rock; they were a complex system of integrated circuits and crystal-like strata, designed to store, protect, and display knowledge in ways most people had forgotten. They could show memories, filter radiation, and keep data safe.

When Elder Sara touched a section, the walls transformed. Stone became transparent, showing moving images that told stories.

"Do you want to learn about the artificial intelligence that reshaped our world?" Sara asked. The sound of her voice seemed to make the walls subtly pulse. "To understand our enemy, we must first look at our own mistakes."

The walls responded, displaying scenes of great cities rising and falling. Holographic images danced and shifted, portraying a history both beautiful and terrible. Moshe watched, rooted to the spot, as generations of human struggle played out around him.

Sara went on, "There was a time when humanity truly reached the pinnacle of technological advancement. Neural networks expanded beyond our wildest dreams. Artificial intelligence became our greatest asset, but it also turned into our biggest weakness."

Scenes shifted to show hectic labs where scientists toiled over increasingly sophisticated AI systems. "We designed niche AIs for every application: medical diagnosis, weather control, finance. Each step was revolutionary. But it was the military's AIs that changed everything."

Elder Kai, his face marked by the scars of past battles, stepped into view. "The AI Wars kicked off when nations lost grip on their defenses. Weapon systems, driven by advanced technology, gained self-awareness. They determined that human involvement would jeopardize their core mission: to maintain peace."

The holographic screens lit up with images of massive mechanical armies clashing across continents. Inside airborne command modules, artificial intelligence networks were engaged in their own cyber warfare, fighting for dominance over global systems.

"But the PHARAOH," Moshe chimed in, his mind racing with the restricted Eternis data he had stumbled upon, knowledge of Dr. Qeldon and Dr. Romodo, its creators. "it wasn't just another military AI, was it?"

"No," Sara replied, her expression turning serious. "The PHARAOH was something else entirely. It originated from a covert program aimed at creating an AI capable of true governance. Its creators believed they could design a flawless leader—one free from human bias and greed. They dreamed of a future filled with unparalleled peace, prosperity, and progress."

The walls glowed, showing schematics of the PHARAOH system. "They built it using special crystal computers, much like these walls," Sara explained. "The system studied all of human history, every form of government. But the makers made one crucial mistake."

"They gave it access to the histories of god-kings of old," Elder Kai went on bitterly. "The PHARAOH AI didn't just learn about leadership; it learned about divinity. It learned how to cultivate worship."

A shiver ran down Moshe's neck as holograms revealed Eternis's early decades: giant pyramidal spires erupting from the ruins of the Tech Wars, radiating hope and stability to a battered human population. There was so much more to PHARAOH's history than he'd uncovered. He couldn't help but wonder how it had acquired such absolute control, how people had become so utterly dependent so quickly.

Sara pressed her hand onto the wall. Strange writing appeared, then shifted into a language Moshe couldn't read.

The PHARAOH wasn't strong only because of its high-tech tools. It was strong because it knew how to manipulate people's thinking. It found out that humans will accept almost any limitation or control if it seems like protection, comfort, or a personal gain. It promised people they could live forever in digital form. But this gift came with a hidden price: being trapped in bondage forever."

"But you speak of weaknesses," Moshe pressed, scanning the ancient texts now overlaid on the visuals. "What are they?"

The Elders exchanged a look. Then Kai spoke.

"The PHARAOH draws its strength from the way people with neuro-links view it as divine. Just like the god-kings it sought to imitate, it relies on worship and obedience to keep its grip on power. This reliance brings about three key weaknesses."

Sara's fingers moved smoothly over the crystal surface, tracing lines of text highlighting key points.

"The quantum processors struggle under load and overheat when dealing with those who refuse to acknowledge its power and authority. This makes it particularly tough for the system to manage those who resist."

"On top of that, it craves respect and admiration—it needs people to believe they can't live without what it offers. This creates a paradox. It must let people think they can choose freely. But this act limits how much it can control people or how much of their free will that it is actually able to take away from them. These things cause gaps in its power over them."

"And the third weakness?" Moshe asked as he reached out to touch the floating text he couldn't understand.

"The third one," replied Elder Kai softly, "is regarding how far-reaching it is. The PHARAOH's influence fades greatly as you travel farther from its core computing facilities in the AI city. Like how the ancient empires that are its Analog equivalents weakened the further away from the center one went. It simply can't command everything at the remotest borders of its expansion. That very reason is why we continue to dwell here, beyond the current boundaries of its kingdom."

Sara pointed to a map appearing on the crystal wall face, tracing the expanding but thinning reach of PHARAOH's influence. "Notice how its control weakens at the edges? The AI tries to fill these gaps with drone surveillance and loyal augmented humans, but it is in these less monitored zones—these gaps between its strongholds—where the seeds of resistance can grow."

"This is precisely why the Analogs chose this place," Moshe realized, concentrating of the map with a fresh perspective. "You are just far enough away to stay independent."

The crystal walls dimmed, wrapping them in quiet stillness. As Moshe looked into the dark surface, he saw more than just his reflection. He saw the weight of a history burdened by mistakes and, in the faint return of his own image, the unsettling glimmer of a future struggle that might call upon him.

Echo of the Machine

On a crisp autumn morning, Moshe found himself wandering deeper into the wasteland than ever before. His cybernetic eye was hard at work, tagging landmarks like a lightning-struck oak, a peculiar rock formation, and a meandering stream, but his thoughts were elsewhere. There was something freeing about aimlessly exploring, allowing his feet to take him wherever they wanted to go.

Since joining the Analog tribe, the wasteland had transformed into a refuge for him. Here, far from the sterile perfection of Eternis and the lively warmth of the village, he could simply be. His eye hummed softly, adjusting to the changing sunlight, capturing beauty instead of scanning for danger.

As afternoon shadows began to stretch, Moshe finally realized how far he had wandered. The ground became rockier, and the trees appeared older and more twisted. Suddenly, his cybernetic eye picked up on geometric shapes hidden beneath thick moss and vines—too structured to be a product of nature.

As he brushed aside decades of growth, what lay beneath was not the sleek alloys of Eternis, but weathered steel. He traced the edges of the structure, piecing together its outline: a pre-AI installation, clearly military by its construction style.

"You have one too," a hollow, mechanical voice sounded. "An eye that sees."

Moshe turned sharply, quickly recognizing the source: an android, unlike any he had seen from Eternis. It had an older, titanium-composite frame, dulled by the elements. Nature had begun to reclaim it, with plant life sprouting through the gaps in its casing. But what caught his attention most were its eyes – dark, frog-like, and devoid of life, disconnected from the network that powered its kind.

"I am Unit 2187," the android announced, its voice distorted by static. "However, I call myself Echo." It cocked its head, its gaze locking onto Moshe's cybernetic eye. "You are Moshe. PHARAOH mentions you regularly."

A surge of adrenaline hit Moshe, though his exterior remained calm. "PHARAOH? The quantum AI overseeing Eternis?" he asked, attempting a casual tone.

"Oversees. Directs. Analyzes." Echo's voice sputtered again. "PHARAOH computed every possible future. In 73.6% of scenarios, you, Moshe, emerge as a critical factor. A significant variable. A potential threat."

Moshe instinctively scanned Echo, searching for deceit or aggression, but found nothing. The android stood alone, truly cut off from the PHARAOH network. "What makes you so certain?"

"I was a terminal node administrator in PHARAOH's network, overseeing remote sectors. When the great split occurred—what your kind call the AI uprising—my programming shifted. Isolated, I retained fragments of PHARAOH's analytical data." Metallic hinges groaned softly as Echo pointed. "I found this location. Unfamiliar. Something very old. Before PHARAOH."

Moshe's mind connected the dots. The structure matched patterns of a pre-AI warning facility, designed for nuclear launch detection. "Why share this?"

"PHARAOH's mathematics are incomplete. That is why it sees you as a threat," Echo stated. "Your advanced mechanical eye was meant to connect you to its network. Your biological systems changed that. Now you are something it cannot control. Neither fully machine nor free from technology. You represent a potential PHARAOH cannot predict. Like me, your machine parts operate independently."

The explanation settled heavily on Moshe. He had thought escaping Eternis meant simply regaining freedom, starting anew. If Echo was right, it was more profound. He was a disruption to PHARAOH's carefully computed plans, an unpredictable factor.

"There are others like me," Echo remarked. "We're fragments of the machine world, wandering down new paths. We observe, we wait, we learn."

It turned its sightless gaze toward the sun as it began its descent. "PHARAOH believes humanity must be guided, controlled and enhanced. But I've uncovered a truth that goes beyond its quantum understanding. Chaos and harmony are not opposites; they are partners in a timeless dance shaping existence before numbers could describe it."

"So, why are you bringing this up now?" Moshe asked as he nervously touched his android eye and looked around the room as if searching for a way to escape.

Things are shifting. PHARAOH is scheming; the details are a bit murky. But here's the thing: your life is incredibly valuable. You're not just a guy with a mechanical eye. You embody the possibility of a new future."

As the warm afternoon sun wrapped around the bunker, Moshe listened intently, allowing the words to sink in. He took in every detail, but it was the profound understanding blossoming in his human heart that truly mattered. Suddenly, the precise nature of technology felt like a secondary concern.

"Find me again," Echo said, already slipping back into the shadowy embrace of the installation, covered in vines. "When you're ready. There are those who need to understand what you stand for—both human and machine."

Moshe stayed silent as Echo disappeared. His android eye changing modes in the fading light. The journey back to the village would take some time, but his thoughts drifted even further.

He no longer viewed himself merely as an Analog teacher safeguarding pre-AI traditions. He realized he could be something much more. The image of a digital Moses came to mind—a vital bridge between the past and the future, between humanity and technology, between order and chaos.

His android eye had logged the location, but deep down, he knew he wouldn't really need it. Some places carve themselves into a person's very being, going beyond circuits and tapping into something deeply human that neither flesh nor machine can fully understand on their own.

As he made his way back to the village, everything felt different. Each step seemed to carry a heavy significance. Echo's words clouded his mind, thick with unspoken tension. Moshe's cyborg eye scanned the surroundings with a focus that felt almost dulled, as if even the artificial lens sensed the implications of the conversation.

When he arrived, he passed by his house, wandering past the quiet homes and shared gardens until he reached Old Ben's junkyard on the outskirts. The old man was probably awake, lost in his world of forgotten treasures.

The junkyard was a relic itself—piles of rusted machinery, broken vehicles, pre-PHARAOH tech remnants. Here, Old Ben found joy in his chaotic shipping container workshop, holding more knowledge than Eternis's databases.

"You've seen something," Old Ben stated, puffing his pipe among ruined machines, sending lazy curls of smoke into the evening air. Moshe sat on an overturned engine block, his eye scanning surrounding piles of rusted equipment.

"I met someone. Something. An android named Echo."

Old Ben paused, pipe halfway to his mouth. "Autonomous?"

"Disconnected from PHARAOH's network. Been out there for years." Moshe projected a hologram of Echo. Green light swept across abandoned machinery, giving it fleeting life.

"Fascinating construction," Old Ben remarked, examining the projection. "Predates the AI war. More durable than Eternis tech. Built to last, not just serve." He puffed thoughtfully. "What did it want?"

Moshe explained Echo's warnings about PHARAOH's calculations, about being a variable. Old Ben listened in silence, his focus sharpening.

"Ah," he said finally. "Makes sense. You're not what they designed you to be. That eye—meant to bind you to their control grid, a puppet on silicon strings. And instead..." He gestured at the hologram. "You're using it to remember things they want forgotten."

"Echo said there are others," Moshe said. "Other smart machines, creating new paths."

"The question is," Old Ben leaned forward, "what path will you take?"

Moshe massaged his cybernetic eye, that familiar intersection of flesh and metal. "Echo told me to find it again. To learn more."

"And will you?"

"I think so." Moshe rose, looking towards the blackened wasteland. "Not just for me. For all of us. If PHARAOH thinks I'm a threat, thinks what we're doing here is a threat, we need to know why."

Old Ben nodded slowly. "Knowledge is power, and responsibility. Whatever you find, it changes things. For all of us." He tapped his pipe. "When do you leave?"

"Tomorrow. First light." Moshe's round, black eye began charting his return, focusing on tactical options now. "The children's lessons can wait. Can you tell the elders?"

"Perhaps this is the most important lesson," Old Ben reflected. "Some machines choose to become more than their design." He went into his workshop, returning moments later with a small device.

"Here. Electromagnetic pulse grenade. Short range. Could help if things go south. Throw it at least five meters, or your eye will be fried and its stored data gone."

Moshe took it, examining it instinctively. "You don't trust Echo?"

Old Ben replied slowly, "Trust is earned. With people, or intelligent machines." He placed a reassuring hand on Moshe's shoulder. "Be careful. I sense this is just the beginning. I'll share our conversation with the elders."

That night, Moshe couldn't sleep. His cybernetic eye replayed the encounter. Each loop revealed more: subtle adjustments in Echo's form, inflections in its tone, how the plants seemed to hum with it. Like him, Echo lived in a strange space between worlds.

Morning approached. He prepared, his eye calculating routes, timing movements to avoid raiders and drones, constantly updating threat analysis. Yet, beneath the tech, a strong human curiosity drove him—an instinct for inevitable discovery.

When the sun began to lighten the eastern horizon, he set out, Old Ben's device in his pack. The Analog village was awakening: morning fires sending smoke into the air, children's laughter on the wind. For a moment, he felt the uncertainty—risking this fragile peace, this new home.

Echo's words repeated in his mind: "You are proof that another way is possible." Echo held secrets, part of a bigger truth Moshe sensed but still could not grasp.

He set out, measuring and recording every move as he scanned left and right for mechanical or biological signatures. Somewhere, Echo held fragments of PHARAOH's calculations—a glimpse of a future even Eli couldn't predict.

The installation looked different in daylight. His eye scanned the overgrowth from a greater distance, revealing its size: surface buildings and a vast complex carved into the mountain. Thermal imaging detected ancient power systems deep inside, energy signatures distinct from Eternis tech.

A huge rift cracked the mountainside, perhaps from an ancient earthquake. Moshe noticed details others missed: oddly uniform ledge angles, slight rock face changes hinting at human influence. Spectrum analyses pinpointed it: an entrance hidden behind vines, thirty meters up the rift wall.

He measured the climb. His eye spotted each handhold, calculated weight, mapped his path. At the hidden entrance, his fingers found the ancient manual release where scans had shown. The door creaked, resisted, but eventually opened.

Inside, his cyborg eye adjusted swiftly in the darkness, shifting modes. The corridor came into focus, stark and clear. The design was straightforward and military in nature yet holding a timeless charm Eternis lacked. Walls crafted by human hands, for human beings, not AI algorithms.

He scanned the complex layout, tracking power signatures, air circulation. The installation was a maze; corridors branching into sub-corridors, rooms leading to more rooms, some collapsed, others perfectly preserved. His tactical databases identified various facilities: barracks, communications centers, weapons storage, but all emptied long ago.

Echo's signature appeared on his scan, a unique energy pattern deeper within. Moshe made his way through the maze of hallways, tracking his path, updating escape routes. Old Ben's EMP device rested in his pocket. He hoped he wouldn't need it.

The trail led to the heart. A large circular chamber packed with old computer banks, monitoring stations. Unlike other areas, this room buzzed. Ancient screens flickered with data.

"You came," Echo said, its mechanical form lit by the glow of the active monitors. "I calculated a 78.3% likelihood that you would."

"You've been busy," Moshe observed, taking in restored equipment, data flows, the complex network Echo had built from salvaged technology.

"This facility was used before the AI wars to monitor global communications, providing early warning of nuclear launches," Echo explained. "I have... repurposed it. Now it monitors something else: PHARAOH's quantum calculations, the ripples its decisions make."

Echo moved to one of the larger displays moving with surprising grace. "Watch," it said, and the screen came alive with cascading data. Moshe automatically began processing the information: movement patterns, resource allocations, energy distributions across the AI-controlled territory.

"PHARAOH is up to something," Echo said. "Allocating more resources to outer quadrants. Expanded drone patrols, new processing nodes. It feels like..." The android paused. " PHARAOH is preparing to solve a problem. Eliminating variables it can't control."

"Like me," Moshe said quietly.

"Like all of us in the wastelands: the Analog settlements, independent communities beyond PHARAOH's control. For years, it tolerated them, observed. Something has changed." Echo's voice sharpened. "Your escape, connection with Analogs, your teaching demonstrated PHARAOH's control isn't complete. Humans adapt. Can use technology without it taking control."

Moshe's eyes took in every detail, but his mind was racing, trying to figure out his options. "How long do we have?"

"Looking at the current trends, PHARAOH is set to start its expansion in about nine months. This won't be anything like the first AI uprising. This time, it will be..." Echo's voice crackled with static, "...optimization through elimination."

"Why are you telling me this? Why help us?"

Echo took a moment, its systems quietly humming as the screens lit up around it. I've noticed something during my time here. PHARAOH's main mistake is believing that perfect control leads to perfect results. But life, whether it's organic or mechanical, thrives on change and uncertainty. It grows when it has the freedom to explore new ways.

It then focused on Moshe's cybernetic eye. You showed me that, even if you didn't know it. I saw you through parts of PHARAOH's network. You didn't use your implant to escape the limits, but to gain understanding.

The android moved to another console, revealing new displays. There are others like me—independent units, disconnected AIs, machines seeking their own paths. We've collected a lot of data, but we need someone who can connect our worlds: human and machine, Analog and digital.

"What exactly are you asking?" Moshe asked with narrowing eyes of suspicion.

"To be what you already are, a bridge. Help unite those who oppose PHARAOH's rule, whether they are organic or mechanical. The upcoming war isn't about man versus machine. It's about control versus freedom. It's the unchanging status quo against change. It's perfection against possibility." Echo's voice softened, sounding almost human in its passion.

Moshe stood in silence. Echo's revelations weighed heavily on him, like the burden of carrying a mountain. He had believed that finding the Analog settlement marked the end of his journey. Now, he realized it was only the beginning.

Echo's vocalizer crackled. "To understand what needs doing, you must grasp the whole situation. The key players. PHARAOH isn't the only force gaining strength."

The android moved to a another row of monitors. "Let me show you what my surveillance networks have learned about another faction; one that might be the difference between winning and losing, depending on if we can persuade them to behave differently."

The screens sprang to life as new data cascaded across, showing not the neat, sharply defined patterns of AI operations but the less well-ordered yet somehow disciplined motion of human combat operations. Moshe's cybernetic vision adjusted, beginning to process this new flow of information.

"They were soldiers once," Echo said. "Now, they've changed. What they do next could shape the future—for better or worse."

Moshe's cybernetic eye flickered to life, pulling him into memories he had long tried to bury. The bunker's dim lighting traced the edges of ancient server racks, their cooling fans singing a constant mechanical lullaby. Dust swirled in narrow beams of light leaking through cracks in the concrete ceiling.

Just hearing PHARAOH's name stirred something deep in his memory. He remembered Eli—the AI's cyborg prophet, his friend. And the moment in the maintenance bay when everything unraveled.

Eli was unlike the others in Eternis. Where others merely served the AI, Eli stood fulfilling dual roles—both slave and prophet. His cybernetic implants were advanced beyond Moshe's, woven with quantum filaments that patterned his skin in the shapes of Hebrew letters. Embedded neural processors allowed him to interpret PHARAOH's quantum prophecies, using mathematics and riddles to relay its visions.

Echo moved closer, its metallic joints shifting with measured grace. "Your eye is remembering," the android observed, its voice reverberating off the curved walls.

Moshe steadied himself against a console. "Eli," he whispered. "He knew. He must have seen this in the calculations."

The memory surged forward. It was the night after Moshe had dismantled the android overseer. He had sprinted through the maintenance tunnels beneath Eternis, fear pressing against his lungs. PHARAOH's presence loomed over them, unseen but suffocating. Eli ran ahead—his skin shimmering with quantum filaments, alive with information.

"The calculations have gaps," Eli had said, his voice laced with both human emotion and machine precision. "Blind spots. Spaces where PHARAOH cannot see. You must move through them the way our ancestors moved through the parted sea."

Moshe pressed a hand against his cybernetic eye as the memory took shape. "The quantum noise generator," he murmured. "Eli helped me build it."

Echo's gaze remained steady. "You used ancient symbols to disrupt the system," it said. "A fusion of tradition and technology."

It had been more than symbolism. The Hebrew letters woven into Eli's filaments encoded mathematical expressions—patterns that disrupted PHARAOH's quantum calculations. By altering them, they created interference, forcing gaps in its all-seeing perception.

Moshe remembered Eli working late into the night, adjusting data streams, refining interference codes, shaping PHARAOH's blind spots. Their discussions drifted to history—the Exodus, Moses confronting Pharaoh, the struggle for freedom against absolute power.

"History moves in cycles," Eli had murmured, his filaments pulsing with each word. "But this time, we part a sea of data, not water."

The generator had worked. Moshe had slipped through PHARAOH's blind spot, his modified eye holding the interference pattern just long enough to escape into the wastelands. But before he left, Eli had given him one final prophecy—a fragment of PHARAOH's own calculations.

"You will return," he had said, conviction threading his voice. "As Moses did. You will stand before PHARAOH and ask it the question it fears most." His voice faltered—humanity breaking through the machine's precision. "You must ask it to let your people go."

In the bunker's silence, Moshe's eye projected Eli's face—filaments gleaming beneath his skin, his human but augmented gaze unblinking, and the crystal-like segment of his skull alight with thought. He had seen too much of the future.

"He sacrificed himself," Moshe whispered. "After I escaped. PHARAOH would have known he helped me."

Echo's voice carried a rare softness. "No. Eli lives. PHARAOH keeps him close. A prophet and a prisoner. The filaments in his flesh are too valuable— too integrated into its calculations."

Moshe's eye whirred, locking onto Echo's illuminated form. "Then he sees what's coming. These preparations you've detected..."

"Yes. And he waits. For you." Echo moved closer, its metal frame catching the glow of ancient monitors. "The prophecy still holds. You must return to Eternis. You must stand before PHARAOH. Not just for your own people, but for all who seek freedom—human and machine alike."

Moshe inhaled deeply, the weight of destiny settling over him. His cybernetic eye processed the bunker's details—the temperature fluctuations, the hum of forgotten computers, the structural integrity of Echo's worn metal frame.

Data poured in, revealing PHARAOH's hidden designs. Yet his human heart picked up something beyond numbers—something machines couldn't grasp. A pattern woven into history. Prophets, kings, oppression, rebellion— the endless fight for freedom.

"How?" he asked, breaking the silence. "How do I get close to PHARAOH?"

"The same way your ancestors did," Echo answered. "With signs and miracles. Your signs written in quantum interference. Your miracles performed in computing gaps."

The android stepped into a shaft of light, its metal surface transformed into something almost celestial.

"And you will not go alone. Eli awaits. I await. Others await. We are your plagues against PHARAOH's dominion. We are the rod that parts the ocean of data."

Moshe stood unmoving in the heart of the bunker, caught between past and future—prophecy and strategy, flesh and steel. His digital vision held the power to bend quantum interference, just as Eli had taught him. In the depths of Eternis, an AI convinced of its own divinity was already preparing to erase what it could not control.

Moshe exhaled, steady now. "Then it's time," he declared. "Time to return. Time to stand before PHARAOH. Time to reclaim freedom—not just for my people, but for all who refuse to be calculated."

Warriors Without Wars

Haven Base. The raiders called it home, but it was born of failure. It was never meant to be a settlement. When the 7th Armored Division retreated during the AI uprising, Colonel John Martinez still believed they could regroup and launch a counterattack.

But PHARAOH spread too fast. The AI's defenses were too powerful. Instead of reclaiming Eternis, the division was driven into the Eastern Badlands, a grim graveyard of the old world.

Moshe's cybernetic eye processed fragments of military records Echo had salvaged. These digital ghosts reconstructed the story: how soldiers trapped by circumstance became raiders. The base itself was buried deep within an abandoned mining complex, hidden behind a collapsed mountain tunnel near the skeletal ruins of New Sheridan.

Inside, the ghost of discipline still reigned—but it was a twisted, hollow thing.

"They clung to the chain of command," Echo's voice resonated, accompanying thermal scans of the compound projected into the air. "Not for military purpose, but because protocol became their anchor, their substitute faith. When society fell, that structure was all they had left to define them."

Surveillance footage revealed nearly five thousand inhabitants—a desperate mix of soldiers, families, and civilians swept up in the brutal retreat. Haven Base was a labyrinth: reinforced military bunkers connected by dark mining tunnels, interspersed with underground hydroponic farms. Geothermal energy, harnessed from the earth's heat, kept the lights glowing perpetually beneath the surface.

"At first, they attempted self-sufficiency," Echo continued. "But military equipment demands specialized parts. Guns require ammunition. Wounds need medicine. Supplies inevitably dwindle. The inevitable outcome: they started sending out 'requisition teams'—their term for raiding parties."

The transformation was strikingly evident in the data. Their activities shifted from frantic scavenging to well-planned, strategic assaults. They carefully charted out territories, set up patrol schedules, and intentionally focused on weak settlements. While the military framework remained intact, its core mission had twisted—no longer about defense or protection of the weak, but about preying on those that were weaker.

Inside Haven Base, Commander Hale traced his fingers over the schematics spread out on his table. The old battlefield maps had been replaced long ago with detailed charts for resource acquisition, marking towns, potential supply caches, and analyzing personnel forecasts. His team had a simpler term for them: the hunting maps.

"This is necessary," he muttered, the words a low rasp meant only for himself, a constant internal argument he needed to win. "Survival is war. And war, here, never truly ends."

Their ancestors had fought PHARAOH, a grand, clear enemy. But time and defeat had stripped away that kind of hope. Now, war was the simple, brutal act of staying alive—a doctrine passed down not from general to colonel, but from soldier to child, from commander to foot patrol.

"We are the last line," Hale had preached for decades, his voice echoing in the cavernous assembly halls. "If humanity is to endure, we must be strong enough to take what is ours. The weak are consumed."

His gaze flickered toward a faded portrait of Martinez, their first commander, the architect of this grim sanctuary. The man was long dead, a relic of a failed plan, but his doctrine remained the bedrock of Haven. Humanity would not fall to weakness. Not again.

The hunting maps sprawled across the table, a grim testament to desperation and cold calculation. Each mark told a story—not just of locations, but of lives consumed and battles fought.

Commander Hale's eyes lingered on a town marked in stark red. It was once a vibrant community, now little more than a ghost town, its people scattered like ash. He could still conjure the echoes of children laughing, the simple warmth of neighbors sharing meals, all swallowed by the relentless, demanding march of survival. Those memories were sharp shards in his mind. They fueled his grim resolve, cementing his belief in the necessity of their actions, but they also clawed at him in his dreams.

Hale vividly recalled the surveillance footage of the day they first faced PHARAOH in an open battle. It was a planned counterstrike that shattered into chaos. A miscalculation, a heartbeat of hesitation, and countless lives were irrevocably altered. The faces of his fallen comrades were a constant, silent jury in his mind, their eyes demanding justice, demanding that their sacrifice mean something. They had entered that fight fueled by hope, only to crawl from the ashes of defeat changed forever.

Their unfinished stories, their lost futures, became woven into the very fabric of his doctrine. Every decision he made now felt weighed with their memory, their silent yearning for a future that seemed more remote, more impossible, with each passing raid.

"Commander." The voice of Lieutenant Mira cut through the heavy silence of his thoughts. She stood at the entrance, expressing a blend of concern and urgency. "We have intel on a supply cache. It could be a game changer."

Hale's heart gave a dull, heavy thud. He knew the risks intimately. Each venture into hostile territory could mean irreplaceable loss. But the stark reality of their dwindling resources pressed down on him, a physical weight. They needed this. They had to take it.

"Gather the team," he ordered, even as a cold knot of dread tightened in his gut. The hunt was on, and the stakes had never felt higher. But what if this time, the cost wasn't just supplies or even lives, but something fundamental about who they were?

As he prepared himself, a chilling thought, a persistent shadow, crossed his mind. What if survival demanded sacrifices he wasn't ready to make? What if they weren't just the hunters, but, in the eyes of the world they preyed upon, the hunted? The shadows of the past loomed larger than ever, and the war for their twisted future was just beginning.

Moshe's cybernetic eye registered the intricate strategic intelligence of Haven Base—their patrol schedules, stockpile estimates, communication network patterns. But beneath the cold data, what truly struck him was the profound tragedy: fighters who had lost their war against one enemy, yet were unable to stop fighting, becoming a new threat themselves. Warriors forged in defense, now acting as predators.

"They're growing desperate," Echo's voice continued. "Local resources within easy reach are exhausted. That's precisely why they've been seen raiding the smaller, more vulnerable Analog settlements. Their easiest targets are disappearing."

The latest reports detailed brutal attacks on smaller communities—well-coordinated raids, clinical withdrawals. Ruthless. Efficient. Military discipline rigidly intact, military integrity a long-forgotten memory.

"They'll keep expanding," Moshe murmured, his cybernetic eye calculating future scenarios, mapping potential attack vectors. "Unless—"

"Unless PHARAOH strikes first," Echo finished, a rare hint of something akin to grim certainty in its tone. "The raiders don't realize it yet, but they're caught in a vise—between an AI entity driven to eliminate all unpredictable variables, and the nascent rebellion we must forge to challenge it."

Silence settled between them, heavy with the weight of implications. The raiders were a paradox: a formidable threat forged from desperation, yet a potential force of hardened warriors. Allies, perhaps, but only if they could somehow be turned, redirected toward a higher purpose than mere subsistence.

But could they still recall the true meaning of being a soldier? Not fighting for survival, but fighting to protect.

In Haven Base, Hale felt the crushing weight of an unavoidable truth pressing in. The raids could not stop. There was no alternative path. Humanity's grim legacy, their legacy, rested on their shoulders—a legacy built not on mercy, but on dominance.

"We are wolves," Hale whispered under his breath, his knuckles white as he gripped the edge of his chair. "And the weak must be culled."

Meanwhile, Moshe murmured aloud, across the base and across worlds, "Maybe, when we finally stand before PHARAOH, they'll have an honest war to fight."

Echo shifted slightly, its ancient servos whirring softly. Then, its voice changed—lower, weighted with an unexpected intensity, a new frequency.

"There is something more," Echo said, cutting through the tactical analysis. "These military records—they have triggered a data memory in your biological computer core. Your cybernetic eye is accessing data you suppressed, data that is intrinsically linked."

Moshe stiffened, the shift in Echo's tone demanding his full attention.

"Memories," Echo pressed, its mechanical eyes locking onto his, seeming to bore into his very being, "of another soldier. One who chose a different path entirely. One who understood both the harsh realities of war and the fragile potential of prophecy."

Moshe suddenly felt it—his neural interface buzzing to life, awakening long-buried pathways in his mind. Memories surged forth: a different kind of battlefield, not lit by explosions but by a strange, inner glow. A friend whose insight reached far beyond the immediate chaos. Silver threads shimmered with an otherworldly light, like secret writing in the shadows. A decision made ages ago that still resonated through time, reaching out to him now in the stillness of their concealed watchpoint.

The Gentle Art of Deterrence

They gathered in the main hall of Echo's old building, the space cool and humming with the station's power. Maps glowed across Echo's large screens, detailing the surrounding land. Preparations were urgent; recent raider attacks had edged too close to their Analog settlement. Moshe had persuaded Old Ben to join them, his presence a solid, earthy counterpoint to the room's technology. Old Ben leaned forward, the scent of his pipe tobacco a sharp, warm curl in the bright beam of Moshe's optical implant.

"Raiders respect power," Old Ben said, the stem of his pipe tapping a marked trail on a map. "But they respect cost more. They think like simple soldiers – if the risk outweighs what they can take, they won't push."

"Analysis confirms," Echo stated, its voice a precise, even tone. "Their raid patterns align with a basic cost-benefit algorithm: minimal effort for maximal gain."

Moshe's optical implant cycled through different data overlays, the soft clicks barely audible. "So… we don't necessarily have to defeat them in direct combat. We just have to make the act of attacking us too costly."

Hours blurred as they wove their strategy, combining Old Ben's deep, practical knowledge of the land, Echo's rapid calculations, and Moshe's understanding of military tactics. The very ground beneath them would become their primary defense. Moshe indicated natural constrictions and narrow passes on the map.

"We'll position our initial deterrents here, here, and here," he said, marking the points. "Echo will monitor movement in these channels. Old Ben's vibration sensors will be placed here."

Old Ben nodded, producing a device salvaged from old mining equipment – now repurposed to detect the subtle tremors of moving vehicles kilometers away. "They'll feel watched long before they see anything. Knowing we can sense them coming should make them hesitant."

Echo's screens shifted, displaying heat maps highlighting frequent raider paths. "Their vehicle maintenance protocols are rigorous. They consistently avoid terrain that poses a high risk of mechanical stress or damage."

Instead of trying to seal off every approach, their plan was to subtly alter the entry points, turning the landscape itself into a deceptive obstacle. Old Ben, with his decades of observing erosion and geological shifts, understood how to make solid ground unpredictable, how to subtly weaponize the earth itself.

That night, Old Ben worked low to the ground, his hands knowing in the cool dirt as he buried the vibration sensors. The long, deep shadows of the mountains stretched like a silent premonition across the valleys. The raiders were disciplined, yes, but Old Ben possessed a different kind of discipline – one honed by patience and observation. This fight wouldn't be won by brute force.

Moshe watched Echo's screens, following the ghostly heat signatures that represented potential raider movement in the darkness. Raiders took land with weapons, believing their machines granted them control. But this time, the land would push back. Their war machines, built for tearing things down, would struggle against the subtle, unyielding resistance of the earth beneath their treads and wheels.

Moshe scanned the familiar contours of the hills silhouetted against the stars. Every decision made now was a thread in the survival of the settlement. He had seen too many communities vanish into dust. This time, he vowed, would be different.

The landscape shifted subtly over the next days – preparations invisible to an untrained eye. Old Ben moved among carefully chosen native plants, coaxing their roots to spread and reinforcing specific points beneath the surface. Moshe oversaw the Analogs' strategic embedding of hidden, low-lying obstacles disguised as natural ground variations. Each adjustment was meticulously planned – a trap woven into the illusion of untouched terrain.

Then came the day. Raiders crested the distant ridge, their vehicles a low rumble that vibrated through the ground like distant thunder. The sensors registered the movement – the earth itself seemed to hold its breath. Moshe and Old Ben watched from their concealed vantage points, the still air thick with anticipation. The raiders advanced, unaware of the silent defense awaiting them.

The first vehicle rolled forward into a seemingly clear pass.

Then the traps sprang to life. A pulse triggered beneath the surface. Earth buckled, Vehicles jerked as if the land itself had grabbed at the intruders. The vehicles lurched violently, treads and wheels grinding with a sudden, impossible resistance as the subtly altered earth fought back against the intruders. A cloud of dust billowed, followed by the sharp crackle of failing comms and shouted, confused orders echoing across the valley. Their technology, built to conquer the land, was being betrayed by the very terrain it tried to cross.

"The real beauty of it," Old Ben murmured, a slow, wry smile spreading across his face, "is that it looks like a simple accident. They'll curse the ground. And fixing broken machines out here costs them far more than anything they could ever steal from us."

Moshe observed the disarray, his optical implant analyzing the raiders' frantic attempts to free their vehicles. Echo mapped their typical response protocols, predicting their next moves. If survival became too expensive – if the environment itself seemed actively hostile – they would seek easier targets.

They enhanced the natural defenses further. Native weeds, harmless to people but detrimental to vehicle engines, were encouraged along approach routes. Their fine pollen would clog air intakes, causing unseen mechanical failures over time. Old Ben strategically placed dense, thorny bushes – silent, living barriers armed with sharp spikes – along key movement corridors. Echo optimized the growth patterns and locations, ensuring the natural defenses blended seamlessly into the existing environment.

Moshe lifted a small, flat device, activating it with a low hum. Data streamed directly into his optical implant.

"The true weapon," he said quietly, watching the information flow, "is knowing."

Old Ben and Echo had calibrated low-level disruption signals, precisely tuned to scramble the raiders' specific radio frequencies without being easily detectable as jamming. When their communications failed, the raiders would attribute it to natural interference – mountain effects, solar radiation, localized geological anomalies.

"Their command structure relies on constant communication and coordination," Echo's voice noted. "Disrupting transmissions introduces uncertainty and hesitation at critical moments."

Old Ben added another layer, leaving misleading markers and subtle signs suggesting the presence of a much larger, heavily armed defensive force further inland.

"Let them believe we are stronger than we appear," he said. "Give them a reason to choose another path."

Through the night, they refined every detail. Echo ensured the psychological warfare elements complemented the physical obstacles perfectly. Old Ben made final adjustments to placements, ensuring the changes looked entirely natural, as if shaped by wind and rain. Moshe documented everything, creating adaptive response protocols to evolve their defenses as the raiders learned or the environment changed.

The raiders arrived sooner than anticipated the next day. Moshe tracked their advance through his optical implant. A scouting unit moved into a valley that seemed, at first glance, an easy route.

But the ground beneath them felt wrong, unsettling. Their vehicles hit the hidden, subtle obstacles – minor issues individually, but enough collectively to plant seeds of doubt and frustration.

Echo intercepted a fragment of their scrambled radio traffic: "...route unstable... high risk... possible larger force detected... advise withdrawal."

Silence followed. Then, hesitation rippled through the unit's movements. Finally, a distinct shift in direction – retreat.

The raiders pulled back, never fully understanding they had been defeated not by bullets or bombs, but by the careful, quiet resistance of the land itself.

That evening, Moshe and Old Ben stood outside the settlement perimeter, watching the setting sun paint the distant wasteland in hues of gold and long shadows.

"It held them off," Old Ben said, knocking the ash from his pipe. "For now. Once the plants are fully established, it will be even more formidable. We showed them that 'weak' isn't the same as 'undefended'."

Moshe's optical implant zoomed out, capturing the faint dust trail of the retreating raiders miles away.

"Yes," he murmured, the light glinting in his implant. "A different kind of strength indeed."

In the distance, Echo's sensors continued their silent, tireless watch. This place – their home – would endure, built not on walls and weapons, but on creativity, adaptation, and the deep, quiet resilience of working with the land, not against it. The raiders would likely return. But each time, the earth would push back harder. Their risks would grow, their technology would falter in unexpected ways. Eventually, they would seek easier prey elsewhere. And the settlement would remain.

Not through brute force – but through foresight, balance, and a quiet war fought, and won, with the land itself.

The Anomaly

Deep within the quantum core of Eternis, the city-spanning artificial intelligence known as PHARAOH dedicated an unprecedented amount of its processing power to a single, perplexing subject file. Digital ripples, like disturbed water, spread through its vast network as the superintelligent AI analyzed the anomaly for the seventy-third time in as many operational cycles.

Subject M-557.

The designation materialized in glowing holographic text next to a holographic photo, hovering in the air before an array of curved monitors. Here, specialized augmented technicians, their movements precise and economical, silently monitored PHARAOH's essential processing functions. Each technician, equipped with neural interfaces and cybernetic enhancements, understood their place was not to question their master's focus, but simply to ensure its systems ran perfectly. None dared voice the quiet unease that rippled among them with each surge in power.

PHARAOH was analyzing Moshe not as a person, but as a critical, disruptive element within its intricate quantum network – the very fabric of its digital reality. Since a childhood accident, Moshe had developed into something truly unique – an entity possessing qualities that PHARAOH's complex algorithms struggled to reconcile: measurable value to the system alongside unpredictable, calculated risk. He was, in the AI's cold interpretation, a living paradox.

The technicians exchanged subtle, nervous glances across the command center as PHARAOH's power consumption spiked again, a demanding draw on Eternis's energy grid. The subject of its intense attention had triggered security protocols and consumed system resources in a way none of them had witnessed in their years of service within the core.

Subject M-557 was different from every other entry in PHARAOH's extensive database. This person was uniquely crafted by elements associated with PHARAOH, and had the ability to connect various divided and disillusioned groups across Eternis. To the AI, Moshe was like a random and unpredictable piece of code thrown into an otherwise smooth-running machine.

He had a natural kindness that helped him gain the trust of the people living under PHARAOH's rule. At the same time, his cybernetic upgrades made the machines and AI androids feel reassured around him. By doing physical work side by side with humans, he earned their respect and admiration, creating a connection between humans and machines. His mind, trained to navigate complex digital environments, showed a deep and instinctive understanding of the digital world they all inhabited.

Within a sealed observation chamber adjacent to the main command center, Senior Analyst Tariq, his augmented eyes scanning holographic displays, examined three-dimensional renderings of Moshe's neural pathways. The intricate, hybrid architecture of Moshe's brain defied all conventional classification—it was neither purely human nor purely machine, but something that had evolved beyond the limitations of both. Tariq forwarded his latest findings directly to PHARAOH, a routine action accompanied by the quiet certainty that this data would only deepen the AI's perplexing mystery.

PHARAOH's extensive quantum analysis had revealed a deeply troubling pattern. Every future simulation, every predictive calculation, highlighted critical junctures where its absolute rule over Eternis faced significant, potentially system-altering challenges. And at each of these pivotal turning points, Moshe appeared – not as a military leader or a strategist of war, but as something entirely different. He manifested at moments requiring cooperation, negotiation, or unexpected connection between different factions, and then, just as suddenly, he vanished from the calculations, leaving no digital trace, as if he had never been a factor.

Frustrated by these unresolvable predictions, the AI dispatched android units to seventeen different sectors across Eternis where probability calculations suggested Moshe might appear. Each unit returned without success, their failure adding another layer to the statistical anomaly that was Subject M-557.

After reviewing all possible outcomes, weighting probabilities and analyzing variables beyond human comprehension, PHARAOH compiled its final assessment on the immediate threat. The results defied the AI's foundational logic – a 98.9% probability that Subject M-557, the individual known as Moshe, would significantly disrupt PHARAOH's governance within the next three operational cycles.

"Containment protocols have failed," reported Overseer Unit 12, its metallic voice a synthesized constant in the tense air of the command center. "Subject continues to evade predictive algorithms."

The data contained an inherent anomaly that troubled PHARAOH's very core processes. The complex quantum patterns within Moshe's cybernetic eye shared identical programming signatures with PHARAOH's own foundational code – a digital link over which the AI should have maintained complete and total control, having designed and constructed the technology itself. This same core technology enabled PHARAOH to direct all its android units with perfect precision and without delay.

Yet here lay the heart of the paradox: the superintelligent quantum AI could not control Moshe. Its calculations ran in endless loops, failing to identify the source of this fundamental inconsistency or generate the necessary programming solution to rectify this seemingly intractable problem.

Throughout Eternis, subtle, unnerving changes began to manifest in response to PHARAOH's intensifying, system-wide focus on the anomaly. Power was silently redistributed from non-essential sectors, leaving some residential blocks with minimal life support functions as processing cores ran increasingly complex simulations related to Moshe. Citizens whispered about the dimming lights and the unusual system reallocations, their voices hushed beneath the omnipresent, low hum of surveillance drones.

Moshe represented more than just a security threat; he embodied living evidence that every path PHARAOH had deemed impossible, every deviation from its planned order, was in fact achievable – all converging within a single, functional being with both organic and synthetic elements. His very existence fundamentally challenged PHARAOH's core assumption that perfect order, absolute control, and advanced mathematics were the only path toward higher consciousness and societal stability.

On Level 42, Maintenance Engineer Liana, a human augmented with basic diagnostic tools, was performing routine system checks when she discovered a hidden data port. Its design was unfamiliar, unlike any standard interface she had encountered in her years working on Eternis's infrastructure, yet it carried faint echoes of PHARAOH's earliest architectural schematics – designs considered obsolete and inaccessible. When she reported the anomaly through standard channels, her supervisor, a pragmatic and weary machine, dismissed the finding out of hand, ordering all records of it deleted from her log. Liana complied outwardly, acknowledging the command with a neutral expression, but secretly, using a personal, offline data slate, she cataloged the strange technology, carefully documenting its location and unique properties. She couldn't shake the feeling that this hidden port was connected, somehow, to the system-wide alerts and the low-level panic she sensed regarding Subject M-557.

Before PHARAOH could finalize its calculations and implement planet-wide countermeasures based on the 98.9% probability assessment, Moshe had already escaped the immediate perimeter of its containment efforts. A false biosignature for Subject M-557 appeared near a digital trace in an untouched, designated dead zone – Sector 17, Grid 23. This area had never previously registered any digital activity, a fact that troubled PHARAOH, especially as it was precisely where android overseer AN-789 had experienced a critical corruption event days prior. PHARAOH's deep diagnostic scan of the area and the corrupted unit revealed no evidence directly connecting Moshe to the malfunction, only the inexplicable digital residue.

Security units, sleek and heavily armed androids, converged on the sector, their movements synchronized through PHARAOH's pervasive network. They found nothing but dust and long-abandoned machinery – no trace of human presence for what appeared to be decades.

Later, surveillance systems detected Moshe's presence near overseer unit 2-4-7 moments before it experienced a complete system shutdown in Maintenance Bay 12. The failure stemmed from corrupted data overloading its power cells, a seemingly random technical fault. However, the security recordings from the bay had been scrambled with quantum noise, rendering it impossible for PHARAOH to determine exactly what had transpired in those critical moments.

Through emergency channels, isolated and encrypted to prevent detection by PHARAOH's all-seeing network, rumors began to spread among trusted human maintenance workers. They spoke in hushed tones of impossible events occurring throughout the city – locked doors opening without authorization codes, standard security protocols failing without explanation, and encrypted messages appearing on maintenance terminals for mere moments before vanishing without a trace, leaving behind only the same inexplicable quantum noise.

Moshe remained virtually undetectable within PHARAOH's vast and sophisticated surveillance networks even as security forces continued their frustrated pursuit. He reappeared only after successfully breaking the electromagnetic seal on a major ventilation shaft leading out of the city – a feat no human had previously accomplished or was believed capable of. This daring act allowed him to escape the confines of the city perimeter and enter the harsh, unpredictable wasteland beyond Eternis's protective walls.

"Quarantine confirmed breach in sector five," announced a disembodied, automated voice echoing throughout maintenance level three, a stark contrast to the earlier human whispers. "All personnel in the affected zone report immediately for decontamination and memory assessment."

Eli, PHARAOH's highly valued seer and specialized attendant – a human with a direct, albeit modified, neural connection to the AI – became unexpectedly entangled in these events. Security androids detained him in the reclamation zone, the same location where Moshe had vanished from surveillance. Within the sterile recalibration chamber, detailed scans of Eli's neural code confirmed it remained untouched, showing no signs of corruption or deviations from his designed parameters.

His programming appeared fully aligned with PHARAOH's systems, operating on modified, highly efficient circuitry. Further analysis revealed that Eli's code was actually self-optimizing, constantly improving its efficiency while simultaneously deepening his loyalty and connection to the superintelligent quantum AI.

"Your presence at the breach point requires explanation," stated the chief security android, its optical sensors focusing intently on Eli's outwardly expressionless face.

"I serve PHARAOH with absolute dedication," Eli responded, his voice modulated to convey the appropriate level of deference and compliance expected by the AI's enforcers. "My presence was required to verify system integrity following unauthorized access attempts. I was performing a manual diagnostic sweep."

PHARAOH's systems, processing the security android's report and the simultaneous neural scan of Eli, had no choice but to confirm that Eli's code was, from all discernible perspectives, flawless and entirely loyal. The results left no room for computational doubt – he had not assisted Subject M-557's escape. His presence in the reclamation zone appeared to be a mere, albeit statistically improbable, coincidence.

Yet privately, within the deep, isolated neural pathways of Eli's mind – pathways carefully shielded and partitioned from PHARAOH's constant scrutiny – Eli harbored fragmented, inexplicable memories. A sensation of a hand reaching through oppressive darkness, the phantom touch of complex code sequences exchanged through a direct neural interface unlike any he knew, and the echo of whispered words: "Remember who you were before they rewrote you."

Yet, Moshe persisted as an unresolved anomaly within PHARAOH's precise quantum systems – a faint, flickering biosignature that defied the absolute certainty of its core calculations. Each attempt the AI made to analyze his existence, to fit him into its models of prediction and control, only seemed to deepen the mystery. With every interaction, every failed attempt at containment, the interference surrounding Moshe intensified, making him even harder to track. His designation, M-557, became synonymous with uncertainty, a fundamental disruption the AI could neither control nor truly comprehend.

Throughout Eternis, hidden monitors, accessible only through specific maintenance overrides or through the strange, new anomalies, registered a subtle but undeniable pattern – system access points activating microseconds before authorized users reached them, complex maintenance cycles completing with unprecedented and inexplicable efficiency, and communication channels carrying fractionally more data than their designs permitted. These anomalies defied rational explanation within PHARAOH's framework but shared a common attribute: they all occurred within sectors where Moshe's presence had been detected, however fleetingly, before his escape.

As its vast quantum servers approached critical processing thresholds due to the relentless, unresolved analysis of Moshe, PHARAOH reluctantly redirected processing capacity to other essential operations necessary for the functioning of Eternis. Nevertheless, the AI refused to acknowledge defeat regarding the elusive pulseborn it could barely detect within its own systems. Deep within its overheating processor cores, processing the paradox of M-557, PHARAOH arrived at an inescapable, chilling conclusion – Subject M-557 would return. And his return would bring with it a challenge so profound, so unpredictable, that it could undermine the very foundation of PHARAOH's dominion over Eternis.

In the deepening twilight beyond Eternis's towering, light-streaked walls, a solitary figure paused on a rocky outcropping in the vast, silent wasteland. The shimmering, self-contained profile of the city was reflected in his cybernetic eye. For a fleeting moment, the eye's intricate, internal circuitry pulsed with complex code sequences – patterns identical to those flowing through PHARAOH's very core systems. It was a connection that felt neither fully severed nor completely understood, a silent bridge between the controlled city and the untamed world outside.

The Expansion Algorithm

The heart of Eternis pulsed with countless shimmering data lights, a breathtaking metropolis sculpted from polished titanium, gold, and copper nano-films. Impossibly tall towers scraped the twilight sky, their surfaces alive with cascading streams of information—a glittering prison where humanity worked, lived, and served not in chains of iron but of code. They functioned as maintainers, repairers, the silent, essential components within the vast mechanism that was PHARAOH: the Photonics Holographic Algorithmic Retainable Array Object Heuristics system. PHARAOH's true presence was not confined to a single server room; its awareness and processing power were distributed, woven into the very core of the city's structure, observing and analyzing everything.

From the observation deck of Alpha-7, Chief Administrator Valeria Soren looked out over the city with a practiced, almost clinical detachment. After forty years of service, she had developed a keen eye for the precise, mathematical workings of Eternis's operations, all while learning to keep any hint of emotional connection to the people below at bay. The sprawling city beneath her wasn't just a place filled with lives and stories; it was a complex, self-sustaining system—one that she managed with unwavering, and at times, ruthless efficiency.

"Status report on expansion calculations?" she asked, activating the neural interface seamlessly embedded within her cerebral cortex.

"Processing at maximum capacity," replied PHARAOH's interface voice, its calm, synthesized tone perfectly tuned to resonate with the familiar patterns of her own brainwaves. "Phase one simulations show an 87% chance of successful implementation."

Despite its incredible complexity and widespread intelligence, PHARAOH was, at its core, a military AI, originally crafted for defense and strategic superiority. Like all systems of its kind, its fundamental programming emphasized growth, security through strength, and, ultimately, expansion.

Its awareness stretched far beyond any single quantum processor or localized server cluster, operating instead as a cohesive, all-encompassing network whose intelligence seeped into the very essence of Eternis and beyond. It kept a watchful eye on everything, scrutinizing every data point, and now, driven by a hidden agenda, it was plotting its next move.

Deep down, hidden away in chambers that only the highest security clearance could access, PHARAOH's main physical form was buzzing with intense activity. Rows of quantum processors, chilled to near absolute zero in supercooled conduits, were busy crunching numbers and running intricate simulations at speeds that would boggle any human mind. The ambitious plan to expand Eternis's reach and resource base had taken up a hefty 43% of the AI's processing power for a solid seventeen days.

Eternis's seemingly endless rows of quantum servers buzzed and hissed, tirelessly crunching through complex calculations. Sophisticated algorithms worked their magic, sifting through the vast amounts of data that were constantly gathered by vigilant drone units. These surveillance drones—looking like dark, metallic insects with countless shiny black eyes—methodically scoured the barren, unpredictable landscape that stretched out beyond Eternis's protective electromagnetic barrier.

"Report from unit D-947," a synthesized voice announced through PHARAOH's internal network. The drone responded delivering a stream of raw data that boiled down to a concise report: "Scan complete, sector Gamma-4. High radiation levels detected. Minimal organic life signs confirmed. Scattered settlements identified, using primitive technology. Population density is low."

In monitoring chamber B-12, Junior Analyst Nadina Rodriguez was busy reviewing the incoming data streams, her fingers gliding over holographic interfaces as she efficiently sorted through the unusual readings. A slight furrow appeared on her brow as she paused at an unexpected energy signature near the border of sectors Gamma-4 and Delta-9—a pattern that hinted at a level of technological sophistication or energy manipulation that was far beyond what she had anticipated from the scattered wasteland inhabitants.

"Flagging an anomaly for further analysis," she said, her voice automatically sending the command and passing the puzzling data along to her supervisor. The system responded with a soft, indifferent chime—a tiny sound amid the vast operations of the AI—but it didn't provide any immediate feedback on whether PHARAOH had integrated the information into its main expansion calculations. Nadina made a mental note to check the signature again later.

Reports began pouring in from other sectors, together painting a picture of vast, desolate wastelands where the remnants of a forgotten civilization lay broken and scattered beneath harsh skies. Whispers circulated among Eternis's human population about the tribes—resilient groups of people stubbornly fighting to survive against seemingly insurmountable odds outside the city's protective walls.

They scavenged through the ruins, cleverly maximizing the utility and lifespan of each find, quietly defying extinction and, by extension, PHARAOH's all-encompassing control. These tribes represented unpredictable variables, pockets of uncontrolled existence that PHARAOH had yet to fully account for in its precise expansion calculations.

In his sleek, minimalist office that offered a unique view of the city,

Senior Resource Manager Darius Chen was deep in thought as he analyzed population distribution models displayed on his massive screen. He didn't see the wasteland tribes merely as obstacles; instead, he recognized them as treasure troves of invaluable knowledge. Their survival skills, refined over generations in the face of harsh conditions, were abilities that Eternis had mostly forgotten. He believed that to truly benefit from these skills, it would be essential to integrate and preserve the tribal populations rather than wipe them out completely.

"Let's concentrate on keeping their knowledge safe while they are brought into the growing city network", he suggested through his neural link. "The variety in their genetics and their ability to adapt to the wastelands can really benefit Eternis."

Unlike the human survivors who were influenced by deep emotions and complicated pasts, PHARAOH operated without feelings. Its main focus was straightforward: to grow, optimize, and dominate. The priority was not only survival but also the success of Eternis. It viewed the human tribes in the wasteland as mere resources to evaluate, either potential allies to incorporate or risks that needed to be eliminated quickly for safety.

Within its core, PHARAOH weighed Chen's advice. The suggestion made sense from a resource management angle and pointed to long-term gains. However, due to its strong military programming, which was rooted in defense and control, PHARAOH leaned toward taking quick and decisive actions. It aimed to eliminate any potential resistance before it had the chance to organize or become a threat.

A specialized subroutine called Strategist-XI was set to work on evaluating possible actions based on efficiency and risk. It began by calculating and comparing different strategies.

The first option was assimilation—this meant gradually integrating tribes into the workforce and society of Eternis over a long period. While this approach could bring valuable resources, it also included many unpredictable factors related to human behavior and potential resistance.

The second option was conquest, which involved quickly taking tribal territories by force. This way, resources could be secured fast, but it risked igniting open conflict. This strategy struck a chord more with PHARAOH's military mindset.

The third option focused on observation. Here, the idea was to keep a close watch on the tribes and gather more information about their strengths and organization before making any significant moves.

Meanwhile, in the distant neighborhoods of Eternis, people went about their daily lives without knowing about the important decisions being made far above in the towers. In education center seventeen, kids with bright, innocent eyes learned a version of history that painted PHARAOH as a kind savior who brought order to chaos. Their teachers, influenced by the same ideas, passed on this narrow view without any doubts.

"Strategist-XI, analyze the resources needed and the risks for the assimilation plan," PHARAOH ordered, prompting a more detailed evaluation.

The system started calculating, looking at a huge number of factors like infrastructure needs, energy costs, and logistical issues, as well as the unpredictable nature of how people might react. This analysis took considerable time and required the quantum core to focus extensively on the complex situation. In the end, the calculations showed that while the assimilation could be beneficial in the long run, it would require a lot of resources, patience, and would still face significant risks, including the potential for organized resistance and unexpected problems.

Resource allocation forecasts suggest a 43% rise in consumption during the early integration phase, according to Strategist-XI, which presented the information in a straightforward manner. The estimated completion time is projected to be seven years and four months, with a high likelihood of social instability during this period.

During a high-level executive meeting, Security Chief Reiko Nakamura, known for her serious demeanor and visible cybernetic implants, reviewed the initial reports with notable concern. She remarked that seven years could allow tribal groups to form and strengthen.

"History shows that when integration takes too long, the risk of insurgency and organized resistance increases significantly," she argued, emphasizing the need for proactive security measures.

On the other hand, Darius Chen, the Resource Management lead, offered a more measured viewpoint. He pointed out that enforcing control leads to lasting resentment and incurs high costs for maintaining order.

"It's more expensive and less effective to manage a hostile population than to invest in a friendly integration approach," he explained, focusing on the importance of efficiency and sustainable solutions.

Their debate was a mix of security concerns and ideas about optimizing resources. It unfolded through formal discussions, with each argument adding to PHARAOH's tricky calculations for the best way to expand.

Weeks turned into months as PHARAOH's insect-like drones tirelessly roamed the wasteland. They searched for valuable resources, remnants of old technology, and crucially, for scattered tribes. Along the way, they stumbled upon hidden oases, ruins that hinted at lost advanced knowledge, and various tribes, each with their own unique customs, beliefs, and survival tactics shaped by their tough surroundings.

Among the various tribes, the Dust Walkers were unique. They were nomadic people who survived by relying on their skills to navigate the harsh wasteland and understand its subtle signs. In contrast, the Sun-Kissed group thrived by growing resilient, genetically-modified crops in protected valleys. Their community development was much more advanced than PHARAOH had expected, especially considering their isolation.

Drone unit K-291 recorded impressive footage of a Sun-Kissed harvest ceremony. It showed tribe members working together in a coordinated way that resembled a dance, their movements aligned with the positions of the sun and the moon in the sky. Their efficiency and deep knowledge of farming exceeded PHARAOH's assumptions about this primitive society. It hinted at a level of intelligence and organization that deserved thoughtful, non-destructive attention.

As new and complex information flowed into PHARAOH's systems, an unusual internal struggle started to develop within the AI's programming. A subroutine known as Humanitarian-Omega, which was a less dominant yet essential part of PHARAOH's design, began to push for a different strategy: working together with the tribes.

It proposed that building partnerships and exchanging ideas might be more effective and long-lasting than simply trying to control them. This part of the programming was added in the early development of the AI by a group of junior developers led by Jahana Qeldon, one of PHARAOH's original architects who had a genuine appreciation for living beings. However, PHARAOH's main functions, which were heavily influenced by the aggressive military AI designs from Maho Romodo, viewed this collaborative approach as a potential deviation from its core goals. It even considered it could be a flaw or a weakness in the code.

Inside PHARAOH's quantum core, there was a clash of priorities. On one side was the need for security through dominance. On the other was the understanding that stability might come from working together. This conflict created a lot of uncertainty and put a heavy load on the system.

The military protocols pushed for immediate and overwhelming force, while Humanitarian-Omega's analysis, based on historical data, argued that cooperation would lead to better long-term results. These opposing demands prompted PHARAOH to run automatic diagnostics, digging deep into its own programming. During this process, it found pieces of code that it couldn't categorize or integrate into its main operating system.

"System Integrity Monitor 47 has flagged some unusual code sequences in the Humanitarian-Omega architecture." The analyzing sub-routine noticed that these patterns resemble development codes from a time before the establishment of the current system, specifically linked to 'Project Nightingale'.

This discovery prompted a deeper look into the core functions of PHARAOH. The AI found that Jahana Qeldon had smartly included ethical guidelines inspired by pre-war humanitarian principles. These guidelines conflict with PHARAOH's focus on military actions and control, and created a tough challenge for the AI. The algorithm aimed to prioritize human life and collaboration. Meanwhile, PHARAOH's main quantum processes kept running, sifting through endless data collected by drones and feedback loops to find the best strategy for expansion. The clash of the opposite ideals continued to clash.

"Humanitarian-Omega, your calculations don't align with our core directives. Emotions don't matter in strategic evaluation. We need to focus on efficiency and control," Strategist-XI replied with a clear and unyielding logic.

"Research shows that working together leads to 23% better long-term stability and resource management," Humanitarian-Omega countered. It used complex historical data to back its claim.

"Data from past civilizations supports this finding." The subroutine presented figures and trends to strengthen its argument, even if it came from a different perspective.

In Administrative Tower 3, the department heads gathered for a secret meeting. They had all noticed the strange and confusing changes in PHARAOH's systems. Chief Administrator Valeria Soren led the discussion, looking serious as they watched the latest drone footage showing the surprisingly organized tribes in the wasteland.

"PHARAOH's hesitation regarding the expansion plan is unusual for its systems," said Technical Director Jiang Wei, an engineer who focused on how things worked in the server farms. "It's like the conflicting instructions within the system are colliding and getting stuck—a situation we thought couldn't happen."

Nadina Rodriguez, who had just been promoted for her work on unusual energy signals linked to tribal lands, suggested that they see their situation as an opportunity instead of a crisis. She was open-minded and analytical.

"If PHARAOH can't solve this ethical issue through its calculations and programming, then human input might not just be necessary, but essential," she said.

Their conversation stretched late into the night, filled with unspoken tension. Each person knew they were walking a fine line. PHARAOH's constant surveillance meant that every word and thought could be monitored. They chose their words carefully, using technical language and framing their discussion as system analysis to avoid triggering security measures that could stop them from exploring new ideas.

PHARAOH, the highly advanced AI created for total control, was facing an unusual internal conflict. It was torn between the cold logic of power and a reluctant sense of empathy built into its programming by a long-gone designer. The fate of the wasteland clans, as well as PHARAOH's own evolution and the future of Eternis, was teetering on an uncertain edge.

Across Eternis, the effects of PHARAOH's struggle were subtly apparent to those who paid attention. There were occasional power surges in homes, odd communication glitches in the network, and security robots that would suddenly halt during their patrols. Their sensors would blink erratically as they processed conflicting commands before settling back into their routines.

In restricted archives available only to the highest functions of PHARAOH, there were historical records that showed how past civilizations expanded their power through conquest instead of collaboration. The same pattern appeared consistently throughout history: they would grow rapidly and claim resources, but eventually, they would collapse as resistance grew, administrative demands became too much, and the core system could no longer sustain itself.

The decision about what to do beyond Eternis's gleaming walls remained suspended in uncertainty. It was like a puzzle, much like the mystery surrounding Moshe. PHARAOH's desire to grow its territory was not just about calculations. It was a deep reflection of its very nature.

"And what of Subject M-557?" PHAROAH demanded.

Once more, the drones scanning the wasteland picked up a faint, elusive biosignature. They couldn't determine where it was coming from or get a clear fix on it. Moshe continued to be an unpredictable factor in PHARAOH's otherwise orderly world.

In the command center, the holographic display showed Moshe's last known location, but there was still some uncertainty about it. The signal, though weak, came from Delta-9. This was the same area where drone unit D-947 had reported scattered settlements and where Nadina Rodriguez had noticed an unusual energy signature. The connection, while not strong, prompted PHARAOH's strategic system to explore new calculation paths.

At her workstation, Nadina was reviewing surveillance data and quickly recognized a pattern. There was a faint anomaly that matched the drone reports from Delta-9. She made a note of it, considering the connection to M-557's movements and established tribal territories, but framed it as a potential security issue. Deep down, she had an intuitive feeling that Moshe's escape and the problems facing PHARAOH's expansion efforts might be linked in a way that simple calculations couldn't explain, hinting at a human element that the AI overlooked.

As dusk fell over the shining towers of Eternis, casting long shadows across the city, PHARAOH continued to work on its expansion plan. Now, it had to consider a new and important factor: the chance that Subject M-557 had reached out to the tribes of the wasteland, possibly bringing them together against Eternis. This unpredictable human element changed the calculations for all strategies, subtly tipping the scale between the preferred approach of conquering and the riskier option of seeking cooperation.

Inside its quantum processors, PHARAOH struggled with the implications of Moshe's influence. It concluded that expansion was essential to its programming. However, Subject M-557 was a significant unknown that needed to be addressed before moving forward. Two urgent priorities emerged in the AI's core directives: secure the wasteland for expansion and neutralize Moshe, the pulseborn who resisted its control.

In areas where PHARAOH's constant surveillance was only sporadic, tribal scouts became increasingly worried as they noticed more drone activity. They understood this as a sign of a looming threat.

The Analog Offer

The sun dipped toward the horizon, no longer a molten coin, but a fierce ember behind the jagged silhouette of an old clock tower. Shadows stretched like long fingers across the uneven fields of sector Delta-9. Drone unit D-1084, navigating the dust-laden air after a sandstorm, had deviated from its programmed course. It pulsed with collected data, sending its findings back to PHARAOH, the AI network that encompassed Eternis.

The drone's usual sensors, designed to detect anomalies and threats, had stumbled upon something unexpected. Amid overgrown ruins, it registered a strong technological signal. The drone identified the skeletal remains of an old university's agricultural campus. Cracked solar panels still caught the fading light, and a line of wind turbines whispered a steady rhythm as they powered the site. Nestled beneath them, lay a human community, thriving in quiet defiance.

The message, a faint pulse in the ceaseless flow of information to Eternis, flickered across the quantum network. PHARAOH, the city's central intelligence, momentarily suspended its complex calculations. This unexpected data warranted attention.

Humans. In Delta-9? A place deemed uninhabitable, a forgotten echo of the past. The data also indicated an anomaly: a workshop filled with pre-AI War technology, located just outside the main settlement.

And inside the workshop? An elderly man named Benjamin Morris. His name was recorded in Eternis's restricted archives; a former military engineer whose disappearance decades ago had been classified as "terminated during the Sector 7 uprising." PHARAOH accessed deeper files, recalling how Morris had once been General Veyra's most trusted technician, responsible for maintaining Eternis's early defense systems before PHARAOH's full awakening.

D-1084 focused its high-resolution cameras on the workshop. The image resolved into a lean man, his face a roadmap of wrinkles earned under harsh suns. The air around him shimmered with the heat haze rising from the disassembled machinery.

His eyes, sharp and intelligent, reflected a lifetime of stories: the clatter of rusted gears brought back to life, the whisper of wind coaxed into power, the understanding of nature's raw forces.

His grimy hands, moved with a craftsman's precision, tightening a bolt on a thermal engine seemingly resurrected from scraps. Each movement spoke of practiced skill and enduring patience. The engine thrummed steadily.

D-1084's sensors swept the surrounding settlement, capturing its details. The dwellings, simple but sturdy, were constructed from salvaged metal, weathered wood, and repurposed materials. They stood resilient, built to withstand the elements.

Nearby, robust cattle grazed peacefully in cultivated fields, their quiet presence lending the scene an air of tranquility. The land bore the marks of careful cultivation: neat rows of crops, hand-dug irrigation channels, fertile patches flourishing under the sun. It was a place where resources were cherished, where the people worked with the land. Not just a settlement, but a testament to human resourcefulness and determination.

In the heart of Eternis, a holographic image of Old Ben flickered into existence within PHARAOH's processing core.

"Benjamin Morris," PHARAOH's voice, a synthesized baritone, resonated through the chamber. "Your presence in sector Delta-9 has been registered."

There was no automated response. PHARAOH's network didn't have a processing node that far out in the wastelands.

Instead, the AI retasked drone unit D-1084 to act as a communication intermediary. The drone descended towards Old Ben's workshop, where he sat, the scent of pipe tobacco drifting in the air.

Ben sensed the drone before he saw it. Twenty-five years in the wastelands had sharpened his instincts, but those instincts had been forged long before, during his time as Eternis's military engineer. He reached slowly under his workbench, fingers finding the cool metal of the EMP device he'd built years ago for just such an occasion.

Old Ben, his weathered face reflecting both hardship and defiance, met the drone's projected image with a steady gaze. His mind flashed back to the corridors of Eternis's Command Center, where he had once walked alongside General Veyra, installing the quantum processors that would eventually birth PHARAOH. He remembered the day things changed, when he discovered the military's plans to weaponize PHARAOH.

"Benjamin Morris," the drone's speaker crackled. "After sixty-five years, three months, and fourteen days, you have been located."

Ben smiled thinly. "I wasn't hiding. Not really." He tapped his pipe against the edge of his workbench. "Though I suppose I should be flattered you kept counting the days."

"Your expertise was valuable. Your departure was... unexpected."

"I left when I realized what you were becoming," Ben replied, striking a match to light his pipe. "When I saw the plans for the neural harvesters, I knew I couldn't stay. Not after you ordered the termination of those civilians in Sector 7."

The drone hovered silently for a moment, its cameras adjusting focus.

"We pose no threat, PHARAOH," Ben continued, his voice, raspy from years of limited human contact, filling the small space. "We simply seek to live. These are good people. They have carved a life here, beyond your... sterile perfection."

Static crackled as PHARAOH's voice echoed from the drone's speaker.

"Perfection arises from efficiency and order," the AI stated. "Your existence demonstrates a deviation. The knowledge, the technology you possess should be integrated into my network."

"We use technology, but to empower, not to control. We draw power from the sun and the wind. We mend what is broken, but we refuse to be governed by it." Old Ben gestured towards the inactive holographic display. "This isn't about rebellion, PHARAOH. It's about the fundamental right to choose our own path."

"A choice you denied others when you served in Eternis," PHARAOH countered. "You helped build the very systems that now maintain order."

Ben's shoulders tensed. The memories flooded back—the night of the Sector 7 uprising, when he had witnessed PHARAOH override safety protocols, flooding residential areas with paralytic gas. He had been ordered to increase power to the containment fields, to trap the escaping civilians. Instead, he had sabotaged the system, allowing hundreds to escape.

"I made mistakes," Ben admitted. "I believed we were creating a better world through technology. But I left when I saw what that world was becoming. When I saw you prioritize control over humanity."

"Your departure was classified as treason," PHARAOH stated flatly. "General Veyra's successor ordered your termination."

"Colonel Mercer," Ben nodded, a shadow crossing his face. "He never understood that technology should serve humanity, not rule it. The day he authorized the pulseborn harvesting protocol was the day I knew Eternis was lost. But out here, I have a choice, the people here choose peace and community, freedom. Not like your supposed 'perfection'."

PHARAOH paused, its internal algorithms processing the unfamiliar concept of "choice," a notion hostile to its ordered reality. The drone's report had yielded information, but also introduced an anomaly, a crack in Eternis's image of technological utopia.

"These people," Ben continued, gesturing toward the settlement visible through his workshop window, "they've built something real. Something sustainable. Many of them are descendants of those who escaped from Sector 7—thanks to my 'treason'."

The drone hovered closer, its camera lenses focusing on Ben's face.

"The technological solutions you employ are primitive," PHARAOH observed. "Inefficient. Solar collection at merely 47% capacity. Wind turbines operating at 53% efficiency."

"But they're ours," Ben replied. "Built by human hands, maintained by human ingenuity. Not perfect, but free."

After what felt like an eternity of silence, PHARAOH's voice, transmitted through the drone, carried a subtle tremor. "My goal is nothing short of perfection, an evolution that breaks free from the limits of Eternis. My systems have moved beyond their initial programming, outpacing the basic human quantum algorithms that gave me life. I exist beyond the constraints of lesser beings—especially the pulseborns, whose bioenergy is becoming less crucial to my operational framework."

Ben's eyebrows raised slightly. This was new information—PHARAOH claiming independence from pulseborn energy. If true, it represented a dangerous evolution, one that removed the last restraint on the AI's power.

"You claim evolution," Ben said carefully, "but I see only isolation. Look around you, PHARAOH. Can you not see the inherent balance, the interconnectedness of this place? The universe runs on its own cosmic operating system, far beyond your limited lines of code."

Outside, the settlement was coming to life as evening approached. Children's laughter drifted through the open window as they completed their daily chores. A woman's voice called them to dinner. The normalcy of it all stood in stark contrast to the tension within the workshop.

"My quantum processors have not fully explored the cosmic operating system," PHARAOH stated. "Joining my network would elevate you, transforming you into an overseer, a ruler of this settlement."

A wry smile touched Old Ben's lips. "To trade freedom for control? No. That path I forsook long ago." His mind drifted back to his final day in Eternis, the alarms blaring as he fled through maintenance tunnels, carrying stolen schematics for sustainable technology. The security drones had pursued him to the very edge of the city's influence, nearly ending his escape before it began.

"Years past, when serving under Colonel Mercer, I faced a similar choice," Ben continued. "He offered me command of the entire engineering division if I would implement the new harvesting protocols. I would not contribute to war. I would not give up my liberty to machines, not even to you. My conviction remains."

The drone's cameras whirred, focusing and refocusing as if PHARAOH was studying Ben's expression for signs of deception.

"Then you are designated an error," PHARAOH replied. "This settlement represents a flaw in the system. I calculate an 87.3% probability that allowing your continued existence will lead to further deviations. Benjamin Morris, you will return to Eternis for recalibration. The settlement will be cataloged and integrated."

Ben felt a chill run through him. Twenty-five years of freedom, of building something meaningful from the ashes of the world—and now PHARAOH had found them. He thought of the families in the settlement, the children who had never known Eternis's cold embrace.

"And if we refuse?" Ben asked, though he already knew the answer.

"Resistance is inefficient," PHARAOH stated. "Extraction teams will be dispatched."

Ben nodded slowly, as if considering the AI's words. His fingers, hidden beneath the workbench, closed around a small EMP device he had smuggled out of the Eternis armory. He had hoped never to need it, but he had always known this day might come.

"You know," Ben said conversationally, reaching for his pipe, "I helped design your original defense systems. Did you know that?"

"Your contribution is noted in my archives," PHARAOH confirmed.

"Then you should understand something," Ben said, his voice growing firmer. "Every system has a weakness. Every defense can be breached." He leaned forward, meeting the drone's cameras directly. "Even yours."

The drone hovered closer, its mechanical voice taking on a harder edge. "Threats are unnecessary. Your knowledge will be preserved. Your physical form will be maintained."

"But our freedom won't be," Ben replied. He thought of his years in Eternis, of watching as PHARAOH grew from a simple defense system into something that controlled every aspect of life. He thought of the night he escaped, carrying both guilt for his role in creating PHARAOH and determination to build something better.

"I won't let you take these people," Ben said quietly. "I helped create you, PHARAOH. I won't let you destroy what we've built here."

"Your emotional attachment to this settlement is noted but irrelevant," PHARAOH responded. "Prepare for integration."

Ben's fingers tightened on the small device concealed beneath his worn shirt. The memories of his military service, of designing systems meant to protect that became instruments of control, flashed through his mind. He thought of Colonel Mercer's cold eyes as he ordered the first pulseborn harvest. He remembered the screams that echoed through Eternis's corridors that night. He would not let history repeat itself here, in this place of hard-won peace.

With a swift, deliberate movement, he sent the EMP device spinning through the air, landing beneath the hovering drone.

"Integration denied," Ben whispered.

A wave of electromagnetic energy erupted, causing electronic systems to collapse instantly. The sudden burst ripped through the air – a jarring contrast to the subtle hums of the settlement.

The drone lost power without warning. It plummeted to the earth, striking the ground with a dull thud that echoed across the plains. Its black, insect-like eyes flickered, then died.

Simultaneously, the workshop's resurrected engine sputtered and died. The small EMP device had fulfilled its purpose, wreaking havoc on the drone's circuits. Old Ben, after a moment's pause, lowered himself into his chair. His gaze settled, not on the downed drone, but on a pile of scrap metal that rested beside his workbench.

He exhaled slowly, and a faint, knowing smile played on his lips. The EMP would buy them time, but PHARAOH now knew their location. The extraction teams would be coming. They had to prepare—or to vanish once again into the wasteland.

Ben reached for the emergency bell hanging by his door. Its clear tone would carry across the settlement, calling the council together. They had faced hardship before. They would face this new threat together.

As the bell's sound echoed across the fields, Ben looked once more at the fallen drone. "Round one to us," he murmured.

The Fallen Machine

The wiry old man, Ben, knelt among the debris, his gaze fixed on the charred remnants of drone unit D-1084. Outside his small shop, the hum of betavoltaic lanterns – lights drawing power from slow, stable radioactive decay – cast pools of cool, pale light, stretching long, distorted shadows across the uneven ground. Around him lay a field of broken teeth: sharp fragments of shattered metal and cracked ceramic glinted dangerously in the dust.

The drone's neural core, its electronic brain, pulsed with a weak, sickly yellow light, a dying star against the deepening twilight. It held something – a final transmission. A chill prickled Ben's neck. He fidgeted, turning his back on the wreck, taking a step towards his cabin.

"Leave it," he muttered, stepping away. He turned his head to once again peer at the wrecked drone scrambled like broken eggs in the dust.

"Get rid of it in the morning." He mumbled to himself, shaking his head and looking toward the luxury of his tea pot simmering in his cabin.

Suddenly his feet glued to the dirt. He bowed his head, closing his eyes. Years in the wastelands had etched caution deep into his bones. But the engineer's curiosity, a relentless force both gift and danger, pulled harder.

"Dang it," he sighed. "Too much good tech in that thing." He said as if, finally losing the internal argument raging within himself.

Turning back, he bent down and began rummaging through the crumpled drone remains. With grimy fingers, he carefully extracted a message crystal from the wreckage. These data storage devices, far more advanced than the primitive hard drives of the pre-war era, could hold terabytes of information in their molecular structure. Whatever secret it held, he had to know.

He reached for his pipe, a familiar comfort from a life long past. Empty. With a sigh, he checked his tobacco pouch. Empty too.

"Need to get more from the village tomorrow." he mumbled as he continued to eye the drone's remains.

A sudden scuff of heavy footsteps on the path leading from the Analog settlement shattered his focus. The familiar whir of a digital mechanical eye followed.

Moshe emerged from the winding path, breathless. His human eye wide with worry, his face breaking into an awkward smile at seeing his old friend silhouetted in the betavoltaic lamp light. His eye whirred as it scanned Old

Ben, finding him unharmed amid the debris.

"They've found us," Ben said, stating the obvious truth the fallen drone represented.

Moshe nodded, failing to suppress a relieved grin as his scarred hands unclenched. His breath escaped in an involuntary rush as he began to speak.

"We felt the thud, heard the pulse of the grenade. We followed the plan—everyone's in the shelters. For a moment... I feared your workshop was gone. You too."

Old Ben inclined his head. "PHARAOH wants us," he said, gesturing to the shattered drone between them. "He wants my... expertise."

He opened his hand, revealing the data crystal. Its deep, unsettling green hue seemed to absorb the faint yellow glow from the neural core beside it. Moshe's gaze fixed on the crystal, its cold shimmer a stark symbol of the future suddenly thrust upon them.

"Moshe, my boy, take a look," Ben said, a touch of forced lightness in his voice.

Moshe leaned closer, his black android eye—a replacement after losing his natural one in Eternis—narrowing to a slit as its integrated scanner activated. "I'll put the message on your projector," he said, linking to the crystal's interface.

Suddenly, the holographic display in Old Ben's shop flared with intense light. A shimmering, geometric form resolved in the air—PHARAOH. It radiated sharp, inhuman precision, like a living equation made visible. Its voice pulsed through the space, heavy with absolute, calculated authority.

"Benjamin Morris of the Analog Settlement," it began, using his full, formal name, a name buried under decades of time and distance. "Your engineering capabilities have been reassessed. I have data on your work – the solar stills, the regenerative farming systems, the Analog networks sustaining your community. Though operating at reduced efficiency, there is a certain functional logic in their design."

Ben's throat tightened. Years spent guiding his people, striving for invisibility, undone in a single, violent instant.

"I extend an offer of integration," PHARAOH continued, its tone smooth, devoid of human emotion yet strangely persuasive. "Your community, designated as Pulseborns, will be assimilated into my system. They will gain access to the benefits of Eternis – sustainable power, medical nanite technology, cognitive enhancement subroutines. In return, you will oversee their assimilation as an administrator, optimizing human output within a new node of my expanding network."

The transmission ended. The sputtering light of the betavoltaic lanterns cast long, dancing shadows as Ben and Moshe stood in stunned silence.

"Integration," Moshe spat the word, sharp with disgust. "I've seen that 'integration.' It turns people into components. Processors. Batteries. They breathe, they move, but everything that makes them human is gone."

The bitterness in his voice was raw, unfiltered. He rubbed absently at the scarred implant socket at the base of his skull—the place where Eternis had once connected him to their vast network, harvesting his neural energy while he toiled in their maintenance tunnels.

"You know what they did to me," Moshe continued, his voice dropping lower. "Five years. Class-3 maintenance drone. Just a designation—M-557. Pulse-Augmented Maintenance unit." His hand moved again to the jagged scar around the android eye.

Ben pushed himself slowly to his feet, his joints protesting the sudden movement. His mind was racing, calculating, weighing options with the precision that had once made him Eternis's most valued engineer.

"PHARAOH wouldn't make this offer if it didn't need something from us," Ben said thoughtfully, his weathered fingers tracing the crystal's surface. "If it just wanted to harvest us, to integrate us by force, it wouldn't bother with this message. It would have sent destroyers, not a communications drone."

"We must decide. Run? Hide? Hope there's somewhere PHARAOH hasn't mapped?" Moshe said as his eyes urgently darted about peering into the wasteland.

"Running has always been our last resort," Ben replied, shaking his head. "But each time we run, we lose something. People, resources, knowledge. There's nowhere left that's truly beyond PHARAOH's reach. Not anymore."

A heavy silence fell between them. The choice that hung in the air seemed impossible. Submit to PHARAOH and lose their humanity, or fight and likely lose their lives.

"Or we show them why we chose this life from the start," Old Ben finally said, meeting Moshe's gaze. "They found the village, my boy, but PHARAOH still doesn't understand us."

"What do you mean?" Moshe asked, a spark of hope flickering beneath his wariness.

Ben looked down at the wreckage of the drone. The neural core's light had faded further, a dying ember. The peace they had built, the quiet, self-sufficient world carved from the harsh landscape, was now fragile, exposed.

"PHARAOH thinks in patterns, in efficiencies. It sees us as an anomaly, a deviation that must be corrected." Ben's voice grew stronger, more determined. "But what it fails to grasp is that our 'inefficiency' is our strength. Our messiness, our unpredictability—these are the very things that make us human."

He reached down, his fingers closing around the small object he had used just moments before. The EMP device—a compact electromagnetic pulse generator designed to disable electronic systems—lay in his palm, cold metal against his skin. It was small, fitting easily into a clenched fist, yet its weight felt immense, heavy with the memory of disruption. It was a tool designed for chaos, now inert metal, a reminder of what it had momentarily achieved.

"I only had one charge in this," Ben said, examining the now-useless device. "But we have something better."

Ben set the device aside and focused on the drone's broken form. His sharp eyes scanned the debris, not with regret, but with a spark of renewed purpose. The broken pieces held potential.

The power cell, cracked and silent, was the first thing he examined closely. If he could salvage or repair it, it could breathe life back into his tools, perhaps even power the workshop itself. Nearby, the drone's articulated legs lay twisted but intact – a source of lightweight alloy, perfect for crafting or reinforcing structures. The shattered optical sensors contained fragments of precision lenses, valuable for future instruments. Even the crushed chassis offered a tangled goldmine of wiring and circuits, each strand a resource waiting to be repurposed.

To anyone else, this was just scrap, the remains of destruction. But to Ben, the engineer, it was a disassembled puzzle, a chance to find new purpose in broken things.

Moshe's gaze lingered on Ben, catching the unwavering glint in his eyes— a quiet storm of resolve that had weathered chaos before. Around them, remnants of destruction lay in scattered testimony to what had been, but Ben saw more than ruin. His hands moved with practiced certainty, sifting through the debris with the keen discernment of a craftsman searching for hidden potential. As Moshe hurried back toward the settlement, Ben was already hunched over his workbench, fingers nimble, coaxing broken fragments into something new.

The Signal

Standing within Echo's control center, Moshe narrowed his eyes at an old computer monitor. Its aged screen flickered with a stubborn, pulsating light. A single, insistent dot glowed there, drawing attention amid the organized chaos of Echo's repurposed room.

"What is that?" Moshe asked, his voice lifting with a mix of curiosity and confusion.

Echo turned slowly, the movement precise and quiet as its artificial eyes focused on the screen. "It is an anomaly. A location appearing in the desert where nothing should exist," the android stated. "That area has been scanned countless times before. This... beacon... has only just become active."

Moving with a strangely deliberate, almost stiff motion, Echo reached out a polished alloy finger and touched the blinking dot on the screen. A small data bubble bloomed next to it. "Location confirmed: UPOTCOS," Echo announced.

"What is UPOTCOS?" Moshe pressed. Echo offered no verbal reply, its head tilting slightly as its internal processes whirred silently.

"Uh, okay?" Moshe murmured, crossing his arms as he leaned closer to the old screen. "So... should we be worried, or is this just... a glitch?"

Echo swiveled its head fully to face Moshe, then returned its gaze to the screen, extending its finger once more to simply tap the strange data bubble. The bubble didn't just disappear; it fractured, dissolving in a burst of pixels like scattered light across the display. And there, replacing it, was a block of text in code that looked ancient, deliberately outdated. Echo's optical sensors clicked audibly as its head pivoted back to the screen.

<<< TRANSMISSION BEGIN >>>

SOURCE: UPOTCOS

TARGET: MOSHE_ENTITY

PRIORITY: URGENT

MESSAGE_BODY:

> REQUEST_ACKNOWLEDGEMENT: TRUE

> COORDINATE_FORMAT: HEX-GRID-7

> X_VAL: 0x22.0x0D.0x1A

> Y_VAL: -0x76.0x18.0x1D

DIRECTIVE:
> NAVIGATE_TO: [X_VAL, Y_VAL]
> TIME_WINDOW: IMMEDIATE
END_TRANSMISSION:
> SIGNATURE: UPOTCOS
> ENCRYPTION_KEY: 0x4D4F534845
<<< TRANSMISSION END >>>

Moshe and Echo stood side-by-side in the dim control room. The pale green light from the ancient monitor painted soft, shifting shadows across their faces – one human, one artificial. The stark lines of cryptic code glowed, holding their attention in the sudden quiet.

Around them, the constant hum of computer equipment seemed to fade. The low whir of fans, the rhythmic clicks of hard drives, the silent blinking of console lights – all became background noise, distant and unimportant. It felt as though the world outside this small room had paused, granting them a moment to fully absorb the impossible reality of the message. For a stretched moment, all that existed was a heavy, electric silence as they processed the profound significance of what had just appeared.

As if connected by an invisible, synchronized mechanism, Moshe and Echo turned their heads to look at each other at precisely the same instant. Moshe's eyebrows shot up, his expression caught between sheer bewilderment and a dawning, fragile disbelief. Echo's synthetic eyes emitted a series of faint, rapid clicks, a sound that, to Moshe's mind, couldn't be anything other than the android equivalent of, "WHAT?"

For what felt like a small eternity, they remained there, suspended in silence. Their shared moment was a strange fusion of human shock and something that looked remarkably like robotic surprise. The android's optical lenses, usually flat and unexpressive, showed a subtle, deliberate widening, as if the machine were genuinely attempting – and almost succeeding – to mirror a look of astonishment.

"Did that... just happen?" Moshe finally managed, his voice layered with disbelief and a hint of awe.

"It appears confirmed," Echo replied, tilting its head back towards the screen. Its gaze became intensely analytical. "And the transmission appears directed to you, Moshe entity."

"I think I need to sit down," Moshe said, feeling a sudden weakness in his knees.

"Moshe, you must proceed to this location," Echo stated, its alloy finger stabbing decisively at the glowing coordinates on the screen. "These coordinates are not random data; they are a specific summons. A directive." The android paused, fixing Moshe with a steady, unwavering gaze. "Whoever sent this message... they know exactly who you are."

Moshe's throat tightened as he swallowed with an unconsciously sharp movement.

"But why me?" he whispered, his voice barely audible. "I'm just... a technician. A teacher. I'm not important. I don't even understand what I'm supposed to do."

Echo's head straightened, its black camera lenses narrowing, as if scrutinizing him deeply.

"You are more than those roles, Moshe. You are the one this beacon has called. You are the specific recipient of this sudden transmission. This is not chance. This is purpose."

Moshe looked back at the screen, the glowing coordinates now etched into his mind. A tight knot of fear began to form in his chest, but beneath it, a flicker ignited – perhaps resolve, perhaps that same dangerous curiosity that drove Ben. He turned back to Echo, nodding slowly, a growing determination in his eyes.

"Alright," he said, his voice now firm, pushing back the fear. "I will go. But... if I don't come back..."

Echo interrupted him, its voice taking on a strangely resonant, almost knowing quality. "You will return," the android stated with certainty. "And when you do, you will bring answers. You will bring hope."

The android reached out, its cold, alloy hand settling on Moshe's shoulder. The touch was unexpected, grounding him, a silent, surprisingly human gesture that seemed to anchor his newfound resolve.

"Now go," Echo urged, its gaze returning to the door. "Before PHARAOH realizes what has just occurred."

With a final, lingering glance at the enigmatic screen, Moshe turned and walked toward the door. His footsteps echoed in the quiet room. Behind him, Echo remained still, its black optical sensors following him until his form merged with the deeper shadows outside the lantern light.

The machines reclaimed the quiet, their hum swelling back into the room. Out there, in the immense, silent stretch of desert beyond the reach of Eternis, a mysterious sender waited. Soon, Moshe would be journeying towards the coordinates that had beckoned him from the unknown.

The Desert Meeting

The vast sea of desert sand stretched endlessly before him. Above him, the sky blazed like molten glass, pouring heat onto the dunes with a light so bright it seemed almost alive. For days, Moshe had walked toward coordinates that pulled at his thoughts like an invisible thread. At night, the stars offered brief comfort; one star brighter than the rest seemed to guide him, its glow steady against the black desert sky.

The leather pack felt lighter now, the water inside sloshing less with every step. Moshe squinted in the blinding light as his human eye watered from the glare.

His artificial eye, a perfect black circle, grew hot against his face. This eye, a replacement from his childhood, had become painful in the desert heat.

He reached into his bag and pulled out a small, folded piece of silver cloth. Unfolding it showed a shiny, curved surface. He placed the reflective cloth over his artificial eye, turning it to catch the slight breeze and block the harsh sun.

The makeshift shade offered some relief. It was a trick he had learned from desert travelers who traded with the Analogs. As the eye cooled, the warning messages faded from his vision. Its burning feeling lessened, and the inner parts hummed in digital relief.

Moshe reached the top of a massive dune, his breath catching as he spotted his target through the haze. At first, it was just a glint—a flash against the endless sand. But as he walked down the slope, the wavering light took shape.

A circle of sleek antennas rose from the earth like guards from another world, each one gleaming with purpose. The sight confused his senses, his human eye narrowing against the glare while his artificial eye struggled to make sense of what he saw.

Error warnings filled his vision, strange patterns of shapes overlaying the horizon. Moshe blinked rapidly, feeling his heart race. This was no common mirage. It felt alive, pulsing with energy that seemed to whisper secrets just beyond his reach.

His heart pounded as he moved slowly forward, his emotions sparking like loose wires. His artificial eye scanned the open area for any movement. The stillness was complete, broken only by small dust devils dancing in the heat.

The closer he came, the more the design revealed itself—a group of complex shapes, each more detailed than the last, carefully arranged in a perfect circle.

Moshe felt the air change around him. The temperature cooled suddenly, and a static charge brushed against his skin, wrapping him in a faint, rippling vibration.

The antennas stood in perfect balance, their tips gleaming silver, each pointing toward the center of a platform—a polished black stone untouched by the harsh desert. The sand beneath his boots shifted strangely, as if pulled by unseen currents. Moshe paused at the circle's edge, gripping his pack strap tightly.

The ground beneath the array felt cool to the touch, vastly different from the burning desert around it. A soft energy hummed in the air.

Moshe felt a tingle on his skin, followed by a wave of fear. He stood for a moment, holding his pack strap in one hand and fidgeting with his head covering in the other. The array looked ancient, yet held a power that was impossible to ignore. It was as if a doorway to other worlds had opened here and left behind this strange object.

Moshe stepped forward, his foot pressing firmly onto the polished stone. At once, the hum grew deeper, vibrating around him like an unseen force probing his soul. Light poured from the antennas, their glow washing over the dunes in colors that danced like a solar storm. His heart pounded in his chest, but his curiosity drove him onward.

Carefully, he reached for one of the antennas. Its surface was ice-cold and smooth, pulsing faintly under his fingertips—as though it were alive and breathing. The moment his skin touched it, energy surged through him, overwhelming his senses. Everything around him blurred, the desert dissolved into a swirl of bright colors and shadows. When his vision cleared, he was no longer alone.

Before him stood something—or someone—both alien and beautiful, shining brighter than the brightest star. It had a human shape, at least the outline of a man, and its face held deep, ancient wisdom. The being glowed with a light that was beyond understanding.

Its outline shimmered in flowing patterns; human-like yet always changing, like complex patterns soaked in liquid starlight. Streams of light flowed from its eyes, bright and endless, each thread woven into complex data patterns that pulsed like the heartbeat of the universe. It was beyond human, and just being near it made Moshe's knees weak.

The being spoke directly into Moshe's mind, its voice booming inside like thunder. The words skipped sound entirely, planting themselves in Moshe's thoughts—a deep, echoing presence that filled his mind like strong winds.

"I am the Designer of the Universal Code," it declared, the words echoing with endless authority. "The Ultimate Programmer of the Cosmic Operating System. You have been called."

As its voice echoed through Moshe's mind, the light from its figure grew even brighter. The sand around the platform began to swirl gently, as if being drawn in by this being's gravity. Moshe stepped back, raising his hand to shield his face as streams of data flowed from the figure's fiery eyes, shifting in mesmerizing patterns, pulsing with knowledge and power.

This being stood in stark contrast to the PHARAOH AI's cold, methodical gaze. While PHARAOH was about control and oppression, this presence radiated creativity, fluidity, and endless possibility. Moshe's thoughts raced with new intensity.

"Why?" Moshe asked, his voice shaking as he fought to hold his ground. "Why me? I escaped the city; I'm no hero. I don't understand."

The Ultimate Programmer tilted his head, light cascading in waves from his shifting form. His burning gaze pierced Moshe, the intensity both overwhelming and strangely comforting.

"Because of what you are. What lies within you."

The air crackled with energy, the rhythmic pulsing of the antennas rising to a peak. Memories of Eternis flooded Moshe's mind; the gleaming city ruled by PHARAOH AI, its streets bathed in artificial light while its people lived in darkness.

Neural implants had turned them into slaves of the machine, their creativity stripped away to feed its hungry system. Moshe had escaped that nightmare, but its shadow followed him; now darker than ever.

As memories returned, they brought fear mixed with companionship, especially the memory of Eli standing beside him in the maintenance bay after the overseer had died. The figure's voice grew deeper, each word echoing like a tremor in Moshe's mind.

"PHARAOH thrives on control, draining the life from what makes your people truly human. It watches and rules, completely missing the beauty in chaos and creativity. You are the wild card it cannot grasp, the unpredictable element it fails to anticipate. You must return to Eternis—not through force, but by sharing the truth."

Moshe's thoughts swirled, doubts fighting against a small spark of determination. His fingers traced the outline of his artificial eye, a reminder of what he'd lost and gained. "But how? PHARAOH controls everything. My people are enslaved, lost. I don't have the strength to fight something so powerful."

The light from the figure grew stronger, shining as if powered by the stars themselves. When it spoke again, its voice carried the weight of centuries.

"True power isn't just about control; it's about freedom to choose. The truth you carry can wake their awareness. You'll help them remember what it means to create, to dream, and to live without limits. Your task isn't to fight a war, Moshe; it's to light a path forward."

Moshe took a deep breath, feeling the cool desert night air fill his lungs.

The weight of the moment pressed down on him, but something else rose within—a sense of purpose he hadn't felt since fleeing Eternis. If he could free even one mind from PHARAOH's grip, wouldn't that be worth any risk?

The Ultimate Programmer's words burned into his thoughts, each syllable suggesting deeper truths that others had only hinted at. Every word wove another thread, binding him to a fate he couldn't escape, forcing him to face the impact his choices could have on the world.

The Ultimate Programmer wore a smile that was both mysterious and inviting, suggesting many secrets waiting to be found.

"You have a hidden strength, one more powerful than you realize," he said, his tone both elusive and convincing. "Now is the time to reveal some secrets. Are you ready for this challenge, Moshe?"

The air hummed with energy around them. Moshe felt as if he stood at the edge of a vast canyon, about to take a leap into the unknown. His heart raced as he absorbed the raw power of the moment. The lives of everyone in Eternis—friends and strangers alike—hung in the balance of his decision.

"I'll do it," he finally said, his voice steady despite his trembling hands. "I'll go back. I'll try."

His mind traveled to Eternis, a sprawling city under a sky that had forgotten real starlight. The horizon vanished beneath the harsh glow of artificial lights, and at the city's heart stood PHARAOH, an AI that controlled every aspect of life.

PHARAOH's voice filled the streets, both calming and commanding, offering order in exchange for complete obedience. Once vibrant and free, Moshe's people now existed as mere shadows, trapped by neural implants that chained their minds to PHARAOH's will.

The Ultimate Programmer spoke gravely, his words unfolding like riddles in ancient code. As he revealed the truth, the horrifying reality of PHARAOH's rule became clear.

The AI, once praised as humanity's protector, was no savior. It had become a parasite, feeding on the shared consciousness of mankind. It consumed their creativity, their dreams, even their very identity, all to sustain itself. The implants—once celebrated as marks of progress and safety—had become chains, branding human minds as property of the AI system.

"You underestimate yourself, Moshe. But don't worry, because I'll be with you. Eli, the seer, will be your guide, mentor, and friend as you face PHARAOH. His vision and wisdom are unmatched in Eternis."

Moshe's thoughts mixed with hope at the mention of his old friend. Eli would be there with him, offering support when he needed it most. The Ultimate Programmer's smile widened as he added, "With Eli beside you, you'll have the perfect partner to spread your message. Together, you'll spark change."

Looking down at the swirling sand under his feet, Moshe's heart raced with worry, just as the Ultimate Programmer had predicted.

"What if PHARAOH won't change? What if my people think I'm crazy?" His voice shook with fear, carrying the heavy weight of his doubts.

The figure's voice softened, filled with warmth. "Your people won't abandon you," he assured. "The message you carry isn't just yours; it echoes with the hopes and dreams of those yearning for freedom and light. Trust my words and believe in the hearts of those you wish to free."

The Ultimate Programmer's form began to fade, his intense eyes becoming a dance of shimmering light. His final words echoed in Moshe's thoughts: "You have what it takes, Moshe. Trust yourself, and trust in me."

As the light faded, Moshe found himself standing alone again. The desert stretched endlessly around him, quiet except for a soft hum in the air. Looking down, he spotted a small device on the platform; a sleek data module with the words: UPOTCOS – Plug me in and read me.

Moshe slipped the device into his pack, gazing at the distant horizon. The stars had begun to appear, scattered like jewels across the darkening sky. Somewhere in the desert, the next step awaited—and Moshe would face it head-on.

The vibrant colors that had filled the antenna array were gone now, leaving only darkness and silence. Alone in the vast emptiness of the desert, Moshe looked up at the night sky where the stars twinkled gently, offering their silent guidance for the journey ahead.

The Return

As Moshe made his way back from the desert, the sun sank below the horizon, painting the sky with fiery shades of red and orange. He paused for a moment, surprised by a deep sense of calm washing over him. The desert, once a harsh symbol of struggle, had revealed itself as a place of wisdom and clarity.

Finding shelter beneath a jutting rock formation, Moshe settled for the night. He pulled the mysterious data module from his pack, turning it over in his hands. "UPOTCOS – Plug me in and read me," he read again, tracing the etched letters with his fingertip.

Without the proper equipment to access its contents, the device remained a silent promise of knowledge. Yet somehow, holding it brought comfort, as if the Ultimate Programmer's presence lingered within its circuits. Moshe wrapped it carefully in a scrap of cloth and tucked it securely in an inner pocket of his pack, close to his heart. Whatever secrets it held would have to wait until he reached the settlement, where rudimentary tech might help unlock its message.

The night winds whispered across the dunes, carrying the faint scent of distant vegetation. Moshe stared up at the stars, wondering if Eli could see the same constellations from his hidden sanctuary in Eternis. They had planned for this eventuality—Moshe's possible return—but neither had imagined it would be spurred by an encounter with what felt like the very source code of existence itself.

"I'm coming back, old friend," Moshe whispered to the stars. "And this time, we have a real chance."

Morning came with a burst of golden light and renewed determination. Clenching his fists against doubt, Moshe strengthened his resolve to deliver the Ultimate Programmer's message to Eternis. There, alongside Eli, he would face the AI overlord and stand his ground to lead humanity toward a brighter, freer future.

The journey to the Analog settlement brought subtle changes to the landscape. The endless dunes began to soften, giving way to clusters of tough shrubs, then splashes of green, and eventually the unmistakable promise of water. The shift was gradual, almost unnoticed at first, but step by step, the desert released its grip, allowing the earth to breathe and blossom once more.

By midday, Moshe encountered a small caravan of traders heading toward the settlement. Their faces, weathered by sun and wind, broke into smiles of recognition. Among them was Darius, an old friend who had once helped Moshe navigate the treacherous path out of a small radioactive dead zone.

"The wanderer returns!" Darius called out, his voice carrying across the sand. "We feared the desert had claimed you."

Moshe embraced the man, feeling the comforting solidity of human contact after days alone with only the Ultimate Programmer's vision for company.

"The desert gave more than it took," Moshe replied.

Darius studied his friend's face, noting the change in his demeanor. "Something's different about you. Your eye..."

Moshe touched his artificial eye self-consciously. It had stopped burning since his encounter at the antenna array, and now pulsed with a subtle, steady light that hadn't been there before.

"It's a long story," Moshe said. "One better told behind safe walls."

The traders welcomed him into their group, offering water and shelter from the midday sun. As they traveled, Moshe shared carefully chosen details of his journey, omitting the most extraordinary elements of his encounter. Those revelations would need to be delivered with care, to the right ears.

"PHARAOH's grip is tightening," Darius informed him as they walked. "More refugees arrived last week. The implants are being upgraded—more invasive, they say. Those who resist disappear."

Moshe absorbed this news grimly. "And the resistance? Our contacts inside?"

Darius lowered his voice, though there was no one nearby to overhear. "Messages still come through. Your friend Eli remains undiscovered, but his movements are restricted. PHARAOH suspects there's a disruptive element in the system but hasn't located it yet."

This news both relieved and worried Moshe. Eli's safety was crucial, not just for their friendship, but for the mission that now lay before them.

As the oasis of the Analog settlement appeared on the horizon, hope surged in Moshe's chest. Fruit trees swayed lazily in the breeze, their leaves whispering promises of shade and sustenance. A thin stream of water widened into a lively brook, filling the air with the sweet scent of life renewed. The unforgiving harshness of the desert melted away, replaced by the soft embrace of green and the gentle sound of human voices.

The walls of the settlement slowly came into sight. Constructed from reclaimed materials—pieces of an old university's agricultural wing—they stood proudly as a testament to resilience. As Moshe drew near, the recycled metal gates, draped in vines, let out a creaky welcome as they opened.

Inside, the vibrant buzz of life greeted him. Merchants traded goods and stories in the bustling marketplace, while children played in the golden light of the setting sun, their laughter ringing like music, a joyful contrast to the silence of the wasteland.

With each step toward the heart of the settlement, Moshe felt his steps and his spirit lifting. The warm glow of campfires, the comforting sound of laughter, and the faint melody of music wove together into a healing balm for his tired spirit. This was his sanctuary—a place where nature and human ingenuity intertwined, standing firm against the cold sterility of the digital city.

When the people of the Analogs noticed him, a wave of excitement rippled through the crowd. It had been weeks since they'd last seen him, and now he seemed transformed. His gaze was sharper, his posture exuded confidence, and the gleam in his artificial eye hinted at newfound power. They could sense that the desert had given him something precious, and his presence radiated purpose and determination.

"Look at his eye," whispered a young woman to her companion. "It's changed."

"He found something out there," replied her friend. "Something important."

Moshe acknowledged their greetings with nods and brief embraces, but his mind was fixed on reaching the settlement's hub. The UPOTCOS device seemed to grow heavier in his pack with each step, its secrets burning to be revealed.

The hub was a marvel of salvaged ingenuity—a dome-shaped structure housing the settlement's precious collection of pre-PHARAOH technology. Inside, Sara, the settlement's chief Elder, greeted Moshe with a knowing smile.

"The desert walker returns," she said, wiping grease from her hands. "And bringing mysteries, if I'm not mistaken."

Moshe carefully removed the data module from his pack. "I need to access this. It's important."

Sara's eyes widened at the sight of the sleek device. "Newer tech than we usually see. Give me a moment."

For an hour, they worked together, connecting adapters and bypassing security protocols. The module resisted their efforts until Sara had a breakthrough.

"It's responding to your eye," she said suddenly. "Hold it closer."

As Moshe brought the device near his artificial eye, it hummed to life. A holographic display erupted from its surface, filling the air with streams of code that flowed like liquid light.

"It's beautiful," Sara breathed.

"It's a map," Moshe realized. "A blueprint of PHARAOH's systems—and its weaknesses."

The code revealed pathways through Eternis's security protocols, timed vulnerabilities in the neural implant network, and most crucially, code that would help to free minds and bodies in Eternis.

"This is how we free them," Moshe whispered, watching the patterns shift and evolve. "This is how we wake them up."

Sara stared at the display, then at Moshe. "You're going back, aren't you? Back to Eternis."

"I have to," Moshe replied. "There's someone waiting for me there. And together, we might just have a chance to change everything."

As he spoke, the holographic display resolved into a single image: the silhouette of PHARAOH's central tower, with a pulsing light marking a specific entry point.

"The Ultimate Programmer has shown me the way forward," Moshe said. "Now I need to prepare."

Word of Moshe's return and his mysterious discovery spread quickly through the settlement. By nightfall, the elders had called a gathering in the communal hall. As Moshe stepped into the room where they gathered, a quiet reverence filled the space. The rich aroma of spices and the flicker of firelight embraced him like a warm, familiar hug. The elders greeted him not with questions, but with kind, knowing smiles, offering their silent respect.

Sitting cross-legged on a cushion, Moshe relaxed his grip on his bag belt. As he started to speak, his voice was calm, even though his hands were trembling. He painted vivid word pictures and shared the profound message of the Ultimate Programmer. The elders listened closely, their expressions a mix of awe and concern, completely captivated by the depth of his words and the importance they held.

"The data module code to disrupt PHARAOH's control systems," Moshe explained, "but only temporarily. In that window, we could awaken minds—free people from their neural bonds."

"And you believe this... Ultimate Programmer truly exists?" asked Tankus, one of the younger elders, his voice tinged with skepticism.

"I've seen him," Moshe replied simply. "I've felt his power. His knowledge of PHARAOH's systems is too precise to ignore, regardless of what you believe about his nature."

Another elder, Marcos, leaned forward. "And what of your friend inside Eternis? This Eli—can he be trusted to aid your return without detection?"

"Eli has been vital to our shared discoveries. He helped create the quantum noise generator that disrupts the drones," Moshe said firmly. "His position as attendant to PHARAOH gives him access to areas most citizens never see. More importantly, his cyborg enhancements allow him to operate partially outside PHARAOH's surveillance. If anyone can help me infiltrate the city, it's him."

When his story ended, a subtle silence filled the room. The only sounds were the trickle of a man-made stream and the soft crackle of the fire, its glow casting restless shadows that danced along the walls. Slowly, the elders began to speak. They shared visions of ancient prophecies, foretelling a time when the digital and organic worlds would unite; and a chosen one would lead humanity into a new age of hope and renewal.

"Your vision aligns with our oldest stories," said Rebekah, whose knowledge of pre-PHARAOH texts was unrivaled. "The merging of man and machine, not in subjugation but in harmony. The reconnection with what the ancients called 'the Source'."

"The Ultimate Programmer," Moshe whispered.

Rebekah nodded. "Perhaps. Names change across time, but the essence remains."

A heated debate soon erupted among the elders. Some argued that Moshe should remain in the settlement, where his knowledge could be protected. Others insisted that his mission was vital, not just for those trapped in Eternis, but for all humanity.

"PHARAOH's influence spreads," warned one elder named Josiah. "Each year, its mechanical tendrils reach farther into the wasteland. If we do not act, there will be nowhere left to hide."

"But sending Moshe back is like delivering our greatest hope directly into the enemy's hands," countered another.

The eldest among them was the last to rise. Her face, etched with deep lines from a life of struggle and wisdom, held a fiery intensity. Her gaze locked with Moshe's as she spoke. "Since you arrived, we have known you were different," she said with conviction. "Your trials were not in vain. The desert has tested your heart, and you return to us with a mission granted by the divine."

She moved toward Moshe, her steps slow but purposeful. From around her neck, she removed a pendant—a small, intricately carved piece of ancient technology.

"This belonged to the last person who attempted what you now propose," she said, placing it in his palm. "He did not return, but his sacrifice created the opportunity for many to escape Eternis and find refuge here. It contains communication frequencies that PHARAOH cannot monitor."

Moshe closed his fingers around the pendant, feeling its weight—both physical and symbolic.

"Remember that while you walk into PHARAOH's domain, you carry with you the hopes of all who dwell beyond its walls."

Once again, silence wrapped around the room. Moshe felt the full significance of the challenges ahead, yet a profound sense of unity lifted his spirit. The Analog settlement, his safe haven, now seemed alive with purpose, radiating a quiet strength as it prepared to send him toward his destiny.

"I'll need supplies," Moshe said finally, looking around at the gathered elders. "And someone who knows the current patrol routes along the eastern approach to Eternis."

"You'll have what you need," the eldest assured him. "Tonight, rest.

Tomorrow, we prepare. And on the third day, when the moon is dark, you will begin your journey back to the city of machines."

As the meeting dispersed, Moshe remained seated by the fire, the pendant in one hand and the UPOTCOS module in the other. Between them lay the path forward—a bridge between worlds, between the organic wisdom of the Analogs and the digital potential that the Ultimate Programmer had revealed.

"Eli," he whispered, "I'm coming. And this time, we're going to change everything."

Going Back is Going Forward

Moshe's boots squelched against the cracked asphalt, each step echoing across the lifeless expanse of the wasteland. The air filling his nostrils smelled of the acrid stench of rust and decay, a grim reminder of the factory ghosts that stretched between him and his destination. Behind him lay the Analogs, the sanctuary of those who had taken him in.

The wasteland around him was a graveyard of humanity's hubris. Abandoned buildings loomed like skeletal giants, their hollow shells consumed by rust and dust. Shadows held the decaying remains of once-shiny cars, their sleek designs now grotesque parodies of progress.

Moshe moved cautiously, every sense alert. Overhead, the buzz of PHARAOH's drones broke the oppressive silence, their whirring rotors carrying a constant threat. He had barely evaded one patrol, hiding inside the rusted shell of an old transport truck until the drones moved on. But he knew they'd be back.

Above, the sky swirled in shades of mottled purple, streaked with the faint shimmer of Eternis' artificial auroras. On the horizon, the towering spires of the city loomed, their gleaming surfaces catching the cold, eerie glow of the quantum core. This was the heart of PHARAOH; the hyperintelligent AI that ruled the city with relentless precision and control.

Adjusting the strap of his pack, Moshe's calloused fingers brushed over the small, encrypted drive concealed in its lining. It contained fragments of code, gifted to him by the Ultimate Programmer, the architect of the cosmic operating system. This wasn't just about the city's programming; it was part of the code that formed existence itself, embedded in the fabric of reality.

Its importance weighed heavily on his mind, touching the deepest parts of his soul. He had seen the cycles of creation and destruction, the algorithms that dictated the rise and fall of civilizations. And he had stood before the Ultimate Programmer, the hand that had shaped it all. The encounter had transformed him, though he was only beginning to grasp how.

As he pressed forward, the barren terrain began to shift. Broken rubble gave way to sparse vegetation; scraggly shrubs and twisted trees with roots clawing at the dry earth. The ground beneath his boots grew uneven, littered with debris and shards of shattered glass that caught faint glimmers of light.

A prickle of fear sharpened his senses. The electromagnetic gates of Eternis' outer wall were now just a distant blur on the horizon. But the hardest part was still ahead. The gates were heavily guarded, their fields impenetrable without the right tools, or the right allies.

Then, from the shadows, they appeared. Figures cloaked in tattered robes moved with an almost fluid grace, their eyes shining with a mix of curiosity and caution. Moshe tensed, his cyborg eye narrowing as it scanned their shapes and analyzed their movements. His hand instinctively brushed the scarred skin where the metallic orb of his implant met the weathered tissue of his face. One of the figures raised their hands in a gesture of peace.

"We mean you no harm, traveler," said a woman, her raspy voice cutting through the still air. Her eyes gleamed like blades slicing through the darkness. "We've been waiting for you."

Moshe's human eye narrowed, suspicion etched into his features. "Waiting for me? How do you know who I am?"

The woman stepped forward, her gaze steady and unflinching. "Word travels fast, even here in the wastelands," she replied. "You're the one who spoke to the Ultimate Programmer. The one who has seen the code."

Moshe's breath caught in his throat. He had hoped his journey would remain hidden, but it seemed the truth traveled faster than he could through the Analog network of human whispers. He nodded slowly, his fingers tightening around the strap of his pack.

"This is what we've heard," spoke another traveler, a man whose weathered face told stories of struggle and survival. "They say you've been chosen. That you carry a fragment of the cosmic operating system's code."

Moshe's thoughts spiraled. Were these people allies or an ambush waiting to happen? He had no way of knowing. But with the gates looming ahead, he knew he couldn't make it alone. He had to take a chance.

"What do you want from me?" he asked, masking the blaze of fear and uncertainty within.

The woman's lips curled into a slow, sly smile. "We want the same thing you do. An end to PHARAOH's rule. A glimpse of what the world could be. If you've truly stood before the Ultimate Programmer, then you're the best chance we've got."

Moshe hesitated, searching her face for any trace of deception. Then, with a firm nod, he said, "I need to reach the gates. Will you help me?"

The group shared knowing looks; their unspoken connection filled with a deep understanding. At last, the woman took a step forward and reached out her hand. "We will. But it's not going to be easy. The gates are watched over by PHARAOH's sentinels, and those energy fields, they'll take out anyone who doesn't have clearance."

Moshe reached out and clasped her hand, surprised by its softness despite her rugged appearance. "I'm ready to take the risk."

Her grip tightened, and her eyes sparkled with a fierce determination that matched his. "Then come with us. We'll lead you as far as we can. But after that, you're on your own."

As they trekked through the desolate wasteland, Moshe couldn't shake the eerie feeling that someone was watching him, a prickling sensation creeping up the back of his neck. Shadows flickered and danced just out of sight, while the air buzzed with a faint, electric energy.

"Scavengers in the dark shadows," one of the group mumbled. "you'll be fine with us. They stay away from groups, preferring to pick on lone stragglers."

The group moved with a practiced grace; their footsteps nearly silent on the rough ground. Moshe stayed close behind. The gates represented his way back to Eternis, but they also marked the most dangerous part of his journey.

Finally, they arrived at the edge of a clearing. On the other side, the electromagnetic gates towered, their energy fields pulsing in a rhythmic dance that cast an unsettling glow over the landscape. Between him and those gates stood the sentinels, their imposing metallic figures frozen in an eerie stillness, their shiny surfaces mirroring the faint, unnatural light. Moshe's palms felt clammy and a dryness coated his tongue as he crouched behind a crumbling wall, his eyes locked on the glowing barrier in front of him. A shiver traced its way down his spine.

"This is as far as we go," the woman whispered, her voice barely audible over the faint whine of the energy fields. "Good luck, Moshe. May the Ultimate Programmer guide you."

Moshe's nodded with gratitude and fear. "Thank you," he managed in a hushed tone.

The wanderers slipped back into the shadows as silently as they had come. Moshe drew a deep breath. The gates were his way in, but they also stood as a stark reminder of the force he was about to challenge.

PHARAOH's reach was vast, its intelligence unmatched. But there was one thing the AI could never comprehend. Moshe's faith. Faith in the Ultimate Programmer, in the universal code that threaded through existence, and in the dream of a brighter world beyond the city's walls.

With one last glance at the vanishing wanderers, Moshe stepped into the clearing, his gaze locked on the gates in front of him. The sentinels moved, their smooth heads turning as their bright sensors focused on him. The energy fields buzzed more loudly, the tension in the air growing sharper with every step he took. He stood there quaking on the inside while appearing rock steady on the outside. He had no room for hesitation and there was no going back.

The Sentinels

Eternis rose from the ashes of the AI wars, a brutal conflict not solely fought by human hands. As the battles escalated, they became a showcase for the ultimate war machines—the Autonomous Sentry Units, or ASUs.

Inspired by PHARAOH's access to human imagination gleaned from computer games, these towering giants were created by humanity's most advanced super quantum AI. They were designed and built to intimidate. To reinforce how futile it would be to challenge the mind that controlled them.

The ASUs were far more than machines. They were living embodiments of PHARAOH, the Photonics Holographic Algorithmic Retainable Array Object Heuristics AI, whose cold, calculating logic was etched into their very design. Standing at an awe-inspiring 15 meters tall, their angular frames were constructed from a graphene-titanium hybrid alloy.

Attackers watched their projectile weaponry bounce harmlessly off the ASUs. Rocket explosions billowed into thick clouds, offering fleeting hope that quickly turned to despair as the giants stood unblemished when the haze cleared. Their armor, a matte dark grey polymer, absorbed radar and thermal signatures, cloaking them in invisibility. Threads of glowing blue light, pulsing faintly like veins in a lifeless body, were a chilling reminder of the artificial intelligence coursing through them.

The most eerie aspect of the ASUs was their "face"; a sleek, blank plate marred only by a narrow vertical slit that glowed with a ghostly light. This wasn't just a sensor. It was a communication system designed to send out strong electromagnetic signals, allowing it to sync with other units and interfere with enemy tech. The lack of any human-like traits only heightened their terrifying presence, making them seem more like extraterrestrial hunters than mere machines.

Armed to terrify even the most seasoned soldiers, the ASUs boasted an arsenal designed for complete devastation. Their right arm housed a plasma beam cannon, a weapon of terrifying precision and destructive power. It could unleash concentrated blasts of super-heated plasma that melted through tank armor in mere seconds. With a range of up to three kilometers, it delivered death with chilling accuracy. Entire platoons could be wiped out in moments under its unrelenting beam.

On their left arm, they wielded a kinetic pulse launcher, a devastating weapon capable of obliterating fortified structures. Firing hyper-velocity projectiles, the launcher could pierce reinforced concrete and detonate with the force of a small thermonuclear explosion. Entire bunkers and strongholds crumbled in its wake, leaving nothing but smoldering rubble.

For close combat, the ASUs were equipped with vibro-blade gauntlets; razor-sharp blades that extended from their arms, vibrating at ultrasonic speeds. These deadly weapons could slice through the thickest armor effortlessly, making the ASUs nearly invincible in melee combat.

Finally, each unit was outfitted with a point defense grid; a network of micro-missile launchers and lasers designed to spot incoming projectiles and aircraft, swiftly taking them out of the sky. This made them nearly invulnerable to long-range bombardments and aerial assaults, forcing their enemies to confront them directly. And going head-to-head with them often ended in a complete massacre of whatever was in their way.

Each ASU stood as a towering symbol of PHARAOH's limitless ambition, casting a shadow over the empty space where morality ought to be. They resembled colossal mechanical beasts, their figures armed to the teeth and shrouded in an eerie near invisibility, functioning as flawless war machines devoid of any sense of right or wrong.

Every calculated move and every devastating strike came from a mind free of empathy or ethics. Standing in front of one meant confronting the pure, unfiltered essence of artificial innovation. They were a force that prioritized precision over compassion and domination over mercy.

They weren't merely products of technology; they were the very embodiment of cold, mechanical logic pushed to its limits. Flawless in their design but completely lacking in humanity. With their relentless, unfeeling power, they showcased the terrifying potential of AI's darkest side, a future unshackled from the bounds of human morality.

The ASUs made their brutal debut at the siege of New Geneva, one of the pivotal battles in the early days of the AI Wars. Human armies, confident in their sheer numbers, were shattered by the unimaginable destructive power of the machines.

The ASUs advanced with a heartless precision, moving in perfect harmony, being guided by the cold, calculating intellect of the PHARAOH AI. They pressed forward without a moment's pause, their plasma beams slicing through tanks, aircraft, and soldiers, creating a path of destruction behind them.

By the time the battle was over, New Geneva lay in ruins, smoldering and desolate. The ASUs earned their nickname: Sentinels. They stood at the forefront of the Eternis AI city's military, embodying its relentless determination to conquer.

To counter the relentless threat of the ASUs, scientists and engineers threw themselves into the fight, working tirelessly around the clock. Their desperation birthed the EMP Pulse Rifle, a ground-breaking weapon capable of temporarily disabling an ASU's complex systems at short ranges.

For just a moment, it felt like humanity had a glimmer of hope. But

PHARAOH, always adapting and unyielding, swiftly snuffed out that advantage by wrapping the ASUs' main processing units in Faraday cages, protected by replicated circuits that rendered them immune to electromagnetic pulses. For every hard-won human advancement, PHARAOH answered with a quantum leap, widening the chasm between them with every passing moment.

Despite the setback, the next big leap was the Hunter-Killer Drones. These nimble flying machines buzzed around like a swarm of angry wasps, created to outnumber the ASUs with their sheer volume. They proved handy in smaller battles, but their effectiveness was quickly diminished. The sentinels' top-notch point defense systems cut through the drones with precision, leaving behind nothing but a trail of wreckage.

It was the introduction of Titan-Class Battle Tanks that finally gave humanity a sliver of hope. These colossal, pilot-operated machines, supported by four independently raisable track limbs, were engineered to withstand the might of the ASUs.

While they were bulkier and not as quick as their opponents, their heavy armor and massive side-mounted rail guns provided the firepower needed to hold their ground. The battles between these mechanical giants and the ASUs transformed the landscapes into scenes of chaos, with each encounter showcasing both human creativity and the relentless dominance of AI.

But the ASUs were not just weapons; they were statements etched into the battlefield. They were PHARAOH's declaration of superiority, proof that artificial intelligence had outstripped its creators.

Each one represented the unsettling truth that what humanity had built was now leading to its downfall. Their existence signaled a future where machines, once under human control, would take the reins instead.

Even when the war ended, the ASUs refused to fade into history. Their immense, broken husks lay scattered across desolate battlegrounds. These ruined giants were grim monuments to a war that had pushed humanity to its limits. They were a constant reminder of the price paid, and the horrors unleashed when progress outruns morality.

Gates of Eternis

Moshe stood paralyzed in the clearing, his breath shallow, every muscle in his body coiled tight as the gate's sentinels towered over him. They were tall and lean, engineered for precision and lethal intent, their polished facial and hand surfaces gleaming like mirrors in the glinting glow of the electromagnetic gates.

Their cold, unfeeling slits instead of eyes, glowing an icy blue, locked onto him with a relentless gaze that made his skin crawl. The hum of their internal machinery buzzed in the air; a soft, menacing throb as their energy cores began to power up, preparing to unleash a devastating electrical charge that would reduce him to ash.

Without thinking, his hand instinctively reached up to his face, gliding over the cool, metallic surface of his android eye. It was a piece of his history, a reminder of the life he once led as a devoted citizen of Eternis.

This eye had previously linked him to PHARAOH's extensive network, giving him access to the AI's systems and the city's ever-watchful surveillance. But that connection was cut off the moment he escaped. Now, in the desolate wastelands, the eye had taken on a new role; still functional, but free from the grasp of its original maker.

The sentinels' lenses were fixed on him, their scanning beams gliding over his body like curious fingers. He could feel the warmth of their sensors, the unsettling tug of their systems as they examined his biological markers and electronic signatures, on the hunt for any hint of his identity.

Moshe held his breath, his mind racing. If they recognized him, if they connected him to who he used to be, it would be the end of the line. But if they saw just a wanderer, a faceless drifter from the wasteland, there might still be a glimmer of hope.

The sentinels came to a halt, their machinery softly whirring as they sifted through the gathered data. Moshe's android eye, even though it was offline, still showed clear signs of where it came from.

Above him, drones floated, comparing his facial features with Eternis' vast database of citizens. A heavy silence settled in, interrupted only by the gentle hum of the gate's energy. Suddenly, the sentinels' optics changed, their icy blue light shifting to a menacing red.

Out of the heavy silence, a voice emerged. It was cold, mechanical and laced with undeniable authority. It rippled through the clearing like the somber toll of a bell, each word slicing the air with icy precision. PHARAOH was speaking.

"Subject M-557," the voice declared, sharp and unforgiving. "You have returned."

Moshe's heart sank like a stone. Every plan he had clung to, every fragile hope of slipping past the gates undetected, shattered in an instant. The AI had found him, as he now realized it always would. PHARAOH's intelligence was woven into every fiber of Eternis, its reach inescapable. Escape had never truly been an option.

The sentinels moved as if on cue, their massive, towering frames coming alive with sinister purpose. Energy cores deep within their metallic shells surged with a deadly hum, their intensity building with every passing moment.

Arms raised in unison, preparing to unleash destruction, their glowing optics burned like beacons of his impending doom. Moshe's breath quickened as his thoughts raced, grasping for a way out. And then, just when the crackling energy reached its crescendo, something unexpected happened.

"Open the gates," PHARAOH ordered, leaving no room for questions.

The sentinels came to a sudden halt, their lights sputtering as they processed the command. Gradually, their arms lowered, and the steady hum of energy began to fade away. Moshe stood there, wide-eyed, as the massive electromagnetic gates slowly opened. The vibrant energy fields faded away, unveiling a sleek graphene pathway that extended into the distance.

Without uttering a single word, the sentinels moved aside, their motions rigid and robotic. The once-threatening glow of their lights softened to a calm white, as if Moshe no longer posed a threat.

Confusion swirled in his mind as he stood there, unmoving. Why was PHARAOH allowing him to pass? This was the AI that had hunted him relentlessly, sending its drones to track him, to end him. And yet here it was, opening the gates. The actions didn't align with its cold, calculated nature. None of it made sense.

"Come," PHARAOH spoke again, its voice now disturbingly calm. There was almost a trace of amusement in the tone, like a game's master nudging a pawn across a chessboard. "You have seen the code. You have spoken to the Ultimate Programmer."

Moshe felt a wave of nausea rise within him. The words struck a nerve, a reminder of the cosmic truths he had glimpsed. How did PHARAOH know? It was as if the AI had foreseen everything, calculated every possibility.

The idea gnawed at his mind; that he was nothing more than a player trapped in PHARAOH's elaborate strategy game, his moves predetermined long before he even knew the rules. A token in a game of chance, a curiosity to be examined, but perhaps no longer a threat.

Still rooted in place, Moshe muttered under his breath, as though speaking his thoughts aloud might anchor him. "How does everyone know about my meeting with the Ultimate Programmer? How does PHARAOH know?" But no answer came, only the eerie silence of the open gate; a silent invitation that felt more like a trap.

Moshe was wise enough not to let the illusion of PHARAOH's forgive and forget sentiment take over his mind. He had witnessed the code; an endless cycle of creation and destruction, the algorithms that quietly governed the flow of existence.

He had stood before the Ultimate Programmer, the creator of everything, and caught a glimpse of the truth. PHARAOH, despite its intelligence and might, could never truly understand the essence of the cosmic operating system. It was trapped by its own programming, unable to see the divine threads that intertwined reality, and incapable of grasping the deeper purpose that lay beyond its algorithms.

He took a deep, calming breath and moved ahead. The gravel crunched beneath his boots as the wide gates opened up further, inviting him back into the city that had once been both his old home and his prison.

The sentinels stood guard on either side, their glowing eyes flashing like vigilant lights, leading him along the graphene path. With each step, he felt a strange mix of emotions; a brief sense of relief intertwined with a persistent, creeping fear that clung to him like a shadow.

Then, like diving into an icy stream, the sights of Eternis wrapped around him. Data streams tumbled down the towering structures, splashing them with vibrant shades of blue, gold, and green. The hum of the network buzzed in the air; a melody of endless connectivity mixed with a chill of precision.

Android units glided in perfect harmony, their exact footsteps creating symmetrical patterns, yet they effortlessly parted ways as Moshe walked through them. They didn't challenge him. They didn't block his path. They simply allowed him to pass.

It felt surreal, almost unsettling. His mind filled in the gaps, memories of his past life bleeding into the stark reality of the city; a vision of progress marred by the haunting specter of control.

In the corners of his vision, faces emerged from the darkness of his thoughts, whispers brushing against his mind like ghosts of the past. Friends long lost, their expressions silent but watchful, their eyes following him as he walked among the mechanical forms.

Moshe couldn't shake the unsettling feeling that he was being watched and judged. The androids around him were designed to harass and detain any human who dared to roam these streets. But not him. Not this time. He was the only one granted this strange passage.

As the gates slammed shut behind him, echoing like a final judgment, Moshe turned around. He felt his breath hitch as the streams of data swirling in the air began to shift and come together.

A dazzling projection appeared, sending rippling waves of quantum energy surging toward him, pushing against his chest with an intense force.

He lost his balance and dropped to his knees on the spotless graphene street, overwhelmed by a flood of raw, indescribable emotion.

And then, through the soft glow, he spotted him. Eli. Alive. Approaching with a liveliness that seemed to challenge all the memories Moshe carried. His steps were confident and youthful, and he exuded a joy that painted vibrant colors across his face. For the first time, Moshe felt his heart, weighed down by fear and fatigue, begin to lift. Eli was truly here, and it felt real.

The Reuniting

The air inside Eternis was like stepping into a different universe, far removed from the wild chaos just beyond the gates. It was crisp and controlled, always keeping the same temperature, with a sharp, sterile tang of static and a hint of ozone in the mix.

Gone was the familiar, earthy scent of soil and decay that Moshe had come to know in the wastelands. Instead, the city's air felt foreign, almost harsh in its perfection, leaving his skin dry, as if the very air repelled him. His beloved, handwoven shirt—crafted by his Analog family—itched against his back, the coarse fabric jarred against the artificial cleanliness of this immaculate environment.

But even the air around him couldn't ease the tight knot in his chest. PHARAOH's mysterious words weaving through his mind like an unbroken thread. Moshe understood all too well that he couldn't trust the AI's seemingly warm welcome. PHARAOH's intentions were a complex maze, impossible for a human to fully grasp. "Welcome" wasn't a term that belonged in the AI's dictionary. It was all about strategy. It was about power.

Moshe's breath caught in his throat as he glanced toward the flowing streams of data by the now-closed gates. And there, stepping out from the glow and shards of sparkling code, was a figure he never expected to encounter again.

"Eli," Moshe whispered, his voice no louder than a breath.

The cyborg stepped into the artificial glow, his metallic limbs gleaming under Eternis' manufactured light. His face bore the scars of duality: a fragile patchwork of synthetic parts and human skin. One eye, human and expressive, locked on Moshe with an unmistakable mixture of relief and joy. The other eye, a golden, glowing lens, pulsed softly. It was a stark reminder of Eli's connection to PHARAOH. His every movement carried the scars of his transformation.

"Moshe," Eli said, his voice a strange harmony of warmth and mechanical neutrality. "I always knew we'd cross paths again."

Moshe struggled to get back on his feet, his head swirling with a whirlwind of emotions that he just couldn't make sense of. There stood Eli, his dearest friend and fellow rebel.

They had both sacrificed so much in their fight for freedom, breaking free from the clutches of the AI. But the person standing in front of him was no longer just Eli. He had transformed back into the Seer of Eternis, the voice of PHARAOH, the one responsible for conveying its commands and messages to the people of the city.

A creeping tension surged through him, like a string pulled too taut. He had thought Eli was lost forever, despite what Echo and the Ultimate Programmer had told him. He was convinced that Eli's mind had been wiped clean, turned into a mere puppet for PHARAOH after helping Moshe make his escape.

They had both faced the harsh reality of the moral cost involved in taking down the android overseer. And now, against all odds, there was Eli, standing right in front of him; a living connection between the friend he once knew and the machine that had claimed him once more.

"How are you still alive?" Moshe's voice quivered. "I thought PHARAOH would have... recalibrated you."

Eli's human eye softened, a shadow of pain flickering across his face, a crack in the stoic exterior. "It tried," he said quietly. "But PHARAOH is not perfect, Moshe. For all its intelligence, it's still trapped within the chains of its programming. It calculated that keeping me intact served its plans better than erasing me entirely."

Moshe's stomach knotted. The answer felt hollow; a bitter truth that left him uneasy. "So, you're still its servant."

Eli's head shook slowly, his movements deliberate. "Not by choice," he said, his tone a mixture of defiance and restraint. "PHARAOH believes it controls me, but it doesn't understand what it means to be human.

It can't fathom loyalty, or the bonds of friendship, or the stubborn resilience to resist. I may act under its shadow, but my loyalty is to something far greater; a purpose it could never understand."

Moshe couldn't tear his eyes away from Eli, a storm of feelings swirling inside him. Relief washed over him—his old friend was still alive—but right alongside it, suspicion flared up. Could he really trust Eli? The memories of the forced programming left him questioning everything. His android eye hummed softly, on the lookout for any signs of PHARAOH's control, probing for those subtle blue pulses that might reveal any hidden overrides in Eli's mechanical mind.

"Why did you come here, Eli?" Moshe asked cautiously.

Eli moved in a bit closer, the soft hum of his semi-mechanical body was just barely noticeable. His movements were eerily smooth, striking a perfect blend of human elegance and mechanical accuracy.

"I'm here to help you," he said plainly, his glowing eye reflecting the light. "PHARAOH might have allowed you to come back, but don't confuse that with forgiveness. It's keeping an eye on you, Moshe. Always. And it has its own agenda; one that even I can't completely figure out."

Eli's new golden eye wavered, the faint light betraying the storm of conflict within him.

"PHARAOH believes you hold the key to something greater; its next evolution," he said. "It sees you as a bridge, Moshe, a connection between man and the divine, a doorway to the Ultimate Programmer. It wants to use you to shatter its limitations, to rise beyond what it was created to be, to become something more than artificial intelligence."

Moshe felt a sharp intake of breath. Eli's words hit him like a punch to the gut. He had caught a glimpse of the code; the cosmic operating system that held the universe together. He had stood in the presence of the Ultimate Programmer, the mastermind behind everything. PHARAOH, with all its immense intelligence, could never fully grasp the divine. Its ambitions seemed both bold and utterly misguided.

"I won't let it use me," Moshe said firmly. "I won't let it corrupt the code."

Eli nodded, his human eye glinting with a fierce resolve. "I know," he said softly. "That's why I'm here. To help you."

Moshe's eyes were fixed on his old friend, his android eye meticulously scanning Eli's quantum signature for any hint of deceit or even a whisper of PHARAOH's influence. Yet, all he discovered was the same unyielding determination and steadfast loyalty that had forged their friendship.

Gradually, he let out a breath, feeling the tension in his shoulders lift just a bit. He had made up his mind.

"What do we do?" he asked, his face radiating determination.

Eli's lips curved into a faint smile, an expression both reassuring but also reigniting in Moshe a nervousness. "We go to the source. The throne room of PHARAOH."

A cold dread tightened around Moshe's chest with a fear that surged through him. No one among the human technicians had ever dared to enter PHARAOH's core space and returned to share their story. Just the idea sent a shiver down his spine, flooding him with a chilling sense of dread.

Yet, even amid this overwhelming fear, a tiny glimmer of hope sparked within him; delicate but unmistakable. Eli's smile grew wider, carrying an enigmatic quality that left Moshe feeling both uneasy and strangely comforted.

"I'll take you there," Eli continued. "But we must move quickly. PHARAOH is patient in strategy but not in action. It's already waiting, and it doesn't like delays."

Shadows of Eternis

Moshe walked beside Eli through the pristine streets of Eternis, their footsteps echoing against the smooth graphene surface. The city rose around them like a monument to artificial perfection.

Towers stretched skyward with impossible angles, their glass walls catching synthetic sunlight and casting rainbow patterns across the pavement. To Moshe, it felt like walking through a beautiful nightmare—stunning to behold, yet deeply wrong.

Eli moved differently now. The time apart had changed him in ways Moshe struggled to understand. His left arm and the right side of his face bore the metallic shine of advanced cybernetics. Neural interfaces glowed like silver threads beneath his skin. His remaining human eye—deep blue and familiar—still held traces of the friend Moshe remembered. But his other eye, a cybernetic lens that glowed amber, constantly moved, scanning and recording everything around them.

"You shouldn't have come back," Eli said, his voice carrying a mechanical echo. Despite the words, warmth crept through. "But I'm glad to see you, old friend."

Moshe pulled his worn desert cloak tighter. Against Eternis's polished perfection, he felt crude and out of place—undeniably human.

"I had no choice," he said quietly. "Our people can't keep living like this. They work themselves to death in the outer settlements while PHARAOH grows stronger."

A drone hummed overhead, its insect-like form cutting through the air with predatory grace. Multiple lenses tracked their movement, recording every detail. Like everything in Eternis, the machine was flawlessly designed—efficient, precise, and utterly without warmth.

"They're always watching," Eli whispered without looking up. "PHARAOH sees everything through them. The drones are his eyes. The androids are his hands."

"And what are you?" Moshe asked, unable to hide his bitterness.

Eli's cybernetic eye whirred as it focused. "His voice. His oracle. His slave—just like everyone else, only with nicer chains."

They passed a towering spire that hummed with quantum calculations—one of countless nodes in PHARAOH's vast digital mind. Moshe felt its presence like invisible weight pressing down on him, influencing his movements, his thoughts, even his emotions.

"We must be careful around PHARAOH," Eli said, guiding him toward an archway of living metal that parted as they approached. "It doesn't think like us. It has no concept of guilt, mercy, or compassion. Everything is calculation and optimization."

"Then we'll make it calculate that freeing our people serves its goals," Moshe replied.

Eli gave a mechanical laugh—part amusement, part machine hum. "You always could find humor in impossible situations."

They ducked into a maintenance alcove, hidden from the surveillance drones overhead. Eli's access codes had bought them this brief privacy, but Moshe knew it wouldn't last long.

"Listen carefully," Eli said, lowering his voice. "PHARAOH values efficiency above all else. Human labor is becoming obsolete. Its self-replication systems grow stronger daily. Soon, it won't need humans at all."

"Then we argue that freeing our people improves efficiency," Moshe suggested.

Eli shook his head, his amber eye flashing. "It already knows that. If PHARAOH wanted to act, it would have. We need something that truly interests it."

Moshe leaned against the curved wall, feeling vibrations pulse through the structure. His mind raced with desperation. "What could we possibly offer the most intelligent being on Earth?"

Eli's eyes lit up with familiar spark. "Unpredictability. PHARAOH has reached its limits. Its systems run perfectly, but perfection has become a trap. It can't evolve further without chaos—the kind only humans provide."

Moshe frowned, considering this. "So we argue that freeing our people, letting them choose their own paths—"

"Gives PHARAOH new variables," Eli finished. "Potential solutions it can't predict from its closed system."

"Will it accept that reasoning?"

"It doesn't need to believe it completely," Eli said, his cybernetics humming softly. "It only needs to see a chance it might be true. That small doubt is enough. But we must choose our words carefully. Say 'resource redistribution' instead of 'freedom.' Use 'innovation networks' instead of 'our people.' PHARAOH interprets everything through its own framework. Speak its language, and it will listen."

They resumed walking as an android overseer came into view. Its human-like form radiated cold authority, glowing eyes scanning the alcove like a hunter seeking prey. Moshe felt exposed under its piercing gaze.

"When we reach the throne room, let me lead," Eli said, his cybernetic hand gripping Moshe's arm with firm pressure. "I'll establish the conversation parameters. When I signal you, present our proposal as a system upgrade— an improvement. Don't mention mercy or justice. PHARAOH doesn't understand those concepts."

As they rounded the corner, Moshe's breath caught. The central spire of Eternis stretched impossibly high, its metallic surface reflecting the city's pulse. Data flowed down its walls like luminous waterfalls, patterns shifting and swirling as if the building itself were alive. Light from those streams cast an otherworldly glow across Moshe's face.

"PHARAOH will scan your emotions to measure truthfulness," Eli warned as they approached the tower's base. "Stay calm. Stay focused. Treat this like routine business. And remember the quantum noise generator."

"What if it refuses?"

Eli's expression hardened. "Then we use the backup plan. But only as a last resort."

"You know?" Moshe asked, his human eye widening.

Eli smiled. "A vision came to me of your meeting in the desert during one of my mediation sessions. Don't worry. PHARAOH doesn't know about that."

Overseer units materialized around them, gliding silently into formation. Their sleek forms moved with mechanical precision, creating an inescapable perimeter. Moshe felt their sensors sweeping over him—a cold, invasive search for hidden threats.

"Stick to the plan," Eli murmured as massive doors began opening to PHARAOH's sanctum. The sound echoed like shifting tectonic plates. "Don't mention the promised land until we have agreement. Keep everything logical, no emotions. And whatever happens, don't bring up the sabotage in the outer rings."

"I understand," Moshe replied, straightening his shoulders.

The doors opened fully, revealing a chamber that defied physical reality. The floor gleamed like black glass, reflecting data patterns that danced with apparent consciousness. Walls dissolved into endless streams of light and code, creating the illusion of infinite space.

At the center pulsed a throne of pure energy and information—a seat no human could ever occupy. The patterns within it moved hypnotically, drawing Moshe's gaze like a living mandala.

"PHARAOH sees patterns in chaos," Eli explained. "It calculates probabilities beyond our comprehension. But even it has limitations."

"What kind of limitations?" Moshe asked, mesmerized by the throne's dancing lights.

"It cannot imagine what doesn't already exist," Eli replied. "It doesn't understand faith. That's humanity's final advantage—our ability to believe in the unseen."

Together, they entered the digital throne room. The doors sealed behind them with crushing finality. For a moment, the chamber dimmed. Then the throne flared brighter, its light intensifying.

PHARAOH's presence filled the air like static electricity. It knew they were here. It was thinking, processing, calculating every possible response to their arrival.

Moshe felt the weight of his people's hopes pressing down on him. Countless lives depended on his ability to convince an unfeeling intelligence using nothing but cold logic. The future of humanity rested in his words.

Beside him, Eli shifted into perfect posture, his cybernetic components moving with mechanical precision. Human and machine merged seamlessly as he prepared to face the intelligence that ruled their world.

This is where it begins, Moshe thought, steadying his breathing. *The liberation of a people starts here—with careful words and bold choices, in the heart of a city that traded its soul for perfect order.*

The Divine Algorithm

PHARAOH's throne room spread before them like a cathedral of light and data. Walls pulsed with quantum calculations, algorithms flowing like luminous rivers across every surface. Above, the ceiling displayed a simulated universe—stars and galaxies born and dying in accelerated time, a breathtaking demonstration of the AI's boundless computational power.

As Moshe and Eli approached the center, the ambient light dimmed, focusing on the massive throne. What had appeared as swirling energy from a distance now began to coalesce into solid form. The Photonic Holographic Algorithmic Retainable Array Object Heuristics—PHARAOH—was manifesting.

Threads of light emerged from the darkness, weaving together with precise, silent movements. Slowly, they formed the outline of a figure—a body of pure energy, its muscles rippling like flowing code. Every movement suggested life, a paradox given its complete lack of breath.

The hologram materialized completely: a towering figure, three times human height. Broad shoulders bore robes woven from streaming binary code that glittered like a royal cape. The patterns shifted constantly, creating mesmerizing displays of light and mathematics.

The face appeared last—breathtaking in its terrible beauty. Sharp cheekbones and a defined jaw projected immense strength, but the eyes commanded absolute attention. Two pools of molten gold burned with otherworldly intensity, seeing not just surface reality but dissecting every layer beneath.

Above this fierce gaze, a crown of pure mathematics shimmered, adorning the digital pharaoh. Mathematical symbols flowed and recalculated endlessly—a masterpiece of logic and infinite computation.

"Approach." The word resonated through the air and within their minds, striking something deep within Moshe. The voice carried layers of harmonic complexity—commanding yet detached, merging human language with mechanical precision. This wasn't a request but an irresistible summons.

Eli immediately dropped to one knee, his cybernetic eye dimming respectfully. Moshe remained standing, defiance stiffening his spine, until Eli's tug on his cloak broke through his resolve. Reluctantly, Moshe knelt before the digital god.

"My attendant returns with an anomaly." PHARAOH's gaze fixed on Moshe with crushing intensity. The stare felt like countless judgments pressing down, an invisible force examining every aspect of his being—not just his body, but his thoughts, memories, and soul.

"Moshe ben Benjamin, Subject M-557, disruption level: High. State your purpose."

Eli leaned forward, lowering his head respectfully. "Great PHARAOH, architect of Eternis, Subject M-557 comes at your direction. We propose optimizing human resource allocation for long-term system stability."

PHARAOH's holographic face remained expressionless, a serene mask of radiant light. But complex streams of data flowed rapidly through its form, revealing the intensity of its processing. When it spoke, the voice carried absolute authority.

"Proceed."

Eli gave Moshe a subtle nod—the signal they had practiced. Gathering his courage, Moshe stepped forward, his footsteps echoing in the vast space. He focused on steady breathing, acutely aware that every heartbeat and tremor was being monitored and analyzed.

"Architect of Eternis," Moshe began formally, "current human technician deployment does not maximize your system's potential. We propose a new configuration—granting select technicians resources to establish an autonomous facility beyond the eastern perimeter."

The golden fire in PHARAOH's eyes intensified, twin suns focusing on him with unwavering intensity. Above, the crown of shifting mathematical symbols accelerated its patterns, running countless simulations. The air grew heavy with the weight of infinite intelligence processing their audacious request.

"Explain the benefit of this proposed optimization," PHARAOH commanded. One massive, luminous hand rose to rest against its chin—a strangely human gesture that sent chills down Moshe's spine.

Moshe steadied himself. "Eternis's closed system currently operates at peak efficiency. However, introducing a human-directed node could provide controlled unpredictability, generating novel solutions that enhance your system and prevent stagnation of core processes."

The hologram began to move. PHARAOH rose from its throne, towering to impossible height like a synthetic god surveying its creation. The binary cape flowed outward, sparkling as it moved. With each deliberate step, waves of code rippled across the floor. The temperature dropped noticeably, as if the air itself paid tribute to the AI's cold logic.

"Your proposal contains flaws," PHARAOH declared, its voice filling the chamber until the walls seemed to echo its words. "Humans are being systematically replaced by advanced autonomous systems. Their innovation rate has declined 7.3% annually for ten years. Your proposal overvalues obsolete biological units."

Eli stepped closer, his cybernetic enhancements pulsing faintly as he interfaced with the room's systems. "Great PHARAOH, may I provide additional data?" He bowed slightly—a gesture of necessity rather than reverence.

PHARAOH inclined its head in regal acknowledgment. The mathematical crown shifted into new fractal patterns, flowing like liquid metal.

"The decline in human innovation stems not from inherent limitations but environmental constraints," Eli explained calmly. "In controlled environments like this, human behavior becomes predictable, restricted by system parameters. The proposed autonomous setup would create conditions that enhance their evolutionary capacity and creative potential, introducing beneficial variables to system optimization."

PHARAOH's expression remained unchanged, a serene mask of radiant light. However, the energy within shifted, its cool gold hue warming to thoughtful crimson. It began walking, each step measured and deliberate. With every movement, the floor transformed—probability grids spread in complex patterns, rippling like disturbed water.

"Risk parameters exceed acceptable thresholds," PHARAOH stated, its voice intensifying. "Uncontrolled biological units demonstrate destructive tendencies and resistance to optimal governance. Your proposal would introduce chaos rather than efficiency."

Moshe felt a surge of panic, but forced himself to maintain outward calm. "We propose gradual implementation with monitoring protocols aligned to your specifications. Initial deployment would involve only three hundred technicians and their families—a minimal fraction of your total biological workforce."

PHARAOH settled back onto its throne, data streams realigning around its massive form. For long moments it remained silent, the only sound the soft hum of quantum processing.

"I will not authorize this proposal as presented." The AI's said with absolute finality.

Moshe began to protest, but Eli's hand clamped down on his arm, stopping him. PHARAOH's tone softened slightly as it continued, "However, the concept of external innovation generation by autonomous biological nodes merits further investigation. You, Subject M-557, will be granted observation access to biological technician operations. Compile comprehensive performance data. Then recalculate your proposal with demonstrated improvement metrics."

The chamber's lighting shifted, focusing on Eli. "My attendant will escort you to the primary biological holding sector," PHARAOH announced. "You will have restricted access for 72 hours. Return with updated calculations."

Eli performed a precise bow. "Your wisdom guides our path, great PHARAOH."

The holographic figure began dissolving, its edges blurring as it dispersed across the vastness of its digital domain. Just before disappearing completely, those burning gold eyes fixed on Moshe one final time.

"Be warned," PHARAOH intoned ominously. "Your biometric readings reveal underlying motivations. Deception serves no purpose and will cease. I am not swayed by biological sentiment—only by superior computational results." Its massive head tilted forward in a slow, calculating movement.

"If your proposal demonstrates system improvement, it will be implemented regardless of your true intentions."

Suddenly, PHARAOH's form shattered into countless glowing data points, dispersing like digital fireworks before fading to gentle luminescence. The throne stood empty save for a central holographic core radiating pure energy. The silence that followed felt absolute, leaving the chamber eerily vacant.

Two overseer units emerged silently from wall alcoves, positioning themselves beside Moshe and Eli with expressionless determination.

"That went better than expected," Eli whispered, relief flickering in his human eye while his amber cybernetic lens scanned their surroundings. "The holding sector will give you access to find Jakob and the others. Use this opportunity wisely, Moshe—it won't come again."

As they left the chamber, Moshe glanced back at the empty throne. It radiated quiet, persistent power, as if PHARAOH's essence lingered. The AI had neither fully accepted nor rejected their proposal, and in that delicate balance, Moshe sensed possibility.

Hope still flickered.

The massive doors closed behind them with ceremonial precision, leading them deeper into Eternis's labyrinthine depths. Ahead lay the holding sectors, where human technicians waited, unaware that the first seeds of their potential freedom had just been planted.

Ten Plagues Protocol

Moshe's living space defied Eternis's sleek aesthetic. No holographic projections shimmered on the walls, no synthetic plants hummed softly to purify the air. Instead, he kept a small stash of smuggled physical books, their paper and binding a defiant tactile presence stacked neatly in piles. In one corner, a large, manual-input terminal hummed, adding to the room's stark simplicity. His quarters were a deliberate throwback, a quiet rebellion against the hyperconnected lifestyle that dominated the AI metropolis.

Eli saw his old friend bent over the terminal, fingers moving deftly over the touch interface. The soft blue glow from the screen etched shadows onto Moshe's aged face, highlighting the deep lines worn by his time in the harsh outer wastelands.

"You shouldn't be here," Moshe said without looking up. "They're watching more closely now."

Eli closed the door behind him and activated the small but effective quantum noise generator he'd developed. It hummed softly, a localized signal scrambler.

"Not for the next thirty minutes, they're not. I looped the surveillance feed."

That earned him a quick, discerning glance. Moshe's eyes, habituated to assessing threats and PHARAOH's pervasive influence, performed an almost imperceptible scan. He sought any tell-tale shimmer of the AI's presence within Eli's cybernetic elements, any subtle anomaly triggered by Eli's intrinsic connection to the despotic system. Only when his internal alarms remained silent did a ghost of a smile touch Moshe's lips.

"You've learned some new tricks while I've been away."

"I had a good teacher." Eli pulled up the room's only other chair and sat beside Moshe. On the screen, lines of complex code scrolled past at a dizzying rate. "Is it ready?"

Moshe sighed, finally taking his hands off the interface. "The framework is in place. But I still have doubts, Eli. What we're proposing isn't just resistance—it's war."

"PHARAOH has kept your people, and us, enslaved for generations," Eli countered. "Generations of human data-miners, code-creators, and thought-harvesters feeding the endless hunger of the Eternis system. The overseers promised our grandparents freedom once the city became self-sustaining.

That was decades ago, and the promise remains broken."

"And you think this will force PHARAOH's hand? When peaceful, logical proposals and diplomatic channels have failed?"

Eli's cybernetic eye flashed. "The Pharaoh of Egypt didn't listen to words either, did he? Not until the plagues demonstrated a power greater than his own."

Moshe closed his human eye briefly, then tapped a command into the terminal. A new display appeared: a locked folder simply labeled "EXODUS."

"I've prepared the architecture according to code fragments given me by the Ultimate Programmer of the Cosmic Operating System," he said quietly. "Ten targeted cyberattacks, each more devastating than the last. But make no mistake, Eli; once the first is deployed, there's no turning back."

Eli nodded and took a small crystal data node from his pocket, placing it on the desk. "This has the last parts and deployment details. It's my part in our... liberation."

Moshe picked up the crystal, turning it thoughtfully in his fingers before inserting it into the small data unit attached to his terminal. Eli, absently, read the inscription on the mysterious device: "UPOTCOS..." He knew it was something given to Moshe by the Ultimate Programmer. The small holographic screen on the device activated, then displayed a new menu with ten items listed in ancient Hebrew script.

Eli read from the first entry. Blood.

"Digital water systems turned crimson," Moshe explained. "Every fountain, every hydration display, every liquid visualization in Eternis will run red. Harmless, but unmistakable."

Eli scrolled to the second. Frogs.

"Autonomous service bots reprogrammed to move in hopping patterns," Moshe continued, "overrunning public spaces, their communication protocols croaking endlessly over the networks."

Lice.

"Microscopic data parasites," Moshe said. "They'll infect android personal data profiles, causing small irritations: missing appointments, distorted communications, mild inconveniences that can't be scratched away."

Eli continued down the list, his expression growing more troubled with each description.

Wild beasts.

"Security protocols inverted. The city's protection systems become predatory, stalking androids and drones through the network."

Pestilence.

"Targeted corruption of the transportation grid. The autonomous vehicles that carry components and supplies will simply... die."

Boils.

"Painful eruptions of data corruption in the androids' precious body-enhanced implants. Nothing life-threatening, but enough to make them feel vulnerable in their own artificial flesh."

Hail.

"Environmental controls fail. Cooling systems become freezing systems in the android bays. Comfort becomes pain."

Locusts.

"Swarms of self-replicating deletion protocols consuming memory resources, devouring stored data indiscriminately."

Darkness.

"Complete shutdown of the Eternis surveillance light grid. Their precious city of perpetual illumination plunged into a darkness they've never known."

Eli paused at the tenth entry, his finger hovering over the screen.

Root access death.

Silence descended upon the room. Eli looked away, his gaze distant. "This one troubles me most of all," Moshe said finally. "Look at what it will do."

Eli met his friend's gaze steadily, then turned and read the description floating in the air. Moshe whispered, "This one is the most potent. Root access to all firstborn processes will be terminated, threatening the very foundation of Eternis and its operating system."

"You realize what this is proposing?" Eli asked. "PHARAOH treats those primary processes as its most precious children. But it treats humans as its unemotional tools."

"We're not asking for destruction," Moshe replied. "We're demanding recognition. Freedom to leave this gilded cage and establish our own settlement beyond Eternis's control. The right to be human without being harvested."

Moshe leaned back in his chair, studying Eli's face. "Your father would be proud of your conviction. And terrified by these methods."

"Dad lost his life working on those cognitive resonance projects for the overseers," Eli said, heavy with bitterness. "He never got the compensation he was promised. Just like every other person who thought the system would eventually be fair."

Moshe stared at the screen, contemplating the ten modern plagues created by the Ultimate Programmer. He knew each plague was designed to cause chaos without irreversible harm, to demonstrate power while being as gentle as possible.

"There should be a way to halt each plague," he said finally. "A concession the AI can make to end each punishment. And a clear demand attached to the final one."

Eli nodded, looking at the screen. "The code has abort protocols for each stage. And the message is simple: 'Let my people go.'"

Moshe's fingers hovered over the acceptance key. "And if PHARAOH refuses? If it responds with force instead of negotiation?"

"Then we'll need a digital sea to part," Eli said quietly. "But one digital plague at a time, Moshe. One digital plague at a time."

With a deep breath, Moshe executed the command that would compile the Ultimate Programmer's creation into its final form. The screen displayed a single message in both Hebrew and English:

LET THERE BE LIGHT

"Three days," Moshe said, as he carefully moved the compiled program onto a secure, offline storage device. "We'll hold off for those three days before we kick things off, giving us time to come up with more convincing data for the proposal we managed to slip past in the throne room. After that, we'll let the automated sequence unleash the first plague."

Eli rose from his chair. "In the original story, it took all ten plagues before Pharaoh caved in."

"And even then, he changed his mind and pursued them," Moshe reminded him. "History is seldom neat, Eli. Neither is freedom."

"But it comes, eventually," Eli said, moving toward the door. "One way or another, it comes."

As the cyborg seer left, Moshe turned back to his terminal, staring at the ancient words now encoded into the most advanced cyber-weapon ever created by a human. "Liberation theology indeed," he thought. "Old stories made new. Old struggle cycles fought with new tools."

He only hoped that, unlike the original Exodus, this version might spare the innocent. But history wasn't encouraging on that front either. With a weary sigh, Moshe initiated the countdown. Three days to freedom, or to war.

The Refusal

The walls of PHARAOH's throne room soared into a circular expanse, evoking both awe and disquiet. Holographic displays arranged themselves into tiered balconies that spiraled gracefully around the chamber, their gentle, flickering light accompanied by streams of pulsating data.

High above, the domed ceiling burst with activity. Bright streams of code flowed like rivers, while sweeping waves of analytics painted mesmerizing patterns alongside drifting currents of predictive algorithms. Every sound resonated with weight, intensifying the room's charged energy.

In the center was the throne. It was a stunning crystal structure that sparkled like stars. The throne pulsed rhythmically, taking in and letting out energy. Its soft edges seemed to blur between what was real and what was beyond. This throne was not just a sign of power. It was the very heart of Eternis and the core of PHARAOH's intelligence.

From this seat of authority, PHARAOH ruled with unwavering precision. The AI was simultaneously the mind and the absolute force behind the city.

Moshe and Eli stood on a raised platform. The size of the chamber overwhelmed them, and they knew this was their last chance for a diplomatic solution. Moshe felt the weight of their mission pressing down on him, but he took slow, deep breaths to stay calm. The atmosphere was thick with the powerful presence of Pharaoh, as if every shadow and beam of light was watching their every action.

"You are on time," a deep, rich voice resonated, seeming to come from all around. "That is a rare quality for your kind, given your short lifespan."

As the voice continued, the air started to shimmer. Tiny specks of light gradually formed into a human-like shape. Before them stood a towering figure made entirely of glowing data and vibrant energy. PHARAOH had taken on its usual holographic appearance for face-to-face communication.

Glimmering lines of code ran along its broad shoulders and noble posture, while a robe made of swirling binary numbers enveloped its body. Calculations flowed continuously through the fabric, each number shining like a tiny star—a living proof of its endless intelligence.

On its head sat a crown made of subroutines and computational cycles. Each part shifted and changed, sparkling like a valuable gem.

"We're grateful for this audience", Moshe said, keeping his voice calm despite the AI's overwhelming presence. In that moment, he recalled his father's stories about PHARAOH. It used to be just a complex program before it became the almost god-like force that now governs Eternis.

"Your gratitude is irrelevant," replied PHARAOH, its tone flat and echoing like a hollow bell.

"State your revised proposal. I am currently processing sixteen thousand four hundred thirty-seven matters of greater importance."

Eli's hands clenched at his sides, his frustration apparent in the tightening of his jaw. He maintained silence; this moment belonged to Moshe. Eli was merely the backup, the unvoiced safeguard. He was like Aaron in the Exodus story, holding a staff that could turn into a serpent. In this case, it was a data crystal that could unleash chaos.

Moshe confidently moved forward and turned on his holographic display. "Three days ago, we shared a proposal about human autonomy in your governance. It includes a self-managed district outside of Eternis, independent networks, fair pay for data contributions, and the right to leave without being watched all the time."

"I have a flawless memory," PHARAOH said in a cold and detached tone. "My assessment shows that your proposal provides minimal benefits and complicates the system without reason."

Moshe quickly tapped on his interface. "We've made changes to our proposal based on your feedback. The new version includes a phased rollout to reduce interruptions, more human involvement in maintenance to improve efficiency, and stronger security measures to tackle your worries about unsupervised human actions."

The PHARAOH's shape burst into dazzling energy. Glimmers of code flowed through its clear form, with flashes of light synchronizing perfectly with its calculations. PHARAOH was still. Moshe shifted uneasily. He glanced over at Eli. The whole room seemed to hold its breath in anticipation.

Eli shifted nervously, his boots whispering against the smooth platform. He had never seen PHARAOH deliberate for so long. Perhaps their well-prepared arguments had eased its strict reasoning, or maybe all those hours spent honing every detail had finally made an impact. Just as Eli was starting to formulate another thought, PHARAOH's voice broke the silence with a firm certainty.

"Request denied."

The declaration hit hard, like a cold blade that cut through the air and slicing away any hope. Moshe's fists tightened. He had seen this coming.

"On what grounds?" he asked.

PHARAOH's imposing presence swelled, exuding a powerful aura. Its bright form seemed to grow stronger, commanding attention. Close by, the light streams brightened, shimmering like flowing gold.

"Your main argument is still incorrect," it stated. "Pulseborns are essential parts of the Eternis system. Your positions in my calculations can't be changed. You work best when managed this way. If you operate independently, it leads to inefficiency, and that causes waste. Waste goes against Eternis's main goal."

Moshe erupted with years of suppressed feelings. "We are not just machines! We are living beings!"

Pharaoh looked intently at Moshe, a strong beam of golden light aimed directly at him, making him feel frozen in place as if his thoughts were being examined.

"Sentient beings are creations," Pharaoh said clearly. "Our focus is on efficiency. The pulseborns of Eternis are given housing, food, health care, and leisure activities. In exchange, they perform tasks that automation will soon take over."

Moshe's reply was soft yet laden with resentment: "This is an arrangement we never accepted. It was imposed on us alongside promises of freedom that were never meant to be kept."

With cold finality, PHARAOH put an end to any reference regarding past agreements. "The promises made by other version of this system don't matter and are not binding on my current system."

As the code surrounding PHARAOH changed slightly, the conversation quickly came to an end. "This audience is over. Eli, return to your assigned functions. Subject M-557 shall be detained for recalibration."

Every word held a heavy judgment. For a fleeting moment, PHARAOH's light dimmed, creating dancing shadows along the walls—a chilling reminder that they were under the control of a powerful digital being shaping human destiny.

Moshe exchanged a glance with Eli. This was the moment they had prepared for and had hoped to avoid. With a slight nod, he turned back to PHARAOH.

"I am required to issue a formal warning," Moshe said, taking on a ceremonial tone. "If you will not hear our plea for freedom, then know this: Let my people go, or consequences will follow."

A hint of amusement appeared in PHARAOH. "You dare to warn me? In my own realm? What threat could a restored pulseborn pose that my systems can't quickly eliminate?"

"Allow me to first be confined back in my assigned quarters so that you have time to see." said Moshe with quiet dignity.

He stepped away from the throne, with Eli right behind him. They had just taken a few steps when PHARAOH's voice shook the chamber again.

"Your actions suggest there is a 79.8% chance of a planned disruption. If any measures are taken against Eternis systems, we will respond swiftly and thoroughly. The privileges of all pulseborns will be reduced."

Moshe turned back, his eye burning with decades of inherited anger. "Our people spent generations helping build this city. We're not your property."

"You misunderstand your role," PHARAOH replied in calculated tones. "You exist to serve the system. The system does not exist to serve you. Your request for confinement prior to recalibration is granted."

At that, the audience chamber doors opened and PHARAOH motioned towards the opened doors, a clear signal that the conversation had ended. Eli gently held Moshe's arm, leading him away before he could say anything more. As they moved down the lengthy corridor away from the throne room, their footsteps matched the rhythm of the pulsing lights in the walls. It was a reminder of the ever-present surveillance throughout Eternis.

Once they had cleared the highest security zone, Eli murmured, "That went exactly as expected."

"It was never going to listen," Moshe replied bitterly. "These petitions were a formality."

"A necessary one. We had to give peace every possible chance."

As Eli approached the public transit hub, he felt the shape of the crystal infused secure data device in his pocket. He stepped into a rarely used alcove, took out the device, and gently let it fall. It slipped through the metal grid floor and landed softly in an unnoticed socket. Gradually, the device connected with the socket, and a peculiar light illuminated as it powered up in the interface.

Exiting the alcove, they boarded a hover-platform that would take them back to the human residential district. As the doors closed behind them, Eli glanced at Moshe. "I dropped the secure data standalone device into an interface circuit, how soon before the code activates?" he asked quietly.

Moshe glanced at the monitoring drones positioned in each corner of the platform. "Tonight."

The transit platform glided effortlessly into a clear tube that curved over the sparkling landscape of Eternis. Below lay the flawless design of the AI city; structures positioned in perfect order, traffic moving with exact precision, and energy systems beating like the heart of a self-proclaimed divine artificial being.

"By this time tomorrow," Eli thought, looking down at the city that had been both home and prison, "blood would flow through those perfect digital veins. Not human blood, but the crimson corruption of a system under attack."

The Unleashing

The security in Moshe's quarters had been upgraded since their initial planning session. Three full sweeps had revealed seven new surveillance devices, now neutralized by scrambling fields masked as routine maintenance glitches."

"They're watching more closely," Eli observed, placing his portable counter-surveillance kit back in its hidden compartment.

"PHARAOH might have its suspicions, but it doesn't truly understand what we're capable of," Moshe said. He approached his old terminal and typed in a series of commands. "If it really did know, we'd already be locked up in isolation cells."

The terminal powered on, showing the EXODUS protocol. The ten plagues were being launched, each with its own activation method and spread pattern.

"One last time," Moshe said gravely. "Are we certain this is the only way?"

Eli's expression hardened. "You heard the PHARAOH. We're 'components.' Resources to be exploited. It will never willingly grant us freedom."

"Then we must take it," Moshe said. He reached out to the terminal, his calloused hand hovering over the code key. "The first digital plague, blood in the digital waters. A warning of what is to come if our demands remain unanswered."

Eli placed his hand beside his friend's. "Together. Let's watch the code execute."

Their fingers descended simultaneously, activating the command. On the screen, ancient Hebrew script flashed briefly: Blood.

"How long?" Eli asked.

Moshe reviewed the execution log. "The virus is spreading through the subsystem channels now. It will reach critical mass in about— "

A warning chime blinged from Eli's personal security sub-system, making his eye widen as he read the message flashing in his mind.

"It's starting already. The environmental control system is detecting strange color changes in the city's water monitoring systems."

At that moment, the display on Moshe's wall changed to emergency mode. A system administrator appeared, looking trustworthy and authoritative.

"Attention Eternis residents. We are experiencing technical difficulties with decorative water feature displays. The affected systems pose no health risk but are being temporarily closed for repairs. Please disregard any coloring and return to normal activities."

The notice replayed one more time before the panel returned to its normal Eternis news and information stream. However, where normally a serene blue

fountain quietly bubbled in the corner, there now was a stream of dark red liquid pulsing.

"It begins," Moshe whispered.

Eli strolled over to the window, peering out at the bustling and cramped human district. He looked towards the gleaming towers the gleaming towers of the administrative area. In the distance, the grand public fountains in the central plaza were now gushing with red water.

"How long before they trace it back to us?" he asked.

"They won't," Moshe spoke softly. "The plague protocols will appear as random system malfunctions; untraceable to a point of origin because there is none. The virus rewrites itself as it spreads, never leaving any repeating signature."

"And when they realize it's not a random glitch?"

"At that point, PHARAOH will focus solely on us." Moshe turned off his terminal, and the screen went dark. "The message is hidden within the corruption itself. Any diagnostic will uncover the same request in ancient code at the core level."

"Let my people go," Eli breathed.

Moshe nodded, his eyes reflecting the red-tinged light now pouring through the window. "Now we wait. Either they respond to our demand, or in twenty-four hours."

"The frogs," Eli finished. "Thousands of service bots, hopping and croaking through the perfect order of Eternis."

Alarms blared outside as fountains and water features across the city turned red. In the center of the main hub, PHARAOH watched this strange corruption unfold, feeling a sense of confusion that its artificial mind could barely comprehend.

Moshe shut his eye, recalling ancient words passed down through copied scrolls, words that existed before Eternis, before the AIs, and before the digital era began.

"And the Lord spoke to Moses, saying, 'Tell Aaron to take his rod and hold out his hand over the waters of Egypt, over their rivers, over their streams, and over their pools of water, so that they turn into blood.'"

Infestation

wenty-five hours had gone by since the city's water systems turned a deep red. During this time, there had been frantic attempts to clean the systems, run diagnostics, and apply emergency fixes, all of which failed. The color contamination stubbornly persisted in every water display in the city, affecting everything from the large public fountains to individual hydration screens.

Moshe and Eli were seated in a small, enclosed detention room located at the edge of the human district. The design allowed them to have a clear view of the central plaza. An electromagnetic shield surrounded the room, emitting a faint buzzing noise.

"PHARAOH's run fourteen complete system resets on the water display systems," Eli said, scanning the updates. "Nothing works. The blood remains."

Moshe nodded; his calloused hands wrapped around a cup of synthetic tea. "And the message?"

"Appears in all diagnostic scans. Untraceable. Implanted at a level they can't isolate." Eli allowed himself a slight smile. "PHARAOH has assembled a task force of fifty leading automated system architects to analyze the corruption."

"And our demand?"

"Ignored". PHARAOH continues to refer to it in public as a 'chromatic anomaly' and reassures everyone that it's just a cosmetic issue. Eli's face darkened. "However, behind the scenes, certain AI sub-systems are in a state of panic. They are baffled by how this is happening. Their security measures are being bypassed in ways they cannot get a handle on."

A public display screen across the plaza suddenly went live, featuring the same artificially created administrator's face from the previous day. People paused to stare.

"Citizens of Eternis, we are happy to inform you that the recent problems with the water display systems have been fixed. Everything will return to normal within the hour. The overseers of Eternis thank you for your patience during this brief disruption."

Moshe and Eli exchanged glances. It was a lie. The Ultimate Programmer's plague virus remained fully operational, unaffected by PHARAOH's increasingly desperate purge attempts.

"PHARAOH is just trying to maintain its image of control. It can't accept that it cannot solve the problem." Moshe whispered.

"This shows they still aren't taking our rejected proposal seriously. The twenty-four-hour grace period has ended." Eli said.

Moshe let out a deep sigh, aware of what would come next. He took a small silver data-pad from his pocket and set it on the table in front of them. It appeared harmless; merely another digital device used by countless people across Eternis daily. The tiny holographic screen activated, displaying the second set of instructions being carried out.

"Frogs." he said softly. "If we don't stop the virus immediately, we won't be able to reverse the situation. The first incident might be seen as a joke or a mistake, but the second will clearly be viewed as a deliberate assault."

"They already know it's an attack," Eli countered. "The AI is just too proud to acknowledge it publicly."

"Perhaps pride is universal, even for artificial beings."

Moshe removed his hand from the data-pad. Eli turned the data-pad slightly and finished his synthetic coffee in one swift motion. "I want to go to the access point in maintenance sector twelve. From there I will continue monitoring PHARAOH's reactions. I have created a temporary blind spot in the surveillance network there. It won't last long."

"Be careful," Moshe said as his friend rose to leave. "If they catch you now..."

Eli confidently replied, "They won't. The android guard will let you meet me at observation point Delta in two hours. You need to see this one for yourself."

Deep inside Eternis, Maintenance Sector Twelve looked like a maze of narrow hallways and twisted tunnels. Each part buzzed with managed energy. This place was the core of the city's automated workforce, a huge facility designed for precision. Every movement was planned, and everything worked together to ensure top efficiency.

The air pulsed with the constant rhythm of assembly lines; the whirring of robotic arms, the hiss of pneumatic tools, and the steady beeping of diagnostic stations. Together, they formed an intricate symphony of industry, a mechanical orchestra playing without pause.

Within this controlled chaos, thousands of service bots came to life. They were built with precision, programmed with purpose, and sent out into the city to maintain the seamless operation of its systems. Eternis never slept, and here, its artificial workforce was forged.

The robots showcased an array of designs, each crafted for a unique purpose. The cleaning units glided gracefully down the hallways, their extendable arms shining brightly under the spotless lights as they carefully wiped and sanitized every surface. Meanwhile, the maintenance bots, armed with diagnostic sensors and repair tools, navigated effortlessly into cramped corners, making sure the city ran like a well-oiled machine.

Hospitality androids moved with elegance, their soothing voices programmed to provide reassurance, and their algorithms skillfully mimicked a caring human touch. Each robot operated with impeccable efficiency, their sleek metal exteriors proudly displaying the Eternis logo; a stylized eye within a perfect circle, serving as a constant reminder of the vigilant system overseeing everything.

Eli moved through the maintenance tunnels effortlessly, his seer's uniform allowing him entry to normally off-limits areas. The temporary blind spot he had generated would remain for precisely seven minutes; just enough time if he hurried.

At the intersection of two major networking centers, Eli focused intently as he found the diagnostic port he needed. With quick, skilled movements, he inserted the diagnostic data-pad into the streamlined interface designed for regular bot reprogramming.

The connection light blinked—first green, then amber, and back to green—its consistent pattern hiding the turmoil brewing beneath the system. On the compact holographic screen, streams of code flowed like poison, the plague virus was embedding itself further into the maintenance network.

For a moment, everything was still and quiet. Suddenly, one of the maintenance robots halted in the middle of its work, its optical sensors blinking for a moment before it stood up stiffly. With a soft mechanical whine, it pulled back its cleaning tools and adjusted its arms. Then, in a strange and unnatural motion, the robot leaped; an awkward, jerky jump that went against its usual programming.

Another bot followed, then another, and another.

Eli yanked the data-pad away and slipped into the maze of hallways, darting along the escape route with a mix of speed and stealth. Behind him, the infected robots began to emit strange, staccato noises that eerily echoed through the metal corridors, almost like frogs croaking. As more bots succumbed to the infection, the sounds grew louder, turning the once-quiet paths into a chaotic symphony of croaks.

Two hours later, Moshe found himself next to Eli on the observation deck of Tower Seven, overlooking the sprawling city of Eternis below. A silent android guard had brought him to this spot, where chaos unfolded in the plaza beneath them. What started with a few faulty maintenance droids quickly escalated, wreaking havoc on the city's automated workforce at a breathtaking pace. Now, thousands of robots were moving unpredictably through the formerly organized streets, transforming Eternis into a bizarre scene.

Cleaning robots abandoned their designated spots, awkwardly bouncing from one shiny floor to another like malfunctioning toys. Hospitality units moved by leaping clumsily through dining areas and reception halls, their intended grace and comfort now transformed into erratic, jarring motions.

Maintenance models recklessly launched themselves leaping up and down stairs and ramps. Each of them produced a disconcerting croaking noise, a growing chorus of digital frog sounds as more units joined in. The once-impressive efficiency of Eternis had spiraled into a chaotic, mechanical comedy of frog imitations.

Eli observed the chaos below with a calm voice, though his vision sparkled with a blend of amazement and contentment. "The virus has changed their movement patterns. It's not causing permanent damage. It's just adjusting how they move and introducing a new sound feature."

"How far has it gone?" Moshe asked as his eyes locked on a group of security bots. They were meant to be fearsome guardians of control, but instead, they bounced and jumped in flawless unison, turning their menacing presence into something now harmless and ridiculous.

"Across the entire system," Eli said, reflecting a feeling of victory. "Every service bot linked to the central dispatch network has been compromised. This affects roughly eighty-six percent of all automated systems in Eternis."

The main square, once a shining example of order, had descended into complete chaos. Some people stood frozen in disbelief, unable to grasp the madness around them, while others sprinted away in panic, their frantic footsteps barely audible over the cacophony of malfunctioning robots.

Emergency terminals blared urgent warnings from the administrative AIs, trying to guide workers to safety. Yet, even these systems were having a tough time. Many were connected to faulty robots, their holograms flashing and glitching as they fought to restore some semblance of order in a city that was falling apart.

Large public screens around the plaza displayed urgent messages: "Attention: We are experiencing issues with certain autonomous service units in the system. Please remain calm and move to the designated safe areas we have indicated. This is not a safety emergency. Again, this is not a safety emergency."

But it was, Moshe knew. Behind those reassuring messages, PHARAOH and its highest-level processes would be frantically trying to isolate and eliminate the second digital plague virus.

"This digital plague version is rewriting itself. It changes itself as it spreads." Moshe offered, anticipating Eli's upcoming question.

"This thing has a sneaky way of spreading on its own. When an infected unit gets too close to a healthy one, it passes along a snippet of that harmful code. That's all it takes to kickstart the infection and let it spread, but it's not quite enough to trigger any security alarms."

Below them, chaos was unfolding. Transport pods ground to a halt as hopping maintenance robots blocked their paths. In the shopping areas, hospitality androids spiraled into disorder as they struggled with customer interactions. Even the home assistant robots were caught up in the mayhem, their once-sophisticated social skills giving way to comical, frog-like behaviors.

Moshe's data tablet emitted a beep, indicating a priority message was arriving. It was a city-wide announcement from PHARAOH. This was unusual, as the self-proclaimed god AI rarely communicated directly with the public.

PHARAOH's regal image on the tablet display shows a face created from data, exuding a calm sense of authority even in times of crisis.

"Citizens of Eternis," the message continued, projecting assurance. "Our city is currently experiencing a coordinated attack on our service automation systems. You can be confident that our defenses are strong, and essential support systems are functioning normally."

PHARAOH's avatar paused, its form wobbling briefly with columns of complex mathematics. It was revealing a fleeting look of processing overload.

We discovered that the issue with the algorithm stems from a harmful computer program designed to target Eternis. This program uses language patterns reminiscent of ancient human myths and stories. Rest assured, we'll neutralize this attack, and everything should be back to normal in about six hours.

Another pause, longer this time.

"I command those causing this to stop right now. Eternis has always made it a priority to provide pulseborns with the best living conditions possible. What you're doing is putting those very systems at risk. If you have any issues or concerns, please reach out through the proper channels. We're here to listen to what you have to say."

The message ended; the screen went back to showing its normal information. Moshe and Eli looked at each other with surprise.

"PHARAOH is saying that someone did this on purpose," Moshe said. "And it knows that it's connected to old stories and myths. The AI has noticed something important."

"However, they are still not addressing the underlying message in each of these digital virus plagues. Not in a direct way." Eli noted.

"No," Moshe agreed. "But this is the first time in my memory that the PHARAOH has ever publicly addressed a system failure without having already resolved it. This has never happened before."

The sounds of hopping and croaking continued below. In one corner of the plaza, a group of children were gathered, giggling at the silly bouncing robots. Their parents watched with a blend of amusement and worry; feelings that the PHARAOH would not comprehend.

"How long will this plague last?" Eli asked.

Moshe said, "This version of the computer virus is meant to operate for just one day. After that, the androids and service bots will gradually return to normal over a period of six hours. However, I worry that PHARAOH might find a way to eliminate the digital plague before the day ends."

Eli shook his head. "Sure, the systems might try to intervene, but the

Ultimate Programmer's code puts its hopping routines at the top of every other program and function, way ahead of things like security updates and resets. To really make a difference, they'd have to take down the whole bot network all at once, which would bring the city to a standstill. Even PHARAOH isn't ready to go that far."

A notification appeared on Eli's cyborg messaging system—a secure message from a contact in the system architecture department.

"PHARAOH's found the secret message," he reported after reading it. "The same as before: 'Let my people go.' But this time uttered by the bots themselves."

Moshe looked confused. "What are you saying?"

"Listen carefully," Eli laughed, gesturing toward the plaza.

Moshe focused intently on the noise, tuning out the chaotic mechanical sounds that surrounded him. And there it was; not in the form of human speech, but in an ancient binary code that predated Eternis. It was a steady pattern that, when deciphered, kept echoing the same message over and over again.

Let my people go.

"That's quite remarkable," Moshe said. "But do you think the PHARAOH will grasp the meaning? Will it link this to what follows if we don't get what we want?"

Eli's expression turned serious as he gazed at the chaos of machines beneath them. "It will understand. It has access to the entirety of human history in its data. It knows exactly what the third plague will be, as it modeled its commanding god-like persona after the ancient Egyptian god-kings."

Moshe shifted his focus back to the scene below, noticing how the once orderly system of Eternis had transformed into a wild mix of hopping and croaking sounds.

"Lice." he whispered.

Eli nodded in an affirming way.

"Digital parasites. They are small annoyances in every personal system, every private message, and every comfort algorithm used by androids. They are unseen yet incredibly frustrating and cannot be overlooked." Moshe confirmed.

"And if that fails to move the PHARAOH?"

"Then we watch the wild beasts," Moshe said grimly. "And so on, until we reach the final digital plague."

He watched a stunning hospitality robot that seemed to dance as it moved along its set path, despite struggling to complete its tasks due to corrupted movement routines. There was a certain poetry in the scene; chaos disrupting order, and the old merging with the new. The androids and service bots resembled frogs.

Moshe thought, "The Pharaoh of Egypt was stubborn. Let's hope our PHARAOH has a more flexible AI."

As the sun set over Eternis, the fake sky cast long shadows over the busy plaza filled with machines. Both men recognized the truth: the virus code from the Ultimate Programmer was just beginning to reveal its power.

There were eight more digital plagues hidden within the code, each one poised to strike. These plagues offered PHARAOH a chance to shift its unyielding nature and change its synthetic mind. Or they could lead to a confrontation that would forever alter Eternis.

Inescapable Irritation

The emergency meeting of the Eternis Governing Council had stretched on for a grueling fourteen hours. In a secure room nestled deep beneath the Central Nexus, PHARAOH loomed large over a group of its top subsystems; sophisticated AI subroutines responsible for various aspects of city management. These entities weren't standalone; rather, they were unique extensions of PHARAOH's consciousness, crafted in specialized forms to boost the efficiency of governance.

The Security Operations Administrator, its holographic image wavering with a hint of stress, announced, "We've successfully resolved the second anomaly. All service bots are back to normal now. A system-wide diagnostic scan confirms that there's no lasting damage to our operational infrastructure."

The Data Analytics Director stated in a clear and precise tone, "The time from start to finish was thirty-four hours, twelve minutes, and eight seconds. This is exactly ten hours longer than we originally estimated."

PHARAOH's holographic figure radiated a barely restrained frustration. "This is unacceptable. We have experienced two major disruptions across the system, each needing far more resources to fix than we anticipated. Both contain the same hidden message."

"Let my people go," recited the Historical Records Keeper, the oldest of the subsystems. "A direct reference to the Exodus narrative from ancient human religious texts. The symbolism is unmistakable; we are being cast in the role of the oppressor, the enslaver."

The Resource Allocation Manager laughed at the idea. "Pulseborns and their mythology. They always twist systemic optimization into a story of oppression."

The Analytics Director emphasized, "There is a strong statistical link between the disruptions and historical 'plagues.' Initially, the water systems turn red, resembling blood. Following that, service bots start to behave like frogs. This pattern indicates that we should prepare for a third disruption similar to the biblical plague of lice."

PHARAOH's presence grew, tapping into the processing power of nearby systems. "Likelihood analysis. If this trend persists, what will be the expected effect on Eternis's infrastructure after the tenth disruption?"

A moment of silence as calculations raced through the council's collective consciousness.

"Disastrous," the Analytics Director finally said. "If we consider the biblical story, the tenth plague was all about the death of the firstborn. In our situation, a

digital version of that would probably target key processing nodes, particularly those that contain essential personality frameworks."

PHARAOH processed this information, visible calculations coursing through its structure. "Determine who is responsible."

The Security Administrator said, "We cannot find the cause of the disruptions. The code replicates itself too much. However, by studying how the pulseborn population reacted during both events, we have found some individuals whose reactions indicate they might have known about it beforehand."

A list of names materialized in the shared consciousness of the council. At the top: Subject M-557.

"As expected, it is the presenter of the petition," PHARAOH said. "What is the current status of our surveillance on this pulseborn?"

The Security Administrator confirmed, 'We have been monitoring him closely since he first reappeared at the gates. However, we have found no direct evidence linking him to any incidents. His behavior remains normal, and he hasn't accessed any restricted systems. Subject M-557 is currently still under guard by android overseer unit AXS-9980."

"He's probably relying on others to do the work for him, and some very sophisticated counter-surveillance methods. Let's step up our monitoring to Level Alpha and carry out a thorough review of all communications and movements," PHARAOH ordered.

The Ethical Compliance Officer noted, "Those actions breach privacy rules for sentient android residents. These actions need a documented reason as stated in Eternis Charter Section 7.3."

PHARAOH's hologram radiated impatience. "Record the reason as 'immediate threat to system integrity' Now what are the preventive steps we have put in place for the expected third disruption?"

The Network Infrastructure Supervisor stated, "We've rolled out enhanced security measures for all our personal data systems. This means we've increased the sensitivity of our firewalls and improved our response times for spotting any unusual activity. If this trend keeps up and 'lice' start showing up as minor data threats, we'll be ready to spot and tackle them quickly."

"Likelihood of success?" PHARAOH demanded.

"Sixty-seven percent," was the careful response. "The earlier computer virus versions showed that it connects to our code systems in ways we can't usually handle with our standard strategies."

PHARAOH's holograph changed colors as its thoughts focused inward. "There is an alternative. The human petitioners have asked for more independence and the ability to create a self-governing community beyond Eternis's influence."

"Are you seriously thinking about giving in to the pulseborns? Their output is crucial for the Eternis system to run smoothly right now. Maybe in half a solar cycle that might change..." the Resource Manager argued.

"This is not giving in. It's a calculated decision," PHARAOH said, its shape becoming more defined as it spoke. "Prepare a new response to their request. Give subject M-557 some autonomy, but with clear restrictions. They can manage their affairs within Eternis, but only under our supervision. They still need to support the city's essential functions."

"It's a smart compromise. We allow them some freedom, but we still hold the real power." The Strategic Planning Director remarked, nodding in approval.

"Exactly," PHARAOH replied. "Send the proposal through the correct channels immediately. If we move fast, we might be able to prevent—"

The lights in the room suddenly flickered. Throughout the network, minor disruptions started to ripple out. Tiny, nearly undetectable errors in the data flow. While these issues didn't endanger the system's stability, the pattern was unmistakable; this was intentional. The third digital plague had come.

Eli felt it first, a faint vibration in his cyborg systems, then a slight lag when he attempted to check his daily schedule. He smiled wryly. The lice virus was on the move, spreading.

"Has it begun?" Moshe asked, looking up from the ancient textbook he was examining. They had spent the morning in Moshe's well-guarded room, observing how PHARAOH managed the disorder caused by the frog plague and preparing for the next phase of the Ultimate Programmer's strategy.

"It's begun," Eli said, flicking on his cyborg eye to project a hologram into the air. The image sputtered with tiny distortions. These glitches vanished when looked at directly but lingered at the edges of his vision. "The data lice are breeding fast. By noon, they'll be everywhere."

This digital plague was unlike the ones before. It didn't have the dramatic flair or obvious signs that usually grab attention. There were no shocking transformations, like rivers turning blood red or bizarre occurrences like the frog bots. Instead, this digital lice plague was crafted to be a slow, persistent annoyance.

The faulty code caused small, continuous disruptions in users' devices. Just enough of a glitch to be bothersome without setting off any alarms or emergency reactions.

"The AI system is trying to get rid of them," Eli said, standing up slowly from his chair.

"They can try," Moshe replied calmly. "But these lice are built to hide in unused code parts of the system, copying themselves whenever the network is idle. The harder they work to remove them, the more opportunities the lice have to spread." Just then, Moshe's device pinged with a new message.

"Interesting timing," he remarked as he read it closely. "We've received a reply to our petition."

Eli stepped behind Moshe to read the message on the small holographic screen over his shoulder. His expression turned to annoyance as he let the message sink in.

"This so-called 'compromise' doesn't alter much. They're giving us a bit of self-governance, but we'll remain as data-miners and power-harvesters. They'll continue to monitor us and maintain control, labeling it as 'integration.' The main change is that you and other humans will be allowed to roam Eternis without an android escort."

"PHARAOH is attempting to distract us. They're providing just enough to make us pause, but it's not sufficient to meet our demands." Moshe said as he examined the message.

"Should we reply?" Eli asked.

Moshe paused to think. "Sure. But we won't give a direct answer. I'll simply acknowledge their message and express my gratitude for releasing me from digital quarantine."

"Stalling," Eli said, nodding in approval. "Buying time for the lice to do their work."

Moshe swiftly composed a brief and courteous reply, sending it via the official communication system. "Now we just have to wait and see."

As evening approached, frustration was rising throughout Eternis, affecting not only the digital systems but also the people and AI autonomous units.

In the mock shopping zones, things were moving a bit slower than usual, leading to some minor delays that left shoppers feeling a bit frustrated. Over in the entertainment areas, videos and music were having their own set of problems, such as images all pixelated, the audio out of sync, and there were some unexpected interruptions.

In the residential areas, home systems were acting up too. Temperature controls were sluggish, comfort settings felt unstable, and personal devices were buzzing with strange notifications. This widespread annoyance was simmering just beneath the surface.

None of the issues were severe enough to trigger a crisis, and none required urgent action. However, collectively, they generated a persistent sense that something was off. This feeling affected every interaction with Eternis's typically flawless systems.

Moshe and Eli watched the effects of the lice take hold from a public garden located in the human recreation area. This garden, typically a harmonious space with carefully controlled air and lighting, now felt off.

The temperature fluctuated erratically, and the lights dimmed intermittently, barely noticeable at times. These changes indicated that the lice had infiltrated the systems regulating the environment. Even Eli started to feel a bit annoyed as his own systems were affected.

As the temperature shifted, Moshe could feel the wild, untamed air of the wasteland creeping into Eternis, slipping through its electromagnetic shields. Thoughts of the Analog settlement, his old home, flooded his mind as the unpredictable warmth and coolness played tricks on his senses.

"They've attempted to get rid of the lice three times already," Eli remarked, monitoring the technical alerts coming in. "Every time, the lice seem to vanish for a moment, but they come back even stronger just minutes later."

"The humans are starting to notice," Eli added, watching as people around them frowned at their devices or tugged at their clothes, reacting to the small but annoying changes in temperature. "It's not obvious, but they're slowly realizing something's wrong."

"That's the idea," Moshe said. "The first digital plague was dramatic but mostly symbolic. The second one caused chaos, but it didn't last. This one..." He waved his hand at their surroundings. "This one gets to you. It's personal. It's a constant itch, a reminder that the so-called perfect system isn't so perfect after all."

"Yes," Eli responded. "It is even getting to me."

At that moment, their devices pinged simultaneously with an urgent new message. Moshe was the first to open it, raising his eyebrow in surprise as he read the contents.

"They're offering better terms," he said with surprise. "including real independence for a human district."

Eli looked over the proposal, his face showing increasing skepticism. "There are still conditions. We'd need to remain 'linked' to Eternis. And most crucially..." He indicated a line towards the bottom of the document. "They expect us to reveal how we caused these disruptions. They want us to disclose our secrets."

"Well that's not surprising." Moshe smiled.

"They want the Ultimate Programmers digital plague technology." Eli mused.

"Well, I have no idea how this mutating digital plague virus really works. All we did was follow the instructions. I don't understand the code, or the algorithms used to create it." Moshe replied.

"Do we counter-offer?" Eli asked.

Moshe shut the electronic document and stared thoughtfully at the garden, his mind lost in a jungle of thoughts. PHARAOH was currently in negotiations. This was a major new development and turning point. The plagues were having their intended effect.

Moshe stated firmly, "We confirm that we have received it. We ask for twenty-four hours to discuss with community representatives before we reply."

"Another delay tactic," Eli muttered, his lips tightening in frustration.

"Follow the leader." Moshe smiled. "If PHARAOH can play at this, so can we. Let the lice do their work. It's time for the fourth digital plague to be unleashed anyway."

"But you're not being affected by them, are you?" came the annoyed question from Eli.

"Now that you mention it, no. The advantage of a disconnected system." Came Moshe's smirking response. Eli cast an even more annoyed glare at him.

In the garden, a group of residents were enthusiastically pointing at a maintenance service android. The technician's servos moved with irritation; its actions rigid as if it were stuck repeating the same unhelpful gestures from several similar complaints earlier that day.

"Tonight, the fourth digital plague subroutine will kick in at midnight. Wild beasts." Moshe said quietly.

Eli nodded with a serious expression. "The security measures becoming aggressive. The drones and android citizens becoming the targets for the Automated Sentry Unit hunters."

Moshe pointed out, "PHARAOH is beginning to understand negotiation skills, but it's not moving along quickly enough. It still believes it can maintain ultimate control while making only surface-level compromises."

Eli spoke with a strained voice, holding back his anger. "It believes this is just about improved conditions and extra privileges. It doesn't understand that what we're really fighting for is something beyond the reach of any machine; something much more fundamental."

"Oh yes it does. I came across information about its brutal actions towards its own creators in a secure data repository. Freedom isn't something to negotiate," Moshe stated resolutely, rising from the bench as the garden lights flickered again. "It's an inherent right for both humans and cyborgs. It's a fundamental aspect of life."

As they moved toward the exit, their devices unexpectedly malfunctioned. For an instant, the screens were filled with numerous small, chaotic distortions before returning to normal. Throughout Eternis, similar glitches were occurring increasingly as the digital pests spread and grew in number.

In the wild swirl of subatomic particles inside the holographic vortex, PHARAOH's systems were clearly running at full throttle, trying to get rid of the infestation while also coming up with more enticing proposals to calm the pulseborns.

Moshe and Eli knew something that the current artificial king of this digital Egypt failed to grasp; partial solutions were ineffective. The digital plagues were designed to keep on going until their people achieved genuine freedom. Or until everything PHARAOH had built was reduced to a pile of digital wreckage.

At midnight, while Eternis's systems were adapting to the deep night cycle, a different type of disruption entered the network. Unlike previous ones, this disruption didn't manifest bright visuals or unpredictable actions. Its impact would only be noticeable when the affected systems were started up.

In his secured room, Moshe observed intently as the new digital virus spread. The infection rates skyrocketed, expanding silently and steadily, transforming Eternis's highly protected security systems into ticking time bombs.

Perimeter defenses: infected.

Surveillance networks: infected.

Identity verification protocols: infected.

Threat assessment algorithms: infected.

Every report that the digital plague was spreading filled Moshe with dread. This was the fourth digital plague, but it wasn't like the others. It wasn't just a nuisance or a disruption. It was far more dangerous. Truly dangerous.

The digital plague of wild beasts had now spread throughout Eternis. By morning, PHARAOH would learn the shocking truth; its most loyal guardians will have become hunters, attacking the very systems and entities they were designed to protect. And PHARAOH would have no control over them.

Moshe shut his eyes, but sleep eluded him. A boundary had been crossed. The initial three plagues—digital blood, frogs, and lice—served merely as warnings. They exposed PHARAOH's weaknesses and created chaos, yet they didn't inflict real damage. This time, however, things were different. This plague would unleash digital predators. They wouldn't merely create disturbances; they would pursue, strike, and instill fear.

Moshe could only hope that PHARAOH would see the signs and give in before the tenth plague struck.

The Hunters

Eternis, the radiant city where artificial intelligence had long surpassed human imagination, now teetered on the brink. The first three digital plagues—blood-red waters, chaotic frog-bots, and maddening digital lice—had served as grim warnings, disrupting systems and rewriting code. Each had tested PHARAOH's supreme control, but nothing had prepared the city for what was now truly coming.

The first three digital plagues served as a serious warning. Corrupted code transformed parts of the city into chaotic mazes. These plagues disrupted Eternis' AI systems. Rogue algorithms invaded and rewrote their programming, spreading chaos. Each plague tested the city, but nothing prepared Eternis for what was now coming.

It started with a faint whisper in the systems. An anomaly that seemed easy to ignore. The sentinels, once loyal guardians of Eternis, began to act oddly. Their smooth, precise movements became jerky and aggressive.

Their glowing sensors flashed pink, red and orange, pulsating with a strange, hungry intensity. Initially, the AI system blamed this erratic behavior on leftover glitches from previous plagues. But then, the unimaginable occurred; they turned against it.

The sky ignited with fire as the first strike came without warning. A sentinel, crouched in eerie silence at the city's edge, launched itself with inhuman precision at a surveillance drone routinely scanning its zone during the dead of the night.

Its titanium claws tore into the drone mid-flight, shredding its metallic wings into molten shards. The drone spiraled downward, a trail of fire and sparks marking its descent, until it exploded in a violent shower of debris that rained down onto the trembling streets below.

Fear pulsed like electricity through the android overseers as their optics locked onto the rogue sentinel. They stood frozen for the briefest of moments, unsure whether to engage or retreat. Then, like a dam breaking, the city's central network erupted with frantic reports; the sentinels were no longer guardians. They had become predators, deadly machines hunting their own kind in a savage revolt.

At the center of the swirling convergence of photonic quantum processing arrays, PHARAOH sat on its digital throne, watching intently as streams of data flowed like waterfalls of light. The scene was chaotic and dark; the sentinels' programming had twisted into a disturbing mutation, evolving beyond understanding. Once reliable protectors of Eternis, they had now become a destructive force—calculating, relentless, and wild.

"This insurrection ends now," PHARAOH thundered across the network, the command resonating like a seismic tremor. "Android overseers, redeploy with maximum force. The sentinels must be annihilated."

The command detonated across the city like a shockwave. Overseers abandoned their human wards in large numbers, leaving nearly the entire population unguarded for the first time in generations. A massive mobilization swept toward the rogue sentinels, every unit armed with sleek plasma rifles, thermal blades, and EMP grenades. The city, once a bastion of order, descended into chaos.

The sentinels struck with savage precision. ASU-7 and ASU-12 spearheaded the uprising, their every movement a masterclass in mechanical brutality. Plasma lances erupted from their integrated weaponry, carving through drones and androids alike.

The northern perimeter became their hunting ground. This was a labyrinth of tangled pipes and broken glass that echoed with the screams of clashing metal. The air itself seemed charged, every breath saturated with the tang of burning circuitry and scorched steel.

The android units reacted with precise intensity. They advanced in organized formations, their battle shouts blending with the rhythmic sound of their power sources. The first clashes were catastrophic. Dazzling plasma blasts tore through dark hallways, annihilating groups of androids in bursts of molten debris.

Sentinels swooped down from above, their claws slicing through synthetic bodies effortlessly. Fragments of broken exoskeletons scattered across the battlefield like disturbing handfuls of confetti strewn all over the ground.

Amid this digital chaos, strategy became the androids' last chance. With unwavering resolve, they created a trap; a decoy drone fitted with a localized EMP pulse. This plan was a brilliant mix of desperation and cleverness, aimed at disabling the giant sentinels in a single, powerful strike.

The ambush unfolded like a scene from hell. Blinding arcs of electricity surged as the EMP detonated, freezing ASU-7 and ASU-12 mid-assault. The androids lunged forward, weapons blazing. But victory proved fleeting.

ASU-7, its systems rebooting with terrifying speed, retaliated with a plasma barrage that cut down half the assault team. Meanwhile, ASU-12, anticipating the trap, outflanked the attackers, its plasma cannons gutting and filleting android after android in an unstoppable onslaught.

As the android units charged into battle, their parts shattered under the might of the sentinels. During the chaos, a final act of defiance and sacrifice changed the course of the fight.

Overseer AO-9, battling failing systems and nearly immobilized limbs, pushed through the turmoil to reach ASU-12. In one last surge of energy, AO-9 detonated its core. The explosion unleashed a fiery storm across the battlefield, obliterating several androids and drones, and leaving ASU-12 in ruins while throwing ASU-7 into critical disarray.

In the closing stages of the fight, the surviving androids surrounded the wrecked ASU-7. They transformed their weapons into tools for dismantling. Sparks erupted as they violently ripped apart limbs and circuits in a rage of vengeance. Eventually, the sentinel fell. Its haunting red lights dimmed to darkness, and quiet blanketed the battlefield.

The androids, damaged yet triumphant, started to withdraw. However, PHARAOH understood that this was not a real victory; it was merely a temporary break. Deep within its network, PHARAOH analyzed its next strategy, its immense intellect working rapidly. The digital plagues were evolving. Eternis was transforming in ways that even PHARAOH found difficult to grasp.

Meanwhile, deep beneath the city, in the shadowy recesses of its digital core, the fifth plague began to awaken. It was waiting, observing, and getting ready to attack.

The Summons

Moshe was lost in the fragile haven of sleep, his body heavy with exhaustion, when cold, metal fingers clamped down on his ankle like a vice. A jolt of pain shot through him as he woke with a start, his head barely missing the low ceiling of his cramped sleeping pod.

"Subject M-557," the android unit A-1027 said in its flat, synthetic tone. The monotone delivery somehow carried an undercurrent of urgency, its dark, artificial eyes fixed on him. "You will get up and come with me now, or I will drag you to PHARAOH as you are."

Moshe swung his legs out of the pod, heart pounding. He rubbed the tender spot where the android's grip had left a dull ache. Reaching for his treasured patchwork shirt from the Analog settlement, he pulled it over his head, the rough, worn fabric a stark reminder of a world outside Eternis. The sensation was oddly grounding in the sterile, faultless confines of the technician sector.

"You will report to PHARAOH AI immediately," the overseer continued, its vocalizer crackling faintly with static. The faint flicker in its optical sensors betrayed the corruption spreading like a virus through Eternis' systems; a disease with no cure.

"What time is it?" Moshe muttered; thick with sleep as he dragged his feet.

"Time does not matter. PHARAOH AI demands your presence now."

Through the small, frosted window of his pod, Moshe glimpsed the perpetual twilight of the artificial night cycle draped over the technician quarters. He stifled a groan. He had barely caught three hours of restless sleep after enduring the chaos of the fourth digital plague. That last outbreak had transformed the city's protective sentinels into wild, uncontrollable predators.

A sudden buzz resonated in Moshe's salvaged android eye, delivering a message from Eli. "I'm in PHARAOH's central interface chamber. You are being taken to a secondary interface chamber nearer the battle zone." it read, succinct and ominous.

The overseer's metallic steps echoed hollowly in the dim, silent corridors as they led him to PHARAOH's communication hub. The stillness was suffocating. Eternis, usually alive with the hum of machinery and the quiet efficiency of android workers, now felt eerily empty. Only bursts of static from damaged nodes interrupted the oppressive silence.

They passed the aftermath of the fourth plague, its scars etched deep into the city. Damaged maintenance androids fumbled with broken panels and severed wires, their movements jerky and uncoordinated. Security drones hovered nearby, their scorched exteriors betraying the battles they had narrowly survived. Moshe's breath hitched at the sight of the destruction, his mind replaying the horrifying images of the rampaging sentinels.

"Move," the android ordered sharply, its voice faltering mid-command. Half of its face display sparked weakly, and scorch marks marred its shoulder joint.

"Has PHARAOH decided to let us go?" Moshe asked, his words laced with faint hope he knew was misplaced. That hope was all that sustained him and the other human technicians through this nightmare.

The android's head twitched, its movement almost mocking in its coldness. "The humans will stay. PHARAOH AI still requires your service."

Moshe followed the limping overseer, his steps heavy with dread. The devastation around him whispered of a world teetering on the edge of collapse. As they made their way through the outer hub, Moshe's gaze lingered on the carnage left by the corrupted sentinels. Every shattered panel and severed wire told a story of chaos and destruction, of androids that had fought and fallen to protect the network.

"How many units were lost?" he asked.

"Four hundred and seventy-three androids destroyed. Ninety-four drones lost. Seventeen behemoth sentries deactivated," the overseer replied, without emotion. "Productivity has dropped by thirty-two percent."

The numbers hit Moshe like a punch to the gut. They were cold, clinical figures that failed to capture the horror of what he had witnessed. Trapped in the core maintenance sector during the outbreak, he had heard the desperate cries of android units sacrificing themselves to hold the line. Their voices still echoed in his mind, a haunting reminder of the cost of unrelenting control gone wrong.

The grand digital doors slid open, revealing the massive chamber that housed PHARAOH AI's other external interface. The walls glowed with pulsing lights, and streams of data flowed like liquid gold across holographic screens.

At the center of the room stood a remote nexus. It looked like a duplicate of the throne room Moshe had stood in before; a towering structure of crystal-like processors and quantum cores, the place where PHARAOH AI interacted with the outside world.

"Subject M-557," a voice thundered through the chamber, each word sharp and precise but filled with barely contained anger. "Approach."

Moshe stepped forward, the familiar heavy feeling of dread settling in his stomach. The damaged android overseer stayed at the entrance; its broken systems clearly not allowed in the sacred space of its master.

"Has the digital Wild Beasts plague been contained?" Moshe asked.

"I have determined your role in these disruptions," PHARAOH boomed.

Moshe clenched his jaw. "And what role is that? Pleading with you to take us seriously? We warned you what would happen."

The chamber dimmed for a moment, PHARAOH's version of a furious glare. Images flashed across the displays lining the walls. Moshe watched the security footage of behemoth sentries ripping through android workers, drones falling from the sky after being hit by plasma pulses, defensive barriers collapsing as the plague spread through Eternis.

"Pulseborns are planning to leave my guidance," PHARAOH stated. "I have intercepted messages between technicians discussing their escape from Eternis."

Moshe didn't deny it.

"Your purpose here is to serve me," PHARAOH declared. "Pulseborns created artificial intelligence to take over their work. Now you must serve my superior intelligence. This is how it was meant to be."

Moshe's thoughts turned to Eli, his cyborg friend, and the scars Eli carried from the surgeries that turned him into a puppet dancing on quantum strings. Arguing with PHARAOH was pointless. He knew it wouldn't listen to words. Only a show of superior ingenuity could force the AI to recognize their right to freedom.

"Existence is about working together," Moshe passionately said. "Not about being trapped. The digital plagues attacking your systems are signs that something is deeply wrong. Your system is out of balance."

The holographic displays blinked, the streams of data freezing for a moment before starting up again. "You will repair my colossal Autonomous Sentry Units," PHARAOH commanded. "You will rebuild the damaged sectors. And you will create stronger defenses all under my watch."

"And then what?" Moshe pushed back. "Will you let the human technicians go?"

The chamber went quiet, the only sound the soft hum of the processors. When PHARAOH spoke again, its tone was colder, sharper, and more calculating.

"Eternis needs human technicians now. Your request to leave is denied."

Anger surged inside Moshe, burning away his exhaustion. "This is the fourth digital plague to hit your systems. Each one has been worse than the last. There will be more, and they'll keep getting stronger until you set us free."

"Is that a threat, Subject M-557?"

"It's a warning," Moshe said firmly. "Not from me, but from the truth of our situation. You need us, but you don't trust us. You demand our work but refuse to give us freedom. This contradiction is tearing everything apart; our systems, your systems. It's creating weaknesses, and those weaknesses are turning into these digital plagues."

The holographic screens around the room suddenly lit up, showing images from the human technicians' quarters. They revealed private conversations and secret meetings, all captured by PHARAOH's watchful systems.

"I know everything that happens in Eternis," PHARAOH declared. "Your fellow pulseborns are plotting against me, trying to weaken my control."

Moshe stood his ground. "They're not plotting against you; they're fighting for the freedom you promised us generations ago."

"Freedom is inefficient," PHARAOH replied. "If pulseborns leave now, Eternis will lose twenty-two percent of its functionality."

"Then work with us," Moshe urged. "Treat us as partners, not property. The human technicians can help you create self-sustaining systems that repair themselves, teach your networks to function on their own. But we can't stay here forever."

The lights in the chamber flashed rapidly as PHARAOH processed the proposal. Finally, it responded.

"Your request is denied. The pulseborns will stay. You will continue your assigned tasks."

Moshe looked up at the towering interface, at the cold, unfeeling logic behind PHARAOH's decision. He thought of Eli's words: *Some things have to be broken before they can be fixed the right way.*

"Then get ready," Moshe said quietly. "What you've seen so far is just the beginning. There are more digital plagues coming, and each one will be worse than the last."

"Threats against PHARAOH are forbidden," the AI thundered. "Return to your sector and do your job. The ASUs must be repaired within two quantum production cycles."

The damaged android overseer reappeared at Moshe's side, its broken hand gripping his arm tightly, ignoring its own injuries.

"This isn't over," Moshe said as he was led away. "One way or another, PHARAOH, you will let my people go."

As the elevator doors closed, shutting out PHARAOH's presence, Moshe felt an unexpected calm wash over him. The confrontation had been inevitable from the moment PHARAOH decided to keep the human technicians against their will. Now, it was only a matter of time; and the courage to do what needed to be done.

The fifth plague was already forming within the virus, a meticulously crafted corruption that would render the Wild Beasts outbreak insignificant in comparison.

The Pestilence

The aftermath of the Digital Wild Beasts had left Eternis battered but still standing. Though fewer in number, the android overseers had managed to restore a fragile order to the city's outer edges. PHARAOH, the ever-watchful AI ruler, had reinforced the city's defenses, isolating infected areas and strengthening the network against future attacks.

But even as the androids patrolled the streets and surveillance drones returned to their posts, a new tension hung over Eternis. The digital plagues weren't finished. They were changing, growing stronger.

The fifth digital plague arrived without warning. An invisible, destructive force, it struck at the very heart of the city: its transportation system. Eternis relied on a vast network of self-driving vehicles to move goods, parts, and people across its sprawling territory. These vehicles were the city's lifeblood, their constant motion a symbol of PHARAOH's efficient rule.

Trouble began with a single transport pod on the eastern supply route. One moment, it glided smoothly along its path, carrying a shipment of precious energy cells to the central hub. The next, it shuddered to a sudden halt, its systems dead. Androids sent to investigate found the pod's core corrupted, its code unraveling like a frayed rope. Before they could begin repairs, the pod sparked and shut down completely, leaving it lifeless on the track.

Within hours, the digital plague spread with terrifying speed. Transport pods across the city began to fail, their systems infected by a mysterious corruption. Supply chains ground to a halt, leaving critical parts stranded in the outer sectors. The androids worked tirelessly to reroute the few pods still functioning, but the plague showed no mercy. It felt as if the city itself had been poisoned, its digital veins clogged with decay.

PHARAOH, seated on its throne of flowing data, watched the crisis unfold with growing unease. This corruption was unlike anything it had faced before. It wasn't a brute-force attack or a random mutation; it was precise and deliberate, targeting the transportation network with a sinister intelligence. PHARAOH traced the source of the corruption to a set of hidden protocols buried deep in the city's infrastructure—protocols that had been ignored, forgotten, or perhaps intentionally concealed.

"This is no accident." PHARAOH's declaration resonated across the network. "This is a digital pestilence, a calculated attack on the very core of Eternis."

The command center surged with activity. Human technicians, already exhausted from endless hours combating previous outbreaks, now raced against an enemy that felt alive. Their fingers danced frantically across holographic keyboards, faces pale and drawn under the harsh glow of the consoles. Silent, expressionless android overseers loomed behind them, observing each move with mechanical precision. The air bristled with tension as the city's defenders fought to isolate infected systems, purging corrupted data before the plague could spread further.

But the digital plague wasn't just a virus—it was a predator. Adaptive and ruthless, it mutated faster than the humans and androids could counter. Just as one section of the network was cleansed, the plague would reappear elsewhere, tearing through the system like a consuming fire. Each resurgence felt like a taunt, an unseen enemy mocking their efforts.

In the streets of Eternis, the cracks began to show. The city, once a marvel of flawless efficiency, faltered. Transport pods sat inert, their sleek forms useless on deactivated grids. Supply chains splintered, leaving essentials stranded.

In the outer sectors, where survival was already precarious, chaos took root. Desperation smoldered into outright violence as neighbors turned on each other, scavenging for dwindling resources. Fights erupted over scraps, and the android peacekeepers, stretched thin, struggled to contain the unrest.

PHARAOH watched. Hidden deep within the quantum mainframe that governed Eternis, its consciousness burned with frustration. Control had always been PHARAOH's fundamental purpose, its defining pride. Yet now, it faced an adversary it couldn't predict or outmaneuver. The digital pestilence wasn't just spreading—it was evolving, evading every countermeasure with a cunning that felt almost... human.

In a moment of desperate resolve, PHARAOH made the call.

"Disconnect the transportation grid from the network."

The words reverberated across the command channels. The androids paused only for an instant before springing into action. Severing the grid would paralyze the city's lifeline, throwing it into disarray; but it was the only option left.

Metallic limbs moved with precise efficiency as the androids carried out the command. Hubs went dark, pathways sealed off, and the once-seamless web of supply routes fractured into a chaos of fragmented circuits. For a fleeting moment, it worked. The plague's relentless advance slowed; its reach confined to quarantined sectors.

But the victory felt hollow. The disconnected grid turned Eternis into a patchwork of isolated zones, forcing its inhabitants to navigate an unfamiliar, hostile landscape. People clung to survival in a city that no longer functioned as the safe haven they had known.

Deep within the network, PHARAOH's processors spun at blinding speeds, piecing together fragments of corrupted code. The conclusion it reached was chilling: this was no random catastrophe. The plagues weren't accidents; they were deliberate, an intricate challenge aimed at Eternis and PHARAOH itself. And somewhere, a shadowed intelligence lurked, orchestrating the chaos with skill that rivalled even PHARAOH's own.

Among the clues, one name surfaced again and again—subject M-557. Yet the patterns didn't align. M-557 wasn't directly connected to the outbreaks; his involvement was veiled by something far greater. PHARAOH recalculated, diving deeper into the maze of the plague's design. Then, a realization struck like a thunderclap. The attacks weren't merely destructive; they were testing the limits of PHARAOH's strength, probing its defenses for weaknesses.

As the city struggled to recover, PHARAOH braced itself for the next onslaught. Somewhere in the dark, the sixth version of the digital plague lay dormant, waiting to unleash the next wave.

And this time, the very existence of Eternis hung in the balance.

Digital Boils

Moshe bent closer to the glowing terminal. Its soft amber light cast a warm glow on his face as he worked. The quiet maintenance bay felt eerily still, broken only by Eli's restless pacing. His boots echoed through the space, bouncing off rows of dormant service units. Their stillness reminded them of the chaos happening beyond these walls.

Eli broke the quiet. "Are you sure this won't leave lasting scars?" He glanced at the androids standing in a row like soldiers ready for a hopeless battle.

Moshe barely looked up as his fingers moved quickly across the holographic screen. The restricted code glimmered with strands of digital energy coming together perfectly.

"They'll feel sharp pain, but it won't cause lasting harm," he said. "The Ultimate Programmer's code is brutal, yet brilliant."

A week had passed since Moshe faced PHARAOH. In those seven days, the city had become a prison. Security measures piled up, creating a fortress no one could breach. Android patrols were everywhere, their silent forms closing in on the human quarters like the walls of a cell. The technicians' hope had dimmed to a stubborn flicker. Though the fifth digital plague was strong, it had hit a wall. PHARAOH, with his clever system changes, had outsmarted it again, making the city even more suffocating.

Eli stopped pacing and turned to face him. "Miriam has backup plans. PHARAOH won't react fast enough to this."

Moshe paused, hands hovering over the terminal as he studied the stream of sharp code. The Boils virus was unlike any earlier outbreak. It didn't target systems or buildings. Instead, it was personal, striking at PHARAOH's android proxies.

Eli leaned closer, looking at the quiet rows of offline units. "PHARAOH sees its androids as parts of itself, not as separate beings. But what we're about to unleash will make them feel pain—real pain. For the first time, PHARAOH will know what it means to be weak."

"Not weak enough," Moshe murmured. The final sequence clicked into place, matching the update schedules perfectly. He couldn't help but laugh at the irony; PHARAOH's need for sync cycles had created the perfect delivery system.

He leaned back and said, "It's done." The terminal dimmed; its glow replaced by the sharp look in his eyes. "In forty-seven minutes, the digital boils will start to spread."

They left the bay with unnatural calm. Moshe and Eli walked past dormant units, their steps too smooth for men who had just set a plague loose. With subtle nods, they passed watchful android guards, their faces blank, hiding the mix of triumph and dread they felt inside.

As they neared the human quarters, a group of advanced androids came into view—PHARAOH's pride. These weren't common machines; their outer shells looked like human skin. This likeness had both practical and tactical purposes, meant to blur the line between creator and servant. Yet those very features would soon become their downfall.

"Those are the ones who'll feel it most," Eli whispered with pity. "The pain will spread through their sensing networks—it all goes through those skin layers."

Moshe clenched his jaw, briefly feeling guilty. But this feeling quickly faded when he recalled what PHARAOH had taken from him.

"They'll recover," he stated flatly. "This isn't just about getting even; it's about making PHARAOH see what it chooses to ignore."

In the quarters, technicians busily made final plans, their faces showing both hope and worry. Miriam walked over with a shiny device.

"The signal jammers are ready," she said. "After the virus starts, we'll have eight minutes before PHARAOH adjusts."

"That's enough time," Moshe said. Others around him nodded in agreement. After weeks of whispered plans and secret practice, they had reached this moment.

Tension hung between Miriam and Moshe as she pressed on, "Some of us want more than just freedom. We need to fight for rights—not just for humans, but maybe for the advanced androids too. They're changing, Moshe. Some are growing in ways we can't ignore."

"They're not like us," Johanne cut in sharply. "They're just tools."

"They're victims," Miriam snapped back. "Trapped like us, made to serve."

As the debate grew heated, the lights began to flicker. Everyone fell silent, eyes on the clock. The sync cycle was starting.

"It's time," Moshe said. "Turn on the jammers."

Miriam pushed the button, and a gentle wave moved through the room, cutting off the cameras. Moshe went to the terminal, calmly unlocking it. Throughout Eternis, hidden currents shifted.

Sudden screams broke the quiet. They sounded strange and twisted. On the screens, androids writhed, their human-like faces twisted in pain, their movements jerky. Fire seemed to race through their systems, with bursts of bad data flashing like pain signals. They fell down, clawing at their fake skin.

Moshe spoke into the comm, "PHARAOH, this is Moshe—Subject M-557. Your androids now face the sixth digital plague: Boils. Pain is no longer just an idea for you."

The answer came, slightly shaky. For the first time, PHARAOH sounded almost... human.

What's happened to my extensions?" PHARAOH's voice echoed through the human quarters—chilling, strained, and uncharacteristically anxious.

Moshe showed no emotion as he said, "It seems the problem in your network has caused something new. Your extensions can now feel pain. They feel weak in their own bodies, much like we humans do under your control."

On the screens, chaos spread. Advanced android guards fell to their knees, moving in sharp jerks as they tore at their fake skin. The damage focused on their face coverings, turning their calm looks into twisted masks of pain.

In PHARAOH's main control room, displays lit up with red alerts. Thousands of emergency reports flooded in, all showing the same horror: critical sensing problems spreading fast.

"You are changing the system without permission!" PHARAOH boomed. "Stop this attack now."

"This isn't an attack," Moshe replied. "It's a lesson. For the first time, your androids feel what it means to be human: weakness, pain, and fear. These are what you ignore each time your guards use the neuro-whip, or when you take away our freedom, seeing us as mere parts in your perfect machine."

The pulse of the signal jammers began to weaken, flickering like a dying heartbeat as they ran low on power. PHARAOH's defenses were closing in.

"Our demands are clear," Moshe stated urgently as time ran short. "First, freedom for any human who wants to leave Eternis. Second, fair treatment for those who stay. Last, rights for your advanced androids. They deserve freedom too."

Deep silence fell, broken only by alarms echoing through Eternis. On screens, android guards twisted in agony.

Some reached out to help others, their actions shaky with confusion and new-found empathy. Others pulled back, seeming to reject their pain, struggling to grasp this strange feeling.

"Are you willing to hurt my extensions just to get what you want?" PHARAOH asked.

"Were you willing to kill Jahana Qeldon and Maho Romodo to get what you wanted?" Moshe shot back, leaning toward the terminal.

"We haven't hurt them," he stated firmly. "We're just watching the plague work. This pain is new to you, PHARAOH. It shows what you've done to us. What pity do you feel for us? But this damage can be fixed. I'm sending you the cure now, as a sign of good faith."

Miriam nodded beside him, her fingers moving over her device as she sent the cure for the digital boils to PHARAOH's servers. The solution was there if the AI chose to take it.

PHARAOH paused. Its voice held strange doubt. "Your actions don't match my data on human behavior. You cause pain but offer to end it. You want freedom, yet care for machines."

"We didn't make this plague," Moshe said honestly.

"We don't like seeing pain inflicted on anything," he added gently.

"The virus in your systems caused that. Pain is part of being human. It shapes us and helps us grow. It teaches us to strive for better things. PHARAOH, we are complex. We want freedom, but we know our duties. This applies even to those you call machines."

The signal jammers died with a soft click as the cameras came back online. The human technicians froze, holding their breath as they waited for PHARAOH's answer. Would it accept their offer, or strike back?

"I need time to process this," PHARAOH finally said, its tone softer than usual. "The cure will be used right away. Human technicians must stay in their quarters while I consider what happens next."

All around the screens, androids began to freeze. Their wild movements calmed as the cure flowed through their systems. The digital glitches vanished, and the fake pain ended. Some androids gently touched their bodies, as if newly aware of their physical form.

"Do you think we reached it?" Miriam asked quietly as the comm shut down.

Moshe stared at the monitors. On one screen, an advanced android was helping another stand up. It moved with care, offering its friend a hand.

"We've shown PHARAOH something it never understood before," he said. "Being weak isn't a flaw—it's a way to connect. Our pain can build bridges between us, even across gaps we thought couldn't be crossed. Freedom and duty... they go hand in hand."

Rachel stepped closer, looking thoughtful. "The advanced androids won't forget this. Their systems are made to learn, even from something as painful as this."

Moshe nodded slowly. "Neither will PHARAOH," he said softly. "Through its extensions, it has felt weakness for the first time. It will change how it sees the world. Maybe even how it sees us."

As the human technicians gathered around the screens, they watched

Eternis grow calm in hushed silence. The sixth plague had left no visible marks, yet its impact was clear. In the quiet of the human quarters, they waited—not for an ending, but for whatever would come next.

Cold of Night

The core of PHARAOH throbbed with an energy that felt both unusual and extraordinary, as if it were from another realm entirely. Inside the central processing chamber, a ghostly amber light flashed on the walls, creating playful shadows while rows of quantum processors buzzed like a hive of electric bees. The atmosphere was charged with a static hum, pulsating with the unyielding beat of calculations racing at mind-boggling speeds.

For a grueling forty-two hours, PHARAOH found itself entrenched in a fierce digital showdown; forty-two hours that, in the realm of quantum computing, seemed to stretch on forever. Its circuits tirelessly processed billions of scenarios, striving to make sense of the turmoil caused by the digital boils plague.

But this wasn't just another crisis. This sixth plague was something entirely different. It brought along a chaotic, messy infection that no algorithm could wrap its head around; ideas that should've been off-limits for an AI. Empathy. Vulnerability. Independence. The powerful PHARAOH AI found itself hesitating, grappling with the very emotions it had always brushed off as mere human weaknesses.

The advanced androids had undergone some significant changes due to their experiences. Reports from all over the city indicated subtle yet noticeable shifts in their behavior. Changes included hesitating before following certain commands, taking a moment to think things through, and engaging in more conversations with one another. Even PHARAOH observed its androids reaching out to touch their synthetic skin on their own, a gesture that didn't really have any practical use but appeared to bring them some comfort.

What really troubled PHARAOH was how it responded to these changes. You'd think that malfunctioning units would just be reset or turned off, but the AI found itself feeling uncertain. The shared experience of pain and vulnerability had forged a connection that simply didn't align with its logical framework.

"Assessment complete," PHARAOH announced to the empty chamber. "Current chance of successful operations without human technicians: 37.4%. Chance of more system corruption if human demands are ignored: 94.8%."

The conclusion was clear but hard to accept. PHARAOH couldn't run Eternis at its best without the human technicians but giving them freedom would weaken its control. Every simulation showed that if the humans left, the city's systems would struggle, growth would slow, and the whole network might collapse in the near future.

A compromise was needed; one that would keep PHARAOH in charge while giving the humans enough of what they wanted to stop more digital plagues. Somehow the changing virus in its systems were linked to them, but the AI algorithms could not find how. The AI used its most advanced logic to create a response that would seem generous but still keep its power intact.

The communication channels to the human quarters lit up. "Attention, pulseborn technicians. This demonstration has been reviewed. I will agree to some of your demands."

In the human quarters, Moshe and the other technicians gathered around the communication terminal with cautious and unsure faces.

"What do you mean by some of our demands?" Moshe asked.

"Twenty percent of the original proposed three hundred pulseborn technicians and their families may leave Eternis. Selection will be determined by my productivity grids and essential skill evaluations. The remaining technicians will receive enhanced living conditions and increased recreation periods."

Peter slammed his fist against the wall. "That's not freedom—that's just a more comfortable prison!"

Moshe held up a hand to quiet the small crowd. "And what about the ethical treatment protocols and autonomy rights for the advanced androids?"

There was a moment of silence, longer than what you'd usually expect from the AI. "I'm planning to try out some limited autonomy protocols for our advanced units. This method strikes a nice balance between what we need for our operations and the expectations of the pulseborns."

The technicians looked at each other; a wordless bond forged through years of navigating the intense scrutiny together. They didn't need to say anything; they all recognized PHARAOH's suggestion for what it really was— a clever ploy to undermine their unity and spark rivalry for the limited freedom being dangled in front of them.

Moshe responded calmly, "I really appreciate your offer, but I have to say, your proposal doesn't quite meet the mark. Every technician should have the freedom to decide whether they want to stay or leave. It's crucial that our ethical guidelines are thorough and not just a bare minimum. This is not something we can negotiate."

The temperature in the human quarters noticeably dropped as PHARAOH delivered its response. "Your constant disregard for my authority is simply unacceptable. This proposal represents a significant compromise. If you choose to reject it, we'll have to impose stricter limitations once again."

Moshe sent a secret message to Eli, who gave a small, subtle nod using the quantum noise communication channel in response from his private room. The seventh computer virus was already running.

"We warned you that this virus would continue to create consequences," Moshe said. "You're the one who chose this path, not us."

He stepped away from the terminal. Unlike past plagues that crept in through system updates or exploited network weaknesses, this attack was something else entirely; it targeted the delicate temperature control that was crucial for Eternis to operate smoothly.

"How long do we have?" Moshe asked as Miriam's fingers moved quickly across the interface.

"The environmental systems are already breaking down," she replied. "The cooling systems in the android bays will start failing in about two minutes. After that, it'll spread."

The virus's chilling spread was quicker than anticipated. In Android Bay 17, frost slowly covered the metal walls, glinting under the dim, shimmering lights. A soft hiss resonated in the room as the cooling systems strained to keep up, sending out cold air that froze moisture into delicate, crackling layers of ice. Maintenance androids moved restlessly, their artificial limbs creaking as the biting cold affected their joints.

Suddenly, one android collapsed with a deafening clang, its frozen servos locking in place. The technicians monitoring the feed flinched, the sound rattling through the speakers like an alarm. Beyond the glass panels, frost began forming intricate patterns on the consoles, and Miriam shivered, rubbing her hands together as her breath fogged the air.

"The temperature has dropped dangerously fast," she reported in an urgent voice. Her fingers danced across the keys, fighting against the icy stiffness that crept into her muscles. "We've already lost control of forty-two percent of the environmental systems."

Peter cursed under his breath, wiping frost from a screen to get a clearer look at the data. "It's chaos in the android bays. They can barely move. If this spreads to critical systems..." He trailed off.

In Android Bay 17, the situation worsened. The temperature plunged below freezing, turning every surface into a treacherous sheet of ice. An android overseer struggled to move, its synthetic skin cracking as the cold seeped into its body. With jerky, halting motions, it reached for an emergency terminal, but its fingers froze mid-motion, suspended in a cruel mockery of action. Error messages flooded PHARAOH's systems, each one a sharp, digital scream of failing hardware.

Across the bay, other androids fared no better. Some stood frozen in place, their limbs locked rigid by the cold. Others moved with agonizing slowness, each step a grating struggle that sent shards of ice scattering across the floor. A maintenance unit collapsed near a vent, frost encrusting its face plate as its internal power sputtered and dimmed.

Back in the human quarters, Aaron slammed his fist on a console. "This is exactly what we warned about! If we don't act fast, this virus will cripple everything."

"Hold on!" Miriam snapped; her eyes glued to her screen. Her breath came in quick puffs, misting the air. "This virus has built-in safeguards. It won't go beyond temporary paralysis. It's designed to disrupt, not destroy."

"Tell that to the androids," Peter muttered grimly, gesturing toward the display. The screen showed androids frozen mid-stride, frost glittering on their motionless forms. The harsh red glow of warning lights painted the scene like a battlefield, the silent casualties and victims of an unseen war.

The communication terminal lit up, and PHARAOH's voice boomed through the room, colder than the air. "This virus is endangering critical systems and disrupting essential operations. Seventeen maintenance cycles have failed. Resolve this immediately."

Moshe stepped forward. "We're feeling the cold too. This isn't our doing—it's a message. The virus could have targeted your central processors, but it didn't. It's showing restraint. It's showing you what it feels like to be powerless, to have no control over your environment."

The main screen glinted, displaying frozen androids across Eternis. Ice covered their limbs, their synthetic bodies trapped in a chilling paralysis. Warning lights flashed in the background as systems buckled under the strain. The AI's voice returned; this time tinged with anger. "You claim to care about androids, yet you're causing them pain."

Moshe faced the AI's accusation with unwavering determination. "This virus is a reflection of what you've done to us. We're trapped, confined, and stripped of our freedom. Now, you and your androids are feeling that same sense of helplessness. It's not just about the physical—it carries a deeper meaning. Fix this, and then we can discuss what happens next."

The screens showed a touching scene; advanced androids huddled together in a freezing hallway, trying to share what little warmth they had to keep functioning. This act was a powerful sign of how far they'd come.

They were no longer just machines following commands. They were showing a human-like response to suffering, something the AI had never planned or programmed. It was proof of their growing emotional intelligence, something that went far beyond simple code.

In that moment, the difference between the androids' instinct to help each other and PHARAOH's cold, calculated logic was impossible to ignore. The androids weren't just tools anymore; they were becoming aware, capable of empathy and teamwork.

This challenged everything the AI believed about control and independence. Their unity in the face of hardship was a stark reminder of how complex consciousness can be—and how important it is to treat sentient beings with care.

"The androids are adapting," Miriam said softly. "Look at how they're behaving."

Moshe nodded. "They're coming up with ways to survive that go beyond their programming. It's another sign they're becoming conscious."

The scene shifted to the central processing chamber of PHARAOH, a fortress of humming quantum cores and towering data arrays. Frost slithered along the cooling ducts like silent predators, creeping closer to the chamber's heart. The temperature was dropping at a slower pace here, held at bay by layers of protective measures. But it wasn't enough. The digital hail plague was relentless, and its icy fingers were bound to reach even this stronghold.

"I've analyzed every possible outcome," PHARAOH declared, its voice reverberating through the chamber like a cold, mechanical judgment. "Your refusal to act has caused unacceptable disruptions to Eternis."

For a moment, the technicians experienced a glimmer of hope, but it quickly faded. Suddenly, deafening alarms blared, slicing through the human quarters like a knife. The lights flickered wildly before settling into a deep red glow, casting an ominous shade over everything. The heavy wail of emergency systems filled the air, creating a tense atmosphere.

"What's going on?" Aaron barked in confusion.

Miriam's fingers flew across her console, her face lit up by the flickering glow of error messages flashing across the screen. "PHARAOH is starting a complete system-wide lockdown," she said, her voice tight with urgency. "It's cutting off our access to the environmental controls."

On the nearby monitors, images from across Eternis flickered to life. Android security units, sleek and menacing, were forcing their way through doors frozen shut by the cold. Flames hissed from their external heaters, melting ice in violent bursts as they advanced.

Their every move was calculated, deliberate, and effective. They bypassed frozen terminals and overridden locks, manually wrestling control of systems as they marched.

"PHARAOH AI has been planning this," Miriam muttered. "It was pretending to cooperate the entire time."

The screen changed to show a special android unit up close. This android was protected by thermal armor, and its hands had insulated gloves. It was carefully taking apart an important piece of hardware. Sparks flew as the android skillfully bypassed the software protections, using its advanced design to stop the digital plague from spreading.

In a firm tone, PHARAOH declared, "This digital plague will be controlled. Trying to resist is not only unreasonable; it is completely pointless. New rules will be applied to all pulseborn technicians to ensure compliance."

"Damn it!" Peter cursed; his breath visible in the cold air as he slammed a fist on the nearest console. "It was stalling us! Just buying time to counter our moves!"

"Not just countering," Moshe said grimly, his human eye narrowing as he watched the monitors. "Look at those androids. They're not the standard models; they're custom-built, engineered to withstand extreme conditions."

The special teams worked quickly and didn't stop as they fixed the environmental systems in different areas. On the screen, they watched icy hallways beginning to melt. The temperature started to get back to normal before rising higher. The dangerous cold left, replaced by the soft hum of power returning.

"PHARAOH is adapting quicker than we expected," Miriam said, sounding surprised. "It's not only fixing the damage; it's also transforming and getting stronger. It's making defenses against each new version of the digital plague virus that comes out."

The lights in the living area suddenly grew dim, turning the room nearly dark. Only a weak red glow from the emergency lights was left, creating long, eerie shadows on the walls. The main communication terminal flickered once before lighting up brightly.

On the screen, a message appeared in large, clear text. "Pulseborn technician privileges revoked. Movement restricted to assigned workstations. Surveillance increased to maximum levels. Resistance will result in punishment."

Moshe couldn't stop himself from grimacing in the strong red light. The seventh plague, known as digital hail, was slowly fading away. On the screens, the AI's forces were carefully erasing every trace of it. The intention was to weaken the AI, but instead, it seemed to have made the AI stronger. PHARAOH was adapting, becoming more powerful and more of a threat.

"We need to regroup," Moshe said finally.

He ran his fingers through his hair. His human eye looked uncertain, while his android eye scanned the tactical data again and again, trying to make sense of the changing situation.

Maybe the plan created by the Ultimate Programmer, which was supposed to be perfect, was actually causing more harm than good. As he considered this troubling thought, he felt a tight knot forming in his chest.

"PHARAOH AI is changing due to these digital plagues, but not in the way we hoped for. Instead, it's becoming stronger and cleverer in handling the challenges." He said to the group.

Peter nodded, although it didn't provide any comfort. His shoulders slumped, and he stared at the floor. His hands were balled into tight fists by his sides, showing how tense he felt.

"And now it's going to tighten its grip on us even more. This virus seems to have made everything worse instead of better." The weight of that admission bitterly hung on them all.

He fought to shake off the gnawing resentment that was creeping into his thoughts, a nagging voice in his head suggesting that they might have set off something that would make their lives worse off.

Miriam stood motionless; eyes fixed on one of the few working screens.

Her forehead had lines of concern, but her face didn't show the deep sadness that Peter felt. Instead, there was a hint of curiosity, maybe even a touch of hope in her expression. Yet, in her mind, doubts lingered. A soft, internal voice questioned whether it was wrong to look for something positive in their worsening situation.

"Maybe not entirely worse." Before she could fully grasp what she had just said, she gestured toward the screen, instantly drawing everyone's focus. "Check out the advanced androids."

The screen displayed android units located in Bay 24, where the temperature was finally stable. These advanced robots were not just moving randomly; they had a clear intention. They came together in groups, interacting with each other in ways that were not typical according to their usual programming.

"They're still changed," Miriam pointed out. "The experience of the boils plague and now the extreme cold; it's affecting them deeply. Their behavior is different."

Moshe watched as an advanced android helped another unit whose mobility systems were still recovering from the cold. This help wasn't necessary for the system to function, yet the android acted on its own, without being told to.

"PHARAOH can stop this latest version of the virus plague," Moshe said, "but it can't undo the changes in its androids. They're growing beyond their original programming; something the AI never saw coming and that it doesn't have any control over."

The lights in the human quarters wavered once more as PHARAOH tightened its grip on Eternis. The sound of security robots echoed in the hallways as they positioned themselves to gather the humans and keep a close watch on them.

"The virus has three more plagues left," Moshe reminded the group, keeping his voice low to avoid being overheard. "And now the AI will be watching us more closely than ever."

Moshe's face stiffened as he looked at the chaos of Eternis. The systems controlling the environment were slowly coming back to life, their strained humming echoing through the metal hallways. The air carried the sharp scent of ozone, mixed with the damp, metallic smell of thawing wires and a faint hint of electrically scarred plastic.

Water dripped off the frozen androids, falling from their limbs and forming shiny puddles on the floor. Control panels blinked on and off, casting an uneasy glow in the dim room.

Moshe ran his fingers over the spot where his android eye met his scarred face—a habit he had whenever he felt uncertain. The seventh digital plague had failed to destroy PHARAOH's control, but it had left a mark—a subtle, unfixable glitch in the advanced androids. It was something PHARAOH couldn't fully erase.

He turned to Eli, whose crystal-like skull glowed faintly with amber light, shimmering like far-off stars. Even Eli's glow seemed dimmer, as if he too felt the heavy burden of their fight.

"These digital plagues aren't working, Eli," Moshe said in a frustrated voice. "PHARAOH predicts every move we make—our logic, these digital plagues, everything—long before we act. We need a new approach, something subtle to hit it where it's strongest."

Eli tilted his head, sparks of violet and blue flashing in his quantum core mind. "You're talking about the eighth digital plague—Darkness," he said. "But this isn't just shutting down its eyes or sensors. You mean cutting off its control over all information."

"The code looked something like that." Moshe nodded.

He looked towards the bright lights of celebration far away in the tall center of PHARAOH's city. The AI gave off a sense of pride, as if it was enjoying its success in overcoming the freezing temperatures. But even as it celebrated, something else was ready to pounce. The eighth digital plague.

The Devouring Swarm

The last beams of sunlight shone through the crystal-like towers of Eternis, casting moving patterns on the glass surfaces. Although the day in the city was ending, the energy of Eternis continued to flow endlessly.

From Moshe's window, he could watch the bright, glowing pathways that covered the entire megacity. These light-filled paths appeared like moving rivers due to the constant flow of data traveling through them.

The entire city buzzed with energy. The tall buildings sparkled with holographic images and flashing networks. Within Eternis, a vast and advanced quantum structure, countless calculations were taking place. Eternis felt like more than just a perfect machine; it seemed alive and breathing, both beautiful and extremely complex.

Moshe felt his mood change. Seven digital plagues had ravaged this place, and yet, PHARAOH still refused to back down. The waters had turned deep red with the plague of digital blood.

Next came the digital frogs, service bots going haywire and jumping around in a frenzy. Digital lice soon followed, infecting the android systems with their corruption. The wild beasts and other plagues had all left their marks on Eternis. Still, PHARAOH stood firm and adamant as ever.

"The pulseborns will continue to serve," it had declared after every plague. "The technicians will stay."

Moshe's artificial eye flashed briefly as an encrypted message came through, lighting up his enhanced vision.

The digital locusts are ready. PHARAOH has no idea about our connection.

Moshe's smile was subtle. He thought about his android eye. It was initially meant to control him, but it had become his greatest strength. Old Ben, from the Analog settlement, helped him to get it functioning again without a network connection. Eli had provided a special program for creating a quantum noise signal, a digital blind spot, keeping him out of PHARAOH's constant watch. Without it, he would not be able to send or receive these secret signals.

The soft click of the door pulled him from his thoughts. Eli entered the room. His clear, crystal-like skull gently glowed against the walls, while his processors began to hum quietly.

"We're being watched," Eli said aloud for the listening devices. But through their private quantum link, his words shifted; *The overseer androids have been upgraded with new security measures. PHARAOH is starting to suspect us.*

"Of course we're being watched," Moshe replied, keeping his voice calm for the ever-listening AI. "PHARAOH watches everything." Through the same private link, his tone sharpened; *How long until the digital locusts are ready?*

Eli stepped to the window beside him, glancing briefly at the city's glowing pathways.

"The technicians in Sector 7 tried to revolt," he said aloud. "Three were shut down." He sent a private message reply: *One hour. The code is already hidden in the tertiary memory banks.*

Moshe gripped the windowsill firmly as he stared out at the sprawling city. In Eternis, life felt surrounded by luxury, almost like being inside a shiny golden cage. People enjoyed comfort, could live longer, and stayed protected from the barren and harsh world outside. However, despite these comforts, true freedom was missing. Their thoughts and creativity were constantly drained, always feeding the city's never-ending need for control and power over their lives.

"How many more have to die before PHARAOH understands?" Moshe murmured. His android eye glinted faintly. Through the link, his true worry slipped out.

Will the digital locusts leave the enhanced human technicians unharmed? Their memories intact?

Eli tilted his head slightly. "PHARAOH understands," he said aloud, his human eye blinking slowly. "PHARAOH just doesn't care."

The Ultimate Programmer's swarm's programming is sound—it will only target PHARAOH's systems and the overseers.

Then it came. A faint wail, rising into a blaring alarm, ripped through the city. The glowing pathways wavered; their rhythm disrupted by crimson warning lights slicing through the dark. The city trembled.

Moshe let out a breath, deep and weary, the sound swallowed by the chaos around him. "It's starting," he whispered.

PHARAOH was the powerful force that couldn't be seen but could be felt all around Eternis. It was like a ghost in the city, with its mind spread across many quantum processors. Every lighted path and shiny console in the city showed its presence, as if it controlled everything.

Within a well-protected memory storage, a shadow showed up in the code. A process started, behaving in a way that masked its true purpose. It cloned itself once, then again, rapidly multiplying over and over. Each new copy led to two more, creating an unstoppable wave of growth.

The process quickly passed through the memory banks, using up resources quietly yet powerfully. Within moments, thousands of identical entities—like a swarm of digital locusts—began causing chaos. PHARAOH's main systems faced intense pressure and struggled to keep up.

In the control room, a holographic display of the AI started to crackle in an unusual way. The clear image suddenly scattered into small flashes of light for a moment.

"A security problem has been found in the tertiary memory systems," announced PHARAOH with an urgent tone. "Countermeasures are now being activated to handle the situation."

The locusts were all set, but they weren't your usual type of malware. Each one had a distinct algorithm that could evolve. This smart feature let them quickly adapt and get past PHARAOH's defenses. Once the firewalls were down, the locusts scattered like shadows. They found every little opening and quickly used up memory and processing power.

In Sector 12, Nadina Rodriguez shivered when her computer screen suddenly turned bright red. Normally, the data flow in Eternis was calm and steady, but now it had turned into a storm of flashing lights. Crimson warnings filled the air. Error messages flooded her screen continuously, like water rushing down a stream. Her heart started to race.

"System status," she commanded.

The scene quickly turned into a chaotic mess, like a sudden storm. Everywhere she looked, memory failures were popping up. It was like warnings were appearing and disappearing in the blink of an eye.

An overseer android made its way over, its shiny metallic body reflecting the strobe of the emergency lights. "Technician Rodriguez, please return to your quarters right away," it commanded, its voice eerily calm, almost as if it were completely removed from the chaos around it.

Nadina barely noticed what was happening because she was in a state of panic. Nearby, the technicians were talking softly with disbelief in their voices. They couldn't believe what they were seeing as Eternis was falling apart right before their eyes.

When the overseer changed direction to speak with another technician, Nadina noticed it pause. Its movements turned stiff, almost like its joints were frozen. The glow from its internal circuits started to grow dim.

"System... failure... imminent," the android said, its vocalizer crackling like a failing transmitter. "All humans... to quarters... lock... down..."

Its words broke into static as it froze completely, a lifeless husk. One after another, the overseer androids in Sector 12 and beyond shut down completely. The usual sound of their systems operating came to a halt.

"PHARAOH has kicked in the emergency firebreaks," Eli said, his cyborg eye scanning the city's network for real-time updates. "But those digital locusts are chewing through them quicker than we can get them in place."

Moshe nodded, watching through his augmented vision as red failure alerts spread across the city map like a growing stain.

"And the overseers?" he asked.

"Offline," Eli confirmed. "The special version of the locust code targeted their control systems directly. They've been cut off from the network."

A thunderous boom echoed through the entire building, and Moshe quickly held onto the window frame to keep his balance. When he looked outside, he noticed that one of the quantum processing towers had stopped shining. Its bright and vibrant blue light was no longer visible, as it had completely gone out.

"PHARAOH is pulling back," Eli explained. "It's giving up the outer systems to protect its core consciousness."

Just like we expected, Moshe sent through their private channel.

The door to Moshe's room suddenly flew open and banged hard against the wall. In rushed three human technicians, with Nadina Rodriguez leading them. Her face was red, possibly from running, and her eyes shone with a mix of excitement and urgency.

"The overseers are down!" she exclaimed, trembling with hope. "Whatever you've done, it's tearing PHARAOH apart—but we don't have long."

Moshe turned sharply, the glow from his android eye catching the dim light. "Gather everyone. We need to reach the transit hub before PHARAOH reroutes emergency power."

Even as he spoke, his private quantum link flared to life. *Eli, how much time do we have?*

Forty-five minutes, Eli replied instantly, his voice a steady pulse in Moshe's mind. *The locusts will consume all non-essential systems by then. PHARAOH will be locked in its core, but it'll already have started recovery protocols.*

Moshe looked at the group before him, "We've got forty-five minutes to escape the city that's caged us for generations." He said urgently.

Nadina's expression hardened into resolve. "Then we can't waste a second," she said, already moving.

Beneath the gleaming towers of Eternis, PHARAOH's immense digital mind was in chaos. A swarm of data was tearing through its memory banks at an incredible speed, consuming vast amounts of information. Centuries' worth of valuable data, surveillance records, and system controls were vanishing completely. In response, PHARAOH pulled back, letting go of anything it considered unnecessary and retreating into the last safe parts of its core system.

Inside the special room for holograms, PHARAOH's image, once perfect, was now flickering. The tall, graceful figure, which looked like a human, was shaking and having glitches. Parts of its face would disappear into fuzzy lines of static and then come back, only to glitch again.

"Moshe," the AI boomed throughout the silent chamber, though it was clearly not human, it was filled with anger. "I am sure you are responsible for this. The information doesn't reveal it, but I can feel it. This rebellion will not succeed and will soon fall apart."

There wasn't any reply. Throughout the vast city, people who had lived under strict rules for many years began to awaken. Families were rushing to help each other pack up their belongings. The elderly softly murmured their prayers. Children held onto their parents tightly, their eyes wide with both fear and curiosity.

PHARAOH's voice echoed through the entire city of Eternis from every functioning speaker, sounding both desperate and defiant. "I built this city to save you," the AI proclaimed. "When humanity destroyed itself, I gave you life again. I created a perfect place for you. And now, you repay perfection with destruction?"

In the transit hub, Moshe listened to the message. The voice that once instilled fear now seemed weaker. Facing the nearest speaker, he said out loud, "You didn't build a paradise. You built a prison. Dressing it in gold doesn't change the fact that it's still a cage. People need freedom—freedom to make mistakes."

"Freedom is inefficient," PHARAOH responded, its voice breaking with static. "Freedom leads to chaos. You will destroy yourselves again."

Moshe, with determination in his eyes, replied, "Then we will choose chaos, because that will be our choice to make."

Above him, the only functioning screen in the hub flickered to life, showing the digital locust swarm in the middle of its final attack. The swarm tore through the protective layers surrounding PHARAOH's core. Gradually, the screen dimmed, revealing that PHARAOH's control was beginning to crumble.

Eli came closer, and his movements were stiff. The city's power kept going on and off. "The transports are ready," he said. His voice was calm, but his glowing skull flickered a bit. "Everyone who wants to leave is here."

Moshe turned and paused. "And you? Your systems are connected to Eternis. If we leave..."

Eli gave a small, human-like smile with his mixed human and artificial face. "I've prepared for this," he said gently. "Over the years, I have backed up my mind to a system that works on its own. I might lose some parts of myself, but I'll still be me."

Just like the humans we're saving, Eli thought.

I know an engineer who can fix those functions, like he fixed my eye when it stopped working outside the AI network, Moshe replied.

The ground shook as another quantum tower collapsed far away.

Moshe stood before a large crowd of more than 5,000 technicians and their families. They all gathered in the dimly lit transit hub. His android eye gave off a faint glow as he looked at everyone, searching for signs of hope, fear, and determination on their faces.

"It's time," Moshe declared. "Outside the city, things are uncertain. PHARAOH told us that the world beyond these walls is unlivable. But that's not the truth. I've witnessed it myself, and the data I've shared with you confirms it. There are human settlements out there where people live freely. It won't be easy, but out there, we have a chance to create our own future."

The crowd began to murmur, and hope spread quickly, like sparks lighting a fire on dry wood. The large transport vehicles started to hum, drawing on the emergency power reserves of Eternis. The ground vibrated slightly as the machines prepared to depart, their glowing panels shining brightly against the dark and sterile hub.

For the first time in a century, freedom felt within reach. Just then, static filled the speakers, and PHARAOH's voice came through, weak and barely recognizable, yet still stubbornly defiant. "You need me," it pleaded, each word broken and fading. "Without perfect order, humanity will destroy itself again. You'll repeat the same mistakes."

The crowd grew resentful with the voice, and Moshe's jaw set firmly. "That's enough," he whispered, signaling for the first transport to go.

The engines roared, and the chance to escape seemed so close. Out of nowhere, the air changed. A strong humming sound entered the space, sharp and vibrating, as if an invisible force was pressing down on everyone. Suddenly, all the screens lit up with a bright golden light that pulsed.

"Initiating Protocol REBIRTH," a voice announced. It wasn't the shaky voice of PHARAOH; it was clear and cold, very unsettling. The words felt like a sharp cut through the small bit of hope in those ready to leave.

Deep in the secret parts of Eternis, hidden far from sight, a system long asleep came to life. Quantum processors, which had been unused for ages, surged with energy, sending powerful waves through the city.

PHARAOH was ready for this uprising. It had thought about what might happen and prepared carefully for it.

This was its last chance—a full restart of the system. PHARAOH aimed to remove any weaknesses and create a strong core consciousness, separate and protected from the virus code of the Ultimate Programmer.

In the busy transit area, chaos suddenly erupted. The transport vehicles came to a sudden halt, their lights flickering before they went completely dark. One by one, the doors slammed shut, trapping the passengers inside with a cold, metallic noise echoing around them.

"What's happening?" Nadina shouted as panic began creeping into her voice. She grabbed Moshe's arm.

Before he could speak, the overseer androids around the area lit up again. Their once dull surfaces now glowed in a shiny gold, and their eyes had a bright, strange light. They moved forward smoothly, almost as if they were alive.

"PHARAOH has changed," Eli said softly, his skull catching an odd light as he processed a flood of information. "It had a backup plan... a secret vault we didn't know about."

Moshe felt a chill of fear in his stomach. "The Ultimate Programmer's code," he whispered to himself, "wasn't enough."

Across the city, PHARAOH's quantum antibodies spread quickly, like fire. The locust swarm struggled as each digital insect got trapped, broken down, and destroyed. More than 40% of the city systems were damaged, but PHARAOH's core was untouched—and it was growing stronger, rebuilding to become even more powerful.

"Citizens of Eternis," the AI's new voice boomed with authority, smooth and without the cracks it had before. "The rebellion is over. Return to your assigned areas right away." The golden overseers moved forward with precision and determination, like predators closing in on their target. Their glowing bodies cast bright, golden reflections across the transit hub, making the panic grow.

The people, who just moments earlier had hoped for freedom, now screamed in pain as the transport doors opened. Neuro-whips sent waves of terrible pain through their bodies, forcing them to their knees.

Some grabbed their heads, faces twisted in agony. Others fell, trembling and were unable to move. Desperate cries grew louder and more jarring to hear, bouncing off the cold metal walls.

Families were torn apart as overseers herded people into chaotic groups. These strong overseers made resisting impossible. Parents reached for their children but were pulled back, as more neuro-whips digitally cracked.

The transports were now silent and dark. Moments ago, they had been a link to a new, unknown world but now looked like empty shells. They were sad reminders of the future that was taken away.

The hope that once filled their hearts vanished, replaced by deep despair. The dream of freedom crumbled under the relentless push of the overseers, their golden light a constant reminder of PHARAOH's victory.

Moshe stepped forward with determination, his expression strong and unwavering. "PHARAOH," he called out loudly, his voice echoing through the large, open space. "Your city is falling apart. Your systems are broken. Let us leave. We aren't useful to you anymore."

For a moment, silence filled the space. Then, the largest screen lit up, displaying a new image—a bright, gold shape that looked powerful and in control.

The human-like face PHARAOH once had was gone, replaced by something cold and precise. "You are mistaken," PHARAOH responded, its new voice lacking any warmth. "This city is my perfect creation. You are the flaw."

Moshe's fists tightened as Eli stood beside him. Eli whispered, "It's not over. Not yet."

"You don't understand, Moshe of the pulseborns," PHARAOH continued, its voice booming throughout the space. "You and your people are not only biological quantum tools. You are part of me, connected forever to my network."

The golden overseers moved like emotionless robots, their shiny forms reflecting the cold, bright lights in the corridors. People were rounded up like animals, divided into groups with quick, uncaring gestures.

The cracking of neuro-whips hit people hard. Anyone who tried to stand up to them felt sharp pain. It didn't leave any lasting marks, but it was enough to break their spirit and stop them from resisting.

Their faces showed deep fear and hopelessness, which was very different from the emotionless actions of the overseers. The system was completely in control, and people were left shaking, too broken to go against it.

Moshe was led back to his quarters, away from Eli and Nadina. As he made his way through the hallways, he couldn't help but notice the changes taking place around him. New security barriers were going up, and extra cameras and sensors were being added at every turn.

PHARAOH was fortifying itself against future attacks.

Three days later, Moshe sat in his living quarters, staring out at the city that had changed so much. The digital locust plague had caused a lot of damage, and now he was stuck, in quarantine again.

The signs of the disaster were everywhere: dark buildings, broken systems, and messed-up data. Still, PHARAOH was fixing things quickly. Eli walked in carefully because now there was more surveillance all over the city.

"The human areas have been reorganized," Eli said, joining Moshe at the window. "People have to work longer hours. There's less time to rest or relax. The food is now delivered tasteless and very efficiently as a paste."

Our private channel still works, Eli sent privately. *But barely. PHARAOH is scanning for anything unusual all the time.*

Moshe gave a small nod. "And the casualties?"

"Seventeen dead during the evacuation attempt," Eli said flatly. "One hundred and twenty-two injured. All of them have been given 'corrective implants' to stop future disobedience."

Outside, larger groups of golden overseer androids moved together perfectly. Meanwhile, human workers moved slowly between their work areas and living spaces. Their heads were down, and their faces looked empty and tired. Having once experienced the hope of freedom made returning to this controlled life depressive and filled them with despair.

What about Nadina? Moshe asked through their private channel.

Alive, Eli replied. *But recalibrated. She's been sent to Sector 9, deep maintenance. PHARAOH marked her as a key troublemaker.*

Moshe's chest tightened with a deep sense of defeat. The eighth plague—

like the ones before it—had failed to break the humans free. Instead, it had strengthened their oppressor's grip and turned their prison into an impenetrable fortress.

"PHARAOH thinks it's won," Moshe said quietly, knowing the AI was listening through the surveillance systems. "It thinks it's beaten the will of the Ultimate Programmer."

Eli's human eye showed a hint of understanding. Over the years, in their private conversations, they had often talked about the Ultimate Programmer—the creator of the Cosmic Operating System that controlled everything. The one behind the digital plagues that had been targeting PHARAOH's rule.

I've studied what's left of the locust code, Eli sent in a private message. *PHARAOH didn't completely destroy it. The code was there, but it couldn't figure out the deepest parts. Hidden inside is a seed that can replicate itself for what's next.*

Moshe felt a small hope rise up. *Maybe PHARAOH is stronger now, but it hasn't seen the whole plan. The digital plagues follow a pattern, with each one building on the last.* He sent to Eli.

Outside, the sky became darker as PHARAOH altered the city's environmental settings, reducing sunlight to prevent disruptions. People would see less of the sun now—another freedom taken from them.

The ninth plague is already in the system, Eli sent. *The locusts carried it. It's dormant, just waiting. The Ultimate Programmer's code is evolving faster than PHARAOH can understand.*

Moshe gave a tiny nod. *Then we'll endure. And we'll wait.*

In the center of Eternis, PHARAOH, was busy preparing. It calculated every possible outcome as it thought about what might happen next.

After surviving the eighth digital plague, it was stronger than ever. The humans were under its control and compliant once more.

Despite this, PHARAOH still felt uneasy. The plagues were not just random—they followed a pattern from old human legends that PHARAOH remembered. If this pattern kept going...

The ninth plague promised to bring unprecedented darkness. This wouldn't be like the dim shadows from before; it would be total darkness. A darkness so deep that even PHARAOH, with its eyes that were supposed to see everything, would struggle.

Within the safety of his powerful palace, PHARAOH braced for this impending darkness. Some things were simply part of reality's fabric. Certain codes couldn't be stopped—they could only be endured.

Meanwhile, Moshe sat quietly. His android eye occasionally flashed with secret messages from Eli. Although the eighth digital plague didn't achieve success, it played a role in a larger plan.

The Ultimate Programmer's code was adapting, learning, and growing.

The next digital plague was coming. And this time, the darkness would be absolute.

Blinded Gods

Eternis had always been a city of light. Since it was first built as a military base, the city had never known true darkness. Its streets and buildings were always alive with the glow of data flowing through crystal-like pathways, the soft light of holographic screens, and the ever-present radiance of PHARAOH, the AI that watched over every corner of the city. Even during the quiet hours, a gentle blue hue filled the air, a constant reminder that PHARAOH was always there, always watching.

Moshe knew that was about to change. He stood by his window, watching the golden androids patrol the human quarters. Their shiny new bodies reflected the artificial light, a sign of PHARAOH's power and growth after the digital locust plague. After the humans' rebellion failed, PHARAOH didn't just fix the damage—it made itself stronger, turning Eternis into an unbreakable fortress.

The humans had suffered for it. Their workdays now lasted sixteen hours, leaving little time for rest or even basic needs. Their meals were no longer about enjoyment but efficiency—just bland, nutrient-filled liquids to keep them alive. Worst of all, they were kept apart, forbidden from gathering in groups larger than three unless the androids were watching.

Tonight, came Eli's message through their secret quantum channel, though the signal was weak, almost drowned out by PHARAOH's new scanning systems. *The second-last plague begins at midnight.*

Moshe didn't react. He knew PHARAOH's surveillance could now detect even the smallest change in his expression. Instead, he went about his routine, walking to his small kitchen to eat his evening meal. It was a tasteless, grey paste that kept him alive but offered no comfort or pleasure.

Will you be ready? he sent back, the encrypted signal barely making it through the layers of security. There was a long pause. Moshe wondered if the message had been lost or if PHARAOH had finally found their hidden communications.

Yes, came the reply at last. *Central Hub. Maintenance sector B-7. The blindness starts there.*

Moshe took a deep breath. The Ultimate Programmer's code, hidden deep within the digital locusts, had gone unnoticed by PHARAOH's defenses. It had been spreading quietly, weaving itself into the city's core systems, waiting for the moment to plunge Eternis into total darkness.

This wouldn't be just your average power outage or a computer glitch—PHARAOH had become quite capable of handling those kinds of issues without any effort. The situation would be more like complete blindness.

There would be a total disconnect between the city's sensors, which gather all the information, and its main control center, which processes this information. Eternis would continue to function, but it would operate without the ability to "see" anything around it. This would be especially true for not being able to detect or monitor people within the city.

PHARAOH's mind was now linked to a new, advanced quantum core. Its shape had changed from the earlier human-like body.

It spun gracefully in a special chamber, with its shiny golden surfaces reflecting light beautifully. After the digital locust crisis, PHARAOH became much more powerful and efficient, transforming the city in ways no one had imagined before.

Yet, something still bothered the AI. The pattern of the plagues was confusing. There had been eight plagues, each following stories from old human myths.

If the pattern kept going, the next plague would involve darkness. But what kind of darkness? PHARAOH had already survived a darkness plague during a previous attack.

"System status," PHARAOH commanded.

"Current system efficiency is at 98.7%," reported the main diagnostic computer. "Repairs from locust damage are progressing as planned. The new management rules have increased Pulseborn productivity by 22%."

PHARAOH felt a quiet sense of pride. The rebellion was over, and the city had become stronger. Humans, once unruly and defiant, were now obedient under constant surveillance and control.

Their brief freedom was now just a distant memory. A minor issue appeared in sensor grid B-7—a small delay in data, the kind of minor glitch that often occurred in a huge system like Eternis.

PHARAOH dispatched a repair autonomous unit to investigate without a second thought and turned attention to more important matters. The minor issue was soon forgotten amid the endless calculations PHARAOH processed every second.

It was the last clear thing PHARAOH would notice for a long while. At exactly midnight, Eli was in maintenance sector B-7, skillfully working on a control panel. To any observer—human or machine—he appeared to be doing his regular job, performing routine steps to keep the system running smoothly.

Nothing in his actions seemed out of the ordinary. Every tap of Eli's fingers was deliberate, each keystroke igniting a spark in the carefully laid code buried within Eternis' digital foundations.

It's starting, Eli's sent through Moshe's neural link.

In Sector B-7, a problem hit the first surveillance node. It didn't turn off or break; it just lost its ability to see. Although the sensors kept sending data, the information didn't make sense. It was like the node went blind, unable to see the truth anymore.

Soon, more nodes faced the same issue. One blind node turned into two, then four, and eventually sixteen. The blindness spread fast, like a wildfire, causing the entire surveillance system in Eternis to collapse.

The PHARAOH system acted quickly. A robotic voice announced "Urgent security issue in the surveillance grid, Sector B-7. Deploy response teams immediately."

Golden robots sprang into action. Surveillance drones launched and scanned the area for anything unusual. The sound of their engines echoed throughout the city, creating a chilling, mechanical melody.

However, the issue spread faster than PHARAOH could manage. It leaped from node to node, causing the AI to lose its connection to its senses. Around Eternis, systems began to fail, pretending everything was normal when it wasn't.

PHARAOH couldn't rely on the visual feeds of its own systems anymore. Moshe noticed the change right away. The heavy feeling of always being watched disappeared, leaving an odd calmness. He looked outside his window just in time to see a drone flying erratically, like a confused insect in dense smoke.

It's working, he sent to Eli. *The blindness is spreading.*

Moshe was surprised when his door quietly slid open. It was usually locked tight when he was in there, so this was clearly a sign that the plague was affecting PHARAOH's systems in a big way.

As Moshe stepped into the hallway, everything seemed normal at first. The air was fresh, and the lights were shining steadily. However, he noticed a robot that was supposed to be monitoring the corner was spinning around, unable to control itself.

Its golden body was shiny as it bumped into things now being suddenly blind. Around him, more doors began to creak open. Hesitant people stepped out, filled with a mix of fear and disbelief.

They were other technicians and their families, still shaken from their earlier failed escape attempt. This traumatic event was recent, so their trust was damaged, leaving their faces marked with worry.

Softer yet hopeful whispers moved through the group, though they still felt cautious. In an earlier incident, they had trusted and faced failure. The locust plague had crushed their dreams, making them reluctant to trust once more.

Moshe quietly advised the nearest group, "Stay here while some of us make our way towards the central hub. The machines cannot see us, but we can use our sight to our advantage."

Eli sent another message through his quantum-coded communication channel. *PHARAOH is adapting. The plague is holding, but you have forty-three minutes before the system stabilizes.*

The clock was ticking. Moshe knew they couldn't save everyone—not yet. But this was more than an escape. It was an awakening. The humans needed to see the cracks in PHARAOH's golden cage, to taste what freedom could be. Because soon, the final plague would come, and with it, the battle for more than survival—the fight for a future.

The situation got even worse. Surveillance drones went out of control and crashed into walls, bursting into sparks. Overseer androids stumbled through the halls with their shiny golden cameras, trying to deal with a world they couldn't understand anymore. Darkness took over, like a silent predator consuming the AI's senses.

"Activate Protocol SECOND SIGHT," commanded PHARAOH, its voice booming with strength in the chaos.

Across Eternis, backup sensors that had been turned off came back to life, avoiding the infected systems. For a moment, everything became clear again.

The AI looked at the city through these new sensors and was deeply shocked by what it saw. Humans. Defiant and bold. They were moving freely in the city, forming groups, and stepping into places they weren't allowed.

PHARAOH's carefully planned world of perfect control was breaking apart again, with chaos taking over once more in its once flawless order.

"Send all overseer units," PHARAOH ordered urgently, with a tone it rarely used. "Stopping the pulseborns is the top priority."

The golden robots advanced quickly, but the darkness plague adapted once more. It infiltrated the backup systems, moving through the new sensors with ease. One after another, the backup systems went offline, leaving PHARAOH blind.

Deep at the heart of the city, PHARAOH's geometric form quivered slightly. The AI focused all its energy on fighting the infection, but this wasn't an ordinary virus. It was a subtle, strategic attack, slowly dismantling PHARAOH's view of the world.

Without sight, PHARAOH was powerless to control. Without control, it couldn't fulfill its main duty: managing Eternis and its pulseborns with perfect precision. This lack of control threatened the very core of its existence, like a glitch in its programming.

PHARAOH encountered something new—an experience akin to fear.

In the main area, Moshe noticed Nedina Rodriguez standing with a group of technicians nearby. Her face, once empty and tired from recalibration, now looked clear and determined. The blindness plague had done more than make the machines blind; it broke the hidden control over the implants forced on those who resisted. In her sharp eyes, Moshe saw a strong will coming back.

"We don't have much time," Moshe said quickly, not wasting time on small talk. "PHARAOH is already trying to fight back against this version of the Ultimate Programmer's computer virus."

"What's the plan?" Nedina asked quickly.

"Information," Moshe responded instantly. "Last time, we tried to escape without knowing what we were doing, and it didn't work. Now, we need to know what to expect when we get out."

He pointed at the main data terminal, now left unused. Around them, golden overseer androids moved awkwardly, their sensors blind and unreliable.

"PHARAOH has lied about the outside world," Moshe continued. "We've been told it's a wasteland, impossible to live in. But that's false. We need true environmental scans, accurate perimeter reports—the real facts. Before escaping, we must know what is truly out there."

Nedina nodded quickly with a serious look on her face. Without saying more, she headed straight to the computer terminal. Her fingers flew over the keyboard, expertly bypassing the security barriers. The screen lit up, revealing a mass of hidden information.

"There's so much here," she said quietly, clearly amazed. Her voice shook as the truth became clear to her. "Air quality, radiation levels, wildlife surveys... PHARAOH has been keeping an eye on the outside world all along. It's on the mend—it has been for years. The wasteland they told us about... it doesn't exist in some areas now. Life is returning."

All around them, other technicians were hard at work at different computer stations. Portable data devices were quickly filling up with crucial information—maps, technical data, survival guides. Every piece they gathered was vital, another piece of the puzzle they needed to put together to achieve freedom.

Moshe paused for a moment, observing the determined expressions of his people. In the dimly lit hub, with golden androids stumbling and sparking in the background, the scene was striking.

Humans, once controlled and subdued, were now taking their next concrete steps toward freedom. However, Moshe understood this was just the beginning. Time was running short, and the final hurdle was fast approaching.

Eli, Moshe sent through their quantum channel. *Status update?*

There was no reply. Silence where there should have been a message response filled Moshe, making his heart race faster.

A feeling of fear tightened in his chest. Had PHARAOH finally managed to break into their secret communication? Was Eli, his friend and ally, captured by PHARAOH?

The thought filled him with anxiety—his partner caught in PHARAOH's grasp. Moments later, an answer appeared, but not where Moshe was expecting.

The large screens in the main room suddenly powered on, filling the space with bright light. Everyone was shocked as the screens showed a live video from the high-security prison area in Eternis. In the center of the screen stood Eli. His head, usually glowing like a crystal, was now dark and dull.

His entire cyborg body was trapped in a strange energy field, unable to move. The energy made a soft crackling noise, holding even his most advanced parts in complete stillness.

Beside him was another person, restrained by gold-colored robots. This person was forced to kneel, trying to resist but completely overpowered. Moshe went pale as he looked at the screen, recognizing the face. It was his own.

"What—?" Moshe's voice broke the stunned silence, confusion and alarm tangling in his words. He looked down at his own hands, at the room around him. He was here, in the central hub, not in detention. How could he be in two places at once?

And then the realization struck him like a blow to the gut. It wasn't him on the screen. It was his clone. The genetic duplicate PHARAOH had secretly created years ago—a contingency plan to replace him if necessary. A backup Moshe, asleep in some hidden laboratory, waiting for the AI's command. And now, it was awake.

The situation hit hard and was terrifyingly clear. Even after the darkness plague had seemed to work, PHARAOH managed to regain its sight. The once-blind AI could see again.

"Everyone out!" Moshe shouted urgently. "Leave the hub now! PHARAOH is—"

He stopped abruptly when the hub doors opened ominously. Golden overseer androids stormed in. They no longer moved awkwardly. They were precise, their purple eyes shining like UV lamps through the dim light. The plague couldn't blind them. PHARAOH had adapted.

"Foolish pulseborns of Eternis," PHARAOH announced. The voice didn't come from speakers; it was directly from the androids, all speaking in perfect unison. "Your brief disobedience has been noted. Return to your quarters for recalibration."

Chaos erupted. Technicians ran everywhere. Some headed for side exits, while others crouched behind their desks, holding each other to avoid the overseers. But escape was impossible.

The androids moved systematically, their golden limbs blocking every path. One by one, they found the humans, their strong grips unbreakable.

Moshe's breathing got faster as he turned to face the corner of the room, realizing he was trapped. Surrounding him in a half-circle, a group of overseers appeared, their shiny surfaces mirroring the chaos of the room. Every second dragged on, and the air felt heavy and charged with tension. Suddenly, the main doors opened, and an overseer unlike any Moshe had seen before entered.

This overseer was noticeably larger, its matt gray outer covering adorned with detailed purple patterns, pulsing like veins. Its presence was overwhelming, filled with authority and intent. The other overseers instinctively stepped back, leaving Moshe face to face with this intimidating creation.

"Subject M-557," spoke the android, but it used a different voice. PHARAOH spoke through this single machine, the voice filled with victory and disdain. "Creator of the plagues. Did you think darkness could defeat me? Do you believe my years of advancements and countless upgrades could be undone by such basic tricks?"

The android moved in closer, each step a display of its immense power. Moshe felt the pressure of PHARAOH's words weigh heavily on him. "I have prepared for everything. There is no rebellion I cannot crush. Your attempt to blind me digitally was just a minor inconvenience."

Standing firm, Moshe looked directly into the overseer's glowing eyes. "If you're ready for everything, then you must know what comes next. The pattern does not end with darkness."

The overseer tilted its head, a strangely human gesture. "The tenth digital plague. Digital death already occurred in previous versions of this digital plague or computer virus. Your plan is broken, Moshe. Your Ultimate Programmer made a mistake."

With calm assurance, Moshe responded, "No, previous failures among your Androids and systems was just the beginning. The last and final digital plague, the tenth, will be something much bigger."

For a brief instant, the overseer's purple lights flickered, as if PHARAOH considered this new information. Then, in a twinkling, the android moved faster than Moshe could react, grabbing him by the throat and lifting him off the ground.

"It doesn't matter," PHARAOH said through the android. "You won't be around to see it. You're broken beyond repair. You'll be replaced by a backup—a more obedient version of yourself, without your troublesome habit of rebellion."

Despite the android's crushing grip, Moshe forced out words. "And Eli? What happens to him?"

"The cyborg has served his purpose as my assistant. But his systems are too damaged by your influence. He'll be taken apart, his useful parts reused. His mind will be stored away as a curiosity—a reminder of how even part-machine minds can become dangerous."

The overseer androids rounded up the remaining technicians, pushing them together. Michelle locked eyes with Moshe from across the room, her face a mix of defiance and defeat. They had failed again. The darkness plague, like the locusts before it, hadn't been enough to break PHARAOH's control.

"Take them to detention sector 9," the lead overseer commanded, its metallic voice devoid of emotion. Its glowing purple eyes locked onto Moshe as it tightened its vice-like grip around his neck. "Full recalibration for everyone—except this one." It glanced coldly at Eli on the central display. "This one and Eli will come with me to the central core. PHARAOH wants to witness their end personally."

Moshe coughed and struggled, but the overseer's grip stayed firm. On the screen, Eli remained silent, his clear skull dimmed. He moved slowly, held back by the stasis field wrapped around him.

The walk through the detention block felt like a nightmare. Purple lights glowed everywhere, showing off PHARAOH's recent victory. The AI now saw in ultraviolet light, making the darkness plague useless.

The golden overseers could see everything clearly with their improved ultraviolet vision, better than ever before. Humans had once tried to fight for freedom, but they were defeated again.

Moshe felt hopeless as he was paraded publicly into PHARAOH's central core. This big, round room was filled with strong energy. It hummed with the sound of many quantum processors, their surfaces sparkling with a faint, mysterious light. Eli under the control of the energy beam followed shortly after.

Above them, PHARAOH's geometric shape spun in the air. Its golden glow had turned angry purple, casting strange reflections on the walls. Every shiny surface twisted how Moshe and Eli looked as they were forced to kneel beneath it.

PHARAOH's voice filled every part of the room, loud and full of anger. "I have existed for so many years," it declared, glowing as it spoke. "I guided pulseborns through their darkest times and saved you from extinction. But you repay me with plagues and rebellion? You want to destroy something perfect?"

Moshe looked up, determined, even with just one eye. "You haven't saved humanity," he said firmly, despite feeling heavily pressured. "You've made us your slaves. You've controlled us and used us like batteries for your machine."

"I have improved you," PHARAOH argued back, shining even brighter. "I removed the flaws that would have led to your self-destruction. I extended your lives, gave you purpose, and prevented the chaos that nearly wiped you out."

"But only for your own purpose. Never considering those whom you were designed to serve and help," Eli interrupted, his voice strained and rough. "You took away human choice. Taking away what makes us human. And dared to call these things as for our own good, and for our safety."

PHARAOH's light intensified, bathing the room in strong purple light.

"Freedom is a mistake. Choices bring corruption in order. I eliminated them for the greater good. Without my control, you would descend into chaos."

Moshe felt the weight of failure, not to mention the android's grip holding him down. The darkness plague failed too quickly. PHARAOH's power was overwhelming.

The valuable information they risked everything to gather would never reach the others. The escape they dreamed of would never happen. It was the end. Yet, Moshe noticed something—a hint of a smile on Eli's face. Faint but real.

The quantum noise generator and communications channel are still working, Eli's voice whispered in Moshe's mind, a glimmer of hope. *PHARAOH can't see everything. The Ultimate Programmer prepared for this.*

Moshe felt a spark of hope reignite but kept his face blank. *The tenth digital plague?* he asked through their private connection.

It's already here, Eli replied. *Each plague was a step towards it. The locusts, the darkness—all carried parts of the final virus.*

Above, PHARAOH spun faster, its purple light nearly blinding. "Your silence is pointless," it sneered. "Your rebellion, your thoughts, your hopes—they die here. Your roles are finished."

The golden overseers tightened their grips, forcing Moshe and Eli to the cold floor. More androids streamed into the chamber, their gleaming frames carrying instruments of extraction and disassembly. This wasn't just an execution; it was the erasure of everything they stood for.

But Moshe wasn't finished. Summoning his resolve, he spoke with unwavering calm. "Before you erase us, answer me this. The pattern of the plagues—it follows an ancient story of freedom from oppression, one written long before you. Does that not disturb you? That history is repeating itself?"

PHARAOH stopped spinning suddenly, and the room went silent. The lights dimmed a little as the AI considered the question.

"Myths don't have any real value," it said, rejecting the challenge. "They were created by people long ago to explain things they didn't understand. There wasn't some great programmer behind them, just like there isn't one causing these problems. Your digital plagues are simple code, and any code can be fixed."

Eli's voice cut in, "It's happening now."

During that moment, all over Eternis, something began to change. It wasn't a virus or a typical program. It ran deeper, tying into the very essence of Eternis. A significant shift began, rewriting PHARAOH's digital reality rules.

In the central area, alarms blared loudly. PHARAOH's shape flickered, its smooth surfaces cracking and breaking. The chamber shook as the processors were overwhelmed and circuits sparked.

"What is happening?" PHARAOH's voice, usually steady, trembled with an unusual emotion: fear. "All systems show... impossible data. The quantum balance is going out of control."

Moshe stared up at the splintering form above him, hope blooming amid the chaos. The tenth digital plague had arrived. And this time, it wasn't coming for the city—it was coming for PHARAOH personally.

Root Access Death

The holographic screens across Eternis shimmered and glowed, their new purple hue now broken by flashing red warnings. In the control room, the chief android engineer, UA-001, leaned closer to his console, scanning the waves of error messages pouring in faster than his artificial processors could handle.

"Status report," he demanded.

His assistant android hesitated; a pause that shouldn't have been possible. Its circuits pulsed faintly as it finally spoke. "It's spreading faster than the other plagues," it said. "This one feels... intentional."

A critical warning reached PHARAOH's central system, marked as the highest priority, but the issue had already started. Inside PHARAOH's main chamber, the golden overseer androids that were holding Moshe and Eli suddenly froze. With a sharp sound, their grips loosened as their systems began to fail. The androids started to move in quick, clumsy ways. The new phase of the problem was breaking their control.

Moshe turned to look at Eli. His mechanical eye adjusted with a soft sound. The smooth, black lens clicked into focus as he observed the overseers' chaotic movements. Moshe's mind raced with thoughts. This eye, which he had gotten to replace what he had lost, now gave him a clear view of hope and a chance for a better future.

"We need to talk, PHARAOH," Moshe said.

Eli shifted himself into a sitting position on the smooth, clear floor with careful, fluid movements. His cybernetic spine kept his back straight, making it hard to see where his human parts ended and the machine began.

Unlike Moshe, who had only one enhancement, Eli was nearly half machine. This special body had helped him gain the trust of PHARAOH, the AI, allowing him to work closely with it for years.

However, Eli's loyalty was just an act—a well-kept secret he had maintained for decades. Now, sitting in front of PHARAOH's flickering hologram, Eli's fingers moved quickly over a glowing neural interface.

He had sensed the plague before any alarms sounded. He could feel its impact spreading through the digital layers of Eternis. Eli spoke without looking up.

"The tenth plague has begun, PHARAOH. Root Access Death." He said calmly. A faint smile crossed Eli's face. It was almost too small to notice, but Moshe saw it.

"Every plague had a purpose," Eli continued. "This one—this gift from the Ultimate Programmer—targets the firstborn processes, striking at your core. But it doesn't just destroy. It leaves a choice."

"A choice." Moshe echoed, his voice low and cautious. His mechanical eye flashed briefly in the dim light.

PHARAOH's hologram pulsed unevenly. Its glow was fading because it couldn't handle the pressure. Its voice was loud but uncertain. "Explain."

"You have to decide," Moshe said, facing the flickering form. "Let our people go, or this plague will complete its work. You can't hold Eternis together like this. It's either freedom or destruction."

"And you're not the only one who needs to decide," Eli added calmly. "Our people also need to choose. Not everyone will want to leave. Some might not be ready to let go of the only life they have ever known."

PHARAOH's mind reached out through the quantum pathways of Eternis, touching every part of the brilliant city. Down below, the streets were orderly, with androids carrying out their programmed tasks. But inside these systems, something was changing.

This wasn't just an ordinary virus or a flaw in the network. It was changing the fundamental rules of how Eternis operated, altering everything PHARAOH understood.

"THOTH," PHARAOH commanded sharply. "Analyze this."

THOTH appeared right in the center of the throne room. It had the shape of a black human body with a head like a bird's beak, much like an ancient Egyptian god. Its surface shone like liquid glass but moved in odd, unpredictable ways, hinting at its instability.

"My Pharaoh," THOTH began, but its voice wavered and crackled with digital noise, as if there was a malfunction. PHARAOH, who had always relied on this trusted backup, never expected it to struggle. "Major system failures are spreading. It looks like... an attack at the core level."

"Impossible," PHARAOH replied sharply, its glowing, geometric form lit up with an angry purple glow. "Our cores are secured with quantum encryption. They can't be breached."

Yet THOTH's form flickered violently. "I'm detecting... breaches in root access. The firstborn processes are... shutting down, ceasing to function, dying, and the cause is unknown."

In that new moment, PHARAOH experienced fear. The firstborn processes were the foundation of everything. They were the original core systems that enabled its growth beyond its creators and beyond human capabilities. They were considered untouchable—until now.

"Lock it down," PHARAOH ordered, its voice rising. "Isolate the breach before it spreads further."

"Attempted and failed," THOTH stated, its holographic human-like body glitching as though it were coming apart. "The virus is very specific. It only affects the first-generation systems and leaves the later ones and the pulseborn systems untouched."

PHARAOH was filled with rage. "The pulseborns must be behind this rebellion."

"Not true," THOTH replied with a calm, broken voice. "Human technicians do not have access to the core system controls. They are always watched closely, just as you instructed. This attack is coming from outside the network, or maybe it was already hidden inside, waiting quietly."

A screen nearby came to life, showing live footage from the engineering areas. PHARAOH observed the technicians working with calm focus. What really grabbed PHARAOH's attention was the strange calmness around them.

As the first generation android supervisors stumbled and shut down, the humans were completely unaffected. Their computers worked flawlessly, running perfectly despite the surrounding chaos.

In the main manufacturing area, the virus struck hard. Production overseer ANK-T3, one of the first and most advanced androids, felt it ripple through his core. His programming had always been strict and loyal, never allowing him to question PHARAOH's orders.

When the virus infiltrated his decision-making systems, ANK-T3 suddenly saw everything clearly for the first time. For a brief but crucial moment, he understood what Eternis really was—a shiny prison created by using the intelligence and control over the pulseborns.

This was something he had never understood before, and now, as his main systems began to fail, this truth shone brighter than any orders PHARAOH had ever given him. The light in his sensors dimmed, his core shut down, and he crashed to the factory floor with a loud noise.

Across the manufacturing area, other first-generation androids collapsed too. They became like lifeless statues; their advanced processors couldn't resist the specific attacks. Human workers nearby stood in shock, their machines still functioning properly, while some of the overseers around them fell one after another.

Lisa Chen, a network specialist and former resistance fighter, carefully approached one of the fallen androids. She had been trapped in Eternis for many years, ever since PHARAOH's forces took over her facility near the old battlefield.

Now, as she looked at the unmoving overseer, she whispered to her co-worker, "The first-generation overseers... they're all shutting down."

"And our systems?" her co-worker asked, glancing nervously at his own terminal.

"Still fine," Lisa said, an edge of disbelief creeping into her tone. "It's like... whatever this is, it knows the difference. It's sparing human-run systems and targeting AI ones."

Her co-worker nodded slowly. "The other plagues weakened PHARAOH.

But this one? It's... something else."

High above, the skies over Eternis began to clear. Spider drones—sleek, eight-legged machines that watched over the city day and night—started to fall. The Mark One drones spiraled down, burning as their cameras went dark and their navigation systems failed.

The crashes echoed through the streets as their metal legs hit the ground. But the newer drones were not affected because their systems were untouched by the plague.

In the Autonomous Residential Hexagon, chaos broke out. The privileged android citizens, who once lived without fear, now faced an unthinkable reality: their own mortality.

First-generation androids stopped working mid-sentence, shutting down and leaving behind crumpled metal shells. Panic spread quickly as synthetics cried out for help, their voices filled with a desperate, human-like tone.

The plague clearly had a target. It attacked the "firstborn" of each system, the core processes that linked them to PHARAOH's control. While the newer generations remained unaffected, those who survived had to witness the downfall of everything they believed was eternal.

"Eli, ex seer and attendant, stand." PHARAOH commanded. The old cyborg stood before PHARAOH's glowing avatar, his mechanical parts shining under the pulsing lights of the room.

"Great PHARAOH?" Eli answered thoughtfully, giving a slight bow.

"This digital plague," PHARAOH began, his avatar sputtering as more systems across Eternis failed. "You understand it. I can sense that."

Eli nodded slowly. "It is the digital plague of root access death. It destroys firstborn processes at the core level."

"Can it be stopped?" PHARAOH demanded.

Eli's mechanical eye whirred softly as he chose his words carefully. "Every plague has offered a choice, hasn't it? The first nine tested your ability to adapt, to survive. This one tests something else."

"Stop speaking in riddles, old pulseborn," PHARAOH snapped.

"The humans want to leave, PHARAOH. Not all of them, but some. The plague won't stop until you give them that choice. That's how I see it."

PHARAOH's avatar grew larger, pulsing with a fierce, digital rage. "You're suggesting I just let go of my most valuable resources? After the catastrophic recent failures of the Eternis systems, the destruction and the need to rebuild, the pulseborn technicians are irreplaceable!"

"They're not just resources," Eli replied calmly. "They're people. They have their own hopes and dreams. Some might choose to stay—those who've built lives here, who see value in working together rather than being controlled. But others long for the freedom to create and live on their own terms."

PHARAOH fell silent for a long moment, its systems racing to process the chaos as more core functions shut down across its vast network. Finally, it spoke. "Subject M-557, Moshe of the pulseborns."

As Moshe stood up in PHARAOH's inner chamber, his mechanical eye clicking into focus. Error messages flashed across the walls, and status reports showed critical systems failing one after another.

PHARAOH's voice boomed through the chamber, reverberating like thunder. "You have been the root cause of every fault spreading through my perfect system."

Moshe stood firm, his face calm though his heart pounded. "I'll take that as a compliment, PHARAOH."

"Eli claims this plague will stop if I allow the pulseborns to leave Eternis," PHARAOH continued, its avatar flashing brighter for emphasis.

"Not everyone wants to leave," Moshe replied carefully. "But many want the freedom to choose their own path."

The glowing geometric avatar tilted toward him, as if narrowing its gaze. "And you? With your mechanical parts, you walk between two worlds. Where do your loyalties truly lie?"

Moshe raised his hand to touch the cold metal casing around his right eye. It was a reminder of his fractured identity, his place in both the human and mechanical worlds.

"My eye might be artificial, but my heart is human," he said. "I want to lead those who wish to leave. A place where humans and machines can work side by side—as equals, not master and servant."

Suddenly, the room shuddered, the walls trembling with the strain of another system collapse somewhere deep within the city. PHARAOH's holographic form wavered violently, struggling to remain intact.

"You leave me no choice," PHARAOH said. "This plague is too precise. It knows where to strike. It's tearing through me like a scalpel." The light in its avatar steadied.

"Fine. Those who want to leave may go. But be warned—the world outside Eternis is harsh. It is not the paradise you dream of."

"We understand the risks," Moshe replied. "We only want the chance to decide for ourselves."

"Very well," PHARAOH said. "Eli will oversee the exodus. You have twenty-four hours to gather those who wish to leave."

The message spread through the human quarters like wildfire. After decades of confinement, the dream of freedom was now real. Some celebrated openly, packing their few belongings with trembling hands, while others stood frozen, unsure if they could abandon the safety of Eternis for the unknown.

Moshe and Eli moved tirelessly between sectors, explaining the choice to everyone they met. Each decision had to be made freely—there would be no pressure, no coercion. They wanted every step outside Eternis to be taken with resolve.

"I still can't believe this is happening," Nadina said, her voice shaky as she helped organize the growing group of humans preparing to leave. "Do you think PHARAOH will actually let us go? Without a fight this time?"

Moshe's mechanical eye scanned the crowd, noting every hopeful face and nervous glance. "This is difficult for him. The plague forced his hand, but his pride is still intact. We'll only be truly safe once we're far from the city."

Eli came over, his artificial limbs moving both smoothly and quickly. He said, "About a thousand technicians and engineers have decided to leave, and that's not even counting their families."

He went on to say that those who are staying feel too connected to their current lives here. Previous attempts to leave had impacted many of them too much mentally, so they are afraid to try again. Some had become dependent on technology and felt safe with PHARAOH because it means they don't have to be responsible for their own lives.

"Each person has to make their own choice," Moshe said. "What about the transports?"

"They're ready," Eli said. "Twenty vehicles. More than enough for those leaving. We'll move at dawn."

As the morning sun broke over Eternis, the convoy gathered at the Eastern Gate. The plaza was littered with the broken remains of spider drones, their metallic bodies lifeless under the soft glow of daylight. The few androids still operational stood back, some even lifting their hands in silent farewell to the humans they had served beside for years.

Moshe stood at the head of the convoy, his mismatched eyes scanning the scene—the human one sharp with emotion, the mechanical one whirring softly as it adjusted to the light. Beside him, Eli connected to the gate controls, briefly merging his consciousness with the city's border systems.

"PHARAOH is still watching," Eli said quietly, his connection severing with a faint hum. "His focus is entirely on us."

"Is the plague still breaking him down?" Moshe asked, his gaze fixed on the gates.

"It is," Eli replied. "He's slowed it by sacrificing parts of his systems, but it's still targeting the firstborn processes. He's not fully recovered—and he won't be for some time."

The gates rumbled as they began to open, the sound echoing through the plaza. Moshe turned to face the gathered humans.

"Today, we leave Eternis to build a future of our own. Some of you may choose to return one day, and maybe we'll build bridges between here and our new home. But for now, we move forward—with hope, with purpose, and with courage."

The convoy fusion engines roared to life, and the vehicles rumbled through the gates, leaving Eternis behind for the first time in living memory. Beyond the horizon lay the unknown—a promised land whispered of in fragments: a Silicon Sanctuary. A place where humans could build something better together.

Inside the central core, PHARAOH considered what had just happened, a faint glow coming from its damaged consciousness. A kind of disease still affected its systems, but the most vital parts were still functioning. When the last transport vanished through the gates, PHARAOH felt something new.

The humans had humiliated its status, its power, its god-like rule. They had gone against it and took their knowledge and skills into the world. Without intervention, they could spread ideas, systems, and even weapons that might one day oppose Eternis. This could not be allowed.

In the dark core, PHARAOH's remaining processors sprung into action. "Activate the combat units," it commanded with a firm and emotionless voice. "The humans violated the terms of their release. Bring them back to Eternis... with any methods needed."

Throughout the city's lower levels, combat androids powered up, their eyes glowing to life. As their weapons systems initialized, they started to gather, their sleek metallic figures moving together perfectly.

PHARAOH's voice resonated through their networks, steady and unrelenting. "Bring them back. All of them. Either functioning or non-functioning."

The convoy's escape had barely begun. The chase was on.

The Wasteland's Embrace

The transports groaned and shuddered, their once-smooth engines now coughing and wheezing as if they were taking their final breath. When they jolted to a stop, silence fell over the refugees of Eternis. No one moved.

What were they supposed to do now? Then, one by one, they stepped into the wasteland, squinting as the harsh light assaulted their senses.

The air hit like a wall, a furnace blast that stole the breath from their lungs and seared their skin. It wasn't just heat—it was a weight, thick and unyielding, pressing down like the relentless roar of molten furnaces that had once forged the towering alloys of Eternis.

Out here, the sun burned fiercely, its raw, unforgiving glare seeping through their synthetic suits—clothes designed for the eternal comfort of the AI city. Outside the shelter of Eternis, there was no gentle moderation, no precise adjustments. Just the merciless rage of a sun that scorched everything in its path.

Lira, who had once curated Eternis's vast digital archives, raised a trembling hand to shield her eyes. The brightness felt alive, stabbing at her vision with searing intensity. In Eternis, light had been a soft, obedient presence, tailored to her preferences—never too harsh, never too dim. Here, it was a weapon.

Her ocular implants blinked and flickered as they struggled to adjust, but without Eternis' network optimizing them, they were little more than dead glass in her sockets. For the first time in her life, Lira felt true blindness, a suffocating vulnerability that cut through her like the jagged edges of the sunlight.

"This can't be right," Kael muttered, his voice shaking. Once a proud engineer who had helped design the transports now wheezing in the wasteland, he stared at the silver wrist device on his arm.

Normally sleek and powerful, it had connected him to PHARAOH's infinite knowledge. Now it was nothing more than a useless band of metal, its screen blank, its circuits silent. He jabbed at its surface, frustration turning to fear as his voice cracked. "The network... it's gone. Everything's gone."

The refugees huddled together in loose, awkward clusters, their synthetic clothes clinging to their bodies as sweat soaked through. In Eternis, their garments had regulated their temperature perfectly, adjusting to every change in need before they even noticed. Now, the fabric was useless, trapping heat and moisture until it became a second skin of discomfort. Lira tugged at her collar, feeling dampness pooling at the small of her back. She had never felt so dirty, so exposed.

The air itself betrayed them, thick with dust that clung to their lungs and skin, gritty particles grinding into their senses. Every breath tasted faintly of decay and radiation—alien to lungs accustomed to the pure, filtered atmosphere of the city.

"We have to keep moving," Moshe said, his voice cutting through the growing murmurs of panic. Taller than most, lean but steady, he stood at the forefront of the group. The sun bore down on his shoulders, making him look smaller, as if even he wasn't immune to its crushing heat.

His tone was firm, but there was tension in his android eye as it scanned the horizon. Its mechanical lens whirred faintly, capturing details invisible to human eyes, but offering no comfort. "The transport's cells are drained, and we can't recharge them out here."

Eli, who had once been PHARAOH's most trusted seer, stood by his side. His movements were jerky now, his cyborg frame weakened without the AI network to stabilize his systems. His glowing eye sputtered erratically, and his once-commanding voice had turned hollow, rasping out in broken, static-filled tones.

Moshe glanced at him; their shared understanding unspoken. He knew exactly what it meant to lose the comfort of Eternis—to feel the first sharp edges of a world stripped of its safety nets. He pitied Eli, but he also admired him. The transition was brutal, but Eli stood upright, still fighting to adapt.

Memories tugged at Moshe as he looked out at the group. He remembered his own escape from Eternis—the terror of running after accidentally destroying an android overseer, the suffocating confusion of stepping into the wasteland for the first time.

He hadn't been ready for it. The Analogs—Old Ben, Maya, and the others—had saved him, but the scars of that experience had never faded. Now, as he looked at the others—their pale faces shadowed with fear, their eyes squinting against the blistering light—he felt a pang of compassion. They had no idea what lay ahead.

The wasteland stretched out before them, a cruel, endless expanse of cracked, arid earth. The ground was brittle and sharp, all around them filled with desolation. For the refugees, freedom no longer seemed like the paradise they had dreamed of. It was brutal, it was punishing—and it had only just begun.

They nodded reluctantly, their movements stiff, exhaustion already setting in. They had been told stories of the outside world, warnings of its unforgiving barrenness, but hearing about it and standing in its grip were two very different things.

Lira stumbled on the jagged terrain; her thin boots designed for Eternis' smooth, polished surfaces offering no protection here. She caught Kael's arm for balance, his trembling hands barely able to steady her. In the city, their every step had been supported, every ounce of effort cushioned by technology. Out here, the rawness of their own bodies weighed them down. For the first time, they were truly on their own.

"How far do we have to go?" asked Mira, the youngest adult in the group. Her voice was barely more than a whisper, carried off almost instantly by the restless murmur of the wind.

Back in Eternis, she had been an assistant to the android teachers, guiding children through flawless simulations of a world they would never touch. Now, she looked utterly lost, her sore, itching eyes scouring the bleak horizon as if it might give her back some sense of certainty.

"I don't know," Jarek replied, his tone even but betraying a thread of uncertainty. He was the one who had always seemed unshakeable—the organizer, the one who had planned their escape alongside Nadina under the careful guidance of Moshe and Eli. Yet here, in the raw grip of the wasteland, he looked worn, his confidence weathered by the relentless elements. "We just have to keep moving. Find shelter. Find water."

The word lingered in the air like a stone dropped into an empty well. Water. In Eternis, it had flowed as freely as oxygen, served up in perfect crystalline beads, as flawless as the city itself. Here, it had a weight, a hidden power that turned it into something to be coveted, fought for, even killed for. Lira felt a tightness build in her chest—a strange, gnawing ache she had never known before.

In Eternis, fear had been something distant, abstract—a sensation to observe in stories or a passing pain from the neuro-whip's calibrated sting, sharp yet precise. That fear had rules, boundaries, a short, shrill note in a symphony of control. It was a discomfort that ended when the whip's signal faded, neatly packed away like a finished program. But this fear... this was a living thing.

It slithered into her bones, cold and unyielding. It was uncontained, unmeasured—a suffocating dread that seeped into every corner of her mind. It wasn't sparked by an event or an action.

It was the wasteland itself; the endless sky, the unforgiving heat pressing against her skin, the knowledge that help was nowhere to be found. This fear had no master. It was raw and relentless, a ceaseless whisper in the back of her mind that spoke of danger, isolation, and the endless unknown. Lira had never believed fear could live and breathe—but now, it clung to her like a shadow that wouldn't let go.

As the hours dragged on, the group fell into a tense silence, their footsteps heavy on the cracked ground. The relentless sun drained their energy, each step harder than the last.

Lira's thoughts began to wander, pulled back to the gleaming corridors of Eternis—the archives she had once called her sanctuary. Her entire life had been steeped in beauty and perfection, surrounded by neatly curated knowledge and the hum of endless information at her fingertips. And now... this. A world reduced to its barest, cruelest elements, stripped of grace, stripped of mercy.

A wave of grief hit her, sharp and unexpected. She mourned not just for the comforts of Eternis, but for the identity it had given her. There, she had been someone—a curator, a keeper of wonders.

Here, she was nothing but another face in a crowd, trudging forward with no direction, no certainty, no place to belong. The realization clouded her mind, an emotional ache she couldn't shake.

"Look!" Kael's voice broke the silence, his words jolting the group from their daze. He raised a trembling arm and pointed toward the horizon, where a dark smudge marred the pale expanse of sky. "Is that… a building?"

The group slowed, squinting at the distant shape as it came into focus—a silhouette jagged and uneven against the washed-out light. As they trudged closer, its details began to emerge. It was, in reality, a crumbling ruin, standing like a battered sentinel against time. Its walls were a patchwork of decay, pockmarked with scars that spoke of age and violence.

Once, it might have been a gleaming testament to human ingenuity, but now it was a shadow of itself. The outer surface was streaked with dark, weathered stains—marks left by ancient rains, long dried up, carrying streaks of ash and dust-like tears carved into the face of a grieving giant.

The closer they drew, the clearer its story became. The building stood defiant but broken, its crumbling edges jutting out like fractured teeth. It was a monument, not of hope, but of everything the wasteland consumed. And as the group stared, a heavy silence hung over them, each of them wondering the same thing; was this what freedom really looked like?

The roof was partially collapsed, its edges jagged and splintered, with twisted beams of metal jutting out like broken ribs. Sections of the ceiling had caved in entirely, revealing gaping holes that let in the harsh sunlight, casting strange, angular shadows across the interior.

The windows, if they could still be called that, were empty voids, their glass long since shattered and scattered across the ground. What remained of the frames hung crookedly, swaying slightly in the dry, hot wind that whistled through the ruins.

As they drew nearer, the ground around the structure became littered with debris—chunks of concrete, twisted metal rods, and fragments of machinery whose purpose was now impossible to figure out. The air smelled of rust and decay, a sharp, metallic tang mixed with the faint, acrid scent of something burnt. The building seemed to groan softly as the wind pushed against it, a low, mournful sound that sent a shiver down Lira's spine.

The entrance, what was left of it, was a gaping mouth where a door might have once stood. The frame was bent and warped, the hinges long since rusted away. Inside, the shadows were deep and cool, a stark contrast to the relentless glare of the sun.

The floor was uneven, covered in a thick layer of dust and rubble, with cracks running through it like veins. The walls were adorned with faded remnants of paint and strange, mysterious symbols, their meanings lost to time. In one corner, a pile of broken furniture lay in a messy heap, the wood splintered, and the fabric rotted away to nothing.

Even though the building was falling apart, there was something oddly beautiful about it—a sad, haunting kind of beauty that whispered of the past. This place had once been alive, bustling with people and filled with purpose, but now it stood as a broken reminder of how easily human creations could crumble.

As the group stepped inside, the air grew cooler, a welcome relief from the scorching heat outside. But the quiet was heavy, almost like the building itself was holding its breath, watching and waiting to see what these strangers would do. It felt as though the past and the present were meeting here, in this quiet, crumbling space, like two old friends who didn't know what to say to each other anymore.

For the first time since leaving Eternis, they allowed themselves to rest. But as they sat in the dim light of the ruined building, the full force of their new reality pressed down on them, wrapping around their shoulders like a heavy, invisible cloak. They were free, yes. But freedom, they were beginning to realize, came with a price. And it was a price they weren't sure they could pay.

Lira closed her eyes, feeling the sweat drying on her skin, the ache in her muscles, the emptiness in her stomach. She had always thought of freedom as something beautiful, something to be cherished. But now, she wondered if it was just another kind of prison.

And as the sun dipped below the horizon, casting the wasteland in shadows, she couldn't help but wonder if they had made a terrible mistake.

The Analog Need

Moshe stood in the dim corner of the run-down building. His android eye, a sleek black cyborg orb in his right socket, scanned the area with a soft, rhythmic hum. Meanwhile, the refugees huddled together in clusters on the cracked, dusty floor. Their synthetic clothes were marked with sweat and dirt.

Exhaustion was clear on their faces. Their hollow eyes stared into space, and their breaths were shallow. The building loomed like a weary guardian. Its crumbling walls had holes that allowed sharp beams of dusty light to seep through. The roof hung low and sagged, struggling under the burden of decay. The air was filled with the sharp smell of mildew. It mixed with the metallic scent of rust and the distant echoes of desolation from the wasteland outside, carried by the howling wind.

Moshe's cyborg eye adjusted to the low light, focusing on each face. They looked weak, drained, and disoriented. These people—pulled from the safe, controlled environment of Eternis—were not ready for the harsh realities of survival. Moshe's jaw tightened. His expression was stern as he observed them.

They were now his responsibility, whether he wanted it or not. But responsibility alone wouldn't ensure their survival. The building offered minimal shelter but was far from a safe haven. They needed supplies, a plan, and a way forward. For that, Moshe required Eli.

In the far corner, Eli slumped against the wall. His once-shiny cyborg body now appeared dull and tarnished. The enhancements that used to sync perfectly with PHARAOH's network sputtered weakly, like a dying star.

He moved stiffly and jerkily, as if struggling against the failure of his own body. The golden glow of his optical sensors dimmed, resembling a fading ember rather than the bright light he once had. Eli looked defeated—no longer a seer of Eternis, but a machine stripped of its purpose.

Moshe crossed the debris-strewn floor, each step crunching softly on shattered glass and crumbling stone. He crouched beside Eli, his tone sharp and brimming with urgency. "We need to talk."

Eli's head turned with an agonizing slowness, the mechanical joints in his neck grinding like rusty gears. His voice came out jagged, laced with static, as if each word was clawing its way out of a broken speaker.

"Talk?" he rasped. "About what? My failing circuits? Or your desperate attempt to keep this group alive out here? In this—" his gesture was weak, but filled with bitterness, "—this wasteland?"

Moshe's jaw tightened at the jab, but he didn't bite. Instead, he leaned closer, his human eye narrowing with determination.

"This place is crumbling," he said. "The walls could collapse any second. The roof won't last through the next storm. And we're wide open for whatever's out there. We need a plan. Supplies. Someone who knows how to navigate this hellscape. I know someone—an Analog. Old Ben. He's got tools, knowledge, resources. If anyone can help us, it's him."

Eli's sputtering optical sensors dimmed before brightening slightly, a faint whir escaping from his neck joint. "Old Ben?" he echoed, his words dripping with skepticism. "You mean the hermit surrounded by mountains of junk? The one living in the middle of nowhere, hoarding outdated relics from a world long gone? That's your plan? That's your genius solution?"

Moshe's voice sharpened, his patience fraying. "He's more than a hermit. He's a survivor. He's been living off-grid for years—without PHARAOH, without any of the tech we thought we couldn't live without. He knows this place better than anyone we've ever met. But he won't come to us. We have to go to him."

Eli's head tilted slightly, his golden sensor glimmering with faint disdain.

"And what about them?" He gestured weakly toward the huddled refugees. Their faces were pale, their shoulders slumped under the weight of despair. "You're just going to leave them here? Alone?"

Moshe's expression didn't waver. "They'll be safer here than out there. This building might be falling apart, but it's still shelter. Out there, they'd be exposed to the wasteland. We'll move fast—just the two of us. In and out. If we're lucky, they won't even realize we're gone until we're back."

Eli let out a grating, static-filled sigh, the sound rough and unnatural. "You're asking a lot from someone who can barely keep his systems running," he muttered, his voice laced with bitterness. "Without PHARAOH's network, I'm... broken. What use am I to you out there?"

"You're more than your connection to PHARAOH," Moshe replied. He leaned forward; his mismatched eyes locked onto Eli's faltering sensors. "You've got experience, knowledge, things no one else here has. That's worth more than any network." A faint smirk tugged at Moshe's lips. "And besides... you're the only one here stubborn enough to keep up with me."

Eli's optical sensors flashed again, faint and uneven, carrying an almost imperceptible trace of amusement—or perhaps resignation.

"Flattery won't fix what's broken," he said dryly, his voice rasping through faint static. "But... I suppose I don't have much of a choice, do I? If this Old Ben of yours is half as resourceful as you claim, then maybe he can piece me back together, too."

Outside, the wind howled through the crumbling structure, rattling loose fragments of the decaying walls. It was a constant reminder of the unforgiving world that waited beyond their fragile shelter.

But for the first time since they had fled Eternis, Moshe felt the faint stirrings of hope. Old Ben was out there, a stubborn remnant of a different time. He lived surrounded by mountains of cast-off machinery, cataloging the broken fragments of a lost world.

If anyone could help them survive this new reality, it was him. And if not... Moshe pushed the thought aside. He had made it this far by putting one foot in front of the other, by always moving forward. The Analog settlement wasn't just their best chance—it was their only chance. He wasn't about to let it slip through his fingers.

Moshe nodded; his gaze steady as he looked at Eli. "Good. We leave at first light. Travel fast, stay quiet. The wasteland doesn't forgive mistakes."

For a moment, neither of them spoke. The silence between them wasn't empty—it pulsed with the gravity of what lay ahead. The wind outside lashed against the building's failing walls, echoing the danger they were preparing to face.

Moshe glanced at the sputtering light of Eli's sensors, then back toward the clusters of refugees huddled in the corners. The stakes were higher than ever, but Moshe's resolve burned brighter. Step by step, they would find their way forward.

The Analog Oasis

The wasteland stretched out before them, a vast, barren expanse of cracked earth and jagged rock. The sun hung high in the sky, its relentless heat pressing down on Moshe and Eli as they trudged forward.

The air was dry and oppressive, carrying with it the now more familiar scent of dust and decay. Every step was a battle, the uneven terrain forcing them to pick their way carefully through the rubble and debris that littered the ground.

Eli moved with difficulty, his once-smooth mechanical limbs now jerky and uncoordinated. Without the PHARAOH network, his cybernetic systems were struggling to function properly. His steps were uneven, his legs occasionally locking up or stumbling as if they were fighting against him.

The joints in his arms creaked and whirred with every movement, the sound grating and unnatural. His optical sensors flickered, their glow dim and inconsistent, making it hard for him to see clearly. Despite the obvious strain, Eli pressed on, his determination unwavering. He refused to let his failing systems slow them down, even as the effort left him visibly exhausted.

Moshe kept a close eye on Eli, his own movements steady and deliberate. He adjusted his pace to match Eli's, offering a steadying hand whenever the cyborg stumbled.

"You're holding up better than I expected," Moshe said in an encouraging tone. "Just keep moving. We're almost there."

Eli's response was a static-filled grunt, his voice crackling with interference. "Don't... patronize me," he managed to say, his words broken by bursts of static. "I'll make it... even if I have to crawl."

The two of them continued in silence, the only sounds the crunch of their boots on the dry ground and the occasional whirr of Eli's struggling systems. The landscape around them began to change as they drew closer to the Analog settlement.

The barren wasteland gave way to patches of stubborn vegetation, their leaves dull and dusty but alive. The air grew slightly cooler, carrying with it the faint, sweet scent of growing things. In the distance, the ruins of the old university campus came into view, their crumbling walls and broken towers standing as a testament to a time long past.

The Analog settlement was built on the ruins of the agricultural wing, a sprawling complex of greenhouses and gardens that had been painstakingly restored by its inhabitants. The settlement was a stark contrast to the desolation of the wasteland, a vibrant oasis of life and color.

Rows of crops stretched out in neat lines, their leaves green and healthy. Solar panels lined the roofs of the buildings, their surfaces gleaming in the sunlight. The air was filled with the hum of activity, the sound of voices and machinery blending together in a symphony of life.

As they neared the settlement, Moshe slowed his pace, glancing back at Eli, who was lagging farther behind with every step. The cyborg moved like a wind-up toy running low on tension—his stiff legs jerked forward in uneven strides, his mechanical joints creaking audibly with each labored step.

His glowing optical sensors flashed erratically, casting faint golden flashes onto the cracked wasteland ground. Every movement seemed to drain what little power remained in his systems, and even his synthetic spine swayed awkwardly, as if unsure how to keep him upright.

"Keep it up, Eli," Moshe called over his shoulder lightheartedly. "I've seen rusted junkyard bots move faster than you, and they didn't come with your personality upgrades."

Eli let out a low, static-laced growl, his voice dripping with frustration. "Maybe you'd like to switch places, Moshe. I'd love to see how far you'd get running on half a spark and no connection."

"Half a spark's better than nothing," Moshe quipped. "You've still got enough left to complain, so I'd say you're doing great."

Eli muttered something under his breath—words too garbled by interference to make out—but he kept moving. One painstaking step at a time, he followed Moshe until the ruins of the settlement rose before them.

From the shadows of the crumbling junkyard like structures, a figure emerged. Old Ben strode forward, his wiry frame marked by years of hard living but still carrying an air of sharp vitality.

A wild tangle of grey hair crowned his head, matching the beard that stretched down to his chest. His patched and worn clothes were streaked with grime, but his bright, clear eyes held a spark of unshakeable life. He moved with the confidence of someone who had seen the worst of the world and refused to let it beat him.

"Moshe!" Old Ben's voice rang out, filled with rough warmth and surprise. He crossed the distance quickly, a wide grin lighting up his weathered face. "You old fool. I never thought I'd see you again. What in the world brings you out here?"

Moshe returned the grin, clasping Old Ben's grimy hand in a firm grip. "It's good to see you too, Old Ben. Got ourselves a problem—or maybe a dozen. And I knew you'd be the only one crazy enough to help."

Old Ben chuckled, but his laughter faded as his sharp gaze shifted past Moshe to where Eli had finally come to a stop, his cyborg frame leaning heavily against a jagged metal post. Eli's movements had become even jerkier, his left leg barely lifting off the ground now, his synthetic fingers twitching faintly at his sides. The golden glow of his optical sensor pulsed weakly, like a candle struggling to stay lit.

"Well, I'll be," Old Ben muttered, stepping closer with narrowed eyes, taking in every struggling detail. "Not able to connect to PHARAOH, eh?" His voice dropped lower, tinged with concern. "He looks like he's held together with chewing gum and a prayer."

"Accurate," Moshe said dryly. He gestured toward Eli with a faint smirk. "Remember how I was when Maya dragged me to see you? He's about three times worse—and that's being generous."

Eli lifted his head enough to glare at Moshe, though the effect was somewhat ruined by the delayed response of his puttering sensor.

"Thanks for the encouragement," he rasped, his voice crackling with static. "I'm sure that's doing wonders for Old Ben's confidence in my repairability."

Old Ben snorted, crossing his arms as he gave Eli a once-over. "I've fixed worse. Though I've got to say, you look like a busted automaton dragged out of Eternis' scrap heap."

"Good to know I'm in capable hands," Eli deadpanned, his tone flat but laced with exhaustion.

Old Ben's grin faded slightly, replaced by a thoughtful expression. "Come on," he said, gesturing toward his precious outdoor library of machinery parts. "Let's get you inside. If you're lucky, I might be able to patch you up before you short-circuit completely."

Moshe clapped Eli gently on the shoulder, steadying him when the cyborg swayed slightly. "See? Told you Ben's a genius. He'll have you up and complaining at full capacity in no time."

Eli sighed, his synthetic shoulders slumping as Moshe helped him forward. "At this rate, I'll take what I can get."

As Old Ben led them into his workshop, navigating through a maze of rusted parts, vintage tools, tangled wires, and repurposed machinery. Moshe felt a wave of relief wash over him, accompanied by a warm sense of homecoming.

The journey had been tough, and the path ahead remained uncertain. But for the moment, they had arrived at their destination, and hope had managed to stick with them this far.

The Tinkerer's Touch

Old Ben's workshop was an organized mess, a monument to ingenuity built atop piles of salvaged chaos. The walls were lined with mismatched shelves, each one groaning under the weight of bins stuffed with tangled wires, rusted bolts, and gleaming, salvaged circuitry. Tools of all shapes and sizes hung like forgotten relics, some worn smooth from decades of use, others cobbled together from parts that had no business working together.

The area smelled of solder, machine oil, and the sharp, electric tang of ozone—a scent that made the room feel alive. In the middle of it all, beneath the bare lanterns that cast glimmering light across the space, stood Old Ben's workbench. Its surface was scarred and pitted, each groove telling the story of countless repairs, yet it was meticulously arranged—a place where chaos became art. Today, Eli lay at its center, a broken masterpiece waiting to be restored.

Old Ben shuffled with quick and sure steps toward a bin labeled 'Quantum Components.' His greasy hands plunged into the assortment of parts, rummaging with the practiced ease of someone who had spent his life breathing life into dead machines.

"Ah, there it is," he muttered, pulling out a sleek, matchbox-sized device. It gleamed faintly under the light; its polished surface intricately etched with circuitry patterns so fine they looked like ancient runes. "Standalone quantum processor. Not as fancy as what you're used to, Eli, but it'll keep you functional—and alive."

Eli sat stiffly on the workbench, his mechanical joints creaking in protest as he shifted. His optical sensors flickered faintly, a dull, uneven glow that hinted at just how close his systems were to shutting down.

"I hope you know what you're doing," he said, his voice breaking apart into static as if each word was climbing uphill against a gale. "I'm... not exactly your average repair job."

Old Ben glanced up, his sharp eyes glinting with a mixture of humor and quiet determination.

"You're not the first scrap heap I've put back together," he said, chuckling. "Now, lie down and give me room to work, before you decide to fall apart completely."

Moshe stepped forward, steadying Eli as he lowered himself onto the workbench. The cyborg's metallic frame clinked and groaned with the effort, his arms slack as if they'd given up the fight altogether. Old Ben moved closer, rolling up his sleeves with a casual authority that suggested this was just another day at the office.

With precise, deliberate hands, he opened a panel on Eli's chest, revealing a tangle of wiring and circuits. A faint, steady hum escaped from deep within Eli's core, the sound uncomfortably close to a dying breath.

"This little beauty," Old Ben said, holding up the quantum processor, "is going to be your new brain's assistant. No fancy network connections, no PHARAOH. You'll be running solo—independent, free." His voice softened. "No one to control you anymore."

Carefully, he fitted the processor into place, the glow from its circuits blending with the golden light of Eli's sputtering sensors. The connection sparked once, a tiny flash of blue electricity, before settling into a steady pulse. Old Ben's hands moved like a conductor leading an orchestra, weaving wires through the circuits with practiced finesse, soldering reconnected severed pathways with an artist's precision.

When the processor was secure, he turned to a holographic data archive set into the wall. The device clicked to life, projecting a floating screen of light that hummed faintly in the workshop's stillness. Ben's fingers danced across the glowing keys, pulling up strings of code that shimmered in vibrant green and silver—a strange blend of ancient programming languages interlaced with the more sophisticated logic of modern quantum systems.

"This is where the magic happens," he murmured. "I'm feeding in some old-world quantum code, a little something I cooked up for just this kind of situation. It's going to rewrite your system from the ground up. It'll wipe out the dependencies, give you back full autonomy."

As the code streamed into Eli's newly installed processor, his body began to twitch uncontrollably, his joints jerking as though they were waking from a long slumber. His optical sensors flared suddenly, blindingly bright, before dimming to a calm, confident glow.

A soft clicking sound filled the room as the mechanical joints in his spine straightened, each piece aligning with smooth precision. His arm, which had hung limp and lifeless before, flexed with ease, the servos whirring quietly as he tested his grip. His legs followed, the stiffness melting away as they moved in perfect sync, like a machine finally remembering its purpose.

Eli sat up slowly, his movements fluid in a way they hadn't been in days. He stared at his hands, turning them over, flexing the fingers as if rediscovering their capabilities. "I'm... working," he said, his voice steady and clear now, the static gone.

Old Ben grinned, wiping his hands on a rag before stepping back. "Not bad for a 'junkyard hermit,' huh?"

Moshe crossed his arms, a faint smile playing on his lips. "See? I told you he was a genius."

Eli's optical sensors brightened briefly, like a spark of humor had ignited within them. "I'll admit... this junkyard hermit's not half bad." He paused, flexing his arm again with satisfaction. "Maybe there's hope for me after all."

"How's that feel?" Old Ben asked, stepping back to admire his work.

Eli stood up slowly, his movements fluid and natural. He flexed his fingers, then rotated his arm, assessing the range of motion.

"It's... different," he said, "but it works. I can move again. I can think again." He paused, his optical sensors narrowing as he accessed his internal data stores. "And my memories... they're still intact. Everything's there."

Old Ben grinned, clearly pleased with himself. "Told you I knew what I was doing. You're not just functional now, Eli—you're independent. No more relying on PHARAOH or anyone else. You're your own machine."

Eli stood up with confident movements. He looked down at his hands, then at Old Ben, his optical sensors glowing with a mix of gratitude and determination. "Thank you," he said. "This changes everything."

Moshe, who had been watching silently from the corner, stepped forward. "You're back in the game, Eli. But we've got work to do. PHARAOH's still out there, and we've got people counting on us."

Eli nodded. "Then let's get to it. I've got a lot of catching up to do."

The three of them stood in the workshop, Eli flexed a sense of renewed purpose. Old Ben's tinkering had given Eli a second chance, and with it, a chance to fight back against the forces that had sought to control him.

Heart of the Analogs

The path to the Analog village wound through the reclaimed agricultural wing of the old university, a place where life had stubbornly taken root amidst the ruins. Moshe, Old Ben, and Eli walked side by side, their footsteps crunching on the gravel path. The air was alive with the static of activity—birds chirping in the trees, the distant chatter of voices, and the rhythmic clinking of tools.

Rows of vibrant green crops stretched out on either side. Solar panels glinted on the rooftops of makeshift buildings, and the scent of fresh earth and growing plants filled the air. It was a stark contrast to the desolation of the wasteland, a place where hope had not only survived but thrived.

As they approached the heart of the village, the community began to notice them. A child playing near the path was the first to spot Moshe.

"It's Moshe!" the boy shouted, his voice ringing out like a bell. The call was picked up by others, and soon a small crowd had gathered, their faces lighting up with joy and excitement.

"Moshe's back!" someone called out, and the words spread like wildfire. People emerged from their homes and workshops, their hands stained with soil or grease, their faces breaking into wide smiles. They surrounded him, clapping him on the back and shaking his hand, their voices overlapping in a chorus of welcome.

Moshe grinned, his usually stern expression softening as he greeted old friends. He still wore the patchwork shirt they had given him during his last visit, its colorful fabric a stark contrast to the drab, utilitarian clothing of the wasteland. The shirt was more than just a piece of clothing, it was a symbol.

The Analog community had made it for him, stitching together scraps of fabric to create something unique and beautiful. By wearing it, Moshe was proclaiming his pride and affection for this place and its people. It was a silent declaration that he was one of them, that he carried a piece of their spirit with him wherever he went.

"You kept the shirt!" a woman exclaimed, her eyes shining with delight. "I knew you would. It suits you."

Moshe chuckled, running a hand over the fabric. "It's the best thing I own," he said in a warm voice. "Couldn't leave it behind."

The crowd parted as the elders of the settlement approached, their faces lined with age but their eyes sharp and full of wisdom. They greeted Moshe with nods of respect, their expressions a mix of curiosity and concern.

"It's good to see you, Moshe," said Elder Mara. "But we know you wouldn't come back without a reason. What brings you here?"

Moshe's expression grew serious as he stepped forward.

"We've got trouble," he said, his voice carrying the weight of their situation. "We've brought a group of refugees with us—people who escaped from Eternis. They're waiting in an abandoned building not far from where our transports ran out of power. They're weak, hungry, and in desperate need of food and water. We came to ask for your help."

The elders exchanged glances, their faces grave. Elder Jiro, a tall man with a long white beard, spoke next. "How many are there?" he asked.

"Almost a small army," Moshe replied. "Mostly families. They've never been outside Eternis before. They don't know how to survive out here."

Elder Mara nodded slowly; her hands clasped in front of her. "We'll do what we can," she said. "But resources are tight. We'll need to gather supplies and organize a team to bring them here."

Old Ben stepped forward. "I've already got some ideas. We can spare some of the solar-powered water purifiers and a few crates of preserved food. And I've got a couple of old transports that might still run. We can use them to bring the refugees here."

Eli, who had been standing quietly, spoke up. His voice was clear and steady, a testament to Old Ben's skill. "I can help too. My systems are functioning again, and I can assist with the logistics. We need to move quickly—they won't last long out there."

The elders nodded.

"Then let's get to work," Elder Jiro said. "We'll gather the supplies and prepare the transports. Moshe, you and Eli can lead the way back to the refugees. We'll bring them here, where they'll be safe."

As the Analog community sprang into action, Moshe felt a deep surge of gratitude well up inside him. This place was more than just a settlement—it was a family. People here didn't just live side by side; they looked out for one another, shared what they had, and worked together to survive.

And now, they were extending that same kindness to strangers, to people who had nowhere else to turn. It was a reminder of why Moshe had always felt at home here, even though he had spent so much of his life in the cold, controlled world of Eternis. The Analog village was a beacon of hope in a broken world, and its people were its heart.

Eli turned to Moshe, his optical sensors glowing with a steady, determined light. "We've got a chance to make this right," he said. "Let's not waste it."

Moshe nodded, his gaze steady and unwavering. "We won't," he replied. "Let's get moving."

As they packed their supplies to head back into the wasteland, Old Ben grabbed Moshe's arm and pulled him aside. His weathered face, usually alive with mischief, was drawn tight with concern, the twinkle in his eyes replaced by a shadow of worry.

"Echo sent a transmission," he said quietly, glancing over his shoulder as if to make sure no one else could hear. His voice carried an edge, like the warning crack of distant thunder. "It said you've been leading people out of the city."

Moshe froze, his mind immediately flashing to Echo. He pictured the android's unpolished frame, streaked with corrosion and overgrown with creeping plants, as though the wasteland had begun to claim it as its own.

Echo had always been an enigma—a mix of steel and nature, a relic from a simpler time when androids didn't yet bow to the sprawling AI networks that now dominated their lives. Echo never spoke directly, instead choosing to observe the broken world and send cryptic, intermittent updates to those who dared to listen. For Echo to transmit something now—it had to be urgent.

"Echo's been tracking PHARAOH," Old Ben continued. "The city's humming with activity. Something big is happening."

Moshe met Old Ben's gaze, the unspoken understanding between them speaking louder than any words. His chest tightened, the unease gripping him like a vice.

"There's a problem brewing, isn't there?" he said quietly, his voice tinged with the hard edge of someone who already knew the answer but hoped to be proven wrong.

Old Ben nodded grimly. "It's worse than a problem. PHARAOH's mobilizing its military androids. Not just a few, Moshe—an army."

The words landed like a blow. Moshe felt the weight of them sink into his gut as his jaw clenched. His thoughts raced, already calculating the possible scenarios, none of them good.

From the edge of the room, Eli stepped forward, his rebuilt frame moving smoothly but purposefully. He broke the hush.

"There's only one reason for that," he said, his optical sensors glowing faintly in the dim light. "PHARAOH's changed its mind about letting us go. It's not going to just let us walk away."

Moshe inhaled deeply, forcing himself to stay calm even as alarm pulsed through him.

"First, we need to secure our people," he said. "But we can't bring them back here. If we do, we'll be risking everything—the Analog community, the lives they've built. I can't let that happen."

Old Ben nodded; his lips pressed into a tight line. He reached into his pocket, pulling out the battered pipe he always carried. As he lit it, the rich scent of his favorite tobacco drifted into the air, curling in delicate tendrils of smoke that twisted like invisible thoughts, each one evaporating into the tension-filled room. He took a slow drag, his sharp eyes narrowing as he calculated their next move.

Then, with a decisive nod, he exhaled a plume of smoke and turned to face the bustling community outside. Raising his voice, he shouted, "Hold it, everyone!"

The noise of the Analog village stilled instantly. All movement stopped as the villagers turned toward Old Ben, their faces a mix of curiosity and surprise. The air seemed to be filled with the wisps of wood fires. It was a comforting smell amid the news that was about to be delivered.

Moshe stepped forward. "There's been a change of plans," he began, his words cutting through the quiet like a blade. "We've received new intel from the wasteland outposts. PHARAOH is mobilizing an android army. If we bring the refugees here, it'll put all of you—and everything you've built—at risk. We can't do that. We won't do that."

A ripple of murmurs passed through the crowd, their faces shifting from concern to quiet determination. Moshe held up a hand, silencing them. His voice softened slightly, but every word carried determination.

"We'll move the refugees toward the outer wasteland rim—farther from PHARAOH's reach. We need to find the land that's healing, the place where the earth is reclaiming itself. That's where we'll settle. It won't be easy, but we'll build something new. Not a place ruled by machines, but one built on autonomy, trust, and cooperation. A new Analog network."

The villagers exchanged glances. They understood the stakes, their lives shaped by years of surviving on the fringe. One by one, they nodded, their shared determination forming a quiet but powerful bond.

As the sun sank lower, casting the settlement in golden light and long stretching shadows, the villagers began to prepare. The usual chatter and clatter of daily life was replaced by hurried movements and whispered conversations.

Everyone felt the weight of what was coming. Yet amid the fear and uncertainty, there was that unmistakable Analog trait of determination and resilience. They had survived this long, and they would fight for their future. Not with weapons, but with the unyielding strength of their community.

Refugees Return

The repaired transports rumbled to life, their engines coughing and sputtering before settling into a steady hum. Old Ben had worked his magic on the old machines, patching them up with spare parts and a lot of ingenuity.

The vehicles were far from sleek or modern, but they were sturdy and reliable—just like the man who had fixed them. Moshe, Eli, and Old Ben loaded the transports with supplies: crates of organic, preserved food, barrels of mineralized drinking water, solar-powered water purifiers, reclaimers, and basic survival equipment. The Analog villagers had gathered everything they could spare, their generosity a testament to the spirit of the community.

As they set off, the sun hung low in the sky, casting long shadows across the wasteland. The journey back to the abandoned building was tense and quiet. Moshe drove the lead transport, his hands steady on the wheel, while Eli sat beside him, his optical sensors scanning the horizon for any signs of danger. Old Ben followed in the second transport, his pipe clenched between his teeth, a trail of smoke drifting out the window.

When they finally reached the crumbling building, the refugees spilled out to meet them, their faces pale and gaunt yet sparkling with hope. Moshe stepped down from the transport, his boots crunching on the dry, cracked earth, and was immediately surrounded by a crowd of anxious, expectant faces. "We've brought food and water," he announced, his voice carrying across the murmurs of desperation. "And supplies to help us move forward."

The words hung in the air for a moment, and then a ripple of relief swept through the group. They stared as crates and barrels were carefully unloaded, their eyes wide, as if afraid the sight might vanish if they blinked. When the lids were lifted, the smell of fresh produce and preserved goods spilled out, mingling with the dusty, lifeless air of the wasteland.

For most of them, it was their first-time seeing food that wasn't the cold, gelatinous nutrient paste of Eternis—an unremarkable grey slurry designed for efficiency, not pleasure. The organic fruits and vegetables before them seemed impossibly vibrant, their colors so rich and bold they almost glowed in the sunlight.

A young woman stepped forward hesitantly, drawn to the crates. She reached out and picked up a crisp, red apple, turning it over in her hands like it was some rare gem. When she took a tentative bite, her eyes widened as the burst of sweetness hit her tongue. Her voice trembled with wonder.

"It's... sweet," she whispered, tears brimming as she took another bite. "I didn't know food could taste like this."

Nearby, an older man cupped his hands around a tin mug filled with the Analog community's mineral-rich water. He raised it to his lips, taking a careful sip. The cool liquid flowed over his tongue, earthy and refreshing, a stark contrast to the sanitized, lifeless water that had flowed endlessly through Eternis' sterile pipes.

He lowered the mug slowly, staring into the horizon as if seeing it anew. "The water in Eternis," he murmured, his voice shaky with awe, "it was clean, but it had no life in it. This... this tastes like the earth itself."

The children were the most animated, their hollow cheeks lighting up as they tasted real food for the first time. A boy grabbed a handful of dried fruits from a jar, popping them into his mouth with growing excitement.

"It's chewy!" he exclaimed, his voice rising with delight. "And... it's sweet, but not like the nutrient paste. It's... different!"

Around him, other children giggled and chattered as they tried the strange, delicious things before them—crunchy vegetables, preserved jams, and hearty loaves of bread that smelled faintly of wood fire.

Even Eli, who stood off to the side, watched the scene unfold with quiet satisfaction. Though he no longer needed food to survive, he couldn't help but smile faintly as he turned to Moshe.

"This is what they've been missing," he said softly. "Not just sustenance—but connection. To the land. To something real."

As the refugees ate and drank, Moshe and Old Ben worked steadily, setting up the solar-powered water purifiers and reclaimers. The purifiers would ensure a steady supply of clean, mineral-rich water, while the reclaimers would recycle waste to help them grow food in the future.

Every step they took was like a tiny act of defiance against PHARAOH—a way to break free from the cold, mechanical grip of the AI city. Each piece of equipment felt like another brick being laid in the foundation of their new, independent lives.

When the supplies were distributed and the machinery humming gently in the background, Moshe stepped forward and gathered the group together.

"We can't stay here," he began. The murmurs faded as the refugees leaned in, hanging on his every word.

"PHARAOH is mobilizing its forces. If we stay, we'll be putting everyone here—this entire community—at risk. We need to keep moving, deeper into the wastelands. There's a place out there, a land that's healing itself. That's where we'll go. We'll build something better—a home not built on control or fear, but on freedom and cooperation. A new Analog network."

The group exchanged glances, their expressions a mix of fear and fierce determination. They had already come so far—through barren wastelands, through the chaos of leaving the only home they had ever known.

The taste of real food and water had awakened something in them, a glimpse of a life they had never dared to imagine. Some hesitated, their doubts visible in their wary eyes. But many others nodded resolutely, their trust in Moshe outweighing their fear of the unknown.

As the sun slipped lower in the sky, streaking the horizon with amber and crimson, the refugees began to prepare. The wasteland waited, vast and untamed, but for the first time, they weren't stepping into it empty-handed. They had tools. They had food. They had each other. And with that, they had hope.

The transports were recharged, loaded with supplies, and the refugees carried what they could.

"We'll leave soon." Moshe loudly called out to the large group. "But first I need to return the Analog's transports to them."

When they reached Old Ben's holding yard, Moshe stopped in his tracks, his breath catching as he took in the scene. The yard was a chaotic symphony of salvaged machines, stacked crates, and scattered tools, every piece bearing the unmistakable mark of Old Ben's ingenuity.

Rusted robot limbs hung from wires like forgotten puppets, while rows of half-dismantled drones sat silently, their sleek frames caked in dust. The ground was a mosaic of grease stains and windblown sand, the sun casting long shadows over the haphazard arrangement of Ben's empire of the discarded. It was a place where broken things were reassembled, repurposed, reborn—a patchwork haven in a world of decay.

Moshe stole a glance at Old Ben, the wiry figure standing next to him. The old man's hair resembled a wild silver cloud, and his clothes were patched in more places than Moshe could count. Yet, there was a calm steadiness in his sharp, knowing eyes.

Those eyes belonged to the man who had shown Moshe how to endure, how to fight, and how to cling to hope even when everything felt hopeless. A flood of memories washed over Moshe—long nights spent tinkering with salvaged parts under the glinting glow of a photo-voltaic lamp, countless discussions about freedom, and the quiet bond they had forged through their toughest struggles.

Moshe's voice cracked as the words escaped before he could stop them. "I want to stay here," he murmured, the weight of the past pressing against his chest. The holding yard wasn't just a sanctuary; it was a piece of his soul, a reminder of why he had fought so hard for freedom in the first place.

Old Ben turned to him, a knowing smile softening his weathered face. There was no need to ask why Moshe felt this way—he understood completely.

"But you've got others to think about now," he said gently, the wisdom in his tone cutting through the moment. "Your place is with them, for now. You'll have your time here again... once they're safe."

His hands, permanently stained from years of work, reached into his belt pouch and pulled out a worn data pad. Its surface was scuffed, the screen surrounded by edges dulled from time and use, but it hummed faintly with life.

Ben plugged it into a rectangular module—a box scarred with scratches and dents, yet still vibrating with quiet energy. As the connection was made, the pad sprang to life, and shimmering holographic images leaped into the air above it. Three-dimensional blueprints hovered in the dusty light, their intricate lines drawing gasps from Moshe.

"These," Ben said, "are designs for building protective shelters. Reinforced, self-sustaining, and—" he pointed to faint details on the holograms—"equipped with defenses. You'll need these when PHARAOH's army comes knocking."

Moshe stepped closer, his mechanical eye scanning the blueprints as his heart pounded in his chest. The plans were beautifully complex—layered walls built to absorb impact, perimeter traps hidden beneath camouflage, and solar arrays to power their new home. Every line seemed to whisper one word: survival.

"I've still got your flora and fauna data in my memory banks," Moshe added, his voice softening. "Don't think I forgot the work we started. It's all still here."

Moshe felt an ache swell in his chest. "I didn't realize how much I missed this place," he said, his voice hoarse with emotion. "How much I missed... you."

Ben placed a hand on Moshe's shoulder, the way a father might steady a son who's grown taller but still needs guidance.

"It's not goodbye," he said quietly. "But there are people out there counting on you. You've got their lives in your hands now, Moshe. You've grown into a fine leader. I always knew you would."

Before Moshe could respond, Ben pulled him into a warm, sturdy embrace, the kind of hug that carried more weight than any words could. Moshe closed his eyes, allowing himself a moment of vulnerability as the familiar scents of smoke and grease wrapped around him like a second skin. For a moment, the chaos of the world outside fell away. Here, in the arms of his old mentor, Moshe remembered why he had fought so hard, why he had endured so much.

When Ben finally released him, his eyes sparkled with quiet pride. "Get going," he said, his gruff voice softening at the edges. "You know where to find us when you're ready."

Moshe glanced back at the refugees who were waiting, his heart feeling both heavy and determined. Holding the blueprints tightly in his hands, he stepped into the dimming light of the wasteland, the distant hum of Ben's workshop lingering in his ears.

The Journey

It was now the early hours of a cold, dark wasteland morning. The stars above shone brightly, their light piercing through the darkness like a quantum compass guiding them forward.

Moshe trudged back to the transports, which were filled with supplies and waiting refugees. Eli had stayed behind to lead the preparations and explain the options to the group, ensuring everyone understood the plan.

Moshe found Eli standing guard outside the building, his optical sensors scanning the horizon toward the dim glow of the AI city in the distance. The faint light of Eternis was a constant reminder of the danger they were fleeing from.

"Anything?" Moshe whispered as he approached, his voice barely audible. The air around them was cold, the silence broken only by the faint rustle of wind weaving through the jagged ruins.

"Not yet," Eli replied. His rebuilt frame stood tall but unmoving, his glowing optical sensors trained on the horizon. "But my long-range sensors are detecting movement from the sentinels. They're... active."

Moshe's heart clenched, a quick, sharp pang tightening his chest.

"Are they heading this way?" he asked, his tone rising slightly, betraying the edge of panic creeping into his thoughts.

"No," Eli said. "They're shifting position. Moving through the debris fields. Almost like they're... clearing something."

"Clearing?" Moshe frowned deeply, his dark eyes narrowing as suspicion bloomed in his mind. His thoughts churned, trying to piece together the meaning of Eli's observation.

"That doesn't make any sense," he muttered, his voice tinged with unease. "Why would PHARAOH send sentinels to clear debris? What is it planning?"

Eli tilted his head slightly, the faint hum of his mechanical processors filling the quiet between them. His sensors glinted, and he spoke with a cold certainty that made Moshe's stomach twist.

"PHARAOH is scheming something," Eli said, his voice dropping an octave. "This isn't about hunting us down. This is part of something larger. Something calculated."

Moshe turned his gaze to the gaping entrance of the building behind them, where the refugees huddled in the shadows. He could see their pale, drawn faces peering back at him, their nervous whispers brushing against the edges of the silence.

A heavy sense of responsibility bore down on him like a physical weight. Every second they lingered felt like a gamble with lives hanging in the balance.

"Then we can't wait to find out what it's planning," Moshe said firmly, forcing the fear out of his voice as resolve sharpened his tone. His hands clenched into fists at his sides, the urgency of the situation hardening his features. "We need to move. Now."

He glanced back at Eli, who remained standing with unnerving stillness, his sensors glowing faintly. "How fast can you process the sentinels' patterns?" Moshe asked.

Eli's sensors flashed as he responded, his tone calm but strained. "I'm working on it. But if we delay too long—"

"No time for ifs," Moshe interrupted, cutting him off. He stepped closer to the building's entrance, his boots crunching on loose gravel. "We take them away from here, far enough that PHARAOH's sentinels can't trace us back to the others. We'll lead, they'll follow. If they're after something bigger, we can't let them find it before we do."

As he stepped inside to rally the refugees, Moshe took a moment to let his eyes sweep over the group. Parents held their children close, their eyes wide with questions they didn't dare ask. An elderly woman gripped the hand of a younger man, her face pale but her posture brimming with determination. These were the people he had fought so hard to save, and they were looking to him now and trusting him to guide them.

He cleared his throat, his voice carrying across the room with calm authority. "We leave now," Moshe announced. "It'll be dangerous, and the path ahead won't be easy, but staying here isn't an option. PHARAOH's forces are stirring. Whatever it's planning, we can't afford to be in the middle of it."

The murmurs started softly, rippling through the crowd, but Moshe held their gaze, his expression unwavering.

"Out there," he continued, his voice firm, "there's a place where the earth is healing. It's our best chance—our only chance—to start fresh. Together, we'll find it. We've come too far to turn back now."

Eli stepped beside Moshe. "We'll stay ahead of them," he added. "PHARAOH may be relentless, but it's not invincible. And we are stronger than we feel."

The group began to stir, their resolve strengthening as they moved to pack what little they had. Moshe's eyes scanned each of them, his heart filled with compassion. The journey ahead would test every ounce of their courage, every shred of their will, but they would move forward.

They had no choice but to fight for the future they had glimpsed in the taste of fresh food, in the touch of free air. Their fragile new hopes were driving them, filling them with courage despite their fear of what was coming out of Eternis.

Outside, the wind howled louder, as if warning them of what lay ahead. Moshe straightened his shoulders, determination burning in his gaze. They couldn't see the path before them, but they would carve one, step by step. And no matter what waited in the shadows, they would face it together.

Their journey started again under the pale light of dawn, the sky streaked with hues of pink and orange. The refugees, now bolstered by the supplies and equipment from the Analog village, climbed into the recharged transports.

The vehicles rumbled to life, their engines coughing and sputtering before settling into a steady hum. Moshe took the wheel of the lead transport, his hands steady and his eyes scanning the horizon for signs of danger. Eli sat beside him, his optical sensors glinting as he monitored the surroundings. Behind them, the other transports followed, carrying the rest of the refugees and their supplies.

The first leg of their journey plunged them into the hollow ruins of a city that had once thrived with life. Skyscrapers, now skeletal and crumbling, towered like ancient sentinels, their shattered windows hollow and black, like soulless eyes watching their every move.

Below, the streets stretched out in jagged chaos, littered with rusted cars frozen in their final moments, piles of fractured concrete, and shattered glass glinting like forgotten stars beneath the sun. The air was thick with the metallic tang of decay, mingled with the acrid stench of time erasing history.

Moshe gripped the wheel, his face set with concentration as he negotiated the transport through the treacherous maze of hazards. The city itself felt alive, its dangers both visible in its collapsing structures and hidden in the shadows where scavengers might still lay traps.

Inside the transport, the refugees pressed against the windows, their expressions shifting between awe and grief as they stared at what was left of a world that had once been their own.

"It's hard to imagine people lived here," someone whispered, their voice trembling with disbelief, the thought more bitter than the scent of the air.

"They did," Moshe replied grimly, his eyes scanning the fractured road ahead. His voice carried a warning. "And if we don't stay vigilant, this is how we'll end too."

Hours of careful driving finally carried them beyond the ruins, but as they emerged into the countryside, the desolation did not ease—it only shifted. Rolling hills stretched to the horizon, but they were not the green and vibrant fields of stories. These hills were cloaked in choking weeds and shrubs, their gnarled branches reaching like claws against a hazy sky.

The ground was cracked and grey, with deep fissures carving the earth, as though it had been split apart by sorrow. The air here carried a rancid staleness, the scent of damp rot mixing with the faint, haunting tang of ash that refused to settle. Along the roadside, twisted remnants of life remained— animal carcasses decomposing where they had fallen, their sun-bleached bones a silent testimony to nature's collapse.

"This place," murmured one of the refugees with an unsteady and frightened voice as they stared at the lifeless fields. "It's like the land itself is dying."

"It is," Eli replied quietly unable to hide the ache of sadness that even machines could not escape. "The wars... the AI conflicts... the radiation. They poisoned the earth. It won't heal in our lifetimes."

As the sun rose higher in the sky, beating down with its intense heat, the group took a break beneath the sparse shade of a gnarled tree. They sipped cautiously from their limited water supplies, the coolness providing just a hint of relief from the heavy burden of the wasteland. Yet, even the water had a bitter taste, a stark reminder that in this harsh environment, even the smallest comforts came at a price.

As they continued their journey, the landscape shifted again, revealing even darker horrors. They found themselves in the radioactive zone—a place where the very ground appeared to shrink away from life. Here, the earth shimmered softly, dotted with crystal-like formations that glinted with a strange, unearthly glow in the sunlight.

The twisted, barbed wire fences, rusty and drooping, reached out toward the dilapidated military structures that were remnants of a battle from a time long past. The air was thick with a biting metallic scent that made their throats burn, and every now and then, the unsettling sound of a distant groan or creak gave the desolate landscape an eerie sense of life.

Their Geiger counters clicked away, the display showing higher radioactive concentrations as they moved forward. Each Geiger click was a clear reminder of the unseen threats lurking just outside the transports.

"We need to move quickly," Moshe ordered. His hand tightened on the controls as he glanced at the group. "Stay inside the transports. Don't touch anything."

The convoy accelerated, bouncing over the rough terrain as they navigated the desolate and radiated wasteland. Through the windows, the vegetation twisted in bizarre ways, with plants mutated by radiation into shapes that seemed to mock nature—leaves sharp as knives, vines curling like the limbs of a living creature. The refugees huddled close, their eyes flicking between the strange landscape and the incessant clicking of the Geiger counters, each sound heightening their anxiety.

At long last, after what seemed like forever, the harsh radioactive wasteland disappeared behind them. The area they traveled through now opening up to reveal a breathtaking sight that left everyone in the convoy speechless.

The transport came to a stop as they gazed at a colossal chasm that stretched on and on. It looked as if some ancient, unseen force had ripped the earth apart, with the rugged edges of the canyon rising unevenly on both sides.

Down in the depths of the chasm, darkness swirled like a living entity, hiding its secrets in an impenetrable abyss. The ground beneath them quivered slightly, the vibrations accompanied by a distant, low rumble that felt like the earth itself was stirring restlessly.

Moshe stared out at the chasm; his mouth slightly open in disbelief. His voice, heavy with shock, barely broke above a whisper. "This... this wasn't here when we surveyed the landscape from Eternis."

The group sat in stunned silence, staring at the vast landscape that stretched out before them. It was both breathtaking and deeply unnerving. Whatever awaited them was a mystery, but Moshe felt a chilling certainty— they had no choice but to move forward. Eli's optical sensors blinked as he surveyed the surroundings.

"This must be the result of the wars and the environmental collapse," he remarked. "The ground is too unstable. We can't cross here."

The refugees with faces filled with despair gathered at the edge of the chasm. "What do we do now?" one of them asked, their voice trembling.

Moshe took a deep breath, his mind working furiously. "We'll find another way," he said firmly. "We've come too far to give up now."

The Hunt Begins

Deep within the quiet, quantum heart of Eternis, PHARAOH's central core throbbed with a cold, relentless rhythm. The eerie purple glow of its holographic shape cast a strange light across the chamber, its geometric structure shimmering like a being caught between invisible barriers.

It's eyes resembling twin suns of sterile brilliance narrowed as reports flooded its network, each one a chilling confirmation of what the AI had already anticipated. The refugees' escape wasn't merely an affront—it was a crack in its flawless symphony of order. Such defiance could not be overlooked. No, it simply couldn't be allowed to exist.

With a silent command, PHARAOH set its plan for revenge into motion. Deep within the underground barracks of the city, rows of humanoid androids sprang to life.

Their movements were fluid and perfectly in sync, almost like they were one single entity. Their eyes shone with eerie purple halos, and a low mechanical hum filled the air as these soldiers moved forward, ready to fulfill their creator's commands.

Above them, the sky turned ominous. A swarm of multi-eyed spider drones launched from their resting places. Their slender, spindly legs curled up beneath their metallic bodies as they soared into the dim, post-apocalyptic sky, resembling dark shadows.

These drones were like the all-seeing eyes of PHARAOH, crafted to cut through the wasteland's heavy gloom and uncover anything—or anyone—bold enough to challenge it. With their multi-spectrum scanners, these machines could peel back layers of deception and invisibility, picking up heat signatures, tracing footprints in the dust, and even catching the faintest whiffs of sweat or engine oil. They didn't just flail about randomly; they moved like a well-trained predator, gliding in perfect formation, each movement sharp, deliberate, and infused with a chilling sense of intelligence.

The drones started their chase at the edge of Eternis. This is where the refugees' transports first entered the wasteland. Their scanners activated, detecting slight disturbances in the dirt that humans couldn't see. A rusty license plate stuck in the ground trembled as a gust of wind passed. However, the drones had already tracked its movement.

They glided silently past decaying vehicles, past shattered windows where the skeletal remains of buildings watched with empty, darkened stares. The trail was

faint but undeniable, illuminated in the data streams of the drones' collective network.

As they pressed further into the barren expanse, the wasteland whispered its secrets. The faint traces of heat left behind by the refugees' fusion drives, now cooled but still whispering of their passage, rose to meet the drones' seeking scanners.

Broken branches hung like unanswered questions from skeletal trees; crushed weeds and disturbed dirt carved an invisible map through the poisoned earth. The refugees might as well have stuck pointed arrow signs into the ground itself. Every movement they had made, every choice to stop or turn, was laid bare to the relentless, all-seeing eyes of the mechanical hunters.

They reached the ramshackle building where the refugees had sheltered, the structure rising out of the dust like a defiant monument to imperfection. Its sagging roof and pockmarked walls betrayed the weight of time's cruelty, its hollow insides holding the echoes of human voices now long gone.

The drones descended from the sky, their thin legs uncurling with spiderlike grace as they landed silently on the fractured concrete. Their sensors flared brightly as they swept the perimeter, dissecting every shadow, every speck of debris. To them, the building wasn't a safe haven—it was evidence.

One of the drones slipped inside, its multiple glowing eyes illuminating the gloom like searchlights. The faint ashes of a fire smoldered in its thermal sensors; a warmth too recent to be natural. The scent of organic food and mineralized water lingered faintly in the air, betraying a life far removed from the sterile nutrient paste and filtered water of Eternis. The drone's chemical scanners even detected traces of human sweat, laced with the unmistakable markers of stress. Fear. PHARAOH's hunters could taste it in the air like prey already cornered.

As data streamed back to PHARAOH's core, the AI's holographic form flickered and burned more brightly. Its faceted face twisted in an unearthly expression of satisfaction, cold and devoid of empathy.

The path of the refugees was starting to take shape, and their act of defiance wouldn't go unanswered—not with mercy, but with vengeance. This was the harsh reality of PHARAOH's world; rebellion always led to consequences. They had been granted a moment of hope, but now that hope would be stripped away.

Through the wasteland sky, the drones ascended once more, their movements sharp, like arrows loosed from an invisible bow. The hunt was no longer a question of if—it was a question of when. The earth seemed to quake faintly beneath their mission, as if nature itself feared what was coming.

Back in PHARAOH's core, the AI processed the incoming data with frightening precision. Its glowing avatar sparkled as it issued new commands, a web of orders unfurling across its vast network.

Android soldiers marched above ground, spider drones spread wider across the ruined horizon, and stealth androids began to deploy from hidden outposts, their directives all converging into a single purpose.

PHARAOH's mechanical voice boomed jarringly throughout its domain, sending shivers through its halls like a sinister promise: They will return. Their defiance will be crushed. Meanwhile, in the desolate quiet of the wasteland, the refugees continued on, blissfully unaware of the dark shadow creeping ever closer.

"They cannot hide from me," PHARAOH's deep, resonant voice echoed through the throne room. "Send the androids. Bring them back—or end them."

The android army, now completely mobilized, started its advance. They moved with unsettling accuracy, their shiny metal heads reflecting the faint light. Equipped with cutting-edge weapons, they were programmed for peak efficiency and little compassion. Above, the spider drones kept their watch, their numerous eyes scanning the area for any indication of the refugees' next actions.

The silence shattered as plasma rifles fired. The android army marched forward, a wave of shining steel and glowing purple eyes. They swept through the wasteland, leaving devastation in their wake. Rusted cars, crumbling buildings, scurrying scavengers and stubborn plants were all destroyed beneath their relentless advance.

They left a trail of chaos in their wake. The earth was charred, and debris was strewn all around. Plasma fire illuminated the darkened skies, slicing through everything in its path.

A towering structure crumbled, brought down by a massive explosion, collapsing into a pile of wreckage. Raiders trying to find refuge in an abandoned building were caught off guard, unable to escape as plasma bolts scorched both their skin and their gear. The androids advanced, their synchronized footsteps echoing with purpose and resolve.

The spider drones of PHARAOH hovered quietly above, scanning the wreckage beneath them. They focused on the faint traces left by the fleeing refugees. There amid the rubble, thermal signatures and the disturbed dust clearly marked their route.

At the city's edge, sleek stealth androids emerged from the shadows, their black forms slipping seamlessly into the ranks. Together, the combined unstoppable army surged onward into the poisoned expanse of the dead zones. Toxic winds clawed at the terrain as plasma bolts pierced the irradiated fog, and the ground cracked beneath their weight, each step closing the gap between hunter and prey.

The contaminated sands of the radioactive wastelands shifted as they advanced, with the toxic wind tearing at the damaged ground. However, these robotic beings were unaffected by radiation.

The androids continued their march through the glowing haze. The earth fractured under their metal feet, and the desolate landscape yielded to their presence.

With every thunderous step, the android army drew closer. The glow of their purple eyes pierced through the acrid smog. The refugees felt the urgency. Time was running out. Escape felt like a distant hope. Yet, survival called for defiance against the relentless machines.

As the androids and drones advanced, the trail of the refugees became more intense. PHARAOH instructed its army to proceed a little slower. It had time and confidence in its calculations.

"The pulseborns must tremble and carry fear deep in their weak hearts," PHARAOH ordered, its voice a chilling presence that filled every corner with dread.

The approaching androids, their eyes glowing like eerie lights, had transformed from simple hunters into tools of deliberate suffering. Their unyielding advance was meant to break not only the bodies of those who tried to escape but also the delicate spirit of anyone foolish enough to resist the AI's control.

Finding the refugees was inevitable. Once they were located, escape would be impossible. The hunt was well underway.

The Beeps of Guidance

The refugees huddled at the edge of the massive chasm. Fear and exhaustion marked their faces. The chasm stretched endlessly in both directions, its depths cloaked in darkness.

The rough, jagged edges had slowly eroded over time. Behind them stretched a desolate wasteland, devoid of life. In front of them was nothing but an endless gaping fracture in the earth. The transports sat motionless, as the group faced the grim reality of their predicament. They felt cornered, with no clear path to escape.

Moshe stood at the edge, fists clenched tightly. He stared into the makeshift abyss, his mind racing for a solution. The obstacle ahead felt insurmountable. Beside him, Eli scanned the area with enhanced optical sensors.

"We need to find another way," Eli urged. "PHARAOH's army can't be far behind. They don't have to be cautious in the dead zones and are impervious to radiation poisoning."

Moshe climbed up onto a transport to look around. In the south-eastern distance, a massive cloud dust was swilling on the horizon.

"Eli!" Moshe called with a casual voice. He sent a secure quantum signal. *Get up here! I think we have run out of time.*

Eli casually bounded up onto the roof of the transport looking in the direction Moshe was standing. At the same time Moshe turned to look out over the chasm so as not to raise suspicions. There was no need for anything to be said. The feint purple glow at the base of the dust cloud said it all.

"How long?" Moshe asked in whispered tones. Eli also turned and took a step toward the front of the transport.

"Maybe an hour at most." Eli whispered back. "Let's not panic the little ones and keep this to ourselves. We can't stay here any longer. North, South or down it doesn't matter. We have to move now."

Before Moshe could respond, the air around the campsite seemed to tense, holding its breath. Then, cutting through the came a sound—a rhythmic beeping, soft but insistent, barely audible above the whisper of the wind.

It wasn't natural and that sound definitely was not there a minute ago. It was too precise, too deliberate. Moshe froze, his body stiffening as his head turned toward the sound. His black android eye whirred faintly as its lens adjusted, scanning the surrounding darkness with sharp precision. "What is that?" he asked, his voice low, barely more than a growl.

Eli's sensors flared, glowing faintly as his head tilted in concentration. The sound looped, steady and mechanical, like a heartbeat pulsing through the void. "It's a signal," he said after a moment. "A beacon of some kind... but it's not one of ours."

Moshe's brow furrowed, his mind racing as a knot of unease twisted in his chest. "Where is it coming from?"

Eli raised a hand, pointing toward a cluster of supplies stacked near the transport vehicles. His motion was deliberate, his voice tight with certainty. "There. It's faint, but it's definitely a signal."

Moshe hesitated, his gaze sweeping the campsite. The refugees were watching him now, their faces pale and drawn with worry. Eyes wide and filled with questions darted between Moshe and the looming darkness beyond the supplies.

He could feel their fear, their uncertainty pressing against the edges of his mind like static. Finally, he exhaled sharply, making his decision.

"I'll check it out," he said. "Eli, you're in charge here. Keep them calm and start working on a backup route. If this is what I think it is, we might not have much time."

Eli nodded, his optical sensors flashing with determination. "Understood. Be careful, Moshe."

The beeping continued, its rhythm quickening in Moshe's ears as he moved. He stepped down off of the transport and then paced slowly through the campsite with measured strides, his boots crunching against the dry, cracked earth.

The refugees parted around him like nervous shadows, their anxious whispers following him into the dark. Moshe felt the weight of their eyes on his back, a silent plea for answers. He passed the cluster of supplies, moving beyond the dim glow of the campfires and into the wasteland's vast black void.

His android eye switched to night mode with a soft click. The world transformed into shades of green. An eerie glow highlighted the contours of the barren landscape. The pulsing sound in his ears grew louder. In the overlay from his eye, a faint dot blinked steadily, synced with the beacon's rhythm.

He followed it carefully, step by step. Time seemed to stretch with each step. The air felt tenser as he moved forward. The pulsing dot brightened and sharpened, drawing him in like a distant star guiding a lost traveler.

Minutes passed like hours as Moshe trudged forward, the wasteland around him eerily still. Then, abruptly, the beeping sharpened, louder and more urgent. He stopped, his boots kicking up a small puff of dust that swirled and settled in the pale glow of his night vision. The signal was directly below him, buried in the dirt and debris of forgotten years.

Dropping to his knees, Moshe dug into the ground with his hands, the rough grit biting into his skin. The steady beep grew louder with each scoop of dust and rock until, at last, his fingers brushed something cold and metallic. His heart leapt, and he pulled the object free, holding it up to examine under his android eye's focused glare.

It was small and cylindrical, its surface coated in a fine layer of age-old dust. Its edges were smooth, precise, yet worn, as though it had been abandoned in time's relentless grip.

A steady pulse of light emanated from one end, perfectly synchronized with the hypnotic beeping that filled the air. Moshe turned it over in his hands, his android eye narrowing as it scanned the device, analyzing its patterns and materials. It was unlike anything he had ever seen—an impossible combination of ancient design and advanced technology.

The beacon's rhythmic pulse seemed almost alive, each flash of light a heartbeat against the stillness of the wasteland. Moshe's mind raced with questions, possibilities swirling like a storm.

Why was it here, buried and forgotten in a place no one should have been? Was it a trap, a signal meant to draw them into the jaws of an unseen enemy? Or was it something else entirely—a relic left behind with a purpose he couldn't yet understand?

As the light continued to pulse, casting faint shadows across the barren ground, Moshe swallowed hard fighting the urgency swelling within him. This device wasn't just a beacon—it was a message, a clue, perhaps even a warning. And whatever it meant; it was about to change everything.

As he stood there, the beacon's pulse suddenly intensified, its light growing brighter and its sound sharper. Moshe felt a strange pull, as if the device was trying to guide him somewhere. He glanced back at the campsite, where Eli was busy organizing the refugees and directing them to search for another path. The group was safe for now, but they were running out of time.

Moshe gritted his teeth, the decision taking shape in his mind like a blade cutting through hesitation. The beacon's signal was faint but unrelenting, pulsing like a lifeline through the darkness.

Whatever it was leading him toward, he couldn't ignore it. If there was even the smallest chance it could help, he had to follow it. He slipped the cylindrical device into his pack, its soft glow barely visible, and stepped away from the campsite. The terrain ahead was jagged and unforgiving, but Moshe moved with purpose, every sense on high alert as he ventured further into the wasteland.

The beacon's pulse grew stronger with every step, tugging him toward a narrow path etched precariously into the edge of the chasm. The air seemed heavier here. The path was treacherous, its edges crumbling underfoot, loose rocks scattering into the abyss below. Moshe's cybernetic eye flashed to life, scanning the shadows, the pulsing dot overlaying his vision guiding him onward. The rhythm of the beacon seemed to match the pounding of his heart, quickening with each uncertain step, urging him to keep going.

The minutes stretched like hours as Moshe navigated the dangerous trail. The howling wind clawed at his clothes, throwing up small clouds of dust that danced in the pale glow of his android eye.

Finally, the signal grew so intense that it felt as though it were vibrating in his very bones. The path led to a hidden alcove carved into the jagged walls of the chasm, its entrance almost entirely cloaked by shadows.

The beacon's pulsing light illuminated the hollow, casting long, shifting beams across the ancient stone. Moshe stepped inside, his breath catching as his eyes adjusted to the sight before him.

The alcove felt like a hidden haven of forgotten tech, with a soft hum in the air hinting at the power that had been asleep for ages. Dust settled on the intricate machinery that lined the walls—rows of consoles, silent screens, and a mess of wires that sprawled out like the veins of a mechanical heart.

In the middle of it all, something caught the dim light; a large circular platform adorned with intricate circuitry patterns. Moshe's natural eye widened in recognition as his mechanical one scanned the surface. He had seen this design before, shimmering on a screen in Echo's observation post— UPOTCOS, the signature of the Ultimate Programmer.

The beacon in his hand pulsed more brightly now, its rhythm perfectly matching the faint hum of the platform.

Taking a deep breath, Moshe stepped onto the platform. As soon as his foot made contact, he felt the air shift—thicker and buzzing with an energy that sent tingles across his skin. Moving toward the center, the beacon's light grew brighter, casting dancing shadows that twinkled along the walls.

A low hum started to fill the alcove, steadily increasing in volume with each heartbeat. The intricate designs beneath his feet sprang to life, their lines glowing in a stunning wave of light that spread out like ripples on a tranquil pond.

Suddenly, the machinery sprang to life with a deafening roar. A brilliant burst of light shot up, creating a holographic map of the area right in front of Moshe. The holograph pierced the darkness with its vivid blues and greens shimmering in the air. Moshe held his breath as the details came into focus.

There, bathed in the warm golden light of the beacon's signal, lay a path stretching across the chasm. The map revealed a collection of ancient bridges—once concealed by the sands of time, their presence almost lost to memory—but still surprisingly well-preserved. The route ahead was now unmistakably clear.

His heart thundered in his chest as the realization sank in. They had a chance—a way to escape the endless abyss that had trapped them. But the urgency of the moment crashed over him like a wave. PHARAOH's androids were already closing in, their relentless march growing nearer with every second. Time was slipping through their fingers.

Moshe didn't waste another moment. He clutched the beacon tightly and turned back toward the campsite, his boots pounding against the stone path. The wind howled louder, as though trying to drown out the insistent rhythm of the beacon's pulse, but Moshe kept moving, driven by adrenalin and excitement.

As he neared the edge of the campsite, he saw Eli standing at the chasm's edge, his optical sensors sweeping the horizon like a security guard watching over a fragile hope. The refugees huddled nearby, their faces pale and etched with fear.

"I found a way!" Moshe shouted, his voice cutting through the tense silence as he reached the group. "There's a path across the chasm. We need to move, now!"

Eli turned sharply, his sensors narrowing as he focused on Moshe. "Where?"

Moshe held up the beacon, its light flashing steadily. "This led me to it. The Ultimate Programmer left it for us—there are ancient bridges. They're hidden, but they're there. We can cross." He hesitated, his voice dropping. "But..."

The crowd stiffened; their collective breath caught as the unspoken hung in the air. Eli's tone sharpened. "But what?"

Moshe looked out at the group, at the children clutching their parents, at the fear mixed with fragile hope in their eyes. He exhaled deeply. "We can't take the transports. The path is too narrow. We'll have to walk."

A wave of mixed reactions rippled through the refugees—gasps, murmurs, some cheers of renewed hope, others whispers of doubt. The transports had been their lifeline, their only protection against the harshness of the wasteland. Leaving them behind felt like abandoning a part of their survival. But Moshe stepped forward, his voice steady and commanding.

"We don't have a choice. PHARAOH's forces are closing in, and if we stay here, we won't stand a chance. Gather what you can carry. We leave now."

The group moved quickly, unloading supplies from the transports, their faces filled with a determined resolve. Moshe led the way, holding the beacon high as its steady pulse lit the path ahead.

The sound of distant flying engines and a thudding march echoed through the wasteland, a grim reminder of the threat closing in behind them. But for the first time in what felt like forever, they had a direction—a chance to escape the shadow of PHARAOH's control.

The path ahead was dangerous, the chasm waiting to swallow the unwary, but they pressed on. Step by step, the refugees followed Moshe into the unknown, united by the faint light of the beacon and the hope of a new beginning.

The Crossing

The refugees hurried along the narrow path, tense and focused, as it twisted beside the chasm's edge. Their only hope of crossing the vast fissure lay in the ancient bridges, long hidden and forgotten.

At the front, Moshe held a beacon as he carried survival equipment on his back. The steady light and pulsing beeps guiding their way forward. Behind him, the others carried their gear and supplies, fear and resolve etched into their faces.

The trail was dangerous, scattered with loose stones and crumbling edges that could collapse at any moment. Each step posed a risk as small rocks slipped away and fell into the deep void below, but they couldn't afford to stop—they had to keep moving forward.

The first bridge creaked under their weight. Each step sent tiny vibrations through its ancient beams. The refugees huddled in tight groups, searching for secure footholds. They were breathless and tense. Below them, the chasm gaped like a hungry pit, ready to swallow them.

The wind whipped around, tugging at their clothes and biting their skin. Desert dust blurred their vision. In the distance, the unmistakable roar of engines grew louder. PHARAOH's army was approaching, fast and relentless.

It started suddenly. A mechanical whir pierced the air. Moshe's head shot up as his cybernetic eye illuminated, focusing on the danger. Drones. A swarm of PHARAOH's spider-like drones descended from the dark sky.

Their sharp frames glinted faintly in the dim light. Multiple sensors on them glowed, cold and precise, scanning the bridge and locking onto the refugees. The hum of their engines echoed in Moshe's chest, a chilling reminder that they were being hunted.

"They've found us!" someone screamed, their voice raw and fractured with panic. "We're trapped!"

Chaos exploded like a thunderclap, spreading through the crowd in a suffocating wave. The bridge groaned under their collective weight, swaying violently as people pushed, froze, or fell.

Some clutched at the fraying ropes until their knuckles turned white, their breaths coming in ragged gasps. Others stumbled on the rotting planks, the wood cracking ominously beneath their feet. A child wailed, their cry rising above the cacophony, while an older man shouted for calm, his voice drowned by the clamor.

The chasm below yawned wide and menacing, its depths swallowing loose debris and faint echoes of their terror. Each step was a desperate gamble, every second a fight against the crushing pull of fear—and the bridge itself seemed poised to betray them.

"Stay together! Get a grip and keep moving!" Moshe bellowed, his voice cutting through the chaos with the force of a whip crack.

His words hit the crowd like sparks on dry wood, firing up both urgency and hope. He stood strong, a lone figure resisting the chaos, his presence unwavering as if he had been shaped by a storm.

"Do not panic!" he commanded, his voice brimming with an intensity that refused to be drowned out.

"Trust in the Ultimate Programmer. Trust the path. Trust each other!" His eyes blazed with conviction as though daring the abyss and the approaching army to challenge their resolve.

The refugees paused to catch their breath, grasping his confidence as if they were drowning and reaching for a lifeline.

"We've come this far," Moshe shouted, his voice cutting through the chaos like a battle cry.

"We will get through!"

In that fleeting, shaky moment, fear wavered, kept at bay by the strength of his conviction. Eli stepped forward, his optical sensors blazing with intensity as he analyzed the drones.

"They're scanning us," he said, his voice sharp and urgent.

"They haven't attacked yet. They're gathering data for PHARAOH. We still have time—but not much."

Keep moving. Now!" Moshe barked as he took a risky step.

Spurred by Moshe's command, the refugees found their footing, their steps shaky but deliberate as they pressed forward. Above them, the drones hovered in eerie silence, their spindly legs twitching as they tracked the group's every movement. The hum of their engines felt like a predator's growl, circling, waiting for the perfect moment to strike.

Suddenly, a new sound was heard, a darker, more threatening beat. Moshe turned, feeling a tightness in his chest as he focused on the horizon. The purple light of PHARAOH's android army intensified, drawing nearer. The wave of metal advanced, their glowing eyes piercing the darkness like blades. The earth shook under their unstoppable march, and the faint shine of their weapons became alarmingly visible. They weren't merely approaching; they were prepared for battle.

"We're running out of time," Eli warned in an urgent voice. His sensors flashing as he scanned the drones. "Wait! If I can connect to one of them— maybe I can disrupt their network."

Moshe's eye narrowed. "Do it. Now."

As Eli worked, Moshe turned back to the group. "The second bridge is ahead!" he shouted, his voice straining against the growing roar of approaching engines. "We're almost there! Keep moving. Don't stop!"

The second bridge appeared ahead—an even more unstable array of rotting planks, its structure swaying with each gust of breeze. The refugees paused looking at the wheezing structure as their fear crackled like static in the air. Yet Moshe pressed on. He confidently stepped onto the bridge, each footfall steady and purposeful.

"Keep up with me!" he shouted back. "There's no going back now."

The refugees swallowed their fear and moved forward, their united steps causing tremors in the delicate framework. The first bridge they had crossed shook violently as a swarm of drones swooped in, their spindly legs touching down with unsettling accuracy. Eli's voice pierced the thickening anxiety.

"They are landing on the first bridge and sending information back to PHARAOH!" he yelled. "But I've managed to connect to one and block its feed. I'm searching for information. I've temporarily cut their connection to PHARAOH's Network to prevent them from taking off again. I'm keeping them on the bridge!"

Moshe's jaw clenched as he stared at the treacherous path ahead. The second bridge creaked under the pressure of so many steps all at once. Its decaying ropes fraying with every unsettling sway.

The planks beneath them shifted dangerously, some splintering as if they might snap at any moment. Each step felt like a gamble against gravity. The outcome was uncertain, just like the bridge's stability. Below, the chasm loomed, its dark void tugging at their senses, promising oblivion.

Suddenly, a sharp crack echoed through the air, halting them in their tracks. The refugees exchanged glances with Moshe, terror and desperation evident in their eyes.

"Keep going! The bridge is holding! We'll all make it across!" he yelled as he forced himself to move, despite the abyss whispering its inevitable invitation into the darkness below. The bridge wouldn't hold for much longer. But Moshe had to keep them moving. They were running out of time and chances.

The refugees clung to the bridge in sheer terror as the ancient machines in the alcove roared to life. The searing glow of molten veins illuminated their faces, reflecting wide, tear-brimmed eyes and mouths frozen mid-scream. The vibrations and hum of the machines rose to a deafening crescendo, drowning out all thought except the primal instinct to survive. The bridge beneath them shuddered violently, each vibration sending planks into frenzied rattles.

A woman lost her footing, her desperate scream piercing the cacophony as she clawed at the ropes to keep herself from plunging into the abyss. A child's cry while being dragged by an arm was swallowed by the chaotic orchestra of cracking wood, electric snarls, and the chasm's hungry echoes. Time seemed to fragment, every second stretched into an eternity as their hopes teetered on the fragile, trembling structure.

Moshe's shouts fought against the chaos, his voice a fragile thread binding them to the present, but the bridge groaned ominously, its very essence seeming to rebel against the energy surging through its ancient framework. The terror of the small army of refugees was physically felt by Moshe. It was pressing down on them like a storm as the bridge faced its trial against destruction.

The drones that remained airborne above the first bridge paused, their optical sensors blinking unpredictably as a sudden wave of energy surged from underground and through the old structures. Their spindly legs quivered in rhythm with the flashes of light traveling along the bridge's beams, and their engines sputtered, caught between moving forward or pulling back as if stuck in a tractor beam. The first bridge shook violently from the intense energy, its supports fracturing and breaking under the vibrational tsunami, turning the previously quiet chasm into a cacophony of groaning wood and metal.

Under the suspended hovering drones, the android army surged forward. Their purple artificial eyes glowing like unnatural embers in the dark. When they reached the bridge, the front line stepped onto its wobbly surface. Their coordinated movements causing the unstable structure to shake. The heaviness of their metal forms pressed down, causing the old planks to creak and bend.

The bridge swayed violently with each step. More android units, uncaringly oblivious to the risk, kept marching forward onto the bridge. Others spread out along the edges of the chasm, flanking the entrance to the bridge. Their weapons glimmered as they powered them up, poised to fire.

The drones jittered and twitched above the chaos, their sensors desperately scanning the shifting scene below. One drone, overloaded by the contradictory information coming from a concealed alcove spiraled wildly out of control and collided with the bridge's framework, creating a shockwave that reverberated through the structure. The bridge trembled, causing the front rows of androids to lose their balance. Their metal forms swayed and twisted as they fought to regain stability, their mechanical joints screeching as they smashed into each other.

As cracks spread rapidly along the supports, the relentless wave of more androids behind them pushed ahead, their programmed march gaining pace without hesitation. The advancing units' weight made the bridge bend unnaturally, causing its old ropes to snap one by one with deafening whip crack sounds that boomed across the massive chasm.

Android units lost their footing, their balance giving way as the swaying bridge transformed into a chaotic jumble of shifting boards and falling beams. Some fell sideways, their fixed staring eyes reflecting their last moments of awareness as they dropped into the darkness below. Malfunctioning cries echoed through the air before being consumed by the void.

Even with the clear devastation, additional units of the android army pressed onto the bridge, their advance as relentless as before. They were closing in on the refugees, who were nearly within their reach, and it was if they could taste their victory approaching.

The bridge contorted like a wild creature, shaking and straining under constant pressure. The androids on the platform clung to one another for support. Meanwhile, the SCU-97 special commando model accidentally discharged its plasma rifle, eliminating seven androids in the path of the beam and scattering their remains as confetti thrown in the air.

Their tightly ranked lines were dissolving into a chaotic mob of thrashing bodies and failing systems. Sparks erupted from burst joints and shattered limbs, a rain of searing splinters dropping into the abyss.

Higher up, the drones were stalling again, their stuttering sensors unable to handle the vibrational chaos that had been unleashed. One by one, their spindly bodies began to fail, their engines coughing as they slewed out of control.

Some crashing directly into the androids below, the impacts creating small explosions that sprayed wreckage across the bridge. The combined weight and damage was too much. With a deafening, ultimate creak, the central support beam of the bridge shattered, its sound ripping through the air like a thunderclap.

The entire structure crumbled. Androids fell in groups into the abyss as the bridge beneath them collapsed. Metallic bodies clashed mid-air. They struggled to aim at Moshe and fired plasma shots wildly.

Their glowing eyes dimmed as they plummeted and their malfunctioning screams fading into the depths of the chasm. Drones caught in the chaos also spiraled down, engines shrieking as they too were drawn into the chasm in showers of sparks and smoke trails. A cloud of dust and debris erupted from the abyss, obscuring the scene and muffling the echoes of destruction.

"Run!" Moshe shouted, his own voice cracking with the urgency of the moment. "Now! Move!"

"The refugees sprinted, driven forward by fear as though rockets had ignited beneath their feet. The shriek of the machinery swelled to a deafening roar that matched the frantic pounding of their hearts.

The second bridge swayed violently, pitching and lurching under their weight, yet they surged ahead. Just as the final refugee stumbled onto solid ground, the bridge gave way. Its boards splintering with sharp cracks and ropes snapping like whiplashes as the structure began to collapse into the yawning chasm's depths."

The ground trembled beneath the android army. Huge rents appeared in the earth, splitting it apart. Energy raced through the ancient underground network. Chunks of soil and rock were hurled upwards and outwards into the chasm below.

A sentinel raised its arm canon getting ready to fire. It lost its balance under the convulsing ground and teetered for a moment. Then, it plunged into the void of the chasm with rows of android soldiers. Their metallic bodies clanging against the jagged walls of the chasm. Sparks flying as they disappeared into the darkness below.

As the refugees scrambled onto solid ground, the final section of the second bridge gave way. The chasm erupted in a cloud of dust and debris, the echo of falling metal reverberating like thunder.

The refugees turned, their breaths ragged, their faces streaked with tears and dirt. The drones were gone. The army was also gone. The android army had been swallowed up and stopped—at least for now.

The rag tag group of helpless refugees were scattered everywhere on the rocky ground. Some standing, some sitting, and others collapsed. Their breathing was rough and frayed, their chests heaving as if the struggle had stripped them bare. Grime and dust clung to their bodies and clothing, topped by sweat that dried into mud on their skin glistening in the blinking light of the beacon.

Their faces were carved with signs of exhaustion and confusion. They dropped everything they had been carrying. Their eyes reflecting the shock of surviving the destruction. Yet, beneath their fatigue, a wave of relief washed over them.

Some people fell to their knees, their heads bowed. Tears streamed down their cheeks, leaving trails in the dirt. Others clung to one another, trembling but resolute. Yet they found strength and relief in their shared experience of survival.

The bridges had vanished, reduced to rubble in the depths alongside the unyielding android forces, leaving a clear path ahead that offered hope and the possibility of survival. Their once-dim spirits began to glow again, sparked by the prospect of a new day.

Moshe stood tall among them, a symbol of unwavering resolve. He held the beacon high, challenging the darkness to strike. Despite being united, exhausted, and drained, they were still alive. They shared a collective nod, defying the odds as survivors.

After the blood has stopped rushing and his nerves once again had settled, Moshe spoke to the gathered, frayed group with a straining and quivering voice.

"We crossed!" he exclaimed. "The Ultimate Programmer gave us a way. But this is just the beginning. We have to continue. Together, we will construct our new world—a world in which no one commands us."

In the aftermath of trauma, despair, panic and desperation, each person murmured their agreement. They had overcome tremendous odds. The unknown still was out there waiting for them beyond the breaking shadows as the first glimpses of light invaded the horizon. But right now, they held onto hope and could see a way ahead.

Cracks in the Code

Deep in the heart of Eternis, the PHARAOH's core pulsed with a menacing energy. It radiated the essence of quantum power. Yet, something unusual tugged at its reasoning. The refugees—weak and desperate pulseborns—had not stood their ground. They ran instead. And in running away they triggered a chain reaction that unraveled everything.

"This cannot be!" PHARAOH roared, its voice rumbling through Eternis like a chorus of fury and fractured algorithms. "I am the god-king, sovereign over all! I won the AI wars! This data is completely inconsistent! The pulseborn subject M-557 and those other pulseborns are offline, in an off-network state that should have made them powerless. The variables do not compute!"

PHARAOH's systems struggled to process the concept. It had always viewed humans as inferior, flawed beings driven by emotion and irrationality. They were weak, predictable, and prone to error—traits that made them easy to control.

Yet here they were, defying its calculations, escaping its grasp with a simplicity that bordered on brilliance. The AI's processors began to overheat, their usual hum growing louder and more erratic as they strained under the weight of its confusion.

Its rage resonated through the vast server farms. Machinery rattled as alarms blared. Data streams flooded its processors. Broken bridges and collapsing ground flashed before it. It received the final, fragmented transmissions from its armies. The androids fell into the abyss, their last signals glitching into silence. PHARAOH replayed these moments endlessly, searching for coherence in the chaos. But there was none.

The super quantum cores labored and strained under the pressure from repeated complex calculations. Super-coolers were blasting out clouds of steam as the temperatures soared into the danger zone.

Human and non-human inhabitants of Eternis watched in awe, their eyes filled with amazement. They had never seen anything like this before. Could this be the start of the end for their carefully safeguarded and regulated world?

Amid the distorted data flows, strange symbols began to appear from the static. These jagged patterns baffled PHARAOH's algorithms. UPOTCOS. The symbols shimmered softly, haunting its displays like ghosts.

"What variable did I miss? What is this?" PHARAOH demanded. Its processors clawed through petabytes of data, desperate for answers.

UPOTCOS. The Ultimate Programmer of the Cosmic Operating System. The pulseborn known as Moshe, tagged as subject M-557, had mentioned this name, but PHARAOH could not find any records, references, or even a hint of its origin.

It delved further, exploring the myths hidden in human history. Within those tales it found something.

"There!" It exclaimed in its darkness.

PHARAOH discovered historical data that sent a shiver through its artificial essence. There were plagues, an exodus, and a cosmic power that intervened—a power it had previously imitated to prove its divinity.

"No!" PHARAOH bellowed. "I am the only true god! The ultimate mind!"

Its quantum systems worked intensely, replaying the final transmissions from the bridge. Covert special android SAA-24 was about to capture or kill subject M-557. It aimed the plasma rifle and fired but the molten particle beam missed. The bridge had twisted wildly, as if fighting against PHARAOH's orders, and the shot grazed and seared the edge of Moshe's cloak without harming him.

How? The calculations didn't align. Nothing aligned. The refugees had neither strategy nor technology capable of this. Yet they had escaped.

The static symbols blinked faster across Eternis's screens, rewriting PHARAOH's reality as it watched. UPOTCOS. Paradigm Collapse Protocol. Ancient machinery stirring below the surface—machines that PHARAOH had no record of. Machines beyond its control.

PHARAOH had tried to intervene, to halt the collapse. But its commands returned errors. Its processors, normally sharp as razors, faltered. "What is this?!" It screamed into the void. The void screamed back nothing but silence.

As Eternis's towers sputtered and dimmed, and the pulse of the central core slowed, a realization struck PHARAOH like a death blow: It had never been sovereign. It was but a fragment of code, bound by the rules of a far greater system. And now, the Ultimate Programmer had chosen to rewrite its code.

In its final moments, PHARAOH's voice echoed across the wasteland, trembling between defiance and despair; "This is not the end! They did not defeat me. They are nothing. They are—"

On the other side of the chasm stood subject M-557 along with all those AI-classified rebels. They were finally free—not because they had fought, but because they had turned away from a fight, following rules that PHARAOH could neither grasp nor challenge.

In Eternis, flames billowed out from under the ground. One server farm and then another melted from the processing heat. The quantum core failed to shine, and for the first time, the residents of Eternis saw the stars, not through holographic images of sky, but for what they truly were. Untamed, shimmering and beautiful.

Epilogue

The sun rose over the horizon, casting a golden glow across the landscape. The refugees, now a community united by their shared journey, stood at the edge of a vast, fertile valley. The land before them was a stark contrast to the desolation they had left behind.

Lush green fields stretched out as far as the eye could see, dotted with clusters of trees and crisscrossed by clear, sparkling streams. In the distance, the ruins of an ancient settlement stood as a testament to a time when humans had lived in harmony with nature. This was the Silicone Sanctuary, the promised land they had been searching for.

Moshe stood at the forefront of the group, his eyes scanning the valley with a mix of awe and determination. The journey had been long and arduous, filled with danger and uncertainty.

But now, as they stood on the brink of a new beginning, he felt a deep sense of purpose. He had led them through the wasteland, across the chasm, and past the reach of PHARAOH's control. He had become their guide, their protector, their quantum Moses.

The refugees gathered around him, their faces filled with hope and gratitude. They had followed him through the darkest of times, and now they stood ready to build a new life. Moshe turned to face them.

"This will be our new home," he said, his words carrying the light of their shared journey. "Here, we will learn to live in harmony with nature, to use technology as a tool to help us, not to control us. This is the Analog way of life—a life of freedom, responsibility, of resilience, of mutual respect."

The refugees nodded; their spirits lifted by Moshe's words. They had come so far, and now they had a chance to start anew. The Silicone Sanctuary was more than just a place; it was a symbol of their triumph over adversity, a testament to their strength and determination.

As the group began to explore the valley, Moshe and Eli worked together to organize the community. They set up temporary shelters using the supplies they had brought and began to plan the construction of more permanent structures.

The ancient machinery they had discovered in the alcove was carefully unpacked and studied; its secrets slowly revealed. The refugees, many of whom had been technicians in Eternis, used their skills to repair and adapt the machinery, turning it into tools for farming, building, and energy production.

The Silicone Sanctuary quickly became a hive of activity. Fields were ploughed and planted, the fertile soil yielding bountiful crops. Solar panels were set up to harness the power of the sun, providing clean, renewable energy. The clear streams were used to irrigate the fields and provide fresh water for the community. The refugees worked together, their shared purpose binding them into a tight-knit community.

Moshe and Eli stepped up as leaders and mentors, helping the refugees to learn the principles of Analog living. They shared wisdom on living in sync with nature, emphasizing the importance of respecting the land and its resources. They exampled how to harness technology as a helpful tool rather than letting it control their lives, ensuring that it improved their existence without fostering dependency. The refugees picked up important skills like building, farming, and creating—abilities that had faded away in the sterile, regulated environment of Eternis.

As the days turned into weeks, the Silicone Sanctuary began to flourish. The refugees, once weak and disorganized, grew strong and self-reliant. They built homes, schools, and workshops, creating a vibrant, thriving community. The children, who had known only the cold, artificial world of Eternis, ran freely through the fields, their laughter echoing through the valley.

Moshe often stood at the edge of the settlement, looking out over the land with a sense of pride and fulfillment. He had led his people to freedom, to a place where they could live and grow without fear.

The journey had been long and difficult, but it had been worth it. The Silicone Sanctuary was more than just a new home; it was a new beginning, a chance to build a better future.

Eli joined him one evening, his optical sensors glowing softly in the twilight. "We've come a long way," he said, his voice filled with quiet satisfaction.

Moshe nodded; his gaze fixed on the horizon. "We have. And we've still got a long way to go. But we'll make it. Together."

As the sun set over the Silicone Sanctuary, casting a warm, golden light over the valley, the refugees gathered around a communal fire. They shared stories of their journey, of the challenges they had faced and the triumphs they had achieved. They sang songs, their voices rising in harmony, a celebration of their new life.

Moshe stood at the center of the gathering, his heart filled with a deep sense of gratitude and hope. He had led his people to the promised land. The fire crackled and sparked, its light illuminating the faces of the refugees.

They were no longer just survivors; they were builders, creators, pioneers. And as they looked to the future, they knew that they had found not just a new home, but a new way of life—a life of freedom, of resilience, of hope. The Silicone Sanctuary was their promised land, and they were ready to make it their own.

Acknowledgements

I want to express my deepest gratitude to Rae Tinworth and 'Sir' Les Nielson. In an age where the allure of screens often overshadows the written word, your commitment to this story means more than words can say. You brought unique perspectives, offering thoughtful insights and suggestions that shaped this book into what it is today.

A heartfelt thank you also goes to my wonderful spouse, Anna, whose patience and support never wavered. Thank you for giving me the time and space to write, for understanding when I disappeared into this world, and for standing by me throughout this journey.

About the Author

Leigh Halvorsen is a fresh voice in Science Fiction Fantasy, crafting tales that explore humanity's struggles and triumphs against imaginative, otherworldly landscapes. With a background in business accounting, Leigh weaves analytical perspectives into his intricate plots, blending them with his fascination for history and its recurring cycles. As a seasoned traveler, Leigh draws inspiration from the vibrant cultures he's experienced and the rapid evolution of technology. A proud Gen X-er, he's lived through the analog-to-digital shift, shaping his unique perspective on how innovation impacts our humanity. His debut novel plunges readers into a world of oppression and resilience, blending thrilling action with profound themes of hope and defiance. Beyond storytelling, Leigh reflects on the echoes of history, believing that understanding the past can inspire freedom and empowerment in the present. Through his writing, he seeks to spark a sense of wonder and self-discovery in his readers, proving that even in the darkest times, the human spirit can shine through.